SHADOW OF THE CONDOR

It was happening. Hwayna, her beloved, the Lord High Inca, was discarding her, his barren wife, for a new *Coya*. The gist of the message was that he must have sons.

Aolani took her hand from his and moved away from him, hoping that distance would relieve the tension. "Hwayna—I'm sorry. I thought we could go on as before but I can see it is not possible." Aolani lifted her head and tried to keep her tears back. "Please go," she said brokenly.

"Aolani, you know I didn't want this—but by all the gods—you know how important it is that I have children."

Taking his hands in her own, Aolani said, "I know, I know, my love. Believe me, I understand. When is the marriage to be?"

"In three weeks."

A wave of darkness swept over her and she put a hand to her heart.

Hwayna drew her toward him and whispered, "Lani, my love. I'm sorry—sorry this has to be, but this marriage will make no difference between us. You are my heart, part of my very being. I will always love you better than life itself."

Shadow of The Condor

JEANNE NICKSON

LOVE SPELL ◆ NEW YORK CITY

LOVE SPELL®

September 1994

Published by

Dorchester Publishing Co., Inc.
276 Fifth Avenue
New York, NY 10001

Cover Art by John Ennis

The name "Love Spell" and its logo are trademarks of Dorchester Publishing Co., Inc.

Printed in the United States of America.

To my brother Bill Collins and his wife Elinor for a lifetime of love and support.

Acknowledgments:

The author would like to thank Joan Gunter, editor, and Brenda Fickett, typist, for their unfailing support.

Author's Statement:

Shadow of the Condor is a book of fiction. It includes historical figures and actual events, but because of contradictory information in the field, I have manipulated some facts to accommodate the plot.

Shadow of The Condor

PART 1

Trouble in the Inca Empire 1510

Chapter One

Seething with anger, Hwayna Capac, Lord High Inca, sat among his nobles barely listening to the long reports of savage fights along the frontiers and of atrocities committed by the barbarians. Hwayna's mind was elsewhere, obsessed by what he had heard from his Lord Chief of Spies. His shocking rage at the man's report had left Hwayna burned almost out of control, like a tree smitten by a bolt of lightning. As he looked at his nobles seated on the floor below him, he wondered who were the guilty. Some among them had dared to defy him, spreading evil tales that whirled like dust in a strong wind among his people. Their defiance disturbed him. By all the devils of Hopi-Nuni, how could such lies be believed? Hwayna shuddered in his anger, and his mouth felt dry with fear as he thought of Aolani. He had left her this morning, lying pale and tired after her last miscarriage. How would she feel if she knew? How could he possibly tell Aolani about the plot against her?

11

With a stiff neck and an aching head, the Inca rose abruptly, left the council chamber, and headed for his wife's quarters. His aide, Quis-quis, and the guards followed behind him. In the light of the afternoon sun, the gold panels on the cold stone walls gave a gleam and a sparkle to the somber hall. He passed through the guarded gate and entered a small garden, through which a stream meandered. Scattered throughout the garden were many beautiful objects of gold, silver, and decorative jewels. There were fountains, figures of gods, animals, and plants. Small gold and silver birds had been placed in the branches of the molle tree.

Hwayna could feel the tension sapping his strength, and his head pounded painfully as he walked. Entering his wife's room, he walked over to the bed of furs and rugs. One of Aolani's woman attendants sat beside her, holding a cone of white feathers, which she gently waved back and forth. Aolani's disheveled hair gleamed like gold against the dark rugs, emphasizing the pallor of her skin and the dark circles under her eyes.

The swollen mound of her stomach had gone down, Hwayna noticed, and his heart ached. He wondered if she had been told that the child, a boy, had been born dead. They had both been so hopeful, so joyous, for she had carried it well over six months. And then that strange accident! A thought hit him like the strike of a snake's tongue. By all the gods above and below, had it been an accident? After what he'd heard today, perhaps not. The thought devastated him. Frightened and overwhelmed by the horrible possibility, he clenched his fists in fury at the tragedy that had ruined their happiness. How was he to handle this? How was he to find out the truth?

As Hwayna looked at the fragile young woman on the bed, a lump lodged in his throat. She looked so

12

small and vulnerable. In the five years of their marriage, his love for Lani had grown even deeper. Sometimes it frightened him. What would he do without her? It was not just the physical lust that he felt at times for one of his concubines, but a deeper spiritual emotion, for she was more than just another woman. She was a friend in whom he could confide all his secret fears and desires and upon whose loyalty and understanding he could always depend.

Hwayna remembered another time long ago when Aolani had been ill: that agonizing time in Chachapoya when she had lost her memory and had not been able to recognize him for many weeks. It had been as if she were a stranger. Living had been so empty without her that loneliness became like a presence, but a presence without warmth or spirit. The earth was a cold and empty place on which he could walk but gain no strength. Then, when she recovered her memory, her love renewed him, made him more of a man, gave him the courage to face the many problems that sometimes seemed too immense to be borne. Oh, how he loved her! What was he going to do?

Turning abruptly to her attendant he asked, "Does she know about the child?"

The woman was frightened at his harsh voice, and she trembled as she whispered, "Yes." She added hesitantly, "The doctor has given her coca."

Hwayna silently thanked all the gods for Aolani's sleep. There was nothing he could do here. He must talk to someone, but who? Gloomily he tried to think of someone with whom he could talk. There were so few. He wished his mother were here in Cuzco, or his childhood friend, Paco. But they were not, and it would take time to bring them from Sauca Cachi. There was only Uncle Roco, who was old and in poor health, but Roco was wise and was usually aware of

Jeanne Nickson

what was going on at court. Hwayna would send for him.

Later that day, as Hwayna looked at Roco, he could see the erosion of skin and muscle tone that the years had brought. Roco had never been a good-looking man, and his features, in the flickering light of the torches, took on the semblance of a creature emerging from some vast primordial jungle. Hwayna examined the heavily wrinkled face with its bristling gray hairs around the ears and the nose. There was a bluish undertone to his skin that alarmed Hwayna. His uncle's deformed arm was hidden by his cloak. Despite Roco's appearance, Hwayna looked upon him with love, for no man other than his father had so influenced him, so supported him, or given so freely of his loyalty and love.

The Inca went to his uncle and, embracing him, said, "Thank you, Roco, for coming so quickly. Sit down and have some wine."

The two men sat, and as one woman poured their *chicha*, others bustled about bringing fruits, honey cakes, and other delicacies, setting them on a small table in front of Hwayna and Roco.

When the women finally left the room, Hwayna relaxed and smiled at Roco. "Sorry, Uncle, it has been a long time since we've talked. I have tried to solve my own problems, but I admit it hasn't always been easy. Now, something has occurred that distresses me deeply, and I need your help."

Roco's eyes twinkled. "At my age it is flattering to be wanted. The days parade past, ascending and descending with the sun in an endless fashion, filled only with the memory of things long gone. This call is a welcome distraction. How may I serve you?"

14

Before beginning, Hwayna poured them both more wine and wondered just where to start. Troubled, he said, "You know this has been a terrible year for the empire. Great waves of water have destroyed villages and crops along the coast; the trembling of the earth has devastated many inland villages and caused countless deaths. Then, the mountains that spit fire and blow smoke have erupted in several areas."

His uncle interrupted. "I've heard that great fires have destroyed valuable forests that we desperately need. Is that true?"

"Yes, and I've just learned today there is pestilence in our northern cities." He sighed. "It is no wonder that our people, bewildered by the disasters, are convinced that the gods are angry." Hwayna paused and then continued. "Some people claim they have seen apparitions who have told them the gods were angry and would continue to send troubles to earth until they are propitiated. The priests are demanding more and more sacrifices, even human ones. Signs are also disturbing the populace. A few nights ago three rings appeared around the moon, which prophesies more disaster. Yesterday, a condor pursued by a flock of falcons fell in Haucaypata Square, and the city went into a panic."

"Most of this I know, Hwayna, but none of these happenings are unusual in our land."

"That is true, but for so many things to occur almost all at the same time is terribly frightening to our people. I can understand their fear and I can deal with it. But now there are new undercurrents and mutterings that disturb me more. I heard this morning that rumors are spreading rapidly, not just here in Cuzco, but in other cities as well, that the cause of these disasters is—it's so ridiculous I even hate to repeat this aloud." Hwayna swallowed and nervously licked

15

his tongue over dry lips. "They are saying that—that Aolani has caused these disasters. They call her the devil-woman." He looked at his uncle and asked, "How can they believe such a thing?"

A rush of emotion assailed Hwayna. He got up and walked over to the open door that faced the garden. Trying to control his feelings, he looked at the solemn night sky studded with stars and felt the sharp breeze on his hot skin. He felt a painful bitterness at the injustice of this accusation that would so deeply hurt his wife. Who had done this? He had a feeling the rumors had been planted, but why? Rumors such as this seldom broke out simultaneously in several places unless spread by a common source. Could it be an attack on him as well as his wife? Perhaps Roco could help. He tried to arrange his incoherent thoughts into some kind of order.

Facing Roco, Hwayna said slowly, "To be honest with you, Uncle, I am not exactly sure why I feel so terribly disturbed about this matter, for rumors about me and the family are always food for gossip. But I have a strong feeling that this particularly vicious rumor has its origin here in the palace, or perhaps in the temples. Aolani is barely known to the common people. They wouldn't think of starting such a rumor unless it was placed in their minds, but by whom? This is why I turn to you. You know much about palace gossip and intrigue. Can you give me any answers?"

His uncle started to speak, but Hwayna stopped him with his hand. "One other thing, and this frightens me. I was told by Kasque, my Lord of Spies, that he has also heard there might be an attempt to kill Aolani." His hand shook as he picked up his vessel of wine and sipped. "As you know, my wife was involved in an accident yesterday. Now I am wondering if it really was an accident or an attempt to kill her."

Roco rubbed his arm. "By all the gods, Hwayna, are you really thinking that Aolani's accident was an attempted murder?"

"The thought crossed my mind, yes! Quis-quis, my aide, examined the rock and the site of the accident, but there is nothing—no evidence to prove that the rock was pushed—at least, at the moment."

Roco burst out, "I can't believe it, Hwayna. Who would dare?"

"I don't know, but it was a freak accident, such an unlikely thing to occur, that I can't help but wonder. It's hard to believe that a huge rock, well anchored in earth and held by strong ropes, would plunge down the stairs at the exact moment Aolani was alone on the landing. If she hadn't jumped over the side, to the terrace below, she would have been killed."

"How is she, Hwayna?" Roco asked.

"She will be all right but she lost the child. It was a boy. Roco, I am so angry it frightens me. If someone tried to kill Aolani it would have to be someone who knew or had access to her schedule. Who? Why? I know my fears and suspicions are nebulous but nonetheless I believe they are true."

After a long silence, Roco said, "Several thoughts occur to me. Some that make sense, some that do not. I agree with you that these rumors seem unusual, and I do not believe Aolani's name just came out of nowhere. I, too, think she was picked for a reason or reasons." Roco hesitated. "Let's talk about Aolani for a moment, since she appears to be the focus of the problem that is bothering you. Let us admit that Aolani is an unusual woman—very different from our women. Wouldn't you agree?"

Hwayna regarded his uncle and said slowly, "Yes, I suppose so."

"Her appearance itself is extraordinary. In our land of dark, straight-haired people, her honey-gold hair sets her apart. Her eyes and fair skin make her different—not one of us."

"I know," Hwayna interrupted, "but it also makes her fascinating to me. Her difference, however, has always been a problem to Aolani. She feels like an outcast at times."

Roco went on. "In addition to her appearance, she cannot seem to bear a child. This is a serious matter to your nobles since you must have heirs and you won't take another wife. She is a threat to our race." As Hwayna started to speak, Roco stopped him. "Wait! There is something else. She is a well-educated young woman."

Hwayna leaned forward. "I admit that, but don't you see this is what makes her invaluable to me? Aolani speaks twenty-two Indian dialects. In our audiences with people from all over the empire she helps me more than you can possibly imagine. She interprets but she also has a great knowledge of each nation's culture and problems, which is of help when it comes to solving their problems."

"I don't doubt that, my boy. But we are discussing the fact that she has created enemies and we are trying to find out why. Let me go on. This same help she has given you is another reason she is resented. There are those who do not want you to use her help. They feel it is a weakness on your part. *You* are their god! *You* are their ruler. Your decisions are wanted, not hers, which by the way they hold suspect, for she is not one of us."

Hwayna glanced at him angrily. "How dare you say that? All of the decisions are mine. Of course I listen to her, as I do to them. I cannot help it that I agree with her logic rather than theirs."

18

"Perhaps not, but I am afraid they put another interpretation on the matter—one not favorable to you."

Hwayna looked aghast at his uncle. "You mean that some of my ministers think that she makes the decisions? That she holds the power? That she has some magical spell over me? That I need to be saved from this devil-woman? What nonsense!"

"Nonsense or not, why is she called the devil-woman?" Roco, after a short silence, went on. "Now, let me go back a bit. As you pointed out, I hear a lot of gossip. Old friends talk to me, and what has a man of my age to do except watch and listen? For a long time I have known that the nobles of your court, especially those in the Apolina Council, have been extremely jealous of Aolani's influence upon you. They would be jealous of any person who had the power to sway you." Roco took a sip of *chicha* and then said, "I know that to be true, for when I was your father's right hand, I was in that same position. I have heard the poison dripping from their tongues and felt the stinging darts of their anger. Imagine how your top advisers must feel when a nineteen-year-old woman who cannot even give you a child takes all their places in your esteem, when you take her advice instead of theirs."

"That is my business! How dare they be jealous?" Hwayna said coldly.

"Still, it is hard to imagine any of them harming her, daring to risk your anger. They have too much to lose."

Hwayna was thoughtful. "I admit I have used Aolani to expound my own theories. If I talk, the men close up. They remain silent. If she talks, they argue with her, and in arguing and discussing the matters, they learn. I have tried to help them become more understanding of the empire's problems. Most of them are still living back in the days of my father. They cannot

19

grasp the vastness of our empire and the complexity of the hundred nations we govern. Perhaps I am at fault in this matter, causing their animosity toward my wife. But what am I to do?"

"I would suggest that you have been too patient. If your ministers won't change, then change them. Do what your father would do. A ruler must rule. Tupac Yupanqui knew that. He made the decisions and demanded instant obedience—no talk, no grumbling, no criticism."

His uncle's words brought back the specter of his former self. Hwayna thought he'd gotten over his self-doubts, his feeling that his father had made a mistake in selecting him as the next High Inca. Was his uncle right? Had he been too weak and permissive as a ruler? He thought of the things he had done over the past few years. The empire was running smoothly, and despite the catastrophes, the problems were being solved. On the whole he felt satisfied with what he had done as Lord High Inca. But perhaps he had been too easygoing and lenient with the men in his council. He grew angry. If any of his ministers had anything to do with this rumor or the accident, he would find out and they would be punished. But it was hard to believe that the men he worked with day after day would resent Aolani so strongly that they would feel the need to act in order to protect him. It was crazy!

"What about those in the service of the gods?" Hwayna asked abruptly.

Roco was silent for several moments before he said hesitantly, "I doubt if you'll like my comments about them, either."

"Just be frank, Uncle. I can take your comments."

"Most priests are dogmatic; perhaps because they are so dedicated to serving the gods, they forget their fellowmen need serving, too. When your father and I

were young men, the temples sacrificed young children, as well as adults, to the gods at all the ceremonies. I've seen as many as a hundred victims killed
at one time, with the blood running from the altars
down channels to the Huatanay, discoloring the river
for yards downstream. Your father was sickened by
this thirst for blood and finally put a halt to it. But
there are still priests who want those times returned.
Having the power of life and death over their followers
enhances their stature, makes them feel as if they are
more important in the eyes of the people."

Hwayna nodded his head. "I've heard that not only
the priests, but the future victims themselves are
demanding the return of human sacrifice. I've had
various delegations from the temples on this matter
and have refused to listen to them."

"Your father always thought priests were sneaky
devils and kept a keen eye and a firm hand on them
and their thirst for power. I have heard that the priests
in the temples to the Sun resent the time you spend in
Viracocha's temples. I have also heard that they attrib-
ute this odd behavior on your part to the influence of
the Lady Aolani."

Hwayna snorted. "Nonsense! I have my own obligations to Viracocha, the Creator, stemming from my
childhood and my own reasons for honoring him." He
stood up, glaring at his uncle. "How dare you say
these things, implying I am weak and ineffectual, not
only with my ministers but with the priests? You have
been no help," he declared bitterly and started to pace
furiously. "Get out of my sight."

A while later, Hwayna stopped his striding about the
room and stared into the night. He turned around and
saw that Roco had not moved. After several moments
he came back and stood looking down at his uncle. His
anger had dissipated. "What must I do?"

21

With a sigh Roco said, "I think you know what you must do. First, you must appear to repudiate Aolani. Relegate her to the women's quarters until you can send her away. This is for her safety and until you can resolve all of the issues. Second, you must announce your plans to take another wife. Aolani's enemies will think she has lost her power over you and will rejoice. It will provide a grand celebration for the people, taking their minds off the rumors. Third, I would advise you to find the culprits as soon as possible and deal with them. And last, remember you are the Son of the Sun, Beloved of the Gods. Let all of your opponents know their opposition has angered the gods and that you will not tolerate human interference. Be as powerful as your father! Allow no jealousy, no dissension. Demand complete obedience. They will respect you and fall in line with what you do."

By all the thunderbolts of Ilyapa, Hwayna thought, am I going to let that horrible memory of my childhood forever fill me with doubts and fears about myself? He recalled the terrible assault on his body that had almost destroyed him. Was his uncle right? Had he been too permissive? He remembered standing on the terrace at Sacsahuaman and the voice of his father telling him that he would be the next Lord High Inca.

Initially, there had been disbelief and then the unreality of the pronouncement. He had almost forgotten his father's admonitions but suddenly they came back to him. First, Hwayna must be a god on earth, a religious symbol, giving his people solace and faith in the future. Second, he was to remember that he was a god and must expect instant obedience at his every command. Standing in front of his uncle he resolved to set aside all doubts and be the ruler his people expected him to be.

Chapter Two

All the fear and apprehension Aolani had been suppressing ever since her accident four weeks ago overwhelmed her as she saw her husband, the Inca, enter her room. With him were the high priest, two members of the Apolina Council, and Lord Roco. This was an unusual event, for never before had men visited her private rooms.

She thought Hwayna looked magnificent in his royal robes, but her heart sank lower than a stone thrown into a bottomless crevice. He had never visited her so formally. His tunic was a deep red orange, embroidered at the neck and hem with beads of pearl and gold. The red fringe of royalty lay across his brow, hanging from a gold headband. Above his head red and orange feathers swayed gently from the cold draft coming through the open door. Red sandals, red-and-orange armbands and legbands, and enough gold jewelry to outfit three nobles completed his costume. His appearance and the men with him seemed to indicate this was an official visit demanded by court protocol.

Aolani focused her eyes upon his face, hoping to read his innermost thoughts. His dark, brilliant eyes roamed the room, unable to meet hers. The smooth sheen of his black brows formed two perfect arcs above them. She had always liked his rugged face but she saw that he was frowning a bit. It was apparent that he was no longer the boyish young man she had married, the youth who had been so shy and diffident with her. No, he was a man, much more like his father, the great Inca, Tupac Yupanqui, that wonderful man who had saved her from enemies who would have killed her. Hwayna Capac, in his five years as Lord High Inca, had developed the same commanding presence as his father, the same powerful personality as Tupac Yupanqui. But Aolani looked below the surface, seeking the lover—the man with the sweetly curving lips that knew her intimately; the high smooth cheekbones, brown with the sun, that she loved to caress; the cleft chin; the shining hair as blue-black as a raven's wing. She loved him so and knew she was losing him.

Aolani could tell by his averted eyes and the nerve throbbing in his temple that he had something unpleasant to tell her. Throughout the last month there had been many indications here at court that something unusual was happening. The relationship between them had been different since the loss of her child and they had avoided talking about it. But now the moment was here and she felt that her whole life was about to splinter in front of her. She heard the wind howling outside as it cried and wept, hurling itself against the stone parapets.

Wanting to howl and cry, too, she listened to Hwayna's stumbling words. How stupid men were—how blind! As if she hadn't seen this nightmare moment creeping inexorably toward her like an icy mass, a glacier of frozen vastness, waiting to engulf her. It was happening! Hwayna, her beloved, the Lord High Inca, was discarding her, his barren wife, for a new *Coya*. The gist of the message was that he must have sons.

What could she do? What could she say? For all five years of her marriage the gods alone knew how hard she'd tried to give him a son. Looking into his eyes she saw a tear streak slowly down his cheek and she felt his burning hand clasp hers and hold it tight. He looked drained and the shadows under his eyes were dark. It must be terribly hard for him, too, she thought. How he has aged. He looks much older than his 25 years.

She took her hand from his and moved away from him, hoping that distance would relieve the tension. "Hwayna, I'm sorry. I thought we could go on as before but I can see it is not possible." Aolani lifted her head and tried to keep her tears back. "Please go," she said brokenly.

Hwayna said anxiously, "Aolani, you know I didn't want this, but by all the gods, you know how important it is that I have children."

Taking his hands in her own, Aolani said, "I know, I know, my love. Believe me, I understand. When is the marriage to be?"

"In three weeks."

A wave of darkness swept over her and she put a hand to her heart.

Hwayna drew her toward him and whispered, "Lani, my love. I'm sorry this has to be, but this marriage will make no difference between us. You are my heart, part of my very being. I will always love you better than life itself."

The words gladdened her heart briefly, but the pain of losing Hwayna soon returned. How could fate be so cruel? Why, out of thousands of women, was she one of the barren ones? The gods were hard to understand. She had prayed to them all, offering sacrifices time and again, but to no avail. They remained mute and uncooperative. She shivered. What would become of her here at court? Despite Hwayna's words, she would be the discarded wife relegated to the background. Once children came, Hwayna would want to be with them. She would be a scorned and pitied woman with no place in his life. She wanted no part of it. She must beg Hwayna to let her go.

She was hardly aware when the Inca and his entourage made their farewells. Alone in the shadowy room after their departure, she was aware of an immense despair. She felt fear, anger, and a loss of faith in Hwayna Capac. There was also a great bitterness, a feeling that one of the few people who had ever professed to understand her had deserted her in the midst of a cold wilderness.

Aolani knew that her uncommon background had more or less isolated her from most men, and certainly from the women of her world, who had been subjected to a rigid life ruled over by men and forced to submit to their authority for many generations. Considered a goddess in her own country of Chachapoya, she had never thought herself subject to the rules of men. Remembering her unusual education while under the protection of Lord Pinau, the Tupa Inca's brother, she knew that her knowledge was superior to that of most of the men at court. As the wife of Hwayna Capac, Emperor of Tahuantinsuyu, she had felt secure in the knowledge that she was different from most women—

until recently. These last weeks of being kept almost a prisoner in the women's quarters had left her emotionally drained and unsure of herself. How could Hwayna have done this to her?

For over three years she had participated in all her husband's activities. She had shared his anxieties and worries and helped in the administration of the empire. She had even been delegated certain tasks to perform herself. Hwayna had seemed happy with the arrangement. Then, suddenly, everything had changed. Hwayna no longer invited her to be with him. She had nothing to do throughout the long, boring days except listen to women's chatter of clothes, gossip, and men. She couldn't talk to them. She seemed to speak an unknown language, even though every word was in their vocabulary. Aolani felt helpless, angry, almost violent, and still she said nothing to Hwayna. Why she remained silent she did not know.

Was it because she felt a sense of guilt about her third miscarriage? Was it because of her inability to function as a woman? Was it her hurt pride? Or even worse, was she afraid to face the fact that Hwayna had tired of her? Aolani had pondered over the situation for days on end, trying to figure out what had gone wrong. Hwayna still visited her at night and was warm and loving, but when she tried to question him he ignored her or became angry.

Suddenly Aolani's thoughts were interrupted, and she heard Hwayna's voice and felt his arms turning her around.

"I couldn't leave you looking so dejected, Lani. None of this is your fault." His lips sought hers. His hands on her breasts felt like fire and her nipples hardened with desire. "Dismiss your women," he whispered in her ear. She felt him release her and she turned, motioning to her women to leave.

Then they were alone. Aolani had not expected this, but she wanted him, even after all that he had done. The thought crossed her mind that she might be able to persuade him to let her leave after they'd made love. She went to him and lifted the fringe from his brow, kissing his forehead, his eyes, and then his lips, which responded to hers. Kneeling, Aolani unfastened his sandals and ran her fingers caressingly up his legs. She could feel his response. He lifted her to her feet and slowly removed her warm vicuna tunic. Her naked body was cold as he drew her to him. She could feel the beads on his tunic cutting into her skin, but she didn't care.

"Hwayna," she said. "I love you so and cannot bear it. What am I going to do?"

To her shame, Aolani started to cry. Through her tears she saw him roughly pull his tunic over his head and throw it on the ground. Lifting her in his arms he lay down beside her on the furs in front of the fire.

He pulled her close to his naked body, and she felt warm and comforted as he tucked himself around her. "Nothing has changed, my love. Nothing!"

But it had! She knew it had. Then, as if she'd never be able to touch his body again, she threw herself upon him in despair. She wanted to feel everything about him so that she could remember him always. Love was like an avalanche that roared and engulfed her in lightning-like flashes. Ravenous, she met every thrust of his with a wild fury of her own. At last, exhausted, they fell asleep.

When Hwayna Capac opened his eyes, he was immediately aware that Aolani's body nestled close to his own. His arms held her in his embrace and she slept as still as a contented child, her head against his heart. A strand of her hair lay across his nose and tickled his nostrils, and he knew if he didn't remove it, he would sneeze and wake her. Cautiously, he raised his free arm and removed the gleaming strand, then gazed down at her sleeping face.

A painful bitterness almost choked Hwayna as he thought of removing Aolani from his life, but he would have to do it, at least for a time. Aolani wouldn't be safe here in Cuzco, not until all her enemies were found. How he had hated to confront her in front of all those men and tell her that in order to have sons he must marry again. He had felt Aolani's pain as if it were his own—her shock at his betrayal. But he'd had to do it, for it was necessary and all part of his plan to keep her safe and free from harm. He must also send her away from him for a period of time and he felt a lump in his throat at the thought of the emptiness in his life without her. By all the gods, how he loved her! Aolani was one of the few people in his world whom he could feel close to, who was warm and loving with him. He was not a god to her but a man, a man who needed to be loved.

Divine power, thought Hwayna, was a dreadful thing—a black bottomless abyss separating him from all that was human, a steep wall of flint and stone that none could climb, leaving him alone on a frozen peak, forever separated from mankind. Hwayna feared above all else the loneliness of his position, where men feared him, even loved him, but put him upon a pedestal. "Oh, Viracocha, Creator of All Things," he prayed, "bring us back together again."

Aolani stirred beside him and opened her eyes. "Were you talking to me, beloved?"

"No, my darling. Go back to sleep."

Aolani lay quietly in the safety of Hwayna's arms and could still feel the warm embers of their passion smoldering within her passive and tired body. At last she murmured, "Hwayna?"

"Hum?" His finger played with a strand of her hair. "Such beautiful hair. It carries the sun in it."

"I want you to do something for me." She sniffed his body, which smelled fragrant from the oil his attendants smoothed on his skin after bathing him. She nibbled at his ear.

He gave a sigh of contentment. "Anything, my love. Anything in the world."

Aolani said quickly, "I want you to let me go home to Chachapoya for a short visit."

Hwayna sat up on the rugs and looked at her in shock. "You what?" he asked.

Aolani sat up, too. "Please listen to me, Hwayna. This is important! You are getting married. It is only fair to give some time to your new wife without me around to disturb her. It is a perfect time to see for myself what is happening in Chachapoya."

"No, I forbid it." His eyes flashed angrily at her.

Aolani lay back on the pillows and managed a few more tears, feeling that he had no right to be so unreasonable. "You promised me when we agreed to marry that Chachapoya was my country, and I could look after it." She saw that he remembered the promise and pushed on. "How can you be so selfish, Hwayna? Don't you realize how hard it will be for me with another woman taking my place? And think of your new wife, with you hopping back and forth between us like a rabbit. It has been said that a happy woman is more apt to conceive."

Hwayna wiped away Aolani's tears with his hand and looked thoughtful. This seemed like a good sign to her, and she pushed a little harder. "Hwayna, I promise I will stay no longer than six months." Trembling a little, Aolani realized that she might not have told the truth.

Hwayna brushed her hair away from her forehead as she tried to hide her face. Hwayna was thinking. Perhaps this was not such a bad idea. He had to send her someplace but not Chachapoya. There might be trouble there. But Cajamarca would be safe. He would be leaving for there as soon as this present situation was resolved.

"Hwayna, why don't you answer me? What are you thinking?"

Hwayna seemed not to have heard her questions. "No, you may not go to Chachapoya, but I will compromise. I will send you to Cajamarca. It is not too far from your country. Your ministers may report to you there."

She gave a deep sigh. She'd have done anything to get away and she liked Cajamarca. At least she'd be near her own country. She spoke up quickly. "All right. Cajamarca will be fine. Thank you, Hwayna."

Hwayna looked relieved. He took her in his arms and nuzzled her neck. "Nothing will happen to you. I'll make sure of that. Perhaps this is the best thing." He paused. "You know, I don't want you to go. I'll be lonesome without you. However, I am aware of how difficult this situation must be for you, and it might be good to have other things to think about for a while. I know you're unhappy, but there are reasons for what I do. It is more complicated than you think. But, Aolani, I expect you to stay there in Cajamarca. No wandering off to Chachapoya as you did before. Remember, you were almost killed."

She nodded her head and kissed him gratefully, ignoring his last statements. "You are so good to

31

me, even though I have not understood you recently. I adore you, Hwayna Capac." Aolani kissed him again. "Please, my love, is it possible for me to be gone before the wedding or, better yet, before she arrives in Cuzco? Is it possible for you to arrange it that fast, Hwayna?" She quickly added, "Of course, I'll understand if you can't."

Hwayna frowned but answered, "I am Inca. Of course, I can arrange it."

Chapter Three

Aolani awoke to deep depression, to the knowledge that she'd finally stepped over the deep chasm lying between her past and her future. By requesting and obtaining permission to leave Cuzco, she might have taken herself out of Hwayna's life forever. Last evening, Hwayna's childhood friend, Paco, had visited her and told her that the Inca, true to his word, had begun preparations for her departure. Twenty thousand warriors were being gathered to accompany her, along with doctors, musicians, dancers, cooks, servants, hunters, bearers for her litter, and of course thousands of llamas to carry the huge amount of supplies, clothing, and equipment that would be needed. Hwayna seemed to be doing things in a royal fashion, she thought. Perhaps he was relieved that she was leaving, and this gesture was to salve his conscience.

Listless and feeling bored by the thought of another endless day, she arose from her bed of furs and began her morning routine. At times she despised the primitive bathing facilities that existed in the palace, so utterly inadequate compared to the big pools at Sauca Cachi and Cajamarca that were fed by hot springs. After relieving herself in the pottery waste jar she moved toward her bath. Most of the time Aolani was grateful for the deep stone basin that was filled with hot water each morning by slaves, for she could remember a time when she was thankful for a jar of cold water each morning. That was before she married Hwayna, of course. How quickly she had become used to her pampered life.

The room was heated and steam from the hot water further warmed the room. On bare feet she crossed the gleaming floor, inset with gold, silver, and mother-of-pearl, to the pool's edge. Touching the water with her toe, she found that it was pleasantly hot, and she nodded to one of her women who removed her robe.

Slowly, Aolani descended the stone steps and sat down gingerly on the bottom one. The warmth of the water quickly relaxed her, and she leaned her head back and let her long hair float on the surface of the water. It looked like strands of green-gold seaweed floating in the shadowy pool. Two of her attendants shed their tunics and entered the water beside her, bringing a fresh twig from the molle tree and a goblet of water with which to brush her teeth. They also brought sponges and soap made with the roots of aloe to wash her body and hair. As they rubbed the soap into her hair, she could smell the fragrance of the flowers they had ground into it.

When they had finished, Aolani stepped from the bath and was wiped dry by her attendants with warm cotton cloths and her damp hair was wrapped in a long scarf. Over her head they dropped a soft, sleeveless gown of pearl-white vicuna wool, embroidered at the neck and the hem with blue-and-silver leaves.

A beautifully woven *chumpi* of silver cloth was tied around her small waist and an *lliclla* of warm blue alpaca wool, studded with silver beads, was pinned at her shoulder with a large silver *tupus*. She hoped it would keep her warm.

After drying, brushing, and arranging her hair the attendants placed an *uncha*, a small, narrow band of blue, across Aolani's forehead and tied it in back. Looking in the mirror of silver, she was not displeased with her image. The blue and silver colors brought out the gold light in her honey-colored hair. Despite the shadows under her dark-fringed eyes, she looked much the same as usual.

Afterward, there was really nothing for her to do but sit in front of the brazier of hot coals and dream about the past as she waited for her morning meal. The fire offered little comfort today. The cold mist that sometimes enveloped the city crept through the windows and permeated the room. She shivered. Sometimes Aolani wished she were a full-blooded Inca and had grown up in the high mountains. It was strange the way they seemed to be able to withstand the cold. Dressed in short tunics, with their arms bare, they seemed impervious to the weather. Hwayna, she knew for a fact, had a body that was always warm, and she loved to snuggle against him on a cold night.

Hwayna! How could she possibly endure the agony of being separated from him? They had been so close, so very much in love in Cajamarca, and even in Cuzco during those first years. What had happened to them? Why had he suddenly left her to herself day after day, refusing to let her participate in his daily life? And then this marriage without even discussing it with her! She would have understood his need, for even though she hated the thought of another wife, she knew he must have sons. For his sake she could have put up with another woman, but there was more to their estrangement than that. They didn't share many things anymore.

She was no longer asked to attend council meetings or the daily audiences that were so interesting. All the special responsibilities that had been delegated to her were being taken care of by others, except for the Yacha-Huasi. But this college for young princes and sons of nobles didn't require much of her time or energy since it was well administered by wise and capable *amautas*. She felt unwanted, no longer important or needed by her husband. He would not even discuss business with her when they were alone. The court was aware that something was wrong. People regarded her with sly little glances. She felt angry and humiliated, but she couldn't talk about it to Hwayna. Physically they were close, but both of them pretended that everything was the same, even though it wasn't. She couldn't bear it any longer. She had to get away.

Aolani thought about those wonderful days when they had first arrived in Cuzco. It had been so exciting, so magnificent! The whole city had waited impatiently for the Lord High Inca's return from Cajamarca. She would never forget the morning they'd arrived five years ago. On the Chinchaysuyu Road coming into the city the people were packed as far as the eye could see, falling to their knees as the open palanquin passed by in all its shining splendor, shouting, *"Haille! Haille!"* The road in front of them had been strewn with flowers, feathers, and brightly colored yarn balls.

Then there was their entrance into Haucapayta Square, which on ceremonial days was closed to ordinary people. Thousands of Inca nobles in splendid clothes and glittering jewels, priests dressed in white with brilliantly feathered capes, and foreign dignitaries in exotic costumes were waiting for the Inca.

All of them fell to the ground as trumpets erupted and drums beat. The great dais in the midst of the square was covered with gold and jewels that glittered in the light. As Hwayna Capac, Lord High Inca, Emperor of Tahuantinsuyu, mounted the stairs, his tunic decorated with hundreds of gold disks rippled and sparkled in the sun. Trumpeters announced his triumphant return all over the city. Even the urn holding the eviscerated body of Tupac Yupanqui was gaily dressed, sitting like some friendly specter enjoying the festivities on the seat below the Inca. It seemed hard to believe that Hwayna's father, such a forceful and magnetic ruler, was gone.

Someone—Aolani thought it had been Lord Roco, Hwayna's uncle—guided her to a bench a few steps beneath the Inca. Aolani had looked up at the golden figure of her god-husband silhouetted against the mountains. They were not friendly mountains. They seemed almost threatening as they reared like arrogant giants, coldly menacing, watching the extravagant show below.

Aolani had looked around at the mass of bodies on the ground. All this adulation and love flowing out from the people for her husband, Hwayna Capac. She had expected this, but the actual experience was awesome, unreal. She had wondered what it would do to him, to her! She had taken her eyes from the kneeling figures and looked at the buildings around the square. The great stones that formed the walls were incredibly smooth, their seams matching perfectly, and they rose to the height of three men. Friezes of gold adorned some of the walls, but from the distant perch Aolani had been unable to detect the designs. Their glitter added a note of splendor to the magnificent palaces. No wonder this ceremonial center of Tahuantinsuyu was called the heart of the empire. How could mere mortals have built such edifices? How could they have transported such heavy stones?

Even though she had been in Cuzco many years before—for the whole year in which she waited for the young Hwayna Capac's caravan to travel north—she had never seen the city. She had arrived at night and been placed in the Temple of the Sun, and she had not left the temple grounds until she departed in his caravan at last. At that time she'd never dreamed she would someday be sitting here as his wife.

But those magic days when they'd loved, worked, and shared everything together were gone. Abruptly, Aolani got to her feet, ignoring the morning meal that had been set beside her. She couldn't eat! She couldn't stay here all day thinking about the past—those wonderful years when she and Hwayna were partners in ruling an empire. She called her aide, Molque, and asked him to summon her guards as she intended visiting the Lady Cori Picchu, whom Paco had told her had come up from her estate, Sauca Cachi.

While Aolani waited, she went to the small aperture that looked out on the huge square. Once a swamp, it had been drained and paved with large slabs of stone by Hwayna's grandfather, Pachacuti. It was already beginning to be crowded. Sightseers from all over the empire came each day to gawk at the palaces of Pachacuti, Tupac Yupanqui, Hwayna Capac and at the *Acclahuasi*, the buildings that housed the Virgins of the Sun. Several *chasqui* were already clustered at the gate, having brought messages or merely standing by, ready to carry them to wherever the Inca would send them. A detachment of the royal guards in their black-and-red uniforms were marching across the stone bridge that spanned the Huatanay River. They were headed for the Cuntisuyu Road that led to the jungles in the east. Coming from the suburbs that housed the *Curacas*, the highest Inca nobles, as well as the governors of provinces, and special guests, such as the King of Chan Chan, were several well-dressed groups of men and their escorts heading for the palace. There were also dancers and entertainers in colorful costumes hoping for contributions from the crowds.

Aolani heard the sound of footsteps behind her and turned to face Molque. He bowed and said, "My lady, the guard is ready."

Her two favorite ladies, Mountain Star and Bright Fire, followed her as she went down the narrow corridor that looked down onto the courtyard below. It was filled with nobles, guards, and prominent visitors awaiting Hwayna's appearance. As she passed her husband's quarters, he emerged and they stood looking at each other silently. She had seen more handsome men in her life, but none had ever pleased and attracted her so much as did Hwayna Capac. Her heart seemed to stop and she breathed heavily.

"You are going somewhere, Aolani?"

Was he checking up on her again? she wondered. He seemed to be waiting for her reply. "I planned to visit Cori Picchu and say good-bye. I was told by Paco last night that she returns to Sauca Cachi early tomorrow morning."

His eyes softened as she looked at him. "You are taking your guards?" She nodded. "I will not detain you then."

She was excused. What could she do? Aolani hoped tears would not appear in her eyes. She bowed and said, "Thank you, my lord."

As she stepped to one side, he brushed by her and Aolani could smell his familiar fragrance. He was dressed in his favorite white and gold, with red accessories. He looked so impressive and haughty. No one outside herself—except for his mother, perhaps— would ever know how lonely and vulnerable a man he really was. Or maybe she just wanted to think this was so, for then she could imagine that someday he would have need of her.

The guards were waiting at the bottom of the stairs. Why she needed them to walk across the huge square that separated the two palaces from each other was beyond her comprehension. But weeks ago she'd made a promise to Hwayna to go nowhere without them.

They entered the outer courtyard of Yupanqui's palace where Cori Picchu and her daughter, Cusi Rimay, Hwayna's first wife, stayed when they were in Cuzco. Aolani motioned to the guards to remain outside and, followed by her ladies, went to the door leading into the family courtyard. The gatekeeper knew her well and admitted her quickly into the small garden area, which was occupied by only one person, a man whom she was always glad to see.

Greeted by her old friend, Paco, who was now the queen mother's Head of Household, she offered him her hand. He used to be such a healthy specimen but was now looking pale and rather fragile. He had never completely recovered from the stomach wound he'd received when saving Hwayna's life. Fortunately, Paco had married the loving woman who had tended him during his long convalescence, and she'd looked after him until she was killed in a rock slide while on her way to help an injured peasant who had fallen from a high cliff.

Due to Paco's health, which had suffered from the shock of his wife's death, Hwayna had reluctantly transferred his friend to his mother's household. "Paco," Aolani said. "How I've missed your friendly face at court."

"Thank you, my lady. I'm glad you've missed me." Paco gave her a shy smile that seemed to light up his whole face. "The family is with Mama Ocllo." He used the term of affection often given to this great lady, Hwayna's mother.

Aolani was pleased that Cusi Rimay and little Huascar were there, for she had wanted to see them before she left. She had always been very fond of Cusi Rimay, or Sosi as the family called her. Besides, she had brought a present for Huascar. He was only five years old and one of the dearest little boys she had ever seen. He was handsome and intelligent, but Hwayna would have nothing to do with him. Other than his mother, only four people knew the truth about Huascar: Hwayna Capac, Paco, Cori Picchu, and herself. Even though Huascar was thought to be the son of Hwayna and his sister, and was considered by the people to be the heir to the throne, he was really not Hwayna's son but the son of Manco, his older brother.

Suddenly, Aolani wondered if Huascar were here for the wedding. She asked Paco hesitantly, "Has Hwayna invited Huascar to the wedding? Does he plan to see him?"

"No to both questions. You know how strongly he feels about the boy, Aolani."

She felt angry and sad, too. "I know, but it isn't fair to take it out on Huascar. He's just a child. How is he going to feel as he gets older about a father who won't see or talk to him?" She could tell by Paco's expression what he was about to say, so she said hurriedly, "I know—I know Hwayna Capac's not Huascar's father, but the boy thinks he is, and the people think so, too, and always will. They idolize the child."

Paco held up his hand. "Enough, Aolani. I know that it will be hard on Huascar, but you know as well as I do that the Inca has good reasons for his attitude. You also know what he thought of Huascar's real father, his brother, Manco, who was warped and

41

evil. He thinks there is bad blood in the child—and who knows, he may be right."

Aolani was indignant. "Bad blood in that darling child? It's ridiculous! However, by the time he grows up thinking he has a father who hates him, it might come true."

"You're seeing it from your own point of view. Look at it from the Inca's side. Manco tried to kill him, not once, but several times. And look what Manco did to Sosi. Can you imagine how Hwayna Capac feels knowing that his half brother, Manco, sexually molested his young sister and drugged her to the point where she almost lost her mind? She still isn't quite normal and has to live a very quiet and tranquil life at Sauca Cachi."

Aolani didn't need to hear the story again. She knew that Hwayna was justified in hating Manco. She hated him herself. He had almost raped and killed her. But she still thought it wasn't fair to blame the child. Neither did Cori Picchu.

Paco seemed to know what she was thinking again. "We know Huascar is a good boy and innocent of harm as of now, but we must face facts. On his father's maternal side of the family there are many members who were mighty unusual, to say the least. You know that is one reason Hwayna doesn't want Huascar to inherit the throne. There is also the fact that he doesn't want to become too fond of the boy, for it might influence him later."

"But he accepted the possibility that the baby might become Inca when he married Sosi and let everyone think Huascar was his son," Aolani snapped.

Paco smiled ruefully. "Oh, come now, Aolani. You know there was nothing else he could do. Sosi would have been disgraced, perhaps even killed. The scandal might have killed his sick father. He was going off to war. He did what had to be done to save Sosi and to resolve the whole mess."

Aolani shook her head. Poor sad Sosi and poor Huascar. Thank all the gods they had Sauca Cachi and Cori Picchu. Yes, and Huascar had Paco, who was like a father to him. Perhaps Hwayna had thought of that when he had given Paco this assignment.

Her heart felt a little lighter. She had always resented Hwayna's treatment of the little boy. They had reached the door of Cori's chamber and Aolani stopped Paco. "Be good to him."

He nodded as he announced her name.

Chapter Four

As Aolani approached the queen mother, she felt some trepidation, even fear. This was unusual, for she'd always felt at ease with Cori Picchu. The room, despite the many gold and silver objects that filled it, was as dark and gloomy as her own chambers. She walked slowly toward the small, dark-haired woman with the luminous eyes who watched her approach. Cori Picchu was alone. None of her ladies were present. Paco had said that Sosi and her son were with her. Where were they? Cori's chambers were usually crowded. Aolani felt a sinking feeling in her stomach. Something was terribly wrong. She sank down on her knees and, out of respect, waited for Cori Picchu to speak.

A light hand caressed Aolani's hair back from her forehead and the kindly gesture caused tears to well up in her eyes. She forced them back, for she knew that if she began to cry, she might never be able to stop. The gentle, husky voice that was so distinctive said with affection, "Poor child! Come, let me look at you."

Aolani lifted up her face and Cori examined her closely. "You've lost weight and there are deep shadows under your eyes. I am so terribly sorry about the baby."

There was a lump in Aolani's throat as big as a stone. Cori was always so kind to her. Why then did she feel so afraid? She burst out, "Cori, please tell me. What is wrong? Why am I so frightened?"

"Quiet, child, I'll tell you what I know. I think Hwayna should have told you long ago. Sometimes, knowing what the problem is helps us to solve it."

"There is a problem, then, that concerns me?" Aolani asked.

Cori nodded, a frown on her forehead. Aolani waited nervously as Cori seemed to be gathering her strength. Suddenly, she said, "I'm sorry to keep you waiting, but it is difficult to know just where to begin." Suddenly she began to cough a rough, rasping cough that shook her slender body. She pointed at the vessel on the small table. Aolani handed her a gold goblet exquisitely adorned with the figures of two running deer and watched Cori sip from the cup. The liquid seemed to relieve Cori.

Aolani felt a touch of concern for Cori's health, but her own troubles seemed so immense that she found it hard to wait patiently for the spasm to subside.

Finally, Cori placed the vessel on the table and took a deep breath before saying, "Tell me, Lani, have you heard anything at all about the situation? Have your friends or ladies told you of the rumors?"

Aolani shook her head. "No, to both questions."

Cori said quickly, "There is no easy way to say this. For months, rumors have been spreading among the nobles and priests that you have cast a spell on my son, an evil spell. They think you have taken over his power. They consider you a devil-woman sent by the gods of the underworld to destroy the Incas and the

Son of the Sun. They blame the disasters that have happened in the empire upon you."

Aolani looked at Cori with her eyes wide and her mouth open. Finally she gasped. "By Mama Kilya, the Moon, what nonsense! I would never harm Hwayna! The only opinions I voice are those he has asked me to voice."

"I know that. Hwayna knows it, but the Inca nobles and priests are convinced that you are evil. There was a plot to kill you—in fact they almost did."

Aolani was shaking with anger. She stood up and started pacing. She couldn't believe this. It was like a nightmare. Turning to Cori she asked, "You mean the accident was intentional—they murdered my baby?"

When Cori nodded her head, Aolani sank down on the rugs. Putting her head in her lap, she rocked back and forth, racked by shuddering sobs. Cori took her into her arms, holding her close.

When she had quieted down, Cori went on. "Hwayna loves you. Remember that! He is trying to protect you the only way he can at the moment. He must appear to reject you. He must make your enemies feel that you are powerless."

Aolani sat up and looked at Cori intently. It was hard to believe all of this. But Hwayna loved her, or so Cori said. Those words made her feel better.

Cori went on. "He is taking another wife so they will think he is through with you. He is also sending you away to keep you safe."

It was beginning to make some kind of sense. At least it explained Hwayna's actions. "He does still love me?" she asked again.

"Of course he does. He hated what he has had to do, but he did it for your safety. He also needs time to find the murderers and the instigators of the rumors."

"Why didn't he tell me all this?"

"He wanted your reactions to be convincing to your enemies."

"Oh, Cori, what can I do?" Aolani cried. "You know I wouldn't hurt or harm Hwayna. I can't understand why they blame me." She clenched her fists. "It's so unfair."

Cori said patiently, "It all has to do with power. Whoever influences or is close to the Inca is in a powerful position and is a threat to those who are concerned with keeping and maintaining what power they now have. You are in such a position. They fear and hate you because through you they may lose their own power. You are also a woman, and a very unusual one at that. They have convinced themselves that you are a devil and that my son is under your spell. It is an excuse to get rid of you."

Aolani drew a deep breath and tried to take in what her mother-in-law had told her. She was so outraged that she sputtered, "It-it is unbelievable!" She thought for a moment and then looked at Cori. "They think I have power? Ridiculous! What power? I made no decisions. Hwayna asked me to voice his thoughts to the council, and I did. They would get angry and argue with me. He liked to have them talk so he could understand what they were thinking. When Hwayna talked, they just agreed with him." She shook her head in amazement. "The decisions Hwayna made were based on his own ideas; those ideas he told me to discuss with them."

"But the council doesn't know that," Cori pointed out.

Aolani cried out, "You know your son. He is very strong willed. He always makes his own decisions. I can see that maybe the council thought that I—oh! It is all so incredible! Why is it, Cori, that men are so

47

against women? Why do they resent us so?"

"I suppose much of it has to do with the way they are educated," Cori said. "In our society males are educated to be warriors and females to be homemakers. A boy is taught to be competitive, to win over others. Our girls are taught to be quiet, submissive, and passive. But even worse, a boy learns that his mother and the other women of the household are under the power of the males in the family. Is it any wonder that a dominant woman is considered abnormal, a threat to their power? When you didn't act like their idea of a female, even though you were queen, they felt threatened and diminished in stature by you."

"Do you feel it was wrong of me to voice my opinions?"

"Not wrong, perhaps, but unwise. It has certainly brought you trouble. Perhaps someday it will be possible for a woman to have a voice in government. But not now, not here. I know and Hwayna knows that you acted on his behalf but they do not. Perhaps you can do more good by using your influence with Hwayna in the background. I think Hwayna was at fault in asking for your opinions in front of the council."

"Men!" Aolani said rebelliously. "The world is so unfair."

Cori went on. "You must be a channel through which information about the people can reach Hwayna. He needs to know what is going on, but he is often isolated by his position. He doesn't always know what people are saying and feeling."

"I think you are trying to tell me that we've been too wrapped up in ourselves. We've left no doors open so that the people can reach us."

"It is so. I think Hwayna has been much at fault, and so have I, for I have not been here when he needed me. He is young and inexperienced. He has been careless

48

in overlooking and ignoring the various forces that vie for his attention. He has also let them think he is weak." Cori pressed her hand to her head and rubbed her forehead. "Do you know from whom I first had an inkling of what was going on?" When Aolani shook her head, Cori said, "Do you remember Nadua?"

For a moment Aolani was mystified; then suddenly she remembered. "Of course, when I lived in the temple I was close to her. Nadua always knew all the gossip and loved to relate it to anyone who would listen to her."

"I gather you haven't visited the Temple of the Sun or seen Nadua or Nonie, with whom you were so close?"

Thinking of Nonie, Aolani felt guilty. She had loved the young concubine and treated her like a sister when she had lived at Corciconcha. She had used Nonie to gain access to Hwayna, for she was one of his favorite concubines. Why had she neglected Nonie since her marriage? She knew why. She was crazy with jealousy—still jealous of Nonie. She hated the times Hwayna visited the temple and had relations with the women there, but she had learned to bear it. She knew it was expected of him. However, she had no desire to see the many children he had fathered or to see their mothers. She saw Cori watching her and she flushed.

Cori said with pity in her voice, "I can understand your jealousy. I, too, have felt the bitter darts strike my heart. But you must rise above it. If you are to be Mama Ocllo, Hwayna Capac's *Coya*, and chief wife, you must be responsible for the happiness of his household. You should show an interest in the welfare of all his children, those of his wives as well as those of the concubines. Aolani, because you are young, I have been acting on your behalf in the temple for the past few years. But the time will come soon when I can no longer be responsible. I-I am not well."

Aolani felt cold, and a sharp pang of fear shot through her body. She looked at the frail woman before her. Cori was much thinner and her skin looked gray. How could Aolani have been so blind? Cori seldom came to Cuzco anymore, and Aolani had not checked on her. She wondered how long Cori had had the cough. She asked slowly, "Is it the breathing disease?"

Cori was matter-of-fact as she said, "I am not sure, but I find that breathing is becoming more and more difficult for me, especially here in Cuzco where the air is hard to breathe. I feel better in the lower valley."

There was a deep, sad feeling in Aolani's heart. The disease was dreaded but common among the mountain people. Dear Cori Picchu! Aolani had always liked Cori's name, a golden sparrow—light and delicate, glowing with a special, inner happiness. Cori was generous and loving with everyone. Hwayna! Did he know? Aolani asked the question with trembling lips.

"No, not yet. Lani, he will need you more than ever soon. You must do everything you can to help him. Remember the things we have talked about here today. Do not emulate Hwayna but create your own sphere of influence." She gave a small sigh, then smiled at Aolani. "The condor soars at ease in the sky above, and the fish swims easily down to the depths of the sea. Who knows which has a richer world?" She lay back on her pillows, her face flushed, her eyes too bright. After she had rested a moment, she went on. "There are a few things Hwayna has instructed me to tell you. Do you remember Capt. Luasi?" Aolani nodded. "Hwayna has brought Luasi back to Cuzco, and he will be in charge of your household and lead the caravan. On my suggestion he has assigned Nadua as your headwoman. She will guard you well and has chosen a new staff of servants for you. There have been signs that another attempt will be made on your life, so Hwayna has decided the caravan will leave tonight. Luasi is waiting outside my door and will take you by secret ways to Sacsahuaman, where you will remain safely hidden until the caravan leaves."

"You mean now? From here?"

"Yes, my child, watch yourself on this trip. Be careful." She held out her hand, and Aolani kissed it. "Now go. Remember, even here in my palace hidden eyes may be watching. Keep your face down."

Aolani hugged Cori and felt choked up as she said, "Thank you for telling me everything even though I find it hard to believe. If you are right, I now have hope." Aolani started for the door, then turned and smiled tremulously at Cori Picchu. "I love you, dear Cori. I promise you I will try to follow your advice in every way." She opened the door quickly, grief stricken that she must leave and perhaps never again see this wise and loving woman.

Luasi and six men were waiting outside the entrance. Aolani didn't even have time to greet him. He put his finger to his lips and motioned her to follow him. They went through many dark and cavernous passageways, which were made eerie by the flickering light of smoking torches. At last they were confronted by a large, wooden door. Luasi handed Aolani a drab woolen cloak and a veil. After she had put them on, he said in a low voice, "We will go outside into the streets now. There will be no litter, for we do not want to call attention to ourselves. Walk quickly and keep your head down."

Feeling a little frightened by this strange trip, she walked up the steep path to the fortress of Sacsahuaman, which loomed dark and threatening above them. She was taken to a simple and barren room, and Luasi apologized. "My lady, I am sorry to leave you here, but since the caravan leaves before

51

dawn there is much to do. You will have servants here within a few hours."

As Luasi started to leave, Aolani stopped him with her hand. "Luasi, I am bewildered. What is going on?"

"My lady, I too am bewildered. I arrived from Machu Picchu this morning, and my Lord Inca gave me my orders and left. I am sure we'll learn something soon. Now, please, my lady, I must go."

Reluctantly she saw him leave. Feeling like a prisoner, she examined her small dark room and saw a flight of stone steps leading upward. One torch flickered in the corner, and by its light she saw a straw mat and some rugs on the floor, but she was too upset to lie down. Feeling slightly ill and with an aching heart, she moved up the stairs. She found herself standing on a rampart overlooking the city of Cuzco, which nestled below. The air was bitter cold, but it revived her a little.

She remembered with anguish the last time she had visited this mighty fortress—many years ago when she and Hwayna had first returned to Cuzco. The master builder, Hwallpa Rumacho, had sent a message humbly requesting her husband's presence at Sacsahuaman. Hwayna Capac had decided to grant the request and had taken her with him. He told her he had met the man when he was young and had been impressed with him as a great builder and an interesting man.

As she had walked through the mighty buildings with Hwayna, she had been filled with awe. She had felt the same way this evening when Luasi and his men had escorted her into the huge edifice. She had also felt fear for her enemies might even kill her here. Aolani didn't want to think of the present—all of the terrible events of the last month. She tried to think of the past and what she had remembered about the place. How splendid she had thought the buildings—

the most magnificent structures in the world. Built on a great bare hill known as Sacsahuaman, or the Speckled Hawk, the fortress had been erected looking eastward to the *Intip Illocsine*, the Place Where The Sun Springs Up.

They had entered a small room very much like the one downstairs, and she had seen an old man lying on some blankets. He looked frail and gaunt—barely alive. Then he opened his eyes, and she knew his spirit must still be strong.

He had whispered, "Thank you, Great Lord, for coming to see me."

She heard Hwayna say gently, "I am sorry, Hwallpa Rumacho, to see you in such poor health. I have not seen you or the fortress for a long time. It is magnificent! My father, the Sun, thanks and blesses you. Why did you send for me?"

The old man closed his eyes and then said hesitantly, "The *pucara*, your peoples' place of refuge, is now complete—but much must still be done. The gods will soon send for me and I thought you should be aware of the present situation. Chuqui, my plans." A young man came forth from out of the shadows. "My grandson, Chuqui Rumacho," he whispered. "He will tell you."

Hwayna turned toward the young man, who fell to his knees before him. "Rise, Chuqui, grandson of Hwallpa Rumacho, our honored master builder. Speak for your grandfather."

"Thank you, lord," Chuqui said, standing up but not looking at the Inca. With his eyes cast down, he looked frightened, but then he gathered his courage and said, "As you know, Son of the Sun, Lord of Us All, your grandfather, the great emperor, Pachacuti, ordered twenty thousand men sent from the provinces to help build this mighty fortress for the protection of your people. Four thousand were used to quarry, six

53

thousand to haul and roll the stones here, and the rest to shape the stones and erect the walls and towers."

Hwayna cut him short. "I am aware of all this, and I know my father continued supplying the same number of men, but is it not finished? What more is needed?"

"Grandfather believes it will take about thirteen more years to finish the buildings remaining in the original plans."

Hwayna had whistled softly. "Seventy-five years of labor! What will take that much time?"

Chuqui unrolled a skin on which dark lines had been etched. "Here is the main fortress standing on the peak and edge of the hill known as Sacsahuaman. Here is the parade ground below the three main defensive walls. Above this round tower, the *Moyamara*, your own personal palace, needs to be completed. A pressure-piped water channel needs to be led in from underground. The royal baths and the compartments for your women must be constructed and—"

"And," the Inca said, "the holy *huacas'* places of worship need to be enclosed."

Chumpi said hesitantly, "If we are to finish, we must continue to have the man power. For the past year the work has been at a standstill, for we have had no laborers. My grandfather worries. He knew that your father, Tupac Yupanqui, was very ill and did not wish to disturb him. But he feels you should know about the situation and make a decision. Should it be completed or not?"

Hwayna had turned back to the old man and taken his hand in his. "The work shall continue, I promise. In the future all who visit Cuzco will see the magnificence of Sacsahuaman and will revere its builder. I will see to it personally."

Aolani remembered that after leaving the old man, she and Hwayna had gone to inspect the new building sites. Shortly thereafter Hwallpa Rumacho had died and Hwayna had appointed his grandson to succeed him. Now here she was in the fortress again. Would she leave it this time or would her enemies kill her here?

She went slowly down the stairs, and her tears began to flow. She fell to the stone floor and sobbed until she could cry no more. Shattered by all that she had heard from Cori Picchu and petrified by what had happened to her today, Aolani felt hollow, unraveled, as if she were lost, abandoned to all the unknown and dangerous forces around her. Was she really going on a journey north, or had she been brought up here to be killed? The wind swept in and brushed her cheeks with cold, crystal fingers. She gasped, then choked back a sob and tried to grab on to her courage. She had been in such spots before.

Aolani got up from the floor and threw herself on the pile of rugs. She couldn't think anymore. She couldn't face her problems tonight. She couldn't! Perhaps in the morning. She remembered that she had faced many problems and sorrows in her life and had always found courage before. Exhausted, she blanked out every image and at last fell asleep.

Aolani was awakened by a gentle hand shaking her shoulder. She fought to stay asleep, not wanting to face reality, but the persistent movement finally made her open her eyes. She found it difficult to focus at first, and the lights from the torches hurt her eyes. As she sat up she heard a familiar voice say, "Wake up, my lady, we must hurry."

The face looking down at her was one she had known before. Suddenly, she recognized the woman and threw her arms around Nadua. "I can't believe it. Am I dreaming? Nadua, is it really you?" She started to cry.

Nadua laughed and held Aolani in her arms. "None of that, child. Now, don't tell me I've made you unhappy?"

"Oh, no, Nadua. I've never been so glad to see anybody in my life. I don't know why I cry so much lately." She dashed the tears away with her hand. "I think I'm beginning to believe Cori Picchu."

"Come, my lady, you must dress. Capt. Luasi will escort us to the caravan, which awaits us at the edge of the city. I have hot water waiting." She hurried Aolani out of bed and into the small dressing room.

Two strange women awaited her and she listlessly let them wash and dress her. Nadua had honey cakes and fruit waiting for her, but she couldn't eat a bite.

There was a scratching at the door and as Luasi entered Aolani smiled at him. He smiled back, but he looked strained and worried—and sad, too. What had happened to him? What would happen to her on this exile from the man she loved? She felt sick and exhausted as Luasi led them from the room, and she became physically unable even to contemplate the future—which seemed desolate and without hope.

Chapter Five

Aolani could hear herself screaming in the blackness as the snow buried her deeper and deeper in its smothering depths. There was nothing but silence around her. The cold and the loneliness were more than she could bear. Panicked, she tried to claw her way toward the light. As she struggled to the surface, her sobbing gasps sounded harsh in her ears. A pale light barely illuminated the unfamiliar quarters. With her heart pounding, she sat up. The cold air hit her bare shoulders and she shivered.

Where was she? Why was she here? Aolani started to sob. She felt sick to her stomach and wanted to retch. She tried to lift herself from the damp pallet, but one foot was entangled in the heavy alpaca blanket. She fell to the cold floor. She felt a firm hand holding her forehead and heard the sound of voices as she vomited.

When she next awakened, sunlight streaked across the strange room from an aperture in the rock wall. A fire glowed in a stone brazier, the smoke drifting up toward the thatched roof. Aolani felt warm and snug in her sleeping robes and sought again to remember where she was. At first, her mind was blank, but then certain scenes flashed into her consciousness. The room at Sacsahuaman, Nadua's arms around her, a long walk in the darkness, the swaying movement of the litter, the warm drink Nadua coaxed her to drink, and then oblivion.

Suddenly, Aolani sensed someone standing nearby and looked up into Nadua's anxious eyes. "Where am I?" she whispered.

"You are all right, my lady. You have been ill for three days with a fever and chills. But the fever has broken, thanks to the gods and the help of *quina-quina*." Nadua wiped Aolani's face with a damp cloth. "The caravan has been traveling long hours and you have been unconscious most of the time. We have been very worried about you. But now you are in the Inca's lodging at Lima-tambo and soon we will cross the holy bridge that spans the Apurimac River."

Aolani shook her head. It was hard to believe. They had come so far and she had no memory of the journey. She was being carried farther and farther away from Hwayna. Her longing for him was like a deep pain that wouldn't go away. Why had it happened? What could she have done to heal the breach between them? Surely, she was at fault. She should have been more clever and less proud. She should have pleaded with him, using all her feminine wiles instead of encasing herself stubbornly in silence and resentment. It was too late now. She turned her head away from Nadua and closed her eyes, unable to face the day. Feeling weak and sick, overwhelmed by lassitude and self-pity, Aolani lay listlessly as her women bathed her, clothed her in fresh garments, and changed her bedding.

Nadua held a bowl to her lips and coaxed her into swallowing the warm broth. Lacking the strength to refuse, she did as she was told. During the next day she remained the same, spending the time lying in her litter, indifferent to what was going on.

It wasn't until the following day when they reached the switchback trail leading down into the awesome gorge of the Apurimac River that she became aware of her surroundings. She couldn't help but become aware of them for her litter pitched and rolled like a boat on a stormy lake, as the eight bearers attempted to work their way down the steep trail. It was like descending the coils of a snake, and she had to hold on to the sides of the litter to keep from falling out.

As they plunged from the high mountain plateau down deep into the jungle mist created by the fast-flowing waters of the mighty river, Aolani noticed a rapid change in the terrain. The vegetation became lush and flamboyantly green. Exotic flowers in myriad colors glowed like jewels in its depths. A tangle of lianas, vines, and creepers clothed the trees in veils of chartreuse and emerald.

Aolani gasped! A flight of gaudy macaws turned the branches of one tree into a riot of color, and the birds chattered angrily as her litter passed by. Then, the trail became dark and the shade cast by the many layered ceiling of dense growth became gloomy. The air was hot and humid. She felt trickles of moisture on her skin, and her body was wet with perspiration.

As Aolani brushed an insect from her cheek, a group of playful howling monkeys threw handfuls of fetid jungle debris at the bearers. She had to smile at the indecent show they put on, for their bottoms were as pink and bare as a baby's. Suddenly, the trail leveled off and the bearers set her litter gently on the ground. As she looked about, she saw a group of Indian women

59

spinning bunchgrass for siding while the men in another group aligned thick cables to form the base and the handrails of a new bridge that would eventually replace the present one. Aolani remembered seeing them before when she and Hwayna had returned to Cuzco after Hwayna's father died. Hwayna had told her that this tribe of Carahuasi Indians had been assigned by his grandfather, Pachacuti, to spin and secure a fiber-rope bridge, 150 feet long, and to replace it at least once every year, or earlier if it showed any signs of weakness. The villager's work service or *Mita* was fulfilled in this way. They didn't have to leave their homes to serve the Inca as soldiers, workers, or servants.

Aolani saw Capt. Luasi approach her litter with Nadua at his side. It was time for her to cross the bridge over a torrent swollen with summer rain. Aolani gingerly started walking over the swaying bridge with Nadua in front of her and Luasi following closely behind. Being a little weak, she stumbled and would have fallen had not Luasi quickly caught her. She liked Luasi. He had been very kind to her many years ago when he was Hwayna's chief aide. She had to find a way to talk to him soon. She gave a sigh of relief as her feet touched firm ground once again.

During the days that followed the spectacular crossing of the river and the laborious return up to the high plateau, Aolani began to slowly regain her strength and with it her attitude changed. She was tired of feeling wretched, depressed, and full of self-pity. She resolved to quit moping about problems that could not be changed. Regardless of the loss of her husband and her position as his chief wife, she would not be defeated. After all, she was a queen in her own right in Chachapoya and the granddaughter of a god. She would make her own life and leave the past few years as far behind her as possible. Suddenly, she couldn't wait to see her cousins, Chacoya and Aruja, who had been assigned as regents in her absence. She began to eat well and exercise daily by walking part of the time. Her skin regained its luster and her hair, when washed by her women, glowed in the sunlight.

It was magnificent country through which they traveled; the mountain's snowy summits crowned the horizon and the lower slopes were lightly sprinkled with red flowers. Sometimes their only companions were the llamas and the condors flying overhead. Aolani knew they were on the Chinchaysuyu Road that paralleled the coast highway going north. It would take three months to reach Cajamarca following that route. One day they dropped into a deep valley where the weather was warm enough to grow sweet fruits, daisylike flowers, many types of blossoming cacti, and bushes loaded with seeds.

Early one morning they passed through a high, sun-washed village where a group of old women sat beside traditional backstrap looms weaving cloth and gossiping.

Farther on, a group of younger women winnowed quinoa in woven baskets while their men harvested the potatoes and other edible roots on the exceptionally high terraces above them. The caravan passed through high deserts swept by cold winds, through deep ravines red with porphyry, and around deep lakes tucked into mountain basins like bits of turquoise decorating the landscape.

One morning Capt. Luasi approached Aolani's palanquin. "Well, my lady, we will reach Bombon in a few days and Jauja in about a week, which is halfway to Cajamarca. We will get a few days' rest in both places."

Aolani smiled back at him. "I remember Jauja very

well; I found it enchanting. I look forward to our stay there."

Luasi looked stern. "Take care, my lady, while we are there. There is a large temple and there are many priests in the city. There may be danger. Stay within your quarters, if you please." He bowed and left.

Aolani felt a little chagrined that he had issued her an order in a most ungracious manner. Sometimes she felt that she was being treated like a child. Could there be a danger now that they were so far from Cuzco and her enemies there? She would be careful, of course, but she was not going to stay in her quarters all of the time.

Aolani awakened in Bombon to see sunlight shining through an open door, making delicate patterns on the stone floor. The air was soft and balmy, with the fragrance of flowers invading the room. It reminded her of the sunny mornings she and Hwayna had spent when they were here, enjoying the morning meal with the birds singing in the molle trees. She remembered the talks they had shared sitting by the Inca's pool and the afternoon rides in a double palanquin. They would go to the royal zoo, the flower gardens, or to check on the Inca's building programs. There was always something interesting to do with Hwayna. Aolani sighed. It seemed so long ago.

The rays of the sun touched her face. A few years ago she had spent two weeks in this very room, looking out at this same garden. It was here in Bombon that she had first become aware of her love for Hwayna Capac. She sat up and realized that she could not think of him without crying. She loved him, but she had to be strong enough to live without him. She called out, "Nadua."

In an instant Nadua was there. She smiled as she

carried in Aolani's morning fruit and coco. "What is it, my lady?"

The water in the pool sparkled so brightly in the light Aolani had to avert her eyes. She saw the emerald green of parrots in the trees and the beautiful pink birds on their long legs, their snakelike necks twisting around. She wanted to go out into the garden. She wanted to sit in the sun. "Nadua, is it not beautiful here? I can't wait to get outside."

Nadua clapped her hands, her eyes lighting up with mischief. "So, my lady is beginning to like life again. Good! She is tired of being as limp and uncaring as a lifeless bundle. So be it." She went to the door and called, "Mourning Dove, Dark Moon, come at once." Giving orders, she clucked around Aolani like a mother bird.

By the time Aolani's ladies had washed and dressed her, Nadua was back with some fragrant broth, thickened with potato, and a portion of delicate white fish, which had been baked, wrapped in leaves, and placed over an open fire. To Aolani's surprise, the food tasted good, and she was able to finish most of it.

Later, as she relaxed against her pillows, the warm sun soaking into her skin, she decided she felt better. Aolani had been in misery for a long time and was thoroughly tired of the way she had been acting. She had always prided herself on her own strength and feelings of independence. She was alive and young. She was going to stop feeling sorry for herself. Hwayna was probably having a fine time—a new wife, celebrations every night, and relief over ridding himself of Aolani. Tears pricked against her eyelids. She had to stop thinking about him.

Aolani heard Nadua, who was sitting on a stone beside her talking nonstop with her usual enthusiasm, relating all that had happened this past week.

Aolani watched her face. Nadua's eyes sparkled, and she laughed often at the things she told. She had such a zest for life. No wonder Hwayna's father, the Emperor Tupac Yupanqui, had selected her as his favorite concubine. Beautiful and full of fun, she had been the Inca's constant companion until he met Cori Picchu. Nadua must know how it felt to be discarded.

Suddenly Aolani asked, "Nadua, were you happy in the temple?"

Looking astonished, Nadua exclaimed, "Of course! I'm always happy. Why be sad and gloomy? Life isn't all happiness, as everyone knows, but I always find something to be cheerful about. Even as a child I always found much to amuse me."

"I heard that your father gave you to the Inca when you were very young. Didn't that make you sad?"

Nadua laughed. "Heavens, no! I was delighted. My home was small and boring. There was nothing to do all day. My father worked from early morning until late at night. He was in charge of the Chasqui station at the North Gate. It was a very important position, for most of the Inca's messages came through that gate. My two old aunts took care of me, and they were ancient. You see, my mother died when I was born and my aunts tried their best with me, but they were just too old and I was too much of a handful. There was no one to play with, so I was always running away."

She stopped for a moment and then went on. "From my earliest years I was told that I was beautiful. Everyone said so, even my father. Perhaps that is what gave him the idea. Anyhow, my father wanted more for me than he could give. I think he felt I needed to be trained to be a lady, so he took me to Coricancha and gave me to the Inca."

"Then what happened?"

"I thought I'd died and gone to the happy afterworld." Nadua giggled. "I was placed with the youngest group. With so many children to play with, no wonder I loved it. We learned how to cook, how to do simple weaving and sewing. We gardened, sang, danced, and learned how to play an instrument. There was always something new, something exciting to do."

"You didn't find the life a little stifling, even a little threatening as you became older and were assigned, assigned—"

"You mean when I was assigned to the House of Concubines?" Aolani nodded. "Oh, my dear child, it was the most exciting and thrilling thing that ever happened to me. To think that I was considered beautiful and clever enough to join the finest group of women in the empire. I might even be able to win the Inca's favor. To me it was the highest honor I could achieve. My greatest fear was that he would ignore me. That really frightened me. I listened and learned from all of the other girls and from the older *mamacoyas*. We were taught how to please a man with our hands and bodies and ways to make love more exciting. I became quite good. I couldn't wait for the Inca to choose me. Do you know what I did?" She smiled and giggled again.

Nadua seemed so pleased with herself, Aolani had to smile, too. "No, tell me."

"There was a lot of competition for the Inca, believe me. The night we heard that he was back in Cuzco, intent upon visiting the temple, every girl in our house prepared herself all day. I tried to think of something I could do to attract his attention. Since we all wore the same long white tunic, how could I possibly stand out amongst all those beauties?

"I thought about myself. The *mamacoyas* said I had beautiful breasts and a tiny waist. They approved of my small buttocks and long legs. Why not show them,

65

I thought, but how? Finally, I found this thin, gauzy cotton in the costume room. Oh, my lady, you could almost see through it. I made myself a short tunic that barely covered my bottom and cinched it with a gold belt. To make it even more provocative, I draped the material over my right shoulder, leaving my left breast partially exposed. Then I slit my own long tunic all the way down the back so that I could easily slip in and out of it."

Aolani was intrigued. "Don't stop there. What happened?"

"Well, the Inca came in and was seated amidst his pillows with everybody bowing and trying to please him. I was so excited that my heart beat as loudly as a drum. Some of the older girls whom he had previously selected moved forward and he talked to them. I couldn't hear what was being said, even though I crept nearer. Then the head *mamacoya* asked if she might introduce the newest concubines. That was my group. The Inca nodded, and we were brought forth one by one."

She looked a little rueful as she said, "Now that I am older, I wonder how I had the nerve to do what I did. I guess at thirteen you don't think of the consequences. As I stepped forward, I let my long tunic slip to the floor. You can imagine the horrified gasps. The faces of the *mamacoyas* were furious. However, I could see a gleam in the Inca's eyes. I pivoted, and as I did so, I gave him a wink."

"You winked at Tupac Yupanqui?" Aolani was amazed.

"Then the Inca held out his hand and I dropped down beside him on the pillows. I let my breast accidentally touch his hand."

"Accidentally," Aolani murmured. "By all the gods, what courage you must have had."

"And it worked. The Inca dismissed all the others. When they had all left, he broke into howls of laughter. I started to giggle as he asked me to undress him. I'd never taken off a man's clothes before. I was laughing so hard I couldn't manage, so he took off his sandals and tunic himself. Mama Kilya strike me dumb if I'm not telling the truth. It was wonderful, even better than I expected it to be."

Aolani watched Nadua in wonder. That sly, devilish look—almost a smirk—on her face. "There is more to the story, isn't there?" she asked.

"By all the gods, yes. The first experience was very intimate, and I loved it. But what happened next was—" Nadua stopped. "The rest is a little too intimate to relate, but that night was the beginning of five wonderful years. The Inca took me back to the palace, to his personal quarters, and there I stayed except when he left Cuzco on business."

A dreamy expression shadowed her face but then she went on. "I'd never before enjoyed such luxury. The sumptuous banquets, the lavish entertainments every night, and you should have seen my clothes and jewels. I was the envy of every girl in the temple. Even when my two sons and then a daughter were born, the Inca often came to see me. He said he enjoyed my company as much as my body." She sighed. "Tupac Yupanqui was a great man, even though he was a god, and I am thankful and grateful that I was a part of his life, even for such a short time."

"Weren't you jealous when he married Cori Picchu?" Aolani asked curiously. "I understand he became quite faithful to her."

"He did, but I was not jealous because of that. The Inca loved and revered her. Who could blame him? She was, and still is, the most beautiful and loving woman I've ever known. She is so wise and good. If

67

only I could be like her, but I know I can't. Perhaps I am jealous of her perfection. I do not know."

Aolani said thoughtfully, "I agree about Cori Picchu. She is a very unique and special sort of person. When I saw what she had created at Sauca Cachi, I was amazed. It was such a happy and wonderful place. I could see why my husband adored it. I, too, wish I could be like her."

"Oh, my lady, she has been so good to all of us in the Temple of the Sun. She looked after us all."

"Just what did she do, Nadua?"

"You were in the temple for a while, my lady, but you were there when her influence was great. You can have no idea how cruel and mean the priests and the *mamacoyas* can be at times if no one watches over them. Cori Picchu, bless her heart, was a match for them. If anyone was harmed or treated badly, she knew about it, and when she was angry they shook like leaves in the wind. She was like a loving mother to us all."

"No wonder you adored her." As she made the statement, Aolani felt ashamed of her own selfish behavior during the past few years. Far from being loving and kind to those around her, she had simply ignored everyone, thinking only of herself and Hwayna. She said impulsively, "Nadua, you have been wonderful to me. I want to thank you from the bottom of my heart. Perhaps you are more like Cori Picchu than you think."

"I hope so, my lady. I can only try, but now we must get you inside. You've had enough sun for one day."

Chapter Six

Passing a bridge set upon large stone piles, the caravan entered a region of high summits, most of them frosted with snow. It was early morning and Aolani shivered as she cuddled down on her furs inside the luxurious palanquin and glanced outside. Her eight litter bearers in their short tunics, with bare arms and legs, seemed oblivious to the cold, or maybe the coca the men chewed made them immune to the weather. She closed the woolen drapes, hoping to keep out the bitter wind that clawed like a jaguar trying to get through to her. It would be a long, cold morning before they came to the high crest where the village of Parcos perched. But from there on, it would be a downward descent through a beautiful valley covered with fruit trees until they reached Angovaco Pass.

Aolani looked forward to having a bath at Parcos this evening in the warm waters that flowed from springs that bubbled up from the ground. What a joy it would be to wash her hair in plenty of hot water with fragrant soap. She recalled that the Inca's lodgings on the white cliffs above Parcos were large and comfortable, much more so than the one-night lodgings she had been staying in along the way.

With the curtains closed, there was nothing to see and her thoughts returned to the conversation she had had with Nadua a few days ago. Nadua was really quite a woman to have won the Lord High Inca away from all the other beautiful women in the House of Virgins. Not only was she lovely, she was a unique and amusing woman who always saw the humorous side of life.

I should have asked Nadua to accompany me today, she thought, for there is plenty of room for two in the palanquin. They both could have forgotten the jarring of the ride and taken pleasure in each other's company. Aolani should have remembered how miserable and uncomfortable the small hemp litters in which the women traveled could be. It was not too long ago that she had been carried in one of them. That was before the prince, Hwayna Capac, had taken her into his custody. Aolani recalled the many times Hwayna had invited her to sit in his palanquin as they journeyed toward Cajamarca. She remembered feeling like a queen as she sat beside him, the ceiling of the palanquin covered with vivid parrot's feathers. She had been flattered and flustered by his obvious interest.

Thinking of Hwayna brought the old memories back to haunt her. Aolani felt stricken by what had happened to her, lost in a morass of turbulent feelings—hurt, resentful, rebellious, bitter, and alone. Hurt because of Hwayna's desertion and estrangement from her, resentful of the fact that everyone seemed to blame her for what had happened, even Cori Picchu. Perhaps she had tried to influence her husband too much, taken on a large number of responsibilities, but by all the gods of earth, sky, and water, how could she be blamed for everything and called a devil-woman? Her enemies had even killed her unborn child. The memory of the babe gnawed at her body, filling her with unbearable pain. The gods were cruel and inhuman—giving her such hope and then tearing it away. She found it hard to believe in the gods anymore. Perhaps they disapproved of her relationship with her husband and were telling her so.

Aolani remembered the first years of their marriage when Hwayna felt so young, insecure, and deeply in awe of his father, Tupac Yupanqui, God and Ruler of the Empire. Hwayna had convinced himself that he was unworthy, not fit to be a god, and he'd dreaded being his father's heir. He had needed Aolani's support and encouragement and she had given it to him in every way she could. She supposed it had become a habit to serve him. But he was not a boy now. He was a grown man and a strong one at that, more than able to make his own decisions. She should have recognized this and stayed more in the background. As Cori Picchu had said, she should have been more a fish than a condor.

The more Aolani thought about the situation the angrier she became. Hwayna had encouraged her to express herself when the council met, asked for her suggestions, and taken her to all of his meetings. If she had been his brother or a male adviser, she would have been admired for her administrative skills and knowledge. Just because she was a woman, and a very different one at that, they saw her as a devil. Her strange coloring probably had a lot to do with their hatred of her. They thought of her as an outsider in their dark-skinned, black-haired world.

Aolani felt miserably alone and without friends, and tears came to her eyes. All her life she had been alone

71

until Hwayna Capac came into her world. She had thought that at last someone had accepted her for what she was and loved her for herself. Aolani closed her eyes in despair and began to feel angry again. She must be strong. She would return to Chachapoya and work for her people. Perhaps they would learn to love and respect her. All she needed was courage and the help of the gods.

As she felt the warmth of the sun coming through the drapes, she pulled them open. It was cold, but bright and beautiful. She would believe in herself and her own power. Her spirits began to rise. When the caravan stopped at midday, she was glad to step out of the litter and away from her own thoughts.

Aolani saw a gleaming lake in the distance and another one of the small fortresses she had seen earlier in the day. This part of the empire had been a scene of many battles before the Incas had finally subdued the warlike people of the Lake Chincha-cocha region. They had caused a lot of trouble for Hwayna Capac over the past few years. Where were they now? she wondered. There seemed to be no sign of human life in this desolate area where vegetation was almost nonexistent. From time to time gusts of wind blew down from the frozen peaks and she drew her fur-lined cloak close to her.

Although the wind was cold, the sun was warm, so Aolani decided to take a short walk to relieve her stiffness. As she started up a faint path leading through the rocks to a high bald hill, she was joined by Nadua and other members of her retinue. Almost immediately she noticed a small hut in the nest of rocks. As they came closer to the stone dwelling, she saw it looked old and deserted, but for some reason she was drawn to it. Aolani felt a strange and compelling urge to investigate as she approached. Suddenly she heard a faint wailing and thought it must be the wind. Then she heard the sound again.

She started forward, but as she drew nearer, she heard Nadua say, "Wait, my lady, let the guard go first."

Knowing the advice was good, Aolani stopped as the man came forward and peered through the torn animal hide that partially covered the entrance. He thrust it aside and entered the crude dwelling. While they waited the dark clouds swirled over their heads obscuring the sun. Aolani shivered at another gust of wind. A flash of lightning clawed against the sky and she felt a superstitious sense of fear. When Nadua came and stood close to her, she felt comforted.

The guard returned and, beckoning to Nadua, said, "There is a woman and a child in there. I think the woman is dead."

Nadua entered, Aolani following close behind. Aolani gasped as she entered the windowless room filled with the odor of smoke, decay, and human excrement. Aolani would have left if the faint wailing had not become louder. She could see very little in the gloom, but as her eyes adjusted to the light flickering through the poorly thatched roof, she was able to see the dead ashes of a fire pit directly in front of her. A basket and a cracked clay pot, touching relics of a past life, lay beside it.

Aolani moved to where the guard and Nadua stood looking down at the still form of a woman lying on a ragged pallet. She seemed fairly well dressed and around her neck was a gold pectoral hanging from a chain. The woman's face was unwrinkled and her skin paler than that of most people. Aolani saw Nadua kneel down, listen for a heartbeat, and shake her head, for there was no sign of life. The woman's arms lay

across a crying baby, who was wrapped in a thick
blanket. The little face was pinched and it continued
to wail miserably. Nadua stared with concern at the
woman's right shoulder. Aolani followed her gaze, but
in the dark gloom, she didn't see the cause for alarm.
Then she noticed what appeared to be blood staining
the material of the woman's tunic.

Taking the wailing baby from the woman's arms,
Nadua said quickly, "Let us leave. The woman is dead
and whoever killed her may still be around."

Together they went outside, followed by the guard.
Aolani was uneasy. Nadua had said the woman had
been killed. Crimes such as this were almost unheard
of in the Inca Empire. If it had been robbery, why
hadn't her clothes and jewelry been taken? Why was
the baby left with her? Aolani felt a strange premonition that she had been meant by the gods to find this
child. Why?

As she looked at the baby, she heard Nadua say, "No
fever, no rashes, no cough! He's probably just hungry.
Fortunately he appears old enough to eat quinoa and
potato. He is a male child, my lady."

Aolani turned to the guard. "Run quickly and inform
Capt. Luasi of what has happened. We will follow you
back to the caravan." She reached out her arms. "Come,
give me the baby, Nadua. I'll carry him. Go and arrange
for food to be ready."

"Oh, no!" Nadua exclaimed, moving away from
Aolani. "Not in your condition. He may be sick. You
had better stay away from me as well."

"What did you say?"

"I said you must not come near us. A woman in your
condition—"

"My what?" Aolani asked in a bewildered voice as
she followed Nadua, who was heading back to the
caravan almost at a run.

Nadua shouted to her. "The Inca would have me killed if I let anything happen to you now."

Aolani stopped, staring after her. Dazed, she followed Nadua with the others behind her. What was Nadua babbling about? Was she implying that she was pregnant? By all the gods, it couldn't be true. It had been almost three months since Hwayna had bedded her but everything was so vague in her mind. Had she had a monthly flow since then? She couldn't remember. It was possible—the nausea, the weakness. It could be. She was appalled. Why now? Now when she had been discarded by the Inca? Now when Hwayna Capac had selected a new wife? She laughed nervously, almost hysterically. It was unbelievable! There was no understanding the ways of the gods!

A few days later, as the caravan wended its way through the large beautiful Valley of Jauja, Aolani was still dazed by the news of her pregnancy. Her morning nausea and her swollen breasts proved that Nadua was right. Aolani hugged herself. In spite of all her problems she wanted this child. Suddenly, the world seemed a better place. As she looked out at the lush land covered with fruit trees basking in the sun, she felt happy. She noticed that people were beginning to line the roadside, their faces bright with curiosity. As her elaborately decorated litter passed by, they bowed and shouted in joyous voices the same salutation they gave Hwayna: *"Haille!"*

Feeling warm and happy, Aolani directed the guard who walked beside her litter to notify Luasi that musicians and dancers should precede the caravan and that peanuts should be tossed to the people. She knew they were considered a great delicacy by the common folk, and it was one way she could express her joy.

In the late afternoon, Aolani saw the great lodgings of stone at the head of the valley. The outer buildings were huge, round storehouses as high as two men, which she knew held food, clothing, and many other necessities belonging to the Inca. They passed the large Temple of the Sun and the smaller Temple of Viracocha as well as small shops and businesses. At the entrance to the palace buildings, gatekeepers were on guard. They quickly admitted her litter and those of her personal staff into the courtyard, where two rows of armed warriors saluted them. At the far end was a stairway that led to a fountain near a great wall in the shape of a triangle. Aolani descended from her litter with a sigh of relief as the members of her personal staff were taken past the fountain into the Inca's courtyard.

Looking about her, Aolani saw all but five of her 60 women attendants were being escorted into the palace by a *mamacoya*. Most of them were carrying baskets and packages. The dancers and musicians followed them. An elderly gentleman in a splendid uniform that fit loosely on his old bones came forward and made obeisance. "Welcome, my lady. Everything has been prepared for your arrival. If you and your attendants will follow me."

Aolani looked at Nadua, Luasi, and the baby. Nadua and Luasi were talking, seemingly about something important, for their faces were very intent. Aolani was getting extremely tired of being manipulated by those two. She must put a stop to it and the time was now.

Ignoring the old man, Aolani walked to where they were standing and spoke firmly to Nadua. "After I have bathed and eaten, you will bring the baby to me this evening. You have had four days to check his health and I want no further delays in seeing him for myself."

Aolani turned to Luasi. "See what information you can gather about the child's mother and find out what happened to the father. Report to me as soon as possible."

Aolani turned and imperiously entered the palace with the court officials following behind. She felt very pleased with herself. At last she was taking charge of her own life.

Chapter Seven

Rising early the morning after their arrival in Jauja, Aolani entered the Inca's private garden, which was adjacent to her bedchamber. The light from the rising sun was just beginning to permeate the sky. Dawn was a time of enchantment, she thought, as the veils of mist from the river played tag for a moment and then disappeared as the sun touched the earth. After a sudden explosion of feathers, a white-winged dove settled on a ceiba tree, eyeing her in a suspicious fashion. She had probably disturbed its morning bath in the fountain, she mused, smiling a little. Aolani watched with delight the gilded flickers that flew in and out of the thornbush, disregarding the little wrens that played in the dirt beneath them.

Aolani took a deep breath. The pungent smell of molle leaves mingled with the aromatic smell of cassia and the sweeter-smelling caimito, reminding her of previous visits. Noticing the gate leading to the river was open, she walked past the guards and looked down upon the terraced gardens, past the river to the far snow-covered peaks that encircled the city like a string of pearls. According to Luasi, the Inca's grounds were well patrolled and she could safely explore the area. She walked down the steps, her eyes returning again to the vast river with its torrents, cascading waters, and swirling pools.

There were rushes along the river's edge and she saw a llama poised in the stillness, standing motionless, but alert to her presence. The sun touched its shaggy coat and turned its grayish wool into a silvery-textured robe of beauty. As a flock of falcons plummeted out of the nearby ceiba tree, the llama took off, startled. As the llama fled, the small yellow and orange wildflowers waved in excitement as it passed.

Oh, what a wonderful morning! Aolani thought. Later on, we'll have a picnic down here and bring the baby. Then in the afternoon she simply must visit the priest, Moche, at the Temple of Viracocha, for he was an old friend of hers. Moche was a dear man and had been like a big brother to her during those happy years she had spent with old Lord Pinau. How lonely those first days had been when Tupac Yupanqui had sent her to the Temple of Viracocha in the remote Valley of Rojchi. Everything had been strange to her. She had only been ten years of age and frightened. Lord Pinau had been kind and gentle, offering her love and friendship when she had really needed to feel wanted. Moche, his other student, had also been affectionate and understanding with her. Lord Pinau had been like a father to her until the day he died.

As she hurried back to the palace, Aolani saw Nadua, who began scolding as usual. "My lady, you are going to age me before my time. I had your bath ready and I went to wake you up and you had vanished. What was I to think? My heart is still pounding with fear."

Jeanne Nickson

"Don't be grumpy, Nadua dear. We're going on a picnic today. Won't that be fun?"

The picnic they had later that morning was fun, in fact delightful. The baby seemed to enjoy it as much as anyone, especially when Aolani sat on a rock and, holding him, let him dangle his feet in the water. He kicked and splashed until they were both wet. Aolani hugged him close. He patted her cheek with his little hand; then his fingers grasped her gold beads, pulling hard until they broke and flew into the water like fragile gold insects. He looked so pleased with himself that she had to smile. But he was tired and put his head against her breast, his thumb in his mouth. She watched the swirling water.

The river was moving swiftly, and in the middle, the currents looked dangerous. By piling rocks out into the water from the land, a section of the river had been made safe for the Inca and his family to swim, and Aolani took advantage of it. Handing the baby to his nurse, she took off her tunic and entered the icy water. The torrential flow from the far hems of snow cleansed her spirit of all the bad memories of recent days. Aolani felt challenged by the rough water. Swimming out into the savage foam she felt invigorated as she battled her way back to shore. A group of water-darkened rocks, covered with lichen, barred her way.

Aolani carefully worked her way around them. She could see that Nadua was not happy with her as she dried her with a soft cloth and handed her a tunic. She wouldn't worry about it. Her body felt wonderful, tingling, and alive. Such a change after all the weeks of illness.

Later that day, Aolani was greeted by Lord Moche, the High Priest of the Temple of Viracocha, with great affection. He took her hands. "Let me look at you, my dear. It is good to see you, but you have changed. How regal you are! Now that you are *Coya*, I should kneel to you!"

Tears filled her eyes as she took him by the shoulders and raised her face to kiss him lightly on the cheek. "Don't! I forbid it! You are like a brother to me. Oh, Moche, how I have missed you and Father Pinau."

Moche looked at her with sorrow. "I am sorry I wasn't with you when he died."

"I have so much to tell you, my friend. Do you have time to talk?"

"Can you wait for a very short time? I have to perform a ceremonial blessing for the planting season. The people are gathering now out in the fields and there is no one else to do it. I am the only priest here. As you know, the god, Viracocha, is not popular with most of our people."

"I know and am sorry about it. But, Moche, of course you must go. I will wait for you. Could someone show us around while you are gone? I would love to see the temple."

"Of course, my dear." Moche summoned a young man to his side and introduced him as Vanos. Aolani smiled at him.

"Come with me, my lady," Vanos said, bowing low. "The first thing you should know is that the temple was built in Jauja by the Lord High Inca, Tupac Yupanqui, who was devoted to the god, Viracocha."

Aolani was not surprised, for she'd heard Hwayna talk about his father's partiality for the Creator. She was amused at Nadua's sudden interest when she heard Yupanqui's name. They followed the young man down a twisted corridor and entered a large courtyard from which many steps led to a sunken plaza. "This is where we hold our most sacred ceremonies, not like the one

Lord Moche is going to perform in the fields." Aolani thought he sounded a little miffed.

There were high walls around the open area on which sharp, bold lines were cut into the stone; the patterns were convoluted, with an elaborate intertwining of various themes. Amongst them were jaws with prominent feline fangs, pairs of nostrils, and profiles of various snakes abounded. On one wall was a great stylized eye in which the pupil, in the upper center, was raised balefully to heaven. Aolani was not particularly impressed. It was similar to the carvings she had seen at Coricancha, the Temple of the Sun in Cuzco.

They passed through several beautifully decorated rooms and at last entered the main sanctuary, a long narrow room that could hold about 200 people. On one wall were five panels that Aolani recognized. They told the story of Viracocha. She had seen similar ones in the temple where she had studied with Lord Pinau. These panels, though, were more beautiful.

The first panel showed the creation of men and women in Viracocha's own image at Tiahuanacu, the birthplace of the Incas, which was near the southern shore of Lake Titicaca. The next mural showed the god giving the people tribal customs and languages as he sent them to earth with orders to emerge from certain caves, lakes, and hills to make settlements.

Aolani turned to the next panel, which showed the god, Viracocha, as an old man carrying a staff, being stoned by the people of Rachi because they didn't believe his words. The next panel showed Viracocha calling down fire from the heavens to subdue the wicked people and in the last panel the god bid the men and women a sorrowful farewell and set off across the ocean, walking on the water. It must be sad, thought Aolani, like creating a child that goes bad and refuses to listen to you.

She heard Nadua asking her a question. "Tell me, my lady, is Viracocha a greater god than the Sun?"

Aolani was thoughtful as she responded. "Let me tell you the story as told to me by my teacher, Lord Pinau, who was a very wise and famous man. He was the tutor of the Great Inca you knew well, Tupac Yupanqui. He asked Pinau if the Sun was a god. As Pinau was trying to think of an appropriate answer, his pupil, Yupanqui, raised his eyes to the Sun and stared directly at it. Pinau asked, 'My lord, what are you doing? You must not gaze at your father, the Sun, in that way.' But the Inca paid no attention to him. Lord Pinau said again, 'Take care. You may go blind.'"

As Aolani paused, Nadua asked quickly, "What happened?"

"Yupanqui asked two questions of Pinau. The first one was, 'Would one of my subjects dare order me to leave my throne each morning and make me run through the day?'"

"I know what he would have said," Nadua announced. "I knew him well. 'No one would dare!' he'd say. What was the second question?"

"Yupanqui asked, 'And if I ordered the most powerful of my nobles to march to the southern sea, would they obey?'"

Nadua said vehemently, "He'd say, 'of course the nobles would obey the Inca, for he was their ruler.'"

"That's exactly what Pinau told him. Then Yupanqui said to Pinau, 'Very well, our father, the Sun, runs across the sky each day without stopping. If the Sun were the ruler of all things in our world, he would stop when he wished and rest. The Sun would not take orders; he would give orders. Since the Sun does not, he must depend on a more powerful god than himself. He is not the supreme being. Ought we to entrust our lives and the life of our country to the Sun?"

"Oh, by Mother Kilya, the Moon," Nadua said, "now I understand why the Priests of the Sun hate the Priests of Viracocha and their temples. It makes you wonder about things, doesn't it?"

"Yes," Aolani said, "it does make you think and wonder."

Vanos led them to a door and opened it. "This is Lord Moche's study. He will be here in a few moments."

Chapter Eight

As Aolani watched the small lizard basking motionless and content in the hot sunlight, she wished with envy that she could be so relaxed. She felt a vague sense of uneasiness, which bothered her. Perhaps it was because of the two men who had asked for an audience with her last night. Despite her fatigue, she had welcomed the Lord General of Jauja and the High Priest of Inti into her presence. Aolani had met the priest, Sonar, before, when he had visited them in Cuzco. There was a certain physical resemblance to Hwayna Capac, his half brother, but otherwise Sonar was very different from her husband. Hwayna hadn't liked him either, saying he was as fork tongued as a serpent and as slippery as an eel. When Sonar looked at her she had felt a nervous shiver go down her spine. It made her anxious to leave Jauja and start on her journey again.

She picked up the tunic of fine vicuna wool and

started to embroider gold flowers on the hem, but she couldn't keep her mind on her work. Aolani stood up and gazed restlessly out the open window. A flock of birds flew across the courtyard; their flapping wings, a shiny blue black in the light, made no sound. Their ominous shadows touched the earth in silence. A cool wind swept down from the mountain passes and ruffled her hair. As the breeze moved through the foliage and trees, the soft rustling of the palm fronds overhead sounded like the beat of a small drum.

Aolani observed Capt. Luasi coming through the open gate with a number of men and knew it must be time to change the guards. As she watched Luasi, she thought how attractive he was, how virile and strong despite his age. She glanced at Nadua and smiled, for her servingwoman was watching Luasi, too. They would make a good match!

The gurgling noise of a delighted baby interrupted Aolani's thoughts. She went over to the rug and sat down beside him. The child tried to grab her hair as she buried her face in his tummy. When she picked him up, held him high in the air, and pretended to drop him, he squealed with delight. She covered him with kisses.

"I hope that child is not going to be spoiled like a rotten piece of fruit left too long in the sun," Nadua commented. "The way you and the other ladies dote on him is not good for the child." Nadua put down her cutting knife and needle, laying them on the window ledge. She said gently, "I must admit he is a sweet baby—hardly ever cries. Not at all like my three sons."

Aolani laughed and hugged the baby again. "Nadua, I know you dote on him, too."

There was a stir at the door. Aolani saw Capt. Luasi enter the large reception chamber and drop to his knees. With his head bent to the floor, he waited for her to acknowledge him. The long narrow rays of sunlight coming through the leafy foliage outside the window illuminated the gold and mother-of-pearl design on its surface and lighted his face.

Aolani placed the baby on the rug and, turning toward Luasi, asked, "Well, Captain, have you heard any news about the child's parents?"

Luasi sat up and said rather cautiously, "My lady, it has not been easy to collect information. Several people saw a large group of travelers that included a woman and a child, but no one talked to them. The group seemed to be in a hurry. They did not stop here in Jauja. About two leagues away from the hut where you found the baby, we found the unclothed bodies of the men in the party. Everything had been taken from them and there was no way to identify any of them, except for the leader. We think it was the leader, for he had a tight gold ring on his little finger that was overlooked. It looked like an ambush. What little I have found out comes from one source, a priest, who, in the course of his duties in some of the outlying villages, ran into them on his way back to Jauja. He happened to see this group of travelers resting beside the highway, not too far from where we found the babe and its mother. He stopped to exchange greetings with them and the leader informed the priest that they had come from Chachapoya."

Aolani turned pale. Not too many people traveled the distance from her country to Cuzco, especially with an escort of many men. It would have to be somebody important, like her cousin, Chacoya. She felt sick with fear as the horrible thought entered her mind. "Are you positive?" she asked.

"The priest seemed positive about the information. He said the man was in his middle years and well dressed. There was a gold clasp on his cloak in the shape of a jaguar."

Aolani felt faint as she remembered such a clasp holding her cousin's mantle in place. She had given him the clasp long ago. It must have been Chacoya on his way to report to her. He had married the daughter of an Inca noble about two years ago when he had last come to Cuzco. He and his wife could have had a baby about the age of this child by now. It all seemed to fit. By all the gods she wished it didn't! She felt tears welling up behind her eyes. Then she looked at the child. So very sweet and precious and now an orphan—blood of her blood. She felt heartsick and yet amazed at the ways of the gods. It was strange that her caravan had stopped at that particular spot, unusual that she had walked down that path to the rocks rather than toward the lake. And when she had heard that faint sound, why had she felt compelled to move toward that old hut?

Aolani looked down at the sleeping child and then took him up in her arms. He made a soft little sound and turned his head and laid it against her breast. She felt a surge of tenderness overwhelm her. The gods must have meant her to find him. "Poor baby," she murmured. "No mother! No father! Not even a name!" Her sorrow was not only for this child, but for the mother and father who would never see their son grow to manhood. A shadow crept across the floor of the room. It would soon be dusk. She looked at Luasi, her eyes wet. "What about the bodies? Has there been an appropriate burial?"

"Knowing they came from your own people, I had the men build a stone *chullpa* in which the man and the woman were buried together in fresh llama hides. Many provisions and supplies were buried with them so that they may be comfortable in the afterworld. I also had holes dug around the funeral hut in which we buried the servants so that their spirits could find their way to their Lord."

"Thank you, Luasi. I appreciate what you have done for them." Near tears, her voice husky with grief, she said, "I must ask you to leave me now."

As Luasi left the chamber, the baby moved in Aolani's arms and opened his sleepy eyes. "Poor babe," she murmured, "I will call you Sinchi Chacoya after your father. You will be as a son to me." Tears filled her eyes as she gently touched his cheek. "Sleep well, little one."

Nadua moved forward. "Shall I take him, my lady?"

Aolani sighed, stood up, and then said as she handed her the child, "Yes, take him, Nadua. Now leave me. I want to be alone for a while."

Nadua hesitated and then said, "But, my lady, it is not good—"

Aolani held up her hand and said firmly. "Enough! Do as I say. Leave me."

As Nadua left, mumbling to herself, Aolani sat down on the carpeted floor. Hugging her knees, she rocked herself back and forth on the soft rug. Why? Why did all these terrible things happen? Why did she lose everyone she loved? Her father and mother, her uncle and aunt, her foster father, and now her cousin, Chacoya. Death seemed to stalk her family like some devil from Huari-Vilca, and now the last of her blood, except for the child, had been slain by robbers. She bent her head and wept bitterly. But then anger began to build up within her until she felt like a fire mountain about to erupt. She stood up, her disheveled hair falling over her face. Crying was weak and pointless. She must fight back against this evil force. As she brushed her hair back from her forehead with angry fingers, she moved toward the window and looked out at a white dove sipping water from the Inca's gold fountain. Everything seemed tranquil and serene.

As the evening shadows began to deepen, a horrible thought occurred to her. It made her sick to her stomach. Had Chacoya been killed because of his relationship to her?

The sounds of the servants in the next room interrupted her thinking and alerted her to the fact that she would soon be surrounded by people. They were like flies around a honeycomb. She didn't want to see anyone. She had to think. She had to get away—she needed time to herself. The water of the river beckoned to her as the last rays of Inti rippled across its surface. She wanted to be down there by the river where she could be quiet listening to the soothing sounds of the cascading water.

Could she possibly get by the two men who guarded the entrance between the Inca's garden and the path down to the river? She was going to try. Determinedly, she grabbed her *liquida* off the small chest where she had thrown it and put it around her shoulders. As soon as the sun sank into heaven's vast sea, it would grow cold and she would need her cloak. As she scrambled out the window, she spied Nadua's knife on the ledge. She put it in her *chumpi*, which was tied around her waist. Dropping softly to the ground, she moved swiftly into the thick shadow of an old molle tree.

Listening intently, she heard the guards as they marched back and forth across the entrance to the garden. How was she going to get past them? If only she could create some kind of disturbance. What could she do? Aolani looked around her and noticed the gold images of birds and animals clustered around the fountain. The shadows deepened as she crept out of the shade of the tree and grabbed one of the gold replicas of a rabbit. Raising the metal object, Aolani threw it over the heads of the two men in the direction of the north wall, which extended down the slope to the river. Aolani heard it crash against the wall. At first, there was no sound from the men. Then she heard a cautious movement toward the spot from which the sound had come. Aolani crept from terrace to terrace, staying close to the south wall.

She heard one man whisper, "Stay! Keep watch at the gate. I'll go see what it was. Keep alert!"

The guard left behind moved toward the north wall. The first man called back, "There is nothing here except one of those small gold animals. It could have been upon the wall." Taking advantage of their conversation, Aolani slipped farther down toward the river. It was wonderful to feel free, if just for a few seconds. The rushing sound of the river grew louder.

Then, above the roar of the water, Aolani heard a grinding sound behind her and a rustling noise. As she looked back, she saw a black shape hurtle toward her. Fearful, she increased her speed, her breath coming in gasps, as she ran swiftly toward the river. The sound of footsteps seemed close behind as she reached the river's edge. With one last burst of energy, Aolani threw herself into the icy stream. She knew that few could best her in the water, for she was a strong swimmer.

As she moved farther from the shore, she felt a clutch at her ankle and her body being pulled back. Then a powerful hand forced her head under the water. As she struggled, Aolani knew that her assailant would drown her if she didn't break away. Remembering the knife, she managed to pull it from her *chumpi* and struggled to find a target, twisting and turning her body. Finally, grabbing at the hand holding her down, she aimed the knife at the upper arm, cutting as deeply as she could into the flesh.

For a few seconds nothing happened. Darkness began to close down upon her. Then the pressure pushing her

91

down began to weaken. As her head emerged from the water, she gulped down the life-giving air. She began to swim swiftly toward the center of the stream. The current seemed stronger than it had been this morning. The rush of waters must have increased during the day, perhaps swollen by snow from the far-off mountains. She felt the current carry her rapidly downstream. She must stay close to the palace grounds, where help was at hand. Swimming frantically toward the riverbank, she pushed toward a shapeless mass of darkness in front of her. A rock scraped against her knee as she tried to scramble into a crevice she felt in the rocks. She hoped she was hidden in its shadows. Thank the gods, Mother Kilya, the Moon, was still hiding from sight.

Hearing the splashing of a heavy body somewhere near and a man's curse, Aolani lay motionless, numb in the cold water. She heard the shouts of running men approaching, and Luasi calling her name, but she didn't dare answer or move. As the sounds drew closer, the intruder gave another curse. She heard him push himself out into the stream. Luasi and his men apparently heard him, too, for several men were jumping into the water all around her.

Then she heard Nadua's voice filled with anxiety. "I tell you, Luasi, she has to be here somewhere. There was no other place for her to go."

Wearily, Aolani pushed her way to the riverbank. Luasi saw her first and ran toward her, with Nadua close behind crying, "Oh, my lady, are you hurt?"

Exhausted, Aolani was unable to answer. A warm cloak was placed around her shivering body. Dazed and horrified by her miraculous escape, Aolani murmured "Why, by the talons of eagles and the thunder of the gods, am I being hounded by evil and the fathomless mouth of trouble?"

Chapter Nine

Hwayna felt like a man from whom a terrible burden had been lifted. He had exposed Aolani's enemies and destroyed them and now he could breathe easy once again. He was glad it was over, for there were other plans to be carried out, which was why he had summoned Roco. Looking across at his uncle, he felt a great sense of gratitude, for he knew that he might not have been as strong as he'd had to be without Roco's loyal support. Hwayna had invited Roco here today because he was essential to his plans. If Roco refused him it would be difficult. He glanced at his uncle, who waited patiently for him to speak. Hwayna began to pace, not certain where to begin.

"Hwayna, what is the matter? Why did you wish to see me?"

Hwayna stared at Roco and noticed that he looked nervous. He poured both of them a goblet of wine and handed one to Roco. Then he said abruptly, "I plan to leave Cuzco soon and make my permanent home in either Cajamarca or Tomebamba. Eventually, I plan to build a new capital city in the north."

Roco stared at him in surprise. "I am sure you have reasons for this decision."

"Of course, I have reasons. However, I am making this decision immediately."

Roco frowned. "This is a big step to take. Why the hurry?"

"There is no reason to wait. The northern area has been newly acquired, is well populated, and causes the most problems. I need to be there. Besides, I heard today that Aolani is pregnant. I want to be there when the baby is born."

He saw Roco looking at him again with a surprised expression upon his face. Then Roco said quietly, "This is a big decision, Hwayna, a decision that will have a tremendous effect on the people and the future."

Hwayna was getting annoyed with his uncle. He started pacing again. Abruptly, he turned and asked, "Are you, too, telling me what I can and cannot do?"

Roco said hurriedly, "No, of course not. If this is your decision—fine!"

Hwayna picked up a small gold figure of Viracocha and fingered it gently. "I am glad to hear you say that, Uncle. This decision is necessary, and I have been planning it for some time. True, I am leaving earlier because of Aolani, but I have long thought of making my home in the busy north. It makes good sense to make my permanent residence there. It is our most heavily populated area and the nations are new to the empire."

"Does anyone know of this decision besides myself?"

"A few, but I will announce it to our people in Cuzco very soon." Hwayna walked over and placed the image of Viracocha back in its place.

Roco said slowly, "Would you mind, my dear nephew, sitting down where I can see you? It's hard to follow your thoughts when you stride around so."

Hwayna sat down beside Roco, saying, "I think I'm a little nervous. It's because I can sense your concern, Uncle. But, remember, it is you who urged me to stand firm and make my own decisions."

"That is true, Hwayna, but let us consider how it should be done. Your decision is made and I can accept it, but let's talk about some of the problems. Your people are nervous and frightened by these recent events. They need reassurance and to feel secure in your favor again. Your announcement of creating a capital city in the north will rock the very foundations of our society."

Roco paused, then said, "Hwayna, you can do as you like. No one questions your comings and goings. Your decision can be made without robbing the city of its pride. It is the capital city of the Incas. This is the sacred place of our ancestors and the heart of our empire. It is here the golden staff of the first Manco sank deep into the earth and the gods ordered that a city be built here. All of your ancestors rest in their palaces and belong here in Cuzco. It is not right to change this."

Hwayna said defensively, "None of that will change just because I live in the north."

"No, of course not," Roco said. "All I'm suggesting is that you not make any announcement of this decision, at least for a while. Let it come about gradually." Roco sighed deeply. "Let the country return to normal. Let the scars of the past few months heal. Do not stir up the savage waters of disharmony at the present time, when our people are still bewildered and confused by what has happened."

Hwayna was thoughtful. "Uncle, you are a wise man. It is true that what our countrymen need right now is not a lightning storm to excite and frighten them, but a gentle south wind that will nurture them. I will make no announcement, I promise. Cuzco will continue to be a sacred place to the members of our race. I will visit often, never fear. In the meantime, I need to have a man of our *ayllu* in charge of the city, to keep an eye on the south and east provinces. I need you, Uncle. You will take my place and be my voice, my eyes, and my ears in Cuzco. The others will be under your command."

Roco looked bewildered, but Hwayna went on. "I know you are going to say, Roco, that you are too old for such an assignment. Perhaps. But as you have proved just now, your mind is alert and you have the experience and the knowledge to rule. Besides, I know I can trust you. You ruled here in Cuzco when my father was gone and he depended upon you for all things, just as I do. You will have plenty of support and help."

Roco said in a choked voice, "But, I—"

Hwayna held up his hand and continued, "Right now, there is no one else. Prince Auqui, my brother, has a head that is either in the clouds or up in the stars, depending upon whether it is day or night. However, he will provide a good image. My half brother, Prince Meyta, is too fond of the pleasures of this world, but he can help with people, projects, and materials. He seems to be very good with them. His brother, Sinchi, is a good general and skilled in warfare but is not wise enough to rule. He will help Quis-quis, who is of royal blood, efficient, and fair, but of a cold and heartless temperament." Hwayna stopped and looked intently at Roco. "Will you help me, Uncle?"

Roco was silent for a few moments before saying, "You flatter me but I don't know whether I'll have the strength for it. However, I will obey you, my lord."

"Good!" Hwayna said with a satisfied smile. "Come with me."

Hwayna left his private quarters, followed by Roco, and they proceeded to a large room containing four flat wooden containers filled with clay. The clay had been molded into a three-dimensional map of the entire empire. Hwayna saw that the other men he had just mentioned were all there.

The Inca took a seat and Roco sat down beside him. Hwayna said, "You all know why you are here. However, so that all of you are clear as to the individual responsibilities each will bear, I will repeat myself. My uncle, Lord Roco, will be in supreme command and all of you will obey him. Prince Auqui, however, will officiate at all rituals and festivals, and he will hold daily audiences for the people." Hwayna looked at Quis-quis. "As you know, Quis-quis is an excellent administrator with a great deal of experience. He is also one of my best generals. In military matters he is without equal. He will be in charge of the army and will maintain order and discipline in the southern part of the empire and will be militarily responsible for the city of Cuzco. He will also handle the Chasqui control stations and the messages received from the south and east."

Hwayna turned to Prince Meyta, his half brother, who was just the opposite of Quis-quis. Hwayna knew Meyta was a happy, self-indulgent man but he had one outstanding ability. He was excellent in handling men and materials. Most of the major building projects of the last few years had been done under his supervision. "And you, Meyta, will continue with the present projects and others that I will speak of later. You will also handle the storing and the distribution of all products."

Hwayna turned to Roco. "Our uncle will supervise

all of your work and offer advice and support. Be wise enough to take it." He smiled at Roco. "Even I have learned to listen to his advice. He is a man of great experience and will give you good counsel."

Taking up a gold pointer lying in front of him, he idly traced the Chinchaysuyu Highway between Cuzco and Cajamarca. "I will leave seven days from today." There was a moment's silence, and then he went on. "I will take with me the north's Chasqui Message Center with all runners and administrators. As soon as I reach Cajamarca, I will take over the Coastal Chasqui Message Center. That area will extend from Nazco to Tumbes. The remaining business from the south and east regions you will handle here in Cuzco, Roco, unless there occurs some national disaster that might affect my plans. Keep me informed of everything you do."

"What disasters do you have in mind?" Roco asked quietly.

"Mountain eruptions, forest fires, droughts, waves that engulf the land, or wars." Standing up, Hwayna began pacing the floor. Turning to Roco he said, "I want you to continue to increase the exchange of our cold-land products, such as potatoes, chuno, oca, quinua, ulluco, anu, and dried meat for those products of the lowlands such as maize, manioc, aji, avocados, tomatoes, squash, beans, and lima beans. Get more of the delicacies such as peanuts, honey, fruits, and some of those sun-dried preserves made of bananas, guavas, and honey. Trade is good for the empire and variety in food adds spice to life."

Turning to Meyta he said, "There are two other building projects that are important to me. I have allocated enough man-hours to continue the work on Sacsahuaman this year and will continue to allot them until the fortress is finished. See that the work is well-done. One other thing I charge to you, personally. It is ridiculous that we have only one *Huaca-chaca* over the Appurimac, which is the largest and most dangerous river we have to cross going north. It is a tediously slow process sending an army across that narrow bridge in single file. It has occurred to me that the village of Curahuasi needs to be enlarged and enough workers moved there to work on an additional bridge."

Meyta frowned. "Some problems, my lord. If I move new people into Curahuasi to help, they must be trained by our present staff. This takes time away from our regular workers. Those *Cabuya* cables must be woven as thick as a man's body, which is a difficult task. Remember, it is a two-hundred-and-fifty-foot span of woven bridge that crosses the canyon, and it must be replaced at least every two years, sometimes sooner. The Chancas are excellent at the work, for they have been doing the weaving for many years. It will take time to recruit and train new workers."

"Do it. It is your problem. Find a way to handle it. And by the way, don't forget road repairs, especially on the Collasuyu Highway south. That road into the jungle always causes problems. Estimate how many additional man-hours you are going to need."

Out of the corner of his eye Hwayna saw his chief aide enter the room with a troubled expression. Hwayna motioned him forward and as he listened he felt cold with shock.

Hwayna let out a deep sigh and said in a low voice, "That will be all for today, my lords." With eyes closed he went on, "I am sorry to inform you that the queen mother, Cori Picchu, is dead." He turned his back on the group and stood motionless.

The men quietly left the room, all but Roco. He sat quietly, his face a mask of grief. Hwayna put his hand over Roco's. He felt his uncle start to fall and called for help. An aide rushed in and Hwayna ordered, "Send for the healers and bring me some *chicha*." He held Roco in his arms until his aide came back with the wine. The aide handed the goblet to Hwayna, who held it up to Roco's lips. He managed to get some of it down the old man's throat.

Roco's eyes opened and he asked, "Is it true? Cori Picchu is dead?"

Hwayna said gently, "Are you all right?" Roco nodded. "I'm sorry I was so abrupt. You didn't know she was ill?"

"No. I've heard nothing! Not even a rumor. It was a terrible shock! Why, Hwayna? Why? She was a young woman. I'm—" He began to sob, unable to go on. After he had quieted down he gasped. "I'm sorry to break down like this, but—"

Hwayna said gently, "I know you cared a great deal for her, as we all did. My mother was a very special person."

Roco took a deep breath. "Yes," he said softly. "She was special—in every way. And so beautiful. I loved her, you know, as a man loves a woman." He smiled bitterly. "Can you imagine a twisted, grotesque figure like myself in love with a woman such as Cori Picchu?"

"She loved and respected you, Uncle. We all did. When I was very little I thought of you as my father. Did you know that?"

"No!"

"I was frightened of my real father. He was like a mysterious stranger. All of my friends were frightened of him, too. I used to pray to the gods to keep the Inca away from our beautiful valley, Sauca Cachi."

Roco said gently, "Your father loved you very much, Hwayna. You were always special to him."

"I learned to love him, Uncle. But you have always been very close to me. I depend upon you."

Roco was touched. "It is kind of you, Hwayna, to tell me this. It makes me feel less lonely."

Suddenly Hwayna looked at Roco intently. "Tell me, Uncle, do you believe in the afterworld?"

Roco shrugged his shoulders. "I don't know. You should be more able to answer that question than I. You are a god yourself."

"I sometimes wonder. Am I a god? The people look upon me as someone special descended from gods. They wait for my pronouncements as if they were holy. But truthfully, Uncle, I listen, but I hear no voices. I make up things in my own mind, for I do not want to disappoint all those supplicating people. Are there any gods, Roco?" he cried in a despairing voice.

Roco said slowly, "There is a strange order in the world we live in, and even in the sky above. The sun comes and goes, as does the moon, and the seasons change. Plants and trees grow because water, warmth, and soil nourish the seeds. I look at my body, ugly as it is, and marvel at its design. Legs for walking, arms and hands that manipulate, eyes that see, ears that hear. We live, we breathe, we love. There must be a god or gods to plan all this. Perhaps they have also planned an afterworld." He was quiet for a moment and then added, "Perhaps they have planted their desires and wishes into your mind and you do but utter them. Who knows?"

Hwayna was very quiet. He seemed to be intent upon his own thoughts. He looked at his uncle with a great deal of respect. "It is true, Uncle. Life is all about us and all is planned, in the air, on earth, and in the sea. Everything lives, not just plants, animals, and people but even mountain crags, desert sands, and rippling streams. I believe in one god, the Creator,

Viracocha, and that he designed the world. So why not an afterworld?"

They sat quietly, each alone in his thoughts, but there was a warm silence between them that Hwayna did not want to break. He watched a great white butterfly with wings of snow drift through the open window. The brilliant sky of twilight changed the color of the butterfly into an iridescent lavender. It fluttered down and for a moment, hovered over Roco's shoulder, and then disappeared. Hwayna wondered if it was the spirit of Cori Picchu passing through with a blessing on her way to another world. Hwayna thought of Roco's unrequited love for his mother. He thought of Aolani and her brush with death and felt a vague sense of disquiet. He felt an urgent need to rush to her side. His plans were in motion. He must hurry them along, for he knew he must reach Aolani soon.

Chapter Ten

Standing in the small tower above the courtyard, Aolani looked down upon the fires being lighted in preparation for the evening meal. She had climbed the stairs to the Inca's private sanctum earlier in the afternoon so she could enjoy some solitude away from her servants and companions. Paying no attention to the commotion below, Aolani looked out over the vast fertile valley whose boundaries dissolved into shadowy mountaintops in the distance. The foreground was dominated by many buildings and temples whose thatched roofs gleamed like gold in the setting sun.

Within Aolani's line of vision she could see the growing fields of maize, quinoa, and *ullucu*. Closer to the river, stands of blossoming fruit trees stood out like glowing jewels on the valley floor. Brightly clad workers returning to their small huts after a long day could be seen wending their way home on the various paths and roads. Because of the flat width of the valley floor the usual terraces were barely visible in the distance.

It was so different from the brooding, gloomy citadel of Cuzco. Her thoughts were disturbed by the noisy flutter of waving palm fronds near the palace. The breeze that was beginning to blow was cold and she shivered in her thin tunic.

Feeling a movement in her stomach, which was getting larger by the day, Aolani put her hand on her belly and felt the babe move. It aroused a sense of excitement, for she couldn't help but think that this time she would succeed in bearing her child. Then a silent fear came over her as she remembered all the times in the past she had also been hopeful.

Superstitiously, Aolani had come to believe that the infant she carried would grow along with the child, Sinchi Chacoya, and arrive safely in this world as long as Sinchi was alive and well. Taking every precaution, Aolani had commanded that her little cousin be watched day and night by those she trusted most. Some nights she let him sleep with her and enjoyed his small cuddly body next to her own, his fragrant smell, and his soft little sounds when he woke up. It was hard to believe that in another few moons she might be carrying her own child in her arms.

She must soon go below, but how she loved to come up here! As Inti began to sink in the sky, a new burst of cold wind hit her. Perhaps later she could dress in warmer clothes and come up to see the city clothed in misty fog. She knew that, as soon as the scalding hot waters that flowed from the Inca's baths collided with the cold wind sweeping down from the icy peaks in the far distance, a veil of mist would cover Cajamarca, transforming it into a mysterious land of strange amorphous shapes, a wasteland of filmy clouds.

Reluctantly, Aolani started to leave the small stone tower. Then she was suddenly aware of a huge commotion in the large entrance courtyard. The great gates were swinging open, which was unusual at this time of the day. Who could it be?

Aolani hurried down the stairs, went to her quarters, and entered her bedchamber. She was greeted by a dark shape jumping on her shoulder, chattering in excitement. "Tutu," Aolani said in a startled voice, "you are a naughty little monkey to jump out at me that way." She reached up and pulled the monkey down into her arms, calling Nadua as she did so. "Nadua, they have opened the gates. Have you heard yet who is arriving?"

"No, I haven't heard a thing. Here, let me take that pesky one outside where he belongs. Tutu has the whole garden to play in. Besides, I know he is covered with mites. He has been itching and scratching himself all day. Another thing, I won't have him jumping at you like that. He could have done harm to the child." Nadua grabbed the monkey, who pulled her hair as she carried him outside.

Perhaps, Aolani thought, there would be guests tonight for a change. She moved over to the large sheet of smooth silver metal hanging on the wall and looked at herself. Taking a bone comb, she ran it through her hair. The new dress was of a beautifully woven blue material and embroidered at the neck and hemline with gold and silver birds. It was a lovely dress and the color was becoming. Even though Aolani was far along in her pregnancy and the baby bulged a little, she still looked presentable.

As Aolani went into the reception room, she saw Capt. Luasi enter from the opposite door. There was someone with him! Even though the torches were lit, it was too dark for her to see the face of the other man. Aolani went quickly forward and, as she came closer, saw Luasi's companion. She let out an excited cry and ran toward him and kissed him on the cheek.

"Moche, by the ancient god of lightning, what are you doing here? No, don't tell me yet. Sit down." As she sank down on the soft rugs, the men sat down as well. She motioned to her women to bring wine. "Now, tell me. I can't wait to hear."

Moche took a jeweled vessel of wine from a serving-woman and then before answering put the bundle he was carrying down on the floor beside him. "My dear Aolani, I am still bewildered by what has happened." He took a deep breath. "Where to begin?" The smile disappeared from his face. "About one moon after you left Jauja, a group of the Inca's warriors arrived led by a man named Quis-quis."

Aolani looked startled. "I know him well. He is an important member of my husband's staff. Why would Hwayna Capac send him to Jauja?"

Moche went on. "On the same day they arrived, I was ordered by this General Quis-quis to report to the palace. I must tell you I was uneasy about being confronted by such an important person. I wondered if I had done something wrong. When I arrived in the reception room of the palace, the general was seated on the dais with two other men. Quis-quis eyed me like a falcon eyes its prey. My legs felt weak and I could hear the rapid beat of my heart."

As he paused, Aolani said quickly, "Well, go on."

"This Quis-quis seemed to be in charge. He questioned me closely about your visit to the Temple of Viracocha, your health, what you discussed with me, who was with you—he was thorough, believe me. Then all three men began asking questions about Jauja, the governor-general, the people, High Priest Sonar, his use of human sacrifices, his friends, how the people felt about him—well, just about everything. It seemed a long time before they were through."

Aolani looked thoughtful. She turned to Luasi. "Did you send a message to the Inca about my narrow escape from death?"

"Of course," Luasi replied. "I was told before I left Cuzco that I was to report daily to him. The Lord High Inca knows about the attempt on your life, the deaths of Chacoya and his wife, the child you adopted—even now I constantly send reports."

Aolani was silent. Perhaps Hwayna really did care for her. Or was he just trying to find all the men involved in the plot against him? She turned back to Moche. "Did anything else happen?"

Moche spoke again. "Several things. I heard General Quis-quis order some men to bring High Priest Sonar to him; then he turned to me and told me that I was being transferred to Cajamarca as high priest in the Temple of Viracocha and that I would be given an escort to take me there the next morning. He signaled to one of his aides who brought him a leather bundle, which he handed to me saying, "Take this to the Lady Aolani and hand it to her personally." Moche picked up the object beside him and handed it to her.

Curious, Aolani unfolded the bundle. Upon pulling aside the leather she picked up the heavy object wrapped in a soft cloth. Her eyes opened wide in surprise as she unwrapped a silver statuette and placed it on the floor beside her. An exquisitely carved llama about two hands high stood before her, its beautifully etched coat shining in the light from the torches, its black eyes and nose gleaming as they looked at her.

"Boti," Aolani gasped. "It's Boti!"

Luasi nodded as he, too, looked at the gift. "It does look like Boti, doesn't it?"

"Who is Boti?" Moche asked.

Aolani closed her eyes remembering Hwayna's love for his childhood pet, a white llama named Boti. She explained to Moche. "My husband had a llama when he was a boy; it helped him through a difficult time. You see, he was kidnapped by two evil men and taken from his home in Sauca Cachi. They used him as a hostage to ensure their own escape, claiming they would mutilate him if the Lord High Inca, Hwayna's father, refused to clear the main highway north of all people and evacuate all cities and villages along the Chinchaysuyu Highway."

Moche looked amazed. "That must have been a massive effort."

"It was," Aolani said. "Even the Chasqui Message Stations and small isolated huts had to be deserted. It is a long story but the Lord High Inca acceded to their demands, for Hwayna Capac was the most favored of his five legitimate sons. It was Cori Picchu, Hwayna's mother, who, sick with worry, had her husband send food, clothing, and Boti to one of the deserted stations that would be most apt to be used by the kidnappers. She hoped the men would keep the llama to ease their own burdens and that it would give Hwayna some comfort. It worked out as she had planned."

Luasi put a word in. "I was with the Inca as he observed and followed the men from a distance. Boti was taken along by the men, and at one point, an ingenious plan devised by the Inca was almost successful due to Boti. The Inca hid a man inside a contrived rock slide. The path the kidnappers followed narrowed at this point and edged a precipitous gorge. The man in hiding was to push them off the edge if he could. The men who had taken Hwayna hesitated, suspecting a trap. Carrying all their supplies Boti daintily picked her way across the rocks followed by Hwayna. Konar, a priest who was traveling with the Inca, raced after them so fast that the hidden man could do nothing. The other man was killed."

Aolani interrupted. "But most important, throughout the long hard days and the cold lonely nights, Boti was Hwayna's only link with home. When Hwayna was finally rescued by his determined father and brought back to Sauca Cachi, the scars of his experience stayed with him. They are still there. Hwayna has never forgotten how much having Boti meant to him during that terrible time. He has cherished and loved Boti over the years and has one of her offspring living in most of his larger abodes, including Jauja."

"I remember that llama. I always wondered why that one animal seemed to have the run of the gardens," Moche said.

Aolani said, "Hwayna sent a famous artisan to Sauca Cachi to capture Boti's likeness in silver, and this is the piece. I have seen it in his bedchamber in Cuzco and it also accompanied him on his many journeys throughout the empire."

Moche was thoughtful. "Sounds as if it is a *huaca* of his own special spirit whose magic powers protect and frighten the demons away. He must love you very much to send it to you."

Caressing the llama with her fingers, Aolani's heart softened. Maybe Hwayna really did love her. She knew how much he cherished this little statuette. She picked up the llama and held it in both hands as she prayed that Hwayna would someday return to reclaim his precious possession. Perhaps the llama would bring her good fortune.

Another day over and still no sign that the birth was near. According to her calculations she was six suns overdue. Reluctantly, Aolani moved from her bedchamber to the outer room and commenced walking back and forth, as Nadua constantly coaxed her to do. She waddled like a pregnant bear. She put her hand on her back, which ached no matter what position she was in. Her swollen ankles throbbed and burned and she felt the ever ready tears come to her eyes. By the Sacred Mother Moon she was tired of all this discomfort, and no word from Hwayna either. Nothing at all since he had sent her the small statuette of Boti.

Hearing a faint scratching at the door she looked up to see Moche smiling at her. She was so grateful to him. He had helped her so much during the last three moons. No one could have been kinder or more helpful and considerate. Aolani held out her hands.

Moche came forward and held them for a moment. "Still no sign of the babe?"

Aolani was ashamed of herself but she couldn't seem to keep from crying. She sobbed as she leaned against him and said, "Moche, I am so tired of waiting. I am so big and ugly and I hurt all over. I've never been so miserable in my life."

The tears were coming faster now but she didn't care. She felt so alone and deserted. Moche's hand kept patting her back. "It's going to be all right, Lani. Just have patience." She felt him smooth her tangled hair. "I know how hard it must be for you but you're so brave. Come, sweet girl, don't cry." He bent and kissed her forehead as he wiped the tears from her face with his hand and she felt comforted.

There was a crashing sound at the door, the rush of footsteps and suddenly Moche was snatched from her and hurled across the room, falling on the stone floor. Dazed, Moche tried to get up. A tall man with a red-fringed band was bearing down on him. Bewildered as she was, Aolani knew without doubt it was the Lord High Inca. She rushed to help Moche.

Aolani pulled on the Inca's mantle from behind. "Hwayna Capac," she yelled, "get your hands off Moche, do you hear me?" She began beating her husband with both hands.

Hwayna turned to face her and Aolani stamped her foot. "Hwayna, what in the name of the gods is the matter with you?"

Hwayna grabbed her and shook her. "He was kissing you," he shouted. "No one kisses my wife. He dies!"

"By all the devils of Hopi-Nuni, Hwayna Capac, listen to me. Moche is like my brother. I was miserable tonight, crying bitter tears on his shoulder. Moche merely tried to comfort me." Aolani stopped and gasped as a searing pain stabbed through her body. "By all the gods, it's the baby. Get Nadua, Hwayna."

Hwayna shouted loudly enough to be heard at the gates of the palace. Women came running from everywhere. Nadua and two other women helped move Aolani to her bedchamber. Aolani turned toward Hwayna as another pain caused her to gasp. When she breathed easier she looked at the Inca. "Promise me you will not harm Moche."

He immediately said, "I promise!" Then he followed her into her bedchamber.

The Lord High Inca gave every indication of settling down in his wife's bedchamber until the baby was born. Sitting beside Aolani, his legs stretched out on the bed of rugs, he held his wife's hand, oblivious to the fact that his presence was making it difficult for Nadua, the midwife, and her helper to work. He ignored them, making sounds to his wife.

He felt a hand touch his shoulder as Nadua said firmly, "My lord, I must ask you to leave, at least for a few moments. We must disrobe your queen and prepare the bed. We cannot make her comfortable with you settled there."

At that moment Aolani gasped and then screamed as another pain engulfed her body. As her nails cut into the palms of his hands, Hwayna looked at Nadua, his eyes filled with panic. "Isn't there something I can do?"

"Please, my dear lord, leave us and let us attend her. It will be better for her if you wait in the outer chamber."

Hwayna turned anxiously back to Aolani. Her eyes were closed as he said, "I'll be back soon, my beloved." Aolani opened her eyes and gave him a faint smile.

Hwayna Capac, feeling completely helpless, was uncertain as he reached the doorway. He stopped and looked back at his wife. He watched as the women began to wash Aolani and then pulled a soft leather coverlet from under her that appeared to be wet and spotted with blood. The old woman raised Aolani's head and put a cup to her lips.

Hwayna turned nervously to Nadua. "What are they giving her? Where is her taster?"

"It is all right, my lord. The midwife made the medicine herself. I watched her as she did so. She is merely giving my lady coca and some other herbs that will help her withstand the pain. Come now, my lord, sit in the outer chamber, if you must. The baby will not arrive for a few hours yet."

"So long?"

"Really, my lord," Nadua said, her lips pursed in exasperation. "If the child is born in a few hours, thank the merciful gods. Sometimes it can take much longer—even a couple of days." He was speechless as she added, "My lord, please, go change into clean clothing and refresh yourself and leave this to us. The baby is in a good position. My lady is doing fine! You have nothing to worry about."

The Inca said abruptly, "Nadua, leave me be! I have had twenty-two children and never seen a birthing. I want to see this child born, do you understand me? This child and its mother are important to me."

"Yes, my lord," Nadua said with a deep sigh of resignation. "I will come for you." She gently closed the heavy wood door behind him.

As Hwayna moved into the outer room the wavering light from the torches shifted the shadows back and forth. As the light hit the far wall he saw the reclining figure of Moche, his head resting against the wall.

"You," he said, "you are still here?"

Moche got up quickly and asked, "How is she? I am deeply concerned. She is like my sister, my lord."

"I understand! Indeed, that is why I had you sent here. Aolani needed somebody who cared about her." He smiled slightly. "I thank you for helping her."

Hwayna could see how upset Moche was as the other man asked, "About Aolani, please, how is she doing?"

"Nadua told me that she is doing fine. The baby's head is down and in position. It will be a few hours yet. I am tired and need to clean up after the long journey today. I will return shortly. You may stay if you like."

Moche bowed his head. "Thank you, my lord," he said simply.

When Hwayna returned a little later, with wet hair and a loose-fitting tunic, a colorfully woven border at the neck and hem, he felt more at ease and a lot less tired. He sat down near Moche. "Has anything happened?" he asked.

"The door has not been opened since you left and I have heard no sounds," Moche answered as Hwayna's womanservant, who had followed him into the room, handed him a jeweled beaker and then brought one to Moche. The wine had been chilled with ice and tasted delicious to Hwayna, who drank it greedily.

113

Both of the men were silent for a while and then Hwayna broke the silence. "I am curious. Why did my father send you to Lord Pinau, his own tutor, a man who was highly respected and who was never imposed upon because of his age?"

Moche looked at him. "Both Aolani and I were brought from Cajamarca in your father's caravan. The Lord High Inca sent us to Lord Pinau with Capt. Luasi shortly after we arrived in Cuzco. I was eleven years of age and Aolani was ten. I believe he wanted a safe place for Aolani where her enemies would not find her. As for me, Tupac Yupanqui was my father. My mother was one of his concubines in Cajamarca."

Hwayna looked at the other man with interest. "So, you are my half brother. My father must have thought highly of you if he brought you from Cajamarca and then sent you to Lord Pinau." He smiled a little. "He was my tutor, also, and probably the kindest and wisest teacher I ever had."

Moche nodded his head in agreement, his expression thoughtful. "It was amazing how he could challenge one to think. Long after a conversation ended I would mull over what he had said. I loved and admired Lord Pinau and it is my dearest wish that, as I get older and more mature, I will achieve wisdom. I want to be like him."

Hwayna put his vessel down on the floor and stood up. "Why is it taking so long? By all the gods, I wish this were over. During my long absence from Aolani I have been distraught. She is the light of my life."

"I can see that, my lord. You need Aolani but then, too, she needs you."

Hwayna looked at the gentle man who was a brother to him. Then he heard Nadua saying, "Come, my dear lord, your child is about to be born."

*   *   *

From the very moment Hwayna Capac entered his wife's room until the diminutive life was thrust out by a hidden force, his being was bombarded by emotions. Aolani's sweat-drenched face as she labored to bring forth his child evoked his admiration, anxiety, and fear. The first sight of the small babe in Nadua's hands brought him a radiant joy. As he held his first legitimate son in his arms, he was overcome by happiness. The small body, still streaked with blood, cried enough to arouse the gods, but was a miraculous blessing that exulted Hwayna. He felt like climbing the ladders of heaven.

At last his wife lay washed and calm, resting peacefully in the clean bed, her sleeping son beside her. Telling the women to leave the room, Hwayna rested beside Aolani and touched the soft head of the babe, who lay between them.

His son, he thought with happiness. He would name him Atahualpa; the child would be the greatest Inca of them all. Hwayna let his arm gently touch Aolani as he nestled closer, and then like three weary birds, they were all fast asleep.

Chapter Eleven

During the first few days after the birth of her son, Aolani felt weak and exhausted, barely aware of what was going on. But by the third day she had regained her strength and was able to observe her husband on his daily visit. She was amazed. Gone was the formal, elegantly clothed figure of the emperor whose appearance alone was enough to subdue and silence all those around him. He looked younger, more vital and handsome, and in his simple white tunic, joking and laughing with Nadua and the other women attendants, he seemed more like the man she had first married. He helped bathe the child and then wrapped him in clean cloths. The women were all smiling, some even giggling at his words, completely at ease with him.

Hwayna took the baby from Nadua and, carrying it in front of him like a gift, brought it to her bed and placed it in her arms with a smile. "He is a fine strong son, Lani," he said as he bent and kissed her on the brow. "Are you feeling better?" He moved the baby to her breast.

Aolani was overwhelmed. "I think so," she said as she looked at his face. "I can't believe it is really you." She hesitated. "I thought I was dreaming that you were here."

"I am here, Lani, and I mean to stay with you." He turned to the women. "All right, ladies, out with you." As they left, he examined her face tenderly. "You still look pale but much better than you did this morning. By all the gods, I am glad to be with you again, beloved."

As the baby suckled at her breast, Aolani felt like a leaf in a remorseless wind being blown toward a new path that she must follow. She closed her eyes. For several months she had convinced herself that their marriage was over, that the wild, exquisite love they had shared together had been lost somewhere in the past. Therefore, it was hard to believe that Hwayna was here, acting as if they had never been parted. In a way, thinking of all the suffering she had endured made her angry. As she opened her eyes, he walked over to a chest and poured some liquid into her favorite gold goblet, one he had given her.

By Mother Kilya, the Moon, Aolani thought, he is waiting on me like a servant. He never lifted a finger in Cuzco.

Hwayna held the cup to her lips and she sipped the cold fruit juice greedily, for she was very thirsty. Hwayna's hand brushed the baby's head, causing the child to lose his hold on her nipple and he let out a loud wail. His father quickly guided the baby's mouth back to her nipple, then tenderly caressed her breast with fingers like feathers.

"Don't," she said, "I am tired." How could she tell him she was also angry? What right did he have to

Jeanne Nickson

come back now, just when she had finally adjusted
to living without him? He'd take her and love her,
then leave to follow his own pursuits and pleasures.
She knew from past experience Hwayna would soon
take as many women as he pleased, leave suddenly if some province or problem demanded his attention, and spend hours away from her with his chiefs,
generals, nobles, and priests. Her sense of depression
deepened.

"No," she said quietly to herself, as the baby fell
asleep. "I don't want to go through that again."

But as Aolani's health improved, Hwayna spent hours
with her and she found that she still enjoyed being with
him. It was hard to believe how each day could be filled
with the same tender joy and loving companionship
they had known in the first years of their marriage.
As Aolani became physically strong, just being near
him sometimes made her body ache for him. Then,
one night, she awakened from sleep and found Hwayna
beside her, his body firm and strong against hers and
she could not refuse him, for her love was too deeply
entrenched in her heart. He would always be the only
man in the world for her. His mouth felt like a bright
flame and the fire of it burned through her mouth,
traveling through her body like lightning until it found
her heart. She kissed him back with all the passionate
fury that had smoldered within her during her illness,
the months on the road, the last months of waiting for
the child, all the time without him. They tasted each
other with familiar tongues until at last their bodies
came together in a wild frenzy of desire.

From then on their nights were filled with love-
making, and their days, too, as they touched and
fondled, seeking to find each other again, relating
all their hidden thoughts and desires. They swam

together in the pool, their naked bodies glistening in the sun, and they were drawn to each other by a power they could not resist. When they drank and ate the delicately prepared meals, they had eyes only for each other, eating quickly and sparingly, impatient to satisfy an even deeper hunger. They shared everything and it seemed to Aolani that Hwayna's love lit a torch in the darkness that had been her world.

But always present in Aolani's mind was the depressing knowledge that Hwayna's other life would claim him soon, for he belonged to his people, not to her. Hwayna Capac, according to Moche, was neglecting his council meetings. Messages were arriving from all over the empire that needed his attention, and the number of people waiting to see him grew day by day. But Hwayna kept insisting that he was weary of his other life. He needed time to recapture her love and forget the many lonely nights he had spent in despair of ever seeing her again. He wanted to enjoy every moment with her. What could she do but join him? They· talked over the many problems they had had in the past, played with little Atahualpa and Aolani's cousin's child, visited the town of Cajamarca and nearby villages, started a zoo, and hunted llamas in the province of Huamachuco, where one of the royal hunting reserves was located.

One day, as they walked through the lush growth below the palace, they said very little, content to be by themselves. Silently, hand in hand, they wandered through a field of young maize plants and then entered a grove of flowering mimosa trees. They smelled the sweet fragrance of the blossoms, heard the soft buzzing sound of the bees, and the whirr of wings as birds swooped over their heads. They stood and marveled at the beauty of a large silken web and the spider swaying in the center of it like a queen. As one silver line broke,

Jeanne Nickson

the spider would throw out another thread as thin and
delicate as she could make it.

Hwayna said thoughtfully, "What wondrous beauty there is all about us that I've seldom had time to
notice. In even the simplest of life's forms there is a
complexity that is awesome."

Aolani nodded. "It always amazes me how hard all
living things work to survive. The spider constantly
rebuilding its web; the bee moving from flower to
flower to collect nectar, seldom stopping; the birds
searching all day for food. They never seem to stop."

The Inca said pensively, "I wonder what the gods
see in men as they gaze down from wherever they are.
Do they look upon us in the same way we look upon
insects, birds, and animals? I must admit the lower
life-forms seem to know exactly what they are doing,
which is more than I can say for men."

Aolani smiled at him. "Coming from you, a god himself, that is a strange thought. But truthfully, I think
men and women are more complex, especially as they
find leisure time. Their emotions and desires seem to
influence and govern their existence rather than the
basic needs of survival. They seem to want more than
just to sustain life."

Hwayna looked at her with interest. "If so, perhaps
it is important, then, that men seek an answer to life,
or at least try. It may be that in addition to survival,
men must exert effort to seek life's meaning, or their
place and duty in the scheme of things, or their own
self-understanding." Hwayna moved restlessly to the
edge of the stream. "I sometimes ask myself just why
I am exerting such effort to build this huge empire.
Have the gods given me this task or am I just deluding
myself?"

"I don't think I can answer that," Aolani said seriously. "But I know we must exert a greater effort to make

120

our marriage work, my dear husband."

Hwayna Capac drew her close to him and kissed her tenderly. "I love you. I'd give you the sun, the moon, and the stars if I could, but I can't. I'd be with you every minute of the day if I could, but I can't. I am Inca. I'm responsible for Tahuantinsuyu."

He pulled her down on the grass beside the stream. His hand crept over hers. "You know, Lani, that you aggravate me and give me more trouble than any woman I've ever known, and still, I can't live without you. I think of you all the time—all those long months you were away, I've longed for you. Sometimes I think that you are a devil, a witch, that maybe you have put a spell on me." He said nothing for a while and then added, "Lani, I've loved every second we've spent together, but I'm afraid it is almost over."

Aolani was not surprised. She had sensed it coming all day. She felt sad as she said, "I understand."

Hwayna said abruptly, "My eldest son, Ninian Cuyuchi, will arrive this afternoon from Tomebamba."

As startled as a bird hearing a sudden noise, Aolani sat up. "Ninian Cuyuchi? A son? You've never mentioned him before."

"No, I haven't. I almost forgot he existed. He was born so long ago, and at that time, the healers said he would not live. They sent him away to a cool, dry climate and I just put him out of my mind. Despite his sickly childhood, his health began to improve and about two years ago I received a very favorable report about Ninian. I wanted to see him but the healers advised against his making the long trip to Cuzco. When I knew I'd be coming to Cajamarca, and with Tomebamba only two weeks' journey away, I sent a message requesting his presence here."

Scrutinizing Hwayna with the intensity of a rock cutter preparing to split a stone, Aolani wondered if

121

she would ever really know this man. She shook her head. Here he had a son of whom she had never heard. However, with his countless other sons and daughters, why should she be surprised? A fleeting comparison between the Inca and his concubines and a queen bee and her drones flitted through her mind and she almost laughed. "How old is he and who was his mother?" she asked with weary resignation.

"Look, Aolani," he said impatiently. "It happened when I was very young. I have never seen him. No one thought he would live. I doubt if many people even know of him."

"Is he a legitimate son?"

"Yes, I suppose he is," Hwayna answered uncomfortably.

"Why do you say you suppose he is? Don't you know?"

"Yes, he is!" Hwayna said but he looked concerned. "The marriage was a quiet one and I doubt if most people know of it. My father, Tupac Yupanqui, brought his two sons and a daughter by his second wife to Sauca Cachi for a visit. My brother, Auqui, and I were there as well. As I have told you before, this country palace was a wonderful place for the children in our family. It was a completely enclosed valley, carefully patrolled, and safe for all of us to play in an atmosphere of freedom not permitted in Cuzco."

Aolani looked at him, frowning. "I presume the two sons were Tupa Huallpa and Paullu. Didn't they have a sister named Azaipay?"

"Yes, let me continue. All of us, Azaipay included, sailed boats on the lake, fished in the stream, played with the llamas in the meadows, and enjoyed lazy days of fun, free of supervision. Azaipay became very attached and followed me around like a shadow. At first I was irritated, and then I began to feel flattered.

She was the first girl who made me feel I was almost a man. Azaipay was very precocious and I—and, well, I was young and hot-blooded and we—well, it happened."

"And then she found herself pregnant. How old was Azaipay?"

"She was about twelve and I was fourteen."

"What did your mother and father do?" Aolani asked.

"I can't remember exactly." Hwayna paused. "I know Mother made me feel a little ashamed but Father just laughed and decided we should marry since we were related and marriage was acceptable between us, so we were married at Sauca Cachi. It wasn't a formal wedding in the temple at Cuzco."

"And so Azaipay died giving birth to a son the healers felt might not live?" Aolani felt sad for Azaipay but knew it was not an unusual incident in the royal family. She knew young girls of ten in the House of the Virgins who had been taken by the Inca in the past. She thought of Nonie, who at 12 had been given to Hwayna on his sixteenth birthday.

Hwayna continued. "My mother kept Ninian with her at Sauca Cachi for a while. But finally she was persuaded to send him to a cool, dry area at a lower altitude where it would be easier for him to breathe. Tomebamba was selected. He is now a young boy of eleven. And he arrives today."

Aolani had been irritated for a few moments when Hwayna had told her of Ninian Cuyuchi but it was only because there were so many hidden facets to her husband's life always surfacing. But why be angry? To be honest about the matter, Aolani was neither too surprised or upset. She had realized even before she married Hwayna Capac that she could not expect the life of the Lord High Inca to follow the traditional patterns of lesser men.

"You must be excited about seeing your son," Aolani said as she stood up. "Come, it is growing late and our own little son must be fed."

They walked toward the palace gates, hand in hand. Capt. Luasi was waiting for them at the entrance. He bowed as they approached him and Aolani thought he appeared pleased and excited. "The young prince has arrived, Son of the Sun."

Aolani felt Hwayna's hand tighten on hers and she could sense his excitement but she heard him say calmly, "Have Ninian Cuyuchi attend me in my quarters in one hour's time. I will speak with him alone first. Have musicians and dancers and perhaps acrobats in the main hall during the evening meal and let the cooks prepare a special banquet. Invite all my staff." Turning to Aolani he said, "Come, my dear. I think you need to rest." He escorted her to her door and asked softly, "Are you feeling well enough to attend the banquet tonight, beloved?"

Aolani shook her head. "I don't think so. It has been a long day and I am very tired. Besides, Hwayna, you need time alone with your son. Bring him to me in the morning." Hwayna gave her one last lingering kiss and left reluctantly but with a gleam of anticipation in his eyes.

Aolani walked into her bedchamber and asked the two women who awaited her, "Is my son awake?"

"Not yet, my lady."

"Hurry and disrobe me. I wish to swim before I feed him."

The water was sweet and cool, and her weariness seemed to vanish as she swam alone. She felt the presence of a benign spirit in the evening sky, which glowed like a luminous pink shell above her. How vast was the solitude and the silence in the heavens above. She mourned the days of magic that were now over—

the days the gods had sent. Those beautiful days that had been woven into her life and whose brightness she would never forget. They had made her believe that Hwayna truly loved and needed her, and she would act in that belief from now on. She knew that his attachment to her was exceedingly strong.

Aolani prayed for the wisdom of Cori Picchu. What had she said about the condor and the fish? Something like the condor soars at ease in the upper world while the fish swims easily in the depths of the sea. Which life is really best? Cori had implied that she must change. Aolani recognized this but didn't know where to begin.

Realizing from childhood that she was descended from the gods and was the rightful Queen of Chachapoya had given her a strong belief in her own worth, so it had not been easy for her to accept a secondary place in the Inca world. But now she must.

Feeling it was important that she face up to the realities of her position, Aolani tried to analyze it. She was not Hwayna's only wife, but she was the favorite wife of the most important and powerful man in the world. Hwayna would never allow her to return and live her life in Chachapoya. She must give up that childish dream. Aolani was not sure, even if Hwayna discarded her, that she wanted to return to her small country after being so totally involved in the grandeur and excitement of the royal court of the Incas. Even though Hwayna Capac would not let her return to her own people, she knew at this time and place in her life he would give her anything else she wanted, within reason.

As *Coya,* Queen of the Four Quarters of the World, she had great power herself, if she could only learn to use it. Her thoughts returned to Cori Picchu's wifely observations.

Cori Picchu had suggested that Hwayna was a condor, the empire sheltered in the shadow of his wings. He soared over all. How could he really know what was going on below? Cori had said that Aolani could help Hwayna in this respect by letting him know what his people were really thinking and feeling. Granted it sounded a little ridiculous but it was true that few people really talked to him. Aolani could gather information from many different sources. True, he had his own spy system that let him know what was happening in every province of the empire, but most of the information was related to administrative detail or campaign decisions.

As Aolani heard the loud, angry cries of her son, she pulled herself out of the water and let the women pat her dry. As they placed a lightweight mantle over her shoulders, she moved quickly to her bedchamber and sank down against the pillows with the child in her arms.

Aolani mulled over her problems as the baby suckled at her breast. Knowing she must have Hwayna's understanding and support if she was to succeed, Aolani decided to discuss her idea with him at the first opportunity. She would repeat the words of Cori Picchu. He loved his mother and respected her. He often took her advice. He would be amused by the story of the condor and the fish, and knowing Hwayna, she felt confident he would agree to her plan.

Chapter Twelve

Nadua bustled in with Aolani's morning meal, a beaming smile on her face. Even though she was no longer Aolani's chief woman, she still came in every morning to gossip with her. Hwayna, unable to deny the pleas of two women, especially after hearing about all that Nadua had done for Aolani, had granted Nadua's wish and given her to a slightly reluctant Luasi. Aolani smiled as she looked at Nadua, for her friend appeared happy, well satisfied, and contented. Obviously, her relationship with Hwayna's old friend, Luasi, was a good one.

"Well, my lady," Nadua said as she put the gold tray down beside Aolani, "I expect you want to hear all the gossip. Things are really happening around here today. Most important, the Lord High Inca is most pleased with his son, Ninian Cuyuchi. They talked a long time last evening. The Inca allowed me to serve them, and so, fortunately, I was able to see and hear the boy. The prince is really a fine lad, not given to loose or wandering speech, thank the gods." She shook her head. "Many misfortunes can be brought on by an uncurbed tongue. He spoke to the point and in a manly fashion when the Inca asked him questions. I could see the Inca was impressed. Wait until you see him, my lady. He looks so much like his father did at that age that it startled me."

Aolani laughed as she looked at Nadua. "I see the boy has found favor in your eyes."

"Of course, my lady. The Lord High Inca is the tree that has produced a seed that will grow into a healthy, strong man, regardless of what the healers say. Prince Ninian Cuyuchi is the Inca's firstborn son and, in my opinion, will become our lord's heir."

"My! My! My! I can't wait to meet this paragon," Aolani said as she finished her fruit. "What is my husband doing this morning?"

Nadua didn't hesitate. "Well, the Lord High Inca is busy planning a great hunt at the Royal Wildlife Station in Huamachuco for his son. He has ordered that three thousand men be gathered as beaters and sent to the site, and one thousand hunters be assigned. Oh, I do so want to go. Luasi says that only a few people, such as nobles and special acquaintances of the Inca, will be invited and he doubted I would be able to attend. I've never been to a hunt," Nadua said longingly.

Aolani grimaced. "Well, I hope I won't have to go, but if I do, I will take you along. I thoroughly enjoy llama hunts where no killing takes place. But these big hunts for wild beasts can be very bloody." She got up from her bed. "Anything else happening?"

Nadua thought for a moment. "Luasi told me that the men from one of the Inca's expeditions sent north to explore the land arrived yesterday and the Lord High Inca intends to see them today."

Aolani looked up with interest. "Do you know at what hour?"

"No, my lady."

"Inform my women I will bathe and dress now. The Inca will visit this morning." She hesitated. "No! Wait. Have them bring Atahualpa to me first. He is bound to drip milk on me." As Nadua left, Aolani knelt and said a prayer to Viracocha, the great god, whose breath blew over the waters and brought life into being. She thanked him for her son.

When Aolani returned to her reception chamber after she had been dressed for the day, she looked out into the garden and saw Hwayna showing his eldest son the pool. She went quickly to the silver mirror that hung on the wall. The soft white tunic clung to her slender form and she thanked the moon goddess that her figure had returned to normal. The red-gold borders at the hem and on the edging of her sleeves made a pleasant contrast with the white. She was glad to see she had lost her grayish pallor and that her skin glowed with health. She touched the amber waves of her shining hair and adjusted her gold bracelets.

Satisfied with her reflection, Aolani went out into the garden. As she approached Hwayna and Ninian, she saw the same look of admiration on their faces and was pleased. It flashed through her head that the three weeks' rest from work had been good for Hwayna. The lines of worry had softened and he was tanned a deep bronze from the hours spent in the sun. His rich brown tunic, embroidered with gold and red pelicans, was elegant and impressive. Even so, she missed the young man in the simple white tunic with bare feet who had given her one of the happiest times of her life.

Aolani bowed slightly as she greeted Hwayna. "May Inti bless you this day, my dear husband."

Coming quickly to her, he bent and kissed her brow. "This, Lani," he said proudly, "is my son, Ninian Cuyuchi."

He was certainly an impressive boy, she thought, with a royal air of distinction that would make him stand out from others. She could understand why Nadua was so taken with him. Ninian did look like a young Hwayna, the same high cheekbones, cleft chin, and dark eyes bright with intelligence. Right now his eyes were looking at her with surprise and admiration. He bowed and said, "My father called you his greatest treasure and now I can see why. You are like a Daughter of the Sun."

"Thank you, Ninian. That is a compliment and I value it."

Hwayna put his arm around her. "Aolani is unique in all this world, not only for her unusual beauty, but for her intelligence and wit. But now, come, you must make the acquaintance of my newest son, Atahualpa."

As they strolled back into Aolani's quarters, Nadua came forward with the baby. Hwayna took the boy from her and pulling aside the cotton cloth exposed his little son of three weeks dressed in nothing but a loincloth.

Ninian seemed fascinated. "May I hold him, Father?"

As Hwayna put the child into Ninian's arms he said, "Keep your hand under his head so that it won't fall. Sit down. You'll be able to see him better."

Ninian examined the child with great interest. "He is so tiny. I've never seen a child this small and I've never held a baby in my life. Look," he said with excitement, "he just grabbed my finger. How tightly he holds it."

"Perhaps Atahualpa senses you are his brother," Hwayna said. "Ah, here comes another member of the family, Lani's nephew, Sinchi Chacoya, who is now well over his first year."

Aolani placed Sinchi upon the floor. Crawling as rapidly as he could, Sinchi headed straight for the baby and the boy. Pulling on Ninian's free arm, Sinchi attempted to crawl onto the boy's lap, too.

Aolani could see that Ninian was entranced by the two babies. He put Atahualpa down in front of him on a soft rug and took Sinchi in his arms. Holding Sinchi's little hands, Ninian let him stand on his feet and then hugged him. Out of the corner of her eye, Aolani saw Luasi come into the room and whisper something to the Inca, who turned to her.

"Sorry, love, there is an emergency. Will you visit with Ninian until I can send for him?"

She nodded as Hwayna rushed out, followed by Luasi. Aolani hoped nothing too serious had happened.

Ninian was having such a good time with the babies that Aolani hesitated to interrupt him but it was time for Atahualpa's nap and Sinchi's bath. She motioned to his nurses as she said, "Ninian, you are good with children. You will make a fine father yourself someday. Unfortunately, it is time that Ata goes to sleep or he will become as cross as a cougar in a trap."

As the nurses took the children and Ninian stood up she added, "Your father had an emergency. He will send for you soon. Let us go out into the garden and get acquainted, for it is a beautiful day, much nicer outside than in here." Aolani led the way to her favorite place under the shade of a giant molle tree.

"This is a large and lovely pool," Ninian said. "We don't have anyplace to swim in Tomebamba."

"Yes, it is lovely and one of the reasons I enjoy living in Cajamarca. I swim every day, and so does your father."

"I don't know how to swim but I'd love to learn," Ninian said wistfully.

131

"And you shall do so. We'll start later this very day," Aolani said firmly. "I am even teaching little Sinchi to swim."

"That baby?" Ninian asked incredulously.

"Of course. Wait until you see him. Sinchi is like a little fish in the water. The pool is always kept at the same temperature through regulating the flow of water from the Inca's hot springs with the cold water from the river. Cajamarca is one of the few cities in the empire having access to hot springs."

"Tell me a little about this city. I have never been allowed to travel and now I am excited by these new places."

"The climate here is ideal, mild and pleasant. You would appreciate this if you had ever lived in Cuzco, where it is usually bitter cold and very windy. Believe me, I was glad to come back here. We have three different rivers running through this valley, so there is plenty of water for irrigation. The soil is rich and all fruits, vegetables, and grains grow in abundance. The land is unusually flat so there is very little terracing. Many loyal *mitamaes* were brought in to build the temples and palaces, and after they had completed the buildings, they stayed."

"All that you say of Cajamarca is also true of Tomebamba except there are no hot springs. But the palaces are much larger and ornamented with gold and silver in a most beautiful fashion," Ninian said.

"Your father wants to move all of us to Tomebamba because there is not enough room here for all of his staff. This was originally just a pleasure palace. But I hate to leave the place where I was first married and where I have been most happy. To tell you the truth, I hated Cuzco. Not just because of the climate, but because of the people." She made a face. "I am afraid they took a great dislike to me."

132

"Why, in the name of Inti?" Ninian asked in surprise.

Aolani was thoughtful. "I don't know. I was too different, I guess. It is a long story and a sad one. I will tell you someday." She decided to change the subject. "I hear that your father is planning a great hunt in your honor." She saw a troubled expression cross Ninian's face like the faint shadow of a bird's wing. "What is it, Ninian? What is the matter?" she asked in a gentle voice.

"I-I—well, my father expects me to be one of the hunters and I can't," he said glumly.

Aolani was surprised. All young men loved the hunt. "Why not?"

Ninian said reluctantly, his voice barely audible, "I have never been taught how to use weapons. You perhaps know I was quite sick as a child, and even though I look healthy enough now, I find it hard to breathe if I overexert myself. The healer who attends me forbids violent exercise. But I so want to please my father and he expects me to hunt. He even wants me to go on his next campaign. I know I'm going to be a great disappointment to him and it hurts." His eyes were full of unshed tears as he looked at her. "I don't know how to tell him. Do you think he will send me away again?"

Aolani felt a great concern, for the boy was right. Hwayna Capac had received the highest marks given for physical and military exercises in the *Yacha Huasi*, the college reserved for princes. Hwayna had always held those who were proficient in the use of weapons in high esteem. Men deficient in their use, he looked upon with scorn. So did all Inca males. How would he react to a son of his who did not even know how to handle a weapon?

Taking a deep breath, she said, "Ninian, I can see why you are concerned, but it takes time to organize

133

a hunt—many days. We'll think of something, so don't worry. Don't mention it to your father either."

The boy started to look more hopeful. "I won't if you don't think I should."

"Now in the meantime, we'll work on your father and show him how smart you are in other ways. You do have some skills you enjoy, do you not?"

As Ninian hesitated, Aolani's heart sank. Surely, his tutors had taught him some things.

"I've been told that I have an excellent memory. I know all the stories of Inca history by heart and—"

"And," she prompted him.

"Well, I'm good at languages. I can speak fluently in Chimu, Canari, and Chachapoyan. Of course, I know the Inca language as well as Quechuan." He frowned as he added, "I am also very good with quipu cords and I know all the ballads and tales about my father by heart."

"Excellent! Your father is very susceptible to flattery. Do you really know all of his exploits as recited by his storytellers?"

"Oh, yes! Yes, I do."

Aolani gave a deep sigh. "Thank the gods, you are so knowledgeable, Ninian. Leave it to me. We'll overwhelm him with all of your accomplishments. In the meantime, we're going to start working on throwing a spear. It isn't too difficult. We'll try it to see how you do."

Later that morning, Aolani and Ninian entered the large reception hall, and as they did so, Ninian suddenly stopped. He was looking at his father in shock. Aolani wondered if this was the first time Ninian had seen his father as the Lord High Inca, Son of the Sun. He seemed awed and frightened. Last evening in his father's chambers they had chatted in a friendly way and today Hwayna had been very informal with him, and both times he had been simply dressed. But now, Ninian was seeing Hwayna looking magnificent in a long mantle of soft red feathers covered with gold disks. Hwayna paced the floor angrily as he talked to the men kneeling below him. His gold headband with the red fringe of royalty circled his brow. He did look magnificent, thought Aolani, very different from the man in a simple white tunic whom Ninian had seen earlier.

On the wall mosaic in back of the dais, gigantic plants with green shoots like tentacles waved their green leaves; feathery flowers, exotic birds, and creatures of the jungle were entwined and tangled in their midst. Aolani had always enjoyed the splendid scene made of gold, silver, emeralds, turquoise, and other precious stones.

Aolani touched Ninian lightly on the shoulder and the boy followed her up the steps of the dais. She took her seat beside the Inca, who smiled and touched her hand. He motioned to Ninian and patted the seat beside him. Aolani noticed how nervous poor Ninian looked as he sat down next to his father. Poor boy! He was not used to this kind of life.

She heard her husband say, "Aolani, I know you are always curious about the reports of expeditions I have sent to other lands. This present group is returning from the far, far north, way beyond Quito." He beckoned to one of his two aides. "Let them come forward. Bring them close to the dais, for I would hear every word."

For the next hour, Aolani sat enthralled listening to a marvelous tale of survival, adventure, and discovery. After months and months of battling plague, venomous serpents, wild beasts, and insects, and after enduring thirst, hunger, and unendurable heat, the 22 men had reached a pleasant and hospitable land. Eight men had been lost in the journey north.

The leader, Kulan, told of the wonders of Tenochtitlan, the city in the lake, a vast towered metropolis built on water. Great causeways with many bridges led across the lake to this place inhabited by a population of over 100,000 people. The bridges were movable, leaving great gaps of water on the causeway to deter any enemies that might attack them. Kulan told of the many magnificent temples, the largest of which, Teocalli, had 114 steps leading to its summit. There, human sacrifices were made to the gods almost every day.

Kulan described the many splendid buildings and palaces, the broad avenues crossing the city, the great marketplace in which incredible things could be bought and services rendered. Raw materials for craftsmen, stones for jewelers, wood for carvers, medicinal herbs, and many other items such as yarn, deer hides, games, and pottery could be purchased or bartered. There were hairdressers who washed and cut hair, and food and drink were available for a small price. Canoes brought all these things into the city daily as well as all the fresh water needed by the inhabitants, for the lake water was brackish. After he had given information about the city, Kulan added that he had left six men outside the city to observe and listen for at least a year. They were to report back to the Inca immediately if anything important occurred.

While the Inca asked questions, Aolani had an opportunity to observe the other men. Thin and gaunt, they showed the effects of their arduous journey. There were eight men plus the speaker. She did a quick calculation. Several Incas had been killed during the course of the journey. What courage it must have taken to go so far, but think of the wonders they had seen. How she envied them, for she knew she would never be strong enough to endure such ordeals. Sometimes she felt women led boring lives compared with men. It didn't seem fair.

Aolani started listening again. The Inca asked whether the men had seen any of the strangers who lived in big houses on the water. Kulan answered, "There were many rumors in Tenochtitlan, Great Lord, of strangers from the sea. It was said by some that these people from another world had already captured many of the towns and villages in their land and would soon arrive in their city. Few seemed worried or concerned about their presence for they thought the city was impregnable and their emperor, Montezuma, a powerful man who would defend them."

"Did you see any of these strangers?" the Inca asked.

"Not in the city, but later, on our return journey down the east coast, we saw a small group pass us, which I will tell you about in a moment. First, we saw three of these huge houses on water in the distance with sails almost as high as the clouds, heading for the coast. We didn't want to meet up with them and so we kept mostly to back trails. We heard from some natives there was great trouble in the area and many people were sick and dying. One day we heard men's voices and much noise. We quickly hid ourselves in the jungle growth and saw the strangers pass. The leader sat on a frightening black beast with four legs and a waving black tail. The man wore clothing of metal and carried a shield, a sword hung from his waist. Suddenly, a strange thing happened. The leader held up the long pole he carried across his lap and pointed it in front of him. Out jumped the lightning of the gods, which hit a large puma several paces away and killed it."

Hwayna was tapping his foot on the floor, a sign he was greatly disturbed by what he had heard. If these strangers could capture Ilyaph, the Thunder, God of

137

Weather, who would be able to stand against them? Aolani was frightened by this news. She wondered if the lightning of the men who lived on the water made a noise. Hwayna must have wondered the same thing for he asked, "Did you hear a sound or did you see a light?"

"There was a large boom, which echoed like the beat of a drum. There was smoke. Some of the men saw what could be fire. I didn't see the fire myself."

The Inca kept a passive face but Aolani knew he was disturbed. He said calmly, "Kulan, you and your men must keep silent on this matter. Do you understand?"

"It will be as you say, my lord."

Then Kulan continued. "I want to repeat something that I think is important. From many Indians we heard stories of a great illness that follows the strangers like a dark cloud. Thousands die wherever they go. Because of that, I do not know whether I did the right thing or not. As we turned to the west and were about to cross the narrow strip of jungle separating the two seas, we came across one of the strangers lying half dead on the trail. He was sick, but not with a strange disease. One that I know well—the jungle fever. I gave him broth made from cinchona bark and he gradually recovered. Then we ran out of the bark and the fever returned. There were times I didn't think he would make it here alive, but he did. He is in the hands of your healers now, and he is isolated in a remote hut until they decide he is free of disease."

When Kulan finished, the Inca said, "I congratulate you on your good sense, Kulan. He may be a valuable prisoner. You and your men have done well and have successfully completed your mission. Your information is important and I will dwell on it. Your services will be well rewarded and in the meantime, you will enjoy the hospitality of the court. Landarco, my aide, will see that you have good accommodations, clothing, food, wine, and women. I will talk to you again, Kulan. Did you hear what I said, Landarco?"

One of his aides stepped forward. "Yes, my lord."

"See to the sick stranger, and when he is returned to health, send him to the *Coya*."

As the men all left, Aolani turned to Hwayna in amazement. "Why me? Don't you want to interrogate him yourself?"

"How can I, my dear wife, when he speaks in another tongue? I will trust you to see that he learns Quechuan. I think you should learn to speak his language as well." His eyes went to Ninian. "My son, you are excused. I will see you at the evening meal. In the meantime, Luasi will show you around the palace."

Ninian bowed and said hesitantly, "Thank you, my father. May I make a request?"

"What is it?"

"The Lady Aolani offered to help me learn to swim this afternoon. Will that be possible?"

Hwayna glanced at his wife, who nodded her head. "Luasi, return him to my wife later this day." He turned to the remaining two aides. "Leave us now."

Hwayna rose and threw off the hot, feathered mantle and then lifted off his headdress and dropped it to the floor. He almost knew what his wife was thinking. Lani thought it was ridiculous to wear spectacular costumes and put on a performance in front of his audiences and it irritated him. She didn't seem to understand that the people expected an awesome and powerful god and would be disappointed if he didn't live up to their expectations. His father and grandfather before him had known this to be true and he had taken their advice and found they were right. He removed his soft sandals and let his feet sink gratefully into the soft Nazca rug.

Jeanne Nickson

Nervously, he began to pace across the dais. Hwayna's mind was full of all he had heard and he wanted to discuss it with Aolani, but there was too much to be done. "Lani," he said abruptly, "the Canari have destroyed two of the three fortresses we set up on the border. After hearing what I heard today, I am convinced more than ever that it is important to strengthen our borders and keep them strong. I cannot let this one nation constantly harass us. They must be taught a lesson and I must be there. I leave tomorrow for Tomebamba."

Hwayna Capac knew his wife was shocked and displeased. He watched her lips narrow as she stood up and turned her back to him. He went to her and gently turned her around to face him. He saw that her eyes were filled with tears, but she brushed them away as she said, "I knew our life could not continue on its present course, but I can't believe it has changed so radically. Do you have to go?"

"Yes, I do," he said firmly. "It is time I resume command of the army. I have to go to Tomebamba."

PART 2

Dark Clouds
Gather
1523

Chapter Thirteen

It was hard to believe, thought Aolani, that their seven years in Tomebamba had passed as swiftly as a raging wind through a mountain pass. Beyond the courtyard garden the gray stone terrace, with its inlaid gold design of small suns traveling across its surface, shone brilliantly in the hot sun. The familiar scene with its colorful flowers and cheerful appearance offered little comfort to Aolani as she listened to the sordid stories about Huascar's violent and unpredictable behavior in Cuzco. It was hard to believe that Hwayna's sister Sosi's son, so shy and charming as a young boy, was turning into an ambitious and ruthless young man. It made her fearful as she thought of the future.

Involuntarily her hand came up, interrupting Hasco, as she asked, "You have proof of these allegations?"

Hasco's round face looked embarrassed. "No, not yet, my lady. But I would not be telling you of these things if I did not feel sure they were true. Moche, here, will vouch for the killings of the five nobles, for he investigated the matter. Huascar is clever and no one has proof that he was behind the murders. However, all five men were members of the highest council in the empire, and as you know, the Apolina Council ratifies the succession. It is quite a coincidence that Huascar now has five of his own men on the council."

"But it all sounds a little unbelievable," Aolani protested. "Hwayna Capac is Lord High Inca and he is comparatively young. Why would Huascar be planning for something that is so far in the future? Besides, Ninian Cuyuchi is the Inca's heir."

Hasco said grimly, "And that could be easily changed, my lady."

Apprehensively, Aolani looked at Moche, whom she trusted implicitly. "Do you agree with Hasco?"

Moche looked at her with tired, red-rimmed eyes. "Yes. Yes, I do. I believe that Ninian Cuyuchi is in danger, grave danger."

Aolani noted his weariness and said, "Look, my friends, you've had a long journey home from Cuzco. You are exhausted. We will discuss this again tomorrow."

After the two men left, Aolani, deeply troubled by what she had heard, stared out at the garden. Hwayna must know about Huascar. She must send an urgent message to Hwayna in Quito requesting his return to Tomebamba as soon as possible. Perhaps she should ask him to bring Ninian. Aolani rose and paced the floor, aware of something the others did not know. She was frightened and alarmed, for few people knew that Hwayna Capac, only 37 years of age, suffered from the same heart problem that had killed his father. If anything happened to Ninian and her husband, Huascar, though not Hwayna's son, might indeed be the next Lord High Inca.

Feeling depressed and unhappy about what was happening in Cuzco, she stood quietly, listening to the familiar sounds around her. The lonely wail of the conch shell announcing the arrival of visitors approaching the palace gates could be heard in the distance. In the courtyard outside, the chattering of monkeys, the squawking of parrots, and the cooing and trilling of doves and birds rose to an unbelievable level. She could hear the chatter of childish voices raised in disagreement in the schoolroom just down the corridor.

Remembering the handsome, sweet boy she had known as a child, she again found the stories about him hard to believe. Was Huascar really capable of such atrocious acts? By the good god, Viracocha, the Mighty Creator, he was only 18. She felt like weeping.

Aolani thought of her own children and her heart was heavy. So innocent and precious now, but they, too, would grow up and change. Her biggest worry concerned Atahualpa. Thirteen years old and already strong, stubborn, and determined to have his way. Despite all Aolani's remonstrances, Hwayna, his staff, and especially his military aides had spoiled Atahualpa since the day he was born. Stocky, handsome, marvelous in sports, capable, even at his age, of winning prizes for his skill with weapons, he was a son most men would look upon with pride. Aolani knew Hwayna was proud of him but also worried, as was she. Unfortunately, their son was the despair of his wise old tutors and simply would not listen to them. His lessons bored him and he made no effort to learn. It filled Aolani with dismay.

Thinking of her children, Aolani felt a need to be close to them. She walked down the dark hall and stood silently in the shadows watching the scene before her. Atahualpa, his tongue clenched between his teeth, was trying to tie the knots in his quipu cord, as his *amauta*

145

watched. It must be a military problem or he wouldn't be exerting such an effort.

At the other side of the room, Sinchi Chacoya, a good student, was listening to his teacher and repeating the historical tale he was expected to learn by heart. Although Aolani loved Atahualpa and was proud of some of his accomplishments, she wished he could be more like his cousin, Sinchi. She was very fond of him. He was a good-looking boy, his skin color much lighter than that of her son. But then, most Chachapoyans were noted for their pale skin. Sinchi was always polite and kind; whereas Atahualpa was always in a hurry and quite rude to people. Aolani wished Sinchi was destined to be Cusi's future husband, for he was kind and gentle. She was positive that Atahualpa and Cusi would not suit each other at all.

She looked at her lovely little daughter, Cusi Hwaylas, a child of sunshine who had given Aolani and Hwayna so much pleasure and happiness. Two years younger than Atahualpa, she was a very thoughtful and sensitive child, always anxious to please. She was so good to her little brother, Manco, too. Cusi was an even better student than Sinchi, having a very inquisitive mind. Being a compassionate girl, she was interested in people and their problems, always wanting to help them. Aolani watched her as she conversed in Spanish with Juan de Montaro. Aolani knew Cusi felt very sorry for Senor Juan, for he had no family or friends and always looked so sad. Suddenly, the solemn expression of the Spaniard changed, and he smiled at Cusi. He was usually aloof and very formal, but the smile changed him. He seemed to become warm and very human. As Aolani examined his familiar profile from her place in the shadows, she was aware that his aquiline nose and high forehead had an air of nobility about it. His body was strong and well developed; his muscles were well defined and sinuous. He presented quite a different picture from the gaunt, emaciated man who had been brought before her ten years ago. She vividly recalled that first day she had seen him.

Luasi had brought him in, and the foreigner looked at Aolani in an odd way. He spoke rapidly to her in his own language. Then he started moving toward her. Aolani was shocked. The guard grabbed him, slapped him across the face, and then threw him on the floor.

As the guard hovered over Juan, Aolani had spoken sharply to the guard and told him to stand by the door. The stranger raised his head, his dark blue eyes looking defiantly at her out of his thin face. He was young, perhaps 18 or 19 years old, and she felt a great sympathy for him. He was alone in a strange world, unable to speak or understand their language. She must try to help him learn Quechuan. She motioned him to come closer and sit down on the rug near her. She offered him some wine and smiled at him. He sipped the wine tentatively, not sure what it was. Then he took a bigger gulp, as if he really liked it.

"Chicha," she said, pointing to the wine. He repeated the name and drank the rest of the wine. And so began what grew to be a very special relationship between them.

Many months later, when she had mastered his language enough to understand him, he explained that, upon first meeting her, he had thought she was of his race and also a prisoner of the Incas. Aolani had a hard time explaining about her grandfather and it was a long time before Juan was really able to understand what she was telling him. Aolani had been slow to learn the Spanish language despite the fact that she had always learned Indian dialects quite rapidly. Many of the sounds were unfamiliar to her. But gradually,

Jeanne Nickson

her Spanish improved and she began to converse with him in his own tongue.

Aolani could not help but be intrigued by Juan. He was so absolutely different from anyone else in the empire, just as she was. Fascinated at first by the light color of his skin, the deep, startling blue of his eyes and the reddish-brown curls, so different from Hwayna's black, straight hair, she could hardly keep her eyes off him. She often felt the urge to touch his hair to see if its texture was similar to her own.

With the passing of time, she began to know Juan and feel his loneliness. His problems were similar to her own. She was an outcast herself because of her appearance and knew what it was like to be considered an oddity. She sympathized, but in those beginning years, she had very little time to spend with this man from another world, for her life was busy with her children, her husband, and her duties as a queen. There had also been her project for setting up some form of communication network to gather information that would be helpful to the Inca. Hwayna had agreed to the plan she'd devised in Cajamarca and even helped her in every way he could. When Hwayna Capac was in Tomebamba, which was seldom these days, he was as attentive and loving a husband as she could ask for.

Every once in a while she would recall those miserable days after she had left Cuzco, when she had come close to being destroyed by Hwayna's apparent desertion. She had bewailed her fate and acted like a spoiled young girl until she'd finally begun to mature, and she had to give Nadua a lot of credit for her change in behavior, and Cori Picchu as well. It was then that Aolani had started to accept the fact that she couldn't change her husband into something he was not. He obviously could never be an ordinary

148

man. She had recognized that Hwayna Capac was a man whom the gods, or destiny, had selected to rule over 100 nations and countless numbers of people, a man with many responsibilities and obligations. Aolani knew she couldn't hang on to him and live his life. She didn't want to be a burden to him. But as Cori Picchu had suggested, she could change herself and acquire an inner strength and wisdom, a way to help carry her husband's burdens and lighten the load he carried.

Thanks to the gods and Lord Pinau, that wonderful and wise old man, she had been given a good education, taught to think for herself, and have confidence in her own abilities. Most women were never given such a chance—a chance to feel strong and worthwhile. Aolani had made a decision at that time to help and encourage all the women with whom she came in contact, here in the palace or in the temples, to broaden their knowledge and take pride in themselves. She wasn't sure she could do much, but she would do what she could. And, of course, there was her own daughter, Cusi. Aolani had carefully selected her tutors and insisted she be well instructed in all subjects.

Her reveries were interrupted by the patter of running feet and the sound of Cusi's voice. "Mama, we're through for the day. May we swim in the bath, please?"

Cusi threw herself into her mother's arms and kissed her. Atahualpa and Sinchi stood looking at Aolani with pleading eyes. She found it hard to resist them, but her husband was on his way back from the borders outside Quito. He might even arrive today. He had installed the large bath for her because she so longed for the pool at Cajamarca. Of course, he enjoyed the bath, too, and the first thing he did after a long trip was bathe.

Hugging her little daughter, she said, "Well, my darlings, if I get a good report from your teachers and if the Lord High Inca, your father, does not arrive today, you may swim later this afternoon."

"They all tried very hard today, my lady," said a familiar voice. Juan de Montaro had followed the children into the room as he did each day at this time to converse with her in Spanish.

"Very well, children, I will send for you when I can get away. I have a few things to attend to after lunch. Leave us now and go to Nadua."

Excitedly, they chattered to themselves as they dashed away. Aolani told Juan to sit down and rang a bell for her attendant, Renpo, to join them. Aolani always made sure that she was not alone with Juan, for with the passing of years, Juan grew more dear and she cared deeply for him. She felt an affinity for him because they were both treated as outsiders, and she knew the relationship between them was growing ever more intimate and close, and it made her fearful.

With Hwayna gone so much of the time, Aolani sometimes wondered what it would be like to be in Juan's arms, to make love to another man. The thought was impossible to contemplate and she shivered as she considered what might happen if she were to succumb to her desire. Juan would die a terrible death and she—well, it could never happen! She wouldn't let it. But once in a while, when she had the courage to face her feelings, she knew she was drawn to Juan and the burning desire she saw in his eyes. She must never, never let down her defenses.

She was coldly formal with him as she said in Spanish, "Sit down, Juan. I want to continue the discussion we were having yesterday about the propagation of children. You were telling me that your god prohibits the marriage between brother and sister, father and daughter, and even between cousins. The Incas, too, have a similar law, that all must obey, except the Inca, Son of the Sun, who must marry one of his blood. Why do both groups prohibit this intermarrying?"

As Juan explained how interbreeding produced anomalous progeny, Aolani listened intently, but interrupted him to ask for explanations for certain words he used. After he had done so, she was thoughtful for several moments. In the royal family, she thought, there were quite a few abnormal members. Huascar, Hwayna's sister Cusi Rimay, his brother Manco, and even Paullu and Tupa Huallpa were lacking in intelligence. There were perhaps more.

"Do your royal families intermarry?" she finally asked.

Juan explained how some did, but rarely and then only with cousins. He explained how royal families used their sons and daughters as bargaining agents in bringing about successful treaties. He told of the Catholic Church's reluctance even to marry cousins and Aolani began to worry. It was planned that Cusi would wed Atahualpa when she was 14, and he was her brother. She must tell Hwayna about what she had learned when he returned home.

"Pour me some *chicha,* Juan. I don't usually drink wine but today has been difficult. I think I need something to sustain me."

Nadua burst into the room crying, "My lady, come quickly. The Inca is arriving. The good gods have brought him home safely."

Aolani jumped up and ran with Nadua toward the great outer courtyard. Juan, anxious to see the overwhelming spectacle, followed them up the steps to the rampart.

The sweepers of the highway came first, clearing it of every blade of grass, every bit of dust, and every scrap of rock. A vanguard of dancers, women, and musicians preceded the Inca Emperor. Finally, the ruler entered the vast courtyard. The Inca always traveled with great pomp, riding in a rich litter set upon long, smooth poles of the finest wood and adorned with great intertwined serpents of gold and silver on the sides. Over the litter rose two high arches of gold set with precious stones, and long curtains hung from all sides of the litter. They were open now, but they were hung in such a way as to cover the litter, if the Inca so desired.

Around the litter and alongside it came the Inca's guard with the rock hurlers, spear throwers and, behind them, an equal number of body fighters with their axes and maces. All the people in the palace knelt in the courtyard shouting out, *"Ancha hatun apu, intip-chari, canque sapallapu tucuy parcha ocampa ugau sullull,"* which Juan could now translate: Most great and mighty lord, Son of the Sun, thou art our lord. May the entire world hearken to you.

As the litter was set gently upon the ground, the Inca stepped out, a splendid and gorgeous figure. Juan saw his eyes move across the crowd and finally rest upon the figure of Lady Aolani standing above him. Juan could see a smile curve the emperor's lips and then the Inca motioned her toward him. She ran down the steps as he strode quickly toward her. When they met, he drew her into his embrace.

Juan saw them disappear into the Inca's courtyard and felt, as he had so often, a surge of jealousy, which he could not stem, overwhelm him. He knew he was possessed of a futile and incomprehensible love for a woman who was impossibly beyond his reach.

Hwayna Capac had been back in Tomebamba for two days and Aolani had found no opportunity to talk to him about Huascar. The night of Hwayna's return, he had been exhausted. After making love to her, he had fallen asleep in her arms. Concerned about him, Aolani had let him sleep late in the morning. Too late, for when he awakened he had no time to talk and had been kept busy all day.

After what had happened to her in Cuzco as a result of her participation in her husband's affairs, Aolani had been reluctant to disturb Hwayna while he was conducting the empire's business with the help of his aides. But today it was late, and after looking in his private quarters without success, Aolani decided that she must interrupt him. She was worried about Ninian Cuyuchi's safety and felt she must talk to Hwayna before dusk fell. He was entertaining important dignitaries at the evening meal and they would stay up eating and drinking for many hours. Aolani moved quickly through the halls and crossed the courtyard, coming at last to the conference room.

Aolani stood quietly at the door, not wanting to disturb Hwayna if there was something important going on. It was gloomy in the room, except where a patch of light shone down on the dais. She couldn't see him in the room but she saw General Quis-quis walking toward her. He would know where the Inca was. As she took a step forward, Landarco, Hwayna's chief aide, called the general. Quis-quis stopped and turned around.

Aolani heard Landarco ask, "Where is my Lord Inca, General Quis-quis?"

"He left a few minutes ago to visit the Lady Nonie. Why do you ask? Do you need him?"

Aolani's hand jumped to her throat. Nonie here? How could she be? She was in Cuzco. Aolani listened intently as Landarco answered, "I need him, but I will wait. How is the Lady Nonie, General?"

"About the same. My Lord Inca will not be long. He merely wanted to let her know he had returned and find out how she was doing."

Aolani moved backward into the shadows, her whole world falling like shattered ice around her. She felt as if she had been hit by one of Llapa's bolts of lighting. Nonie, the gentle, loving woman who had been Hwayna's concubine and his first love. Aolani had known from the very beginning that he was deeply attached to her. But she had thought the affair long over. How could he have done this to her, after assuring her many times that she was the only woman in the world for him, that he couldn't live without her? Ha! Home one day and he was already in Nonie's arms. Aolani felt completely betrayed.

Then she heard Landarco speak again, rather softly. "He never forgets her, does he?"

"The Inca knows how much Nonie needs him, especially now," Quis-quis answered.

"Well, I hope he won't be too long. The Captain General of Cuntisuyu Province and the King of the Canari are both waiting for him."

Not able to bear hearing more, Lani ran through the dark corridors, tears streaming down her face. Finally, breathing heavily, she stopped in the Inca's garden and flung herself down on the soft grass and beat the ground with her fist. That despicable lying beast with the morals of a cat! He had told her over and over again that she was his only love. She moaned. What in the world was she going to do? She remembered just last night he had mumbled as he fell asleep, "For me there is nobody but you—you. You hold me completely in your power." Yet all he had said was a lie, like an illusion reflected in calm waters that disappears when the waters are stirred.

She heard the sound of rushing footsteps and looked up to see Nadua, Renpo, and some of her women. Nadua looked distraught. "What is it, Nadua? Tell me."

"A—a—the young princes, Atahualpa and Sinchi, are gone."

"Gone? Gone where?" She stood up, and she felt her blood turn to ice. "Where are their guards?"

"My lady, you know those balls the Inca gave them yesterday that bounce around with the devils in them? The boys coaxed the guards into taking them to the great outer courtyard, where they would have more room and—" Nadua stopped, unable to go on.

Aolani looked puzzled. "There is nothing wrong with that. They often play there."

"I don't know how they did it," Nadua said, "but they managed to slip through the gates. Luasi saw the back of Sinchi when he was talking to the captain in the hut. Luasi and many men are out looking for them now."

Aolani felt deeply concerned. The boys were out in the city with the darkness of night rapidly approaching. Ordinarily she wouldn't be this worried, but after the stories Hasco and Moche had told her, she couldn't help but wonder if Huascar planned to eliminate Atahualpa as well as Ninian. What more could happen on this terrible day? Was the maggot of fire, the sign of misfortune, dragging her forward to another disaster?

Chapter Fourteen

The sound of low voices calling her name awakened Aolani out of a deep sleep. It was dark in the room except for the flaming torch in the far corner, whose flickering light touched the faces of three of her attendants. Remembering last night, Aolani sat up abruptly, her heart thudding in her chest. The children—were they all right? Then it all came back to her: the waiting, the fear and terror, and finally the arrival of Luasi with the boys. Aolani sank back on her pillows, her head aching, her body bloated, and her back a mass of pain. By all the mighty gods she wished this day were over.

As Aolani stretched her body, she felt moisture between her upper thighs. She groaned. No wonder she felt like a toad's belly. She was getting her monthly flux. Adding that problem to the thought of having to sit for hours in the sun next to Hwayna Capac made her want to fall back to sleep and forget it all.

Aolani felt the soft touch of one of her women. "I'm sorry, my lady, but you must get up. The children have already left for the temple. We must get you ready for the ceremonies."

With a sigh, Aolani allowed herself to be helped from the bed. This was going to be one of those terrible days and she would just have to endure it. Hwayna would be incensed if she missed the most important festival of the year, Inti Raymi, without good reason. The Sun God must be brought back from his travels in the heavens and returned to his people on earth. Hwayna knew his people were disturbed when the sun went too far north or south. It was his duty to pray for it to return and Aolani's duty to be there as well.

Resigned to her part in the day's proceedings, Aolani let herself be bathed, dressed, and taken to her litter. It was still totally dark when they reached the large, finely built temple made of stones laid one upon another with great skill. The ceremonies took place in the Inti Huatana, the sacred hitching post of the sun. To reach this point there were two stairways of 30 stones each, a public entrance and a private one. Her guards hurriedly escorted her to the Inca's private staircase, and at the top, she paused for a moment. A faint glowing halo in back of the dark mountain peaks announced the imminent arrival of the great sun. The throbbing of drums and the haunting, five-toned melodies of pipes filled the air. Hwayna Capac must already be seated, for the music did not begin until he was present. It was hard to see in the faint light and Aolani stifled a sigh as she was guided by a priest to the throne at the top of the shrine.

Made of a single stone so large that it was longer than the height of two men, the throne had seats cut into it for the Lord High Inca and his *Coya*. The throne was inlaid with gold and silver, and fortunately, soft cushions embroidered in red, black, and gold had been placed upon it.

157

Aolani took her place silently beside her husband and felt Hwayna's hand close over hers. She sensed his excitement as he tried to anticipate the exact moment when he would stand. The timing must be perfect, for the sun must first touch his head and then creep gradually down until it inundated his body with golden light. Aolani knew he had fasted and prayed all night, as he always did before such an important occasion. If he followed his usual routine of drinking *chicha* on an empty stomach with each noble who approached him this day, he would be inebriated by this afternoon. He would return to his quarters and sleep the sleep of his ancestors and there would be no time to talk to him. She must see him today. Perhaps she could manage to be in his bedchamber when he awakened in the late afternoon.

Aolani felt Hwayna's warm hand leave her own as he stood up and faced the sun. The frenzied beat of the drums reached a towering crescendo. The noise was deafening. Her headache became almost unbearable. The beat of the drums suddenly ceased, and in the ensuing silence, all eyes focused on the Lord High Inca.

Raising her eyes, Aolani gasped as she saw her husband. The light was touching his face and illuminating the gorgeous headdress of feathers, which had been dipped in liquid gold and encrusted with sparkling crystals. The feathers cascaded down his back and, as the light hit them, sparkled like rays of sunlight. There was an opalescent quality to the morning sky that was awesome in its intensity. The Son of the Sun was bathed in its beauty, endowing him with an overwhelming majesty.

Even knowing the amount of time and effort spent in planning one of these spectacles, Aolani could not help but be impressed by the scene. She heard her husband chanting the usual prayers to the returning sun and averted her eyes as a llama was sacrificed to the God of the Sun. Then there was collective rejoicing as all the people chanted to the sound of the drums.

After the nobles and priests concluded the chant, Aolani knew that she, as Mother Kilya, the Moon, must stand beside her husband and help dispense the sacred wine to all the nobles. Dressed in a gown strewn with silver strands of beads that moved and shimmered when she walked, Aolani joined her husband. Great silver buckets of wine were brought forward by priests. After the Inca poured wine over his hands and blessed the containers, everyone moved forward in an orderly line to have the gold cups they had brought with them filled with wine by either the priests, the Inca, or his *Coya*. Later, these vessels would be left as gifts to the Temple of the Sun.

The music became lighter and gayer; dancers appeared and began to perform well-known rhythmic patterns. Soon others joined them and Aolani knew that in a short while she would be able to leave. Hwayna, however, would have to sit for several hours before his people and bless them as they passed before him. By the end of the day, his part would be over but the festival would then last for a riotous week of animal sacrifices, divinations, and ritual drinking.

With some surprise Aolani watched her husband step once again upon the dais at the foot of the throne. He looked down at the richly clad nobles, the somber priests, and the musicians and dancers in their colorful costumes. Then he raised his arms. The music ceased, the dancers stopped, and everyone looked toward the Lord High Inca in astonishment for he was not acting according to tradition. When he lowered his hands, the crowd fell to their knees. This was something unusual, she thought, as he began to pray:

"O far away and ancient Lord, Mighty Viracocha,
Who has created and established all things,
The sun, the moon, the day, the night, summer and winter
Let there be man, let there be woman.
Thou, the molder, thou, the Creator.
Inasmuch as thou hast made and established mankind,
Grant that we may live in peace and safety,
O Lord, O generous and diligent Lord, most excellent Lord,
Protect thy people from their enemies.
I pray thee, O he who has power over all that exists
Guard and watch over us, as strangers approach our borders
This I implore thee, O Creator of Newborn Light.

As Hwayna Capac left the shrine, the silence continued for a few moments. A prayer to Viracocha had never been included in any ceremony held in a Temple of the Sun. Thoughtfully, and with some concern, Aolani made her way down the stairs and returned to the palace.

Aolani awakened from a short nap later that afternoon feeling morose and irritable. She was terribly concerned about Ninian and sick at heart over her jealousy of Nonie, and her indignation at Hwayna's betrayal. But there was no consolation in moping about. She exerted herself to get up from her sleeping pad and commanded that her ladies bathe and dress her. She would go to Hwayna's quarters and wait. Aolani decided she would limit the conversation with Hwayna to the problem of Huascar alone. She was too upset to talk about Nonie.

Hwayna was still asleep when she entered his bed-chamber, so she sat down to wait. Sitting in the shadows beyond the flames burning in the brazier, Aolani observed her husband while she waited for him to awaken. In repose his face was still as young and vulnerable as the face of the young prince she had married. Her face softened as she remembered his agony at defying his father because of his love for her. How she had loved and admired his courage. She still did. But then there was Nonie. How could he have kept such a secret from her for so long? Everybody in the palace must know of his liaison except her. His face was in shadow now. Night was closing in and the light was becoming dim but still he slept on.

There was a sharp clap of thunder and Aolani saw Hwayna's body move restlessly on his mats. Going to his bedside, she bent down and touched his shoulder. In a second he had her hand clutched firmly in his; then recognizing her, he yanked her down on the bed beside him. Before she could protest, he was kissing her with fervent lips and she could feel her instant arousal.

Pushing him back, she tore herself away and said, "Hwayna, not now. I must talk to you. It concerns Ninian Cuyuchi." As he released her she added, "Besides that, it is my time of the month."

Hwayna rolled over, leaped naked out of bed, and laughed as he dragged her with him. "Come, my love, I need a bath. You can talk to me while I swim."

Aolani had not wanted to talk to him in such an intimate setting, but for Ninian's sake, she had to talk

161

to him right away. She felt a growing sense of urgency, a vague feeling of uneasiness, a premonition that something terrible was about to happen. She'd felt that way ever since Sinchi had told her what had almost happened yesterday to Atahualpa. Sinchi had told her, despite Luasi's order to keep quiet, for Sinchi's first loyalty had always been to her.

Hwayna dismissed the servants and swam the length of the pool several times. Aolani sat at the edge of the pool and slipped her feet into the water as he came up beside her. "All right," he said, "tell me what is wrong."

She briefly gave him all the information about Huascar's activities, the killings and the gossip surrounding him, the attempt to kill Atahualpa, and she ended with the fears of Moche and Hasco for Ninian's life.

Hwayna looked concerned, shocked, and angry. Suddenly he dove under the water, then reappeared swimming rapidly around the pool before coming back to her. He asked several questions and then cursed Huascar. "That damnable traitor! He must be destroyed but it will be difficult. All of Cuzco stands behind him. Do you really think Ninian and Atahualpa are in danger?"

"Yes," she said. "If he is making plans to be the Lord High Inca as Moche believes, he must want Atahualpa out of the way as well as Ninian."

"All of Huascar's behavior could be partially my fault," Hwayna said abruptly. "At least I provided the provocation that inflamed his anger and encouraged his desire for revenge."

"What do you mean?"

"Two years ago when I was in Cuzco I clearly stated that Ninian Cuyuchi was my heir and that Huascar would never be Lord High Inca."

"How did the prince react to that?"

"On the surface he was submissive and accepting, but I could sense his intense anger at my words, and his eyes when he lifted them were bitter and cold."

"There is one thing more, Hwayna," Aolani said reluctantly. "It is hard to believe, but from what you've just told me, Moche could be right."

"About what?"

"He believes Huascar intends to kill you as well as Ninian."

Hwayna laughed as he got out of the water and wrapped a white cloth around his body. "I wouldn't be surprised, for I stand in the way of Huascar's ambitions."

Aolani stood up and faced him. "How can you laugh about this?" she asked anxiously.

"What else can I do for the moment? I must think about this."

An eerie feeling crept over Aolani. Her world was coming apart and she didn't know how to handle it. Hwayna reached out and held her close.

"I wish I could reassure you, Lani, but these are troubled times, not only here in Tomebamba, but in other parts of the world. Remember the city in the lake and the people called the Aztecs?" She nodded. "Their land has fallen into the hands of the strangers from across the seas. These strangers have ravished and ruined the country and the people have become slaves." Hwayna looked somber. "The strangers will soon be here. With the gods' help, I will seek to defeat them even though the omens are not propitious."

"What omens?" Aolani asked.

"Oh, the usual things: rings around the moon, eagles falling from the sky, tidal waves, anything different that happens is a cause for concern. I am trying to prepare for the problems I see before us, but frankly,

I am worried. For the sake of the people, I must appear strong and confident and you also must appear that way. Now, I must leave you to take care of this matter concerning Ninian."

As he left, Aolani felt as chilled as if she were standing alone on a high mountain peak in the midst of a glacial storm. She had never known Hwayna to be so pessimistic. What would happen to them all?

Chapter Fifteen

Juan awakened to the noise of drums, pipes, and trumpets resounding like a devil's chorus in the small room. A multitude of voices were raised as they screamed, "*Haille.*" Then he remembered. The Festival of Inti was being celebrated this morning. Juan groaned. No one had told him whether he should attend this holy ceremony. Well, it was too late now, though he'd wanted to see it. Besides, after last night's hectic experience he did not feel up to it. He'd spent hours with Capt. Luasi and his guards searching for the boys, Atahualpa and Sinchi. Just as they were about to give up, they had found the boys fast asleep in the rock-splitting yard.

Thank God, they had found them! There would have been hell to pay if anything had happened to either of them, but especially to the son, Prince Atahualpa. It was ridiculous to call them boys. They were young men and knew better than to sneak out. That rebel, Atahualpa, had probably run off and Sinchi had followed along to protect his cousin because he was the eldest. Juan hoped Sinchi wouldn't be blamed for it. He was a fine young man.

It must have been after midnight when they'd brought the two boys back to the queen. Juan had watched the conflicting emotions flash across her face. First, relief and joy, and then as she dashed over to them, he'd seen the anxiety and fear. Her hands and eyes searched for any signs of injury before she kissed and hugged them both. Fifteen-year-old Sinchi hugged her back, but Atahualpa, a tough warrior of 13 years, protested and pulled away from his mother's hands.

Sighing deeply, Aolani stood back and looked at them sternly. "You have both been told that you must never, never leave the big courtyard without guards and you have disobeyed. Your punishment, I'm afraid, will be severe, but for now, Nadua will take you to bed. You must be up before dawn to welcome Inti."

As the chastened young men left the room, she turned to Juan and Luasi. "This escapade could easily have resulted in a tragedy and I want to find out just how those two escaped from their guards, but that must wait. You are dismissed."

Juan and Luasi bowed and left. As they walked down the hall, Luasi said, "Whew! I need a drink. How about you? I have some *chicha* in my room. Will you join me?"

Juan was surprised. It was the first time Luasi had treated him as an equal. He accepted, but later when he returned, tired and dizzy, to his room, he'd had a hard time falling asleep; even when sleep came, it had been fitful.

Juan lay back on his pillow, still tired, but enjoying the solitude. No one would be needing him this morning with everyone at the festival. He lay there thinking how much his life had improved since those first hard years in Cajamarca. There had been many changes since coming to Tomebamba. He was still a slave, but was treated like a respected prisoner.

He thought of the morning he and the others had left Cajamarca. It was that trip that had jolted him out of the apathy and depression he'd felt ever since he'd been captured and it was because of Lord Moche. The huge caravan had started out at dawn, warriors, servants, and slaves walking, nobles borne in their litters, and thousands of llamas trailing behind with their herders. To Juan's surprise he was assigned to a big palanquin with an overhead roof. He knew it must have been because of the Lady Aolani's instructions, but why she had done so had puzzled him.

As he'd approached the palanquin and seen the man inside the double litter, Juan's throat had become fearfully dry. What should he say? How should he react to the lord known as Moche? He had become easily intimidated after some of his past experiences. He and Moche would be on the road for many days in close quarters, and he dreaded it. He would rather walk, but if he did he'd probably insult or even hurt the Lady Aolani. For God's sake, the man he was traveling with was the Lord High Inca's half brother and the Lady Aolani's close friend.

Looking within the litter, Juan saw a man who appeared to be asleep. At least his eyes were closed. Relieved, Juan stepped quietly into the litter, not making a sound. Moche didn't move even when the bearers lifted their heavy burden and began to move forward. Juan was excited. In his three years as a slave at the palace, he had never been allowed off the grounds. He felt as if he'd escaped from prison. A wave of pleasurable excitement engulfed him at the thought of penetrating this strange new world, of examining its people and seeing its splendors. They soon reached the banks of a river that ran through a deep ravine. Trees and bushes, bright frost on their leaves, hung from the cliff at the side of the road, their roots buried in the cracks of the rocks. God, it was wonderful being out in the open again!

Up ahead a narrow rock bridge spanned the rushing water. It appeared to be man-made. The bearers stopped, lowering their burden to the ground. Juan heard a soft grunt and stared into the dark friendly eyes of Lord Moche, who said, "So, we have reached the river already. We have to walk across, you know. Sorry, I fell asleep. I had a late night. Give me a hand up, will you? I always have pains in my joints in this damp weather." Juan held out his hand and helped him out.

They walked across the bridge and while waiting for the rest of the caravan to make the crossing, Moche asked Juan questions about his homeland, Spain. It felt good to have someone interested in him and Juan talked eagerly. He was glad that his command of the Quechuan language seemed adequate to the task. Later, when they were on their way again, Juan felt quite comfortable with his companion. Moche, he found, was very knowledgeable about the country through which they passed. Juan was especially interested when they entered Chachapoya, for it was the country of Aolani's birth. Moche informed him that the land was very fertile and there was an abundance of corn, edible roots, and fruits. In addition there were falcons, partridges, pigeons, doves, and other game. The people were skilled in working with gold and silver, for they had many rich mines in their province. They also wove beautiful cloth, which was in great demand.

"I can see why the queen is so proud of her country. She is also proud that her grandfather was a god. She told me a long story about her grandmother finding him in the sea, tied to a log, and that later she married him. Is that correct?" Juan asked.

"That is the story that I've heard. He was apparently a very wise man and taught the people many things. Aolani's grandmother, a princess, married this man and he later became King of the Chachapoyans. As for his being a god, that I do not know." Shrugging his shoulders, Moche added, "Who can say for sure if a man is a god and if it really matters? I do know he was a very unusual man from what is said. He taught the Chachapoyans many things about weaving, farming, hunting, and protecting their small country. Did you know their warriors defeated the Lord High Inca's fine army three times before Hwayna Capac was at last able to conquer them, and Aolani had a lot to do with that."

Juan said tentatively, thinking it might be too personal, "The Lady Aolani is so different from all the other people I've seen. Her coloring, her features, and her eyes are more like some of the people in Europe. Sometimes I wonder—"

"What? What do you wonder?"

"The queen possesses some of the characteristics of a group of people in our world called Scandinavians. They are magnificent sailors and their vessels roam the world. I just thought that—"

"Her grandfather might have come from the land you speak of? It is possible! But if I were you, I would not mention it to her. She would be hurt and angry. Lani really believes her grandfather was a god, and who is to know? Her belief has made her strong and proud, a fitting queen for the Lord High Inca."

"I would not hurt her in any way, Lord Moche. Believe me! She has been very good to me. I would do anything in the world for her."

"Good! If you are Aolani's friend, you are also mine.

Now, what do you say to walking for a while? I need to stretch my legs."

While they were walking, Juan thought of his first meeting with the queen. She had protected him and offered wine. She was very beautiful, with her golden hair and amber eyes. Was it any wonder that he, a 19-year-old boy, had lost his heart to her? When he was away from her presence, the loneliness of his helpless existence was almost too hard to bear. His obsessive dreams and fantasies about her had comforted him. He still dreamed that someday she would be his, even though he realized that such a dream was impossible. But suddenly he felt like a grown man, perhaps because Moche treated him like one. He could no longer live in a dreamworld. He was no longer the young boy who had sailed to the New World seeking fame and fortune. He would have to find himself in this strange world, for it looked as if he would be here for a long time.

Ten days later, as the caravan moved through the land of the Canari and they approached the end of their journey, Juan felt that he had truly made a good friend in Moche. It was a wonderful feeling. Perhaps, it was for this purpose Lady Aolani had arranged for him to travel with Moche.

As they approached Tomebamba, the young Spaniard was rendered speechless. Juan had thought that the palace in Cajamarca was quite a lovely place, but compared to the Inca's lodgings in Tomebamba it was nothing. "It's amazing," he said.

"I can understand your surprise," Moche said with a smile. "Tomebamba is among the finest and richest cities to be found in the Empire of the Incas. Of course, it can't be compared to Cuzco."

Juan could see that most of the buildings were made of great stones; some of them appeared rough and black and others seemed to be jasper. The fronts of the biggest and finest buildings were beautiful and highly decorated with gold, emeralds, and precious stones.

"You will hear," Moche said, "that most of the stones were brought from faraway Cuzco by order of the Lord Hwayna Capac and were pulled here by great cables. That is not exactly true. However, they were brought here from the mountains east of Jauja, about six hundred leagues to the south."

Juan could only gasp in amazement. The stones were huge. The fact that they had been dragged here by men all that distance was incredible! They went inside the largest building and it was even more beautiful. In the queen's quarters, as well as in the rest of the building, the walls were covered with sheets of the finest gold and encrusted with statues of the same metal. Everywhere Juan looked there were things of great beauty. Gold jugs, pots, and animals, carved walls, many rich tapestries and rugs covered with silver and beadwork. It was awesome. Juan couldn't begin to imagine the wealth possessed by Hwayna Capac, the Lord High Inca.

The Lady Aolani swept by, followed by her guards, retainers, and servants. She looked so beautiful and unattainable, even though slightly pregnant, that Juan was left breathless. When he entered her anteroom, he meekly sat down, his back to the wall, waiting to be called or assigned a place to sleep. Again, Juan realized what an idiot he had been, a stupid young man who had fallen in love with a great queen. It was ridiculous! She was a woman with children, and she was married to one of the richest and most powerful men on earth, who would never let her go. Hwayna Capac was a handsome man who had won her heart. Juan had seen that the Inca loved and adored his wife, and that she loved him.

Juan now knew that if he were to survive he had to

171

change. What was he going to do with himself? He was 29, physically in good shape, and not unattractive to women. He was intelligent and well educated. He knew Aolani was interested in him and enjoyed their conversations. She had gone out of her way to help him and he was grateful. Perhaps he could use her interest to gain the attention of the Lord High Inca. He knew of many discoveries in his own culture that might interest the Inca. As far as Juan knew, the Incas had not yet discovered the wheel or the art of written language, and his knowledge of guns might be of great interest right now. It was something to think about.

He had another thought—a way to get rid of his fixation on Aolani. Perhaps he could find a woman. Nadua had mentioned that to him one day. He would try to see her soon. Juan moved restlessly. He had to relieve himself. He stood up and started for the door leading to the hall and almost bumped into Lord Moche, who exclaimed, "Good! Just who I was looking for. Aolani sent me to find you. She said you are to stay with me for the present."

"Where's that?"

"We'll have to find out. It's a six-room building that houses the Chasqui Message Station and the storage of quipu. I will be in charge of the facility. Come on, let's explore."

A short time later, they had found the building, where the members of Moche's new staff were waiting for him. Moche found time to assign a small room to Juan, who was quite excited to have a place of his own.

Four days later, Juan managed to find the person he'd been looking for. "Nadua," he asked, "could I talk to you for a few minutes?"

"You can talk to me until my lady calls for me. We are very busy trying to settle in, but everything seems to be going along smoothly today. What can I do for you?"

"I've been thinking of something you said to me not too long ago and I think you are right. I do need a woman and I now have a room of my own. Can you advise me?"

"Advise you, no! Get you a woman, yes." Nadua smiled. "I have just the one for you. She is a Chachapoyan and is now too old for marriage, but she is pretty, light-skinned, and of a sweet disposition."

"How old is she?" Juan asked. He didn't want too old a woman.

"Well, she is of about the same age as the Lady Aolani. I would say about thirty. How many years do you have?"

"About twenty-nine years."

"Give me a few days, Juan, and I'll let you know what she says."

"Thanks, Nadua, you're a love." Juan leaned over and kissed her on the mouth. "I'd sure like to have you, but I know I don't stand a chance with Luasi around."

Chapter Sixteen

The next two days after the festival passed slowly and Aolani did not see her husband, for he seemed busier than ever and kept away from her. The normal day-to-day activities lulled her fears and she even managed to put the hurt and anger she felt over Nonie out of her mind most of the time. But at night she worried and fretted over the situation. In a way, it bothered her that Hwayna made no attempt to see her.

On the night of the third day after her talk with him about Huascar, he came unannounced into her presence. Hwayna tried to kiss her but she drew away from him, saying, "Not now."

Hwayna said, with anger in his voice, "You have been staying away from me these past two days, and even before that, you were acting strange. At first, I thought it was merely because of your woman's flux, but I know you, Lani. You are angry with me for some reason, the gods only know what it can be. Let us talk about this now," he commanded.

Aolani looked at him. She did not want to talk to him about Nonie. She was too angry to discuss the situation. "I prefer not to talk about it."

Hwayna grabbed her and shook her, his face hard, angry, and tight lipped. He had never looked so grim. "By all the *huacas* of the family, you are going to talk to me, or so help me I will send you back to Cajamarca, where you can sulk in silence, alone, without your children, your attendants, or your staff. I am under too much pressure at the moment to put up with this kind of behavior from my wife. Do you hear me, Aolani?" he shouted.

Aolani thought quickly. He meant it. He really would send her to Cajamarca in his present mood. Well, she would let it come out. "I have one word to say to you, Hwayna Capac, and that word is Nonie!"

"By all the gods and the blessed Viracocha." Hwayna began to smile. "So you have found out about Nonie, have you? Well, let me—"

"I don't want to hear your lies and excuses," she said bitterly. "I've put up with your women year after year after year but Nonie is just too much. She was always your favorite concubine and you know it. She was very special to you."

"Yes, of course, she was special and still is, but that's not—"

"Not what? You brought her here to Tomebamba ten years ago. Nonie was already housed and waiting for you while I was packing up your household in Cajamarca because you lovingly urged me to come here."

"Lani, if you would just listen—"

"I have listened to you for years. I've tried to understand that you are expected to mate with the Virgins of the Sun and have children with them, but to have you single out one who you hold above all others is just too much—and to have housed her where you can see her all the time is humiliating. I hate you, Hwayna Capac. I hate you." Aolani burst into tears and, sobbing, tried to run from the room.

Hwayna caught her. She tried to kick him and scratch his face. Then she bit into his hand and she heard him call for Luasi, who came running. "Get me a rope so that I can tie her hands and feet."

Luasi left and Aolani started to scream.

Grabbing the thin veil from off her head Hwayna began stuffing it into her mouth. She bit down hard on his finger. Hwayna pulled his finger out and pushed more of the material into her mouth. Aolani tried to spit out the gag but she couldn't. Luasi came back with a piece of rope and held her while Hwayna tied her hands together.

"All right, Lani," he said grimly, "you have asked for this. There is a simple explanation, but I think if I take you to Nonie, it will help you to better understand. This would not have happened if you were not the most fiery, difficult, and obstinate woman I've ever known."

He turned to Luasi. "Have the litter and two guards come here at once. No, wait! Aolani, will you walk quietly beside me to the litter in the courtyard? You must realize that, if the guards have to come here to carry you, the news will spread all over the palace and it could be embarrassing, especially to the children. Will you walk?"

Looking at him, Aolani knew there was nothing she could do. He was determined to do what he said. He meant to take her to Nonie. Aolani hated him but she nodded her head. She looked at him, then down at her mouth, trying to get him to take the nasty gag out of her mouth.

"Oh, no, my little cat. I do not want to listen to your complaints all the way there. It will be good to have silence between us for a change." He opened her tunic and kissed her breast. "Come, little fireball, let's go."

As they traveled down the hill toward the town, Aolani was astounded and enraged by Hwayna's treatment of her. She was miserable with the gag in her mouth and her hands tied behind her back. Hwayna put his arms around her and she jerked away from him. Unable to brace herself against the jolting of the litter made her even more uncomfortable. Damn Hwayna anyhow.

Then a thought slipped into her mind. Did he intend to present her to Nonie, bound and gagged like some criminal? The thought horrified her. Aolani did not want her rival from the past to see her like this. She must do something, but what? Unfortunately there was only one way. Since she couldn't talk, she must use her body to change Hwayna's mind. Aolani snuggled up to him and put her head against his chest. For a moment he remained stiff. Then his arms went around her and he pressed his lips against her forehead. She managed a small groan.

Hwayna said in a husky voice, "If I take the gag out of your mouth, will you promise to talk quietly and reasonably with me?" She nodded her head. "I'll take the gag out, but if you start anything, especially in front of Nonie, I will not hesitate to replace the gag. Do you understand?"

While Hwayna was pulling the cloth from her mouth, Aolani felt sad and dispirited. Her own husband was placing Nonie's feelings above her own. How could he? Tears came to her eyes. This was all his fault but she certainly hadn't handled herself with dignity tonight. Nonie was undoubtedly his favorite, for she was so gentle, sweet, and loving while Aolani was, as Hwayna had said, fiery, difficult, and obstinate.

He had called her other things, too. A cat and a fireball!

Hwayna was gently caressing her hair. She felt his breath on her face. Aolani felt warm and secure in his arms and wondered if maybe he did love her a little bit after all. He brought his head down to her breasts. "Hwayna, did you really mean it when you said I was an obstinate and difficult woman?"

With her hands tied behind her, Aolani could do nothing as he sucked and licked at her nipples until she could hardly bear the torment. Her breath coming rapidly she gasped, "Answer me, please, Hwayna."

He took his time answering her, his lips now nuzzling her neck and ears. At last he said, "I meant it, yes. You are difficult and obstinate, and I love you more than anything else in the world. Don't ask me why!"

"More than Nonie?" she asked in a whisper.

"Yes, more than Nonie." He crushed her to him and pressed his lips on hers, his tongue ravishing her mouth.

Suddenly, the bearers stopped and the litter was lowered to the ground. "Well, my little spark of heaven, we are here. You will now understand about Nonie."

"Please, Hwayna, untie my hands. I promise I will behave."

It was very dark even though a blanket of stars was scattered through the night sky. Hwayna had to fumble with the knots for some time before he could loosen them. Finally, her hands were free; she rubbed and stretched them, for they were numb and stiff. Hwayna held her arm as the guards preceded them toward a fairly large house that loomed before them.

They entered what appeared to be an antechamber furnished simply with Nazca rugs on the floor and beautiful tapestries on the walls. The torches burned brightly in opposite corners. Two young men were standing in front of them, one tall and quite nice looking with Hwayna's cleft chin. He was dressed in a uniform of a captain of the guards. The other male was younger, slender and fine boned, with a shy diffident manner. They both bowed to Hwayna Capac and then to Aolani.

Hwayna said with pride, "These are two of my sons, Chauca and Macon. Nonie is their mother."

Trying to suppress her jealousy, Aolani politely acknowledged the boys and heard Hwayna ask, "Is your mother able to see me?"

The younger boy nodded and said, "Yes, my lord, she is awake."

Leading the way, Hwayna took Aolani into another room. Looking at the small emaciated figure on the pile of rugs, Aolani was shocked. She could find little resemblance to the beautiful young girl she remembered. The face was worn and thin, with deep shadows in the hollows of her cheeks. Only the soft dark eyes, with their incredibly dark lashes, looked familiar. Nonie did not notice Aolani in the shadows, for her eyes were focused upon Hwayna's face. The love she felt for him illuminated her features for a moment, giving her the illusion of beauty.

"My dear lord," she whispered as he gently kissed her on the brow and placed his hand on her hair, which was no longer glossy. Aolani remembered how it had shone like gleaming black water when Nonie was young. Nonie breathed with difficulty and coughed so badly Aolani thought she would choke to death. Her younger son held a cloth to her lips and wiped the blood from her mouth. Then he held a cup to her lips and the potion seemed to help her.

179

Macon propped up her pillows, saying, "You are usually more comfortable sitting up, Mother."

Nonie smiled at him, her eyes filled with tears. "My dear son, what would I do without you?"

The boy said nothing but he smiled shyly as if pleased by her words. "It is almost time for your favorite drink."

His mother made a face. "If that horrible stuff doesn't kill me, it may cure me."

As the boy went out, Hwayna said, "Nonie dear, I've brought someone with me." He motioned to Aolani, who walked toward the bed.

Nonie looked up startled, but then smiled at Aolani. "It's been so long, so very long." She sighed. "I've always remembered your kindness when I was so sick during my first pregnancy."

Aolani was feeling so guilty she could only say, "Oh, Nonie, I did nothing."

Hwayna interrupted. "I will leave you two alone for a few moments, for I want to talk to Macon and the healers I sent over from the palace. I'll be back, Nonie." He glanced at Aolani. "If she starts to choke again, Lani, give her some more of this liquid." He pointed to the vessel Macon had placed on the small chest.

When he had left, Aolani felt so ashamed of herself and so embarrassed she couldn't think of a thing to say to the poor woman. By all the gods, life had been cruel to Nonie. Why hadn't Hwayna told Aolani long ago about Nonie? It hurt to think he had been afraid to tell her.

Nonie broke the silence. "Did my lord tell you?"

"About what?"

"I am dying." Nonie took a few shallow breaths. "It is time for me to leave this earth and, truthfully, I am glad."

Fighting back tears, Aolani whispered, "No, Nonie, I don't believe it."

Closing her eyes Nonie went on, "I am so tired of fighting to breathe and I hate lying in bed all day. And I am so very tired." She opened her eyes. "Perhaps you could help me, Lani. Maybe the gods have listened to my prayers."

Kneeling down beside the sick woman, Aolani took her cold hands into her warm ones. "How can I help you?"

"My lord has been so good but he doesn't understand."

"Tell me what you want."

"It is Macon," she murmured. "My lord plans for him to join his brother in the army. He must not be a warrior as his father wishes. It would—it would destroy Macon." She shuddered. Her breathing became more rapid. Her hands clutched at Aolani. "Help him, Lani. Help my son. He is sensitive, kind—he cannot kill." She could no longer speak.

"I understand," Aolani said and she did, for she had noticed that Macon was different. He seemed like a very shy and sensitive boy. "Do not worry, Nonie. If anything happens to you, I will take him into my own household and have him trained in whatever direction he wishes to go. Now, don't talk anymore. Just rest. Talking seems to tire you out. Close your eyes, little one. Everything will be all right, I promise."

By all the gods, thought Aolani, as she looked down with pity at the sick woman. How could Viracocha be so cruel? Nonie didn't deserve this. Why did Aolani have so much and Nonie so little? It wasn't fair. But then, she thought despondently, life did not seem to be fair to an awful lot of people.

Hwayna came back into the room and Macon followed, carrying a tray. Hwayna took Nonie's hand in his

Jeanne Nickson

and said gently, "It is time for your medicine, Nonie. It will let you sleep and regain your strength. Good night, my dear."

Aolani knelt and kissed her, saying in a whisper, "I will keep my promise."

As she followed her husband, Aolani turned her head back and saw Macon gently lifting Nonie's head to give her the medicine.

Silent and drained of emotion, Aolani sat beside her husband. The thought of dear little Nonie struggling to breathe made burning tears well up behind her eyelids. She tried to hold them back but soon they were streaming down her face. Aolani ineffectively sought to wipe them off with her sleeve. When her husband put a comforting arm around her shoulder and drew her close to him, she broke into sobs and cried out, "Hwayna, how can life be so cruel? Nonie is loving and good. Why did this have to happen to her?"

Hwayna drew her close. "I don't know, Lani. At some time in life almost everyone asks that same question about someone he loves who is at the door of death. No one has ever found the answer, or so the priests inform me."

"But," Aolani cried, "she is in such agony and suffering so."

"I know," Hwayna said sorrowfully. "For many weeks now I have implored the gods to end her life, but to no avail. I was so angry after one very difficult time that I cursed the night sky and all the gods that live there. Perhaps they are punishing me through her."

Aolani was silent for a while and then said, "I know that death and suffering are all about me every day but I have seldom given it thought. The only death that I can truly remember seeing is that of Lord Pinau, who was old and went quickly. Nonie's suffering really touched me. Can't you do something?"

Hwayna took a deep breath. "A drug could be given her that would ease her pain and help her slip into the afterworld but she refuses such help. I promised her I would obey her wishes."

Lani looked at him with love in her eyes, even though he couldn't see her. "You are a good man, Hwayna Capac. I am proud to be your wife." She went on hesitantly. "I want to say how sorry I am about everything. I am sorry that I fought with you, very sorry about my jealous behavior and my refusal to listen to your side of the story. But most of all, I feel for Nonie. I have neglected her for years because of my jealousy and I hurt inside because of it." She held his hand tightly. "I make so many stupid mistakes in life that it shames and embarrasses me. I feel so guilty."

Hwayna's lips brushed her forehead. "I, too, feel guilty many times and it is a hard burden to bear. All people make mistakes, but when I make them, my errors in judgment involve thousands, if not hundreds of thousands, of people. Last year in the withering heat of the jungle, thousands of men died of poisoned darts, snakebites, bleeding sores, festering wounds, and malaria. All because I was stubborn and thought I was right. I wouldn't turn back. Well, you know what happened. I gained absolutely nothing by causing all those deaths and the despicable cannibals still reign supreme in their miserable land. I often feel so guilty about the campaign that I have nightmares."

"I know you do, beloved. I have heard you at night. I know how much you care. But they were attacking our borders and killing our people. You did it for the well-being of the empire."

She heard Hwayna murmur, "I wish I knew."

Lani reached up to touch his cheek and got his nose instead. Her fingers slipped down to his lips and she lightly caressed them. "Hwayna, do you truly forgive

183

me?" She felt him nod and squeeze her hand. "Will you stay with me tonight? I really need you."

He did not answer, for they had arrived at the palace. Instead, he took her into his arms and, with her head on his shoulder, carried her back to his quarters, for his need was even greater than hers.

Later that evening, as Aolani was about to go to sleep, she heard her husband mutter, "And Nonie has not been here for ten years, Lani. Over a year ago Roco informed me that Nonie was very ill and the healers agreed she needed the low country. I had her brought here and I never even saw her. I was in Quito. Now she is dying and I comfort her. That's all!"

Chapter Seventeen

Juan watched the queen record a complex administrative problem onto a quipus. Juan marveled at the Incas' preservation of a wealth of detailed information by using a series of cords consisting of a main cord from which hung colored, woolen threads. As Juan had been told, the position and the number of knots tied on these threads provided numerical information. The *Coya*, Lady Aolani, was sending out a message. She was very adept at what she was doing. But then she was good at everything she did. Look at how quickly she had learned Spanish, not only to speak, but to read and write, though no other Inca could read or write his native language. Juan marveled at Aolani's abilities but he was beginning to wonder how long he would continue to be of use to her.

Having come from a long line of Sephardic Jews who valued education, Juan had been encouraged by his father, but mostly by his young uncles, to read most of Erasmus and Cicero and to at least familiarize himself with Alexander, Hector, and Titus Livius. He had used his knowledge of history to entertain Aolani. Though he cherished his time with her and lived in this splendid palace in such an exotic land, he missed his family. Juan often longed for his home. Though he didn't remember his mother, who had died when he was very young, he remembered his father, Pedro de Montaro, with love and affection. His father had always given him a great deal of time and attention when he was at home, which was not often. As a merchant, his father often left Juan with his grandmother and three uncles while he went to Salamanca, Seville, and even Madrid. Juan had enjoyed living with his grandmother and his young uncles, who treated him with affection, even though they made him work hard at his studies. But his biggest wish had been to travel with his father, to see all the sights of the big cities, especially Seville, the port leading to the New World.

When he was 15, his father had finally decided to let him accompany him on one of his journeys. When they had reached Seville, and he had listened to the exciting tales of the explorers, Juan decided he just had to go to see the New World. He knew his father wouldn't permit him to go but his desire was so overwhelming that he stowed away on a Spanish galleon sailing for the New World. His father had no doubt never forgiven him and probably thought him dead.

The sound of thunder in the distance brought Juan out of his reveries. He saw the quipu master leaving the room just as the music master entered. It seemed to Juan that he spent all his time waiting for the queen to request his service. But it was better than waiting in his small chamber, which had just enough space for a sleeping mat. As he looked at the *Coya,* the sun chose that moment to come out of the clouds. The light from the open door flickered across her features, highlighting her cheekbones, endowing her face with a mysterious beauty. Juan watched her as he did every day when he could do so without being noticed, memorizing every detail of expression, every delicate movement of her slender body. He thought of her almost all of the time. Tonight, he mused, he would be wakeful again, thinking of her pearllike skin, her beautiful hands knotting the cords, her long waving hair with its glints of gold. He was obsessed with her and there was nothing he could do about it. Lady Aolani was out of his reach and always would be. It made him miserable. If it were not for the young cooking girl, he'd go out of his mind.

The woman that Nadua had told him about hadn't been interested in him and it seemed that no one else wanted him either. There was no way out of his dilemma, for if he was to survive, he had to make himself useful to the *Coya* in every way he could so that she would keep him around. He knew his safety was in her hands, for who else in this strange world cared whether he lived or died? Certainly not the Inca, whom he rarely saw. He had enjoyed teaching the *Coya* and now he taught the children. They were all doing well, except for the eldest son. It had been over eight years since he began working with the *Coya* and only in the last five years with the children.

But Juan was frustrated. His thirtieth birthday was near and Juan felt his life was slipping away without his having any control over it. When he'd first arrived in Tomebamba he had tried to change his life and in some ways he had. He had made friends. He had been with women, but here he was, still a man in prison, in a palace, but a prison for all of that. There were only two things that kept him from going mad—his time with the queen and his secret occupation of finding out all he could about the Incas. Since his presence

Jeanne Nickson

had become familiar and nonthreatening, he often overheard conversations and stored them away in his memory. Someday, when his countrymen arrived, he would be useful and become a man of power and wealth, perhaps even have a chance to win Aolani.

Juan's daydream was interrupted as Aolani asked him to bring her musical instruments. She kept them in her bedchamber. As he picked them up, he looked longingly out into the Inca's garden. No one was allowed to enter it uninvited, but he felt rebellious. The big outer courtyards of the palace were devoid of growing things. He brought the instruments to the *Coya* and moved silently into the background. The *Coya*, with the help of the *amautas*, often composed comedies and dramas for her husband's court. Juan knew these plays were treated very seriously and the actors were all members of the elite. The dramas were usually about heroic exploits and wars or the greatness of past Inca rulers. The comedies were concerned with agriculture or household themes.

The *Coya* was planning something a little different for her husband. The story sounded rather like an Inca fairy tale to Juan, for it was about a famous shepherd named Acoya-napa and the beautiful Chuqui-Llantu, Daughter of the Sun, and the shepherd's unrequited love. This was not a story that suited Juan's mood at the moment. It was too much like his own story. The noise was dreadful, he thought, as they tuned their instruments. Never having had much of an ear for music, he soon found that the strange wailing sounds of the flutes and the pipes were giving him a headache. All the people in the room were so intent and busy he doubted if anyone saw him in the shadows. It was a dark, cold day, and he wondered if he could slip into the garden for a moment. He knew it was forbidden territory but he felt like rebelling today. He was just in the mood to try something to cure his boredom. He made up his mind.

Juan edged toward the open bedchamber door, and as the group began listening to the *Coya*, he slipped out of the room. Seeing no one in her personal quarters, he moved swiftly to the door that led to the Inca's garden. Outside, he first looked around for a place of concealment and settled on the small molle tree with its weeping green foliage falling almost to the ground. Planted under it, almost touching its branches, was a thick shrub about three feet tall with dark needlelike leaves that would conceal his body.

As he settled down with his back against the garden wall, he took deep breaths of the fragrant air. He watched the sun playing a game in the clouds, appearing suddenly in all its brightness, then leaving the earth in shadows of darkness. As Juan peered through the leaves, he was impressed by the beauty of the place. A pathway, a mosaic of silver and gold, led around the pool and widened at each end to provide an outside sanctuary shaded by trees and filled with beautiful flowers. Outside of the jungle, he had never seen such an exotic display of plants. He was also impressed by the many gold and silver fountains and statues, as well as the jeweled flowers and animals everywhere he looked. By the Blessed Virgin, what wealth the Inca must have. Even the King and Queen of Spain would envy this garden.

A small fly buzzed irritatingly around his head and he was just getting ready to slap it with his hand when he heard voices. He froze. He stopped breathing and could feel his heart pounding so hard that he thought surely someone would hear it. Juan was petrified as he saw the figures that were approaching his place of hiding. It was the Lord High Inca, the *Uillac Uma*—the highest priest in the land—and Lord Moche, who seemed to be with the Inca a great deal of late. Juan couldn't hear what they were saying.

As they came closer, the first voice Juan could distinguish was that of the Inca, who sounded angry. "I want you to quit talking about my duty, Lloque. Enough is enough. You may be *Uillac Uma* but I am the Custodian of the Sun, and I alone know what my duty is. I will take your suggestion under advisement but I am not happy with it. Now leave me."

After the priest had bowed his head and left, the Inca watched him, then said, "That priest is getting bolder all the time. I think it is time for a change." He looked up at the heavens. "The sky is getting darker and a south wind is blowing. We may have a little rain for a change, if Wilkamaya so decides." He walked over to a rock and sat down. "Decisions! How I wish the gods would make them for me. Perhaps the goddess of the storm will help me. There was a poem about the goddess Wilkamaya. Do you remember it?"

Moche recited:

O Wilkamaya of the stormy skies
When you beat your drums of thunder
And rain pours down in sheets of silver
When the wind howls in interminable anger—

Moche put a hand to his head. "Sorry, my lord. I've forgotten the rest, but the idea was that the empire would fall if all these events happened."

Hwayna said abruptly, "I am worried about the empire and my family. If the strangers from another land invade our world, I want Aolani and the children in a place of safety. I don't want to lose you, Moche, but I trust you, so I must send you with them. Today I learned that men in a large wooden house appeared on the sea and they have gone ashore at Tumbes. These strange people are white with bearded faces and their fierce looks have frightened the people. They sleep in their house on the water at night and come ashore during the day. They demand to see the lord of the land. Can you imagine such a thing." The Inca was scowling. "They entered the royal houses and carried off my treasures. They even went into my zoo and killed the beasts I kept there."

"How bold and threatening!" Moche said.

"The house sailed away two days ago, but they will be back and in greater number. I don't think I have a great deal of time left." The Inca rose slowly. "I feel the burden of my years. I am only thirty-eight but I feel like a man of sixty."

"Your burdens are heavy, my lord."

The Inca turned and faced him. "Do you believe in premonitions, Moche?"

"Yes," Moche said. "I think some people have them."

"I want to tell you a story that my Uncle Roco told to me. This happened many years ago in the time of my father, Tupac Yupanqui. He had been working with his council all day on some serious problems and it was late. He went outside to get a breath of air on the large terrace at Sacsahuaman, for the night was warm and oppressive. The sky was overcast, not a star could be seen. Suddenly, a breeze as cold as ice swirled around him. The earth began to heave and shake like a wounded animal in pain. Then it was quiet—there was an intense silence. He glanced at the sky and saw the clouds part as if swept aside by a giant hand. The moon shone down but it was like no moon he had ever seen. It was encircled by a triple halo, one as red as blood, the second a deep green, and the third as dark as smoke. My father couldn't move but he could see himself standing outside of where he stood. He heard these words: 'Pachacamac, the creator and giver of life, threatens your family, your realm, and your subjects.

191

Sons of your blood will rage a cruel war. Those of royal blood will die and the empire will disappear.' Then the clouds covered the moon and his outside body became a part of him."

Juan watched Moche blink rapidly and lower his eyes. "Pachacamac is not even one of our gods, but he is a respected oracle, I admit. Do you believe this story?"

"I am afraid, Moche. Three times this last month I have dreamed the same dream, heard the same words, and woken up sweating. I want to say it is just a dream, but I can't. I believe, even though I don't want to, that the strangers who destroyed another empire to the north of us are coming here. Atahualpa and Huascar are the sons who will wage a cruel war, and I can do nothing about it, for my time is near. I have tried and I will continue to try but there is nothing I can do that will change the events that are about to happen."

Juan shivered with excitement as his eyes followed the Inca who walked slowly like an old man down the beautiful walk and disappeared into the palace leaving Moche looking worried and disheartened as he headed in the other direction.

Juan sat quietly for several minutes after the two men had left. He felt exultant. Spaniards had already set foot upon Incan soil. Nothing would stop them now. They would soon be arriving—hordes of men seeking to destroy the empire. A sober thought invaded his mind. It might be many years before they could successfully conquer this great land. He might be an old man before they did, if he lived that long. The Inca might even kill him long before his countrymen could rescue him. As he slipped through the shadowy garden he was not elated, but concerned about his own survival.

Peering through the door to the bedchamber, Juan saw no one there but he could hear the sounds of instruments in the next room. Lady Aolani's voice was raised in a sad refrain. He walked softly through her room and made his way carefully into the shadows of the outer chamber.

Within a few minutes the antechamber was empty and Juan was the only one left with the queen. He saw her sitting there with a cold detached expression on her face as if she were in another world. He wondered if she knew he was there. He walked forward and sat down quietly. A kind of dizziness came over him at the thought of being alone with her. It had happened only once before in all the time he had been here, for she usually kept one of her women with her. Erotic thoughts crept into his mind and his whole body ached with the desire to touch her. He closed his eyes, imagining her in the pool, her breasts bared to the sun, her long hair cascading down her back.

His fantasy was brought to an abrupt end with the entrance of Capt. Luasi. Lady Aolani suddenly snapped out of her trancelike state and said, "Luasi, this is a pleasant surprise. What are you doing here at this time of the day?"

"I am here at the Inca's request, my dear lady. He wants you to bring the foreign slave to the reception hall."

Aolani looked startled. "Now?"

Luasi smiled a little. "Yes, now."

"I wonder why." She thought for a moment. "He seemed very interested last evening in your story about the Roman Empire, Juan. Perhaps that's why he wants to see you." She paused and then said softly, "Juan, this may be an opportunity for you to prove your worth. Be as honest with the Inca as you are with me. If you try to conceal anything or lie, he will instantly know."

For a moment her comment encouraged Juan and he felt optimistic. He might have to stay here for years and he didn't want to remain a lowly servant or slave as the Inca called him. He was frightened but the queen was right. He would answer all questions and respond in the best way he could. Perhaps he might become an adviser to the Inca.

"Come," Lord Luasi said as he walked toward the door. Juan and Lady Aolani followed him.

When they entered the large reception hall, Juan looked around in amazement. The room was huge. It could easily hold over 300 people. Two great windows, one on each side of the chamber, let in the light, but not the wind. Their coverings were translucent and glittered and sparkled as Juan walked by. Juan wanted to look at the windows more closely but he saw they were almost in front of a gold dais that stretched across one end of the room. The heads of black pumas, their gaping paws and fearful fangs repeating themselves, were carved along the base of the dais.

An immense funerary mask of hammered gold, gold overlays, and ornaments was directly in back of the Inca's throne and, to Juan, it appeared menacing. Large gold-filigree panels framed it on each side. The Inca sat below, no longer in the simple tunic he had worn in the garden. He was covered with a shimmering mantle of bright red feathers matching the red-fringed band he wore across his brow. Moche had told Juan the fringe was the insignia of the Inca's royal status. Great gold embossed earrings hung from the Inca's lobes, and necklaces and bracelets of the same metal adorned his body.

When Luasi nudged him, Juan followed the other man up the steps leading to the dais. Feeling a slight pressure on his shoulder, he sat down and slowly began to look around. He noticed the Lord High

Inca sat on a low stone throne covered by a thick red rug directly in front of, but above him and the other people. As Juan listened he heard the Inca saying to one of his aides, "Have all messages decoded by dark. I want to see anything that comes in from the Canari at once. You may go."

He then turned to another man, whom Juan recognized as Gen. Quis-quis, who commanded all of the Inca's armies. A serious man, he had a scowl on his face. Though he was stout in build, he sat erect and stiff. Juan felt the man's eyes upon him, and as he looked back, he felt the critical gaze that seemed to take him apart. As the Inca addressed Quis-quis, the general's glance shifted back to the Inca, who ordered him to keep in touch with his aide. "We may have to send another detachment in to make sure those devil-birthed Canari keep the peace."

An assistant came up to the Inca and whispered something to him. The Inca nodded and the man unrolled a piece of material, which the Inca silently studied. It gave Juan an opportunity to look at the other people seated around the Inca. Sitting next to Gen. Quis-quis was Lord Moche, who gave him a friendly smile. Juan noticed that Moche had an air of graceful dignity, as if his interests verged upon the spiritual rather than the real. But there was also a strong human quality about him, a warmth and an interest in people. He was smiling at the Inca; the smile was gentle, but also a little sad.

To the Inca's left sat Capt. Luasi, who was a good deal older than the Inca. His face seemed to carry the entire tale of his years. As the head of the Inca's household, Luasi had often met with Juan and they had become friends. Juan knew Luasi was a practical, responsible man who ran the palace with a stern hand and constant vigilance.

Between Luasi and Juan was the serene figure of the *Coya*, absorbed by what was going on. Juan, who knew what a well-disciplined life she led, thought she was mature beyond her years.

As the Inca dismissed his retinue, except for two aides who sat on each side of him, he turned back to the five people present in the room and looked at them in silence. Juan had never been this close to the Inca, except in the garden. There the Inca had appeared an old and discouraged man. Now he was vigorous, alive, and teeming with energy. There was a magnetism about him that drew everyone's attention.

The Lord High Inca turned toward Juan, who was mesmerized by his brilliant black eyes. "I would like to hear in your own words again the story of the Roman Empire. I want all of you to listen well and think about it for discussion later. Begin," he commanded.

Juan swallowed and began hesitantly, but then with more assurance, to tell of the mighty Romans and the fall of their empire.

When at last he came to the end of the saga and explained the final disintegration of the Roman Empire there was a silence in the room. As the Inca began to speak, Juan listened to him with a measure of uneasiness, fearing that he had failed in some way. The Inca was not speaking to him, but to others in the room.

"I am sure you are wondering why I have had you listen to this story." He paused. "We have an empire that may be faced with an invasion of men from another world. As large and as powerful as our empire may be, we are vulnerable. We must learn how to deal with the problems we will have to face. Many of our Indian nations may side with these strangers, especially people like the Canari who are always causing trouble. Quis-quis, where will these invaders land? How can we keep our nation together? Think about these problems and come up with some answers. Another thing, we may have to destroy their boats. How can we do this?"

He turned to Luasi. "You heard of the chariots and how they moved on huge, round wheels. Have someone make me two wheels attached to a box of some kind. We will need better transportation, if we are attacked. We don't have the Romans' animals to pull these carts, but we have manpower." He thought for a moment. "Moche, I want you to gather some wise men and begin trying to find a way that our spoken language can be made into a written language. That is all for now. Now, you may leave, except for the *Coya* and her teacher."

As the men left the room, Juan sat there amazed at the tasks the Inca had assigned his men. Would this Inca be able to stop the hordes of determined, rapacious men who would overrun his empire?

"One or two more questions, Juan, but first know that I am pleased with you. If you will work with us as an assistant to these men, you will no longer be a slave but an 'Inca by Privilege.' Better lodging, clothes, food, and freedom will be given to you. Do you so agree?"

Juan felt important and needed. He heaved a sigh of relief. He would no longer be a slave. He decided to accept the Inca's offer. "Yes, my Lord Inca, I agree to help in every way I can."

The Inca smiled. "Tell me, is your king powerful, more powerful than other rulers?"

"All kings are powerful. When I was growing up Ferdinand and Isabella were king and queen. They were strong."

"Europe?" the Inca questioned.

Juan explained. "There are many countries in our part of the world that form Europe. Among these countries are France, England, Portugal, and others, but Spain because of her conquests is the wealthiest and most powerful country."

"Were Ferdinand and Isabella brother and sister?"

"No. Our religion forbids the marriage of close relations such as brother and sister; even first cousins are forbidden to marry."

The Inca looked interested. "Why is this forbidden?"

Juan thought for a moment. "I believe it is claimed that the children of such a marriage are often weak, either physically or mentally."

The Inca wanted to hear more but he didn't think it wise to have Aolani begin to worry about what the young man had said, especially with the marriage of Atahualpa and Hwaylas soon to be consummated. He would question Juan later. This belief could be an answer to a lot of his own questions. His father, Tupac Yupanqui, had claimed that of his five sons, the only one he could name as heir in good conscience was Hwayna, the youngest of his sons. He remembered his brother, Auqui, a good but unstable man, his sister Cusi Rimay, strange and unpredictable, and his half brothers, all flawed in some way. His own brood, with the exception of Aolani's children and Ninian, were also a disappointment. Could this be the reason? The Inca looked at this stranger from another world. The gods moved in strange and unusual ways. Perhaps this Spaniard had been sent for a purpose. He would have to think about this. He resolved to talk to Juan more in the future.

Chapter Eighteen

Watching Aolani as she talked with one of the priests from the temple, Juan was as impressed as always by her calm assurance and quiet dignity. A few inches taller than other women, she was at 32 the most beautiful and alluring woman that he had ever seen. However, today, he noticed the dark shadows under her eyes and the tremor in her voice. Suddenly, she seemed fragile and vulnerable. He wondered what was bothering her. She had seemed absentminded and preoccupied ever since the Lord High Inca's return.

Again, he wondered why she had asked him to stay after the lesson today. Well, he'd know soon enough. Juan settled back patiently, his back against the wall, trying to imagine why she wasn't following her usual routine. Every day, after they finished their lesson, she left to join her children. He knew she would spend a good hour or two with them, for she enjoyed her children, and this time was precious to her. She never gave it up without a reason, and it had to be a good one at that.

As the priest bowed and left the room, he saw Lord Moche enter. Another unusual event. Moche always came later in the afternoon to inform Aolani of the day's events. Juan watched Aolani go toward the other man, kiss him lightly on the cheek, and motion him to a seat.

Aolani turned to her servingwoman. "You may leave us, Renpo." Juan saw her looking at him. "Come join us, Juan."

As he moved over to the soft rugs and sat down, Juan noticed that her hands were shaking and her eyes were reddened as if she had been crying. Moche seemed to be aware of her agitation, also, for he glanced at Juan with a questioning look in his eyes.

The door to Aolani's bedchamber was ajar and Juan could see the garden outside. Under the lashing wind, the trees loosed whirlwinds of dry leaves. Suddenly, there came an uproar and flashes of lightning raced across the sky. A chill wind swept through the room and Juan shivered. He wondered if he should close the door.

Aolani broke the silence. "I have a terrible problem and I've asked you both here to help me. You, Moche, because you are the wisest man I know, and you, Juan, because in my agony I feel I can trust you." She said bluntly, "The problem is my son, Atahualpa." She paused and then said in a choked voice, "I've been worried about him for a long time, but like most mothers, I just hoped and prayed that things would right themselves, but instead they become worse day by day."

Standing up, she nervously paced the floor while Juan watched her with concerned eyes. She knelt in front of Moche and asked, "You have known

Atahualpa since he was born. Is he capable of deception, abuse, and even the torture of an innocent child?"

"Aolani, what is this? How can I answer such a question?" Moche asked, astounded.

"All I asked was is he capable of doing a great wrong."

"All people are capable of doing a great wrong, but, yes, I think Atahualpa, more than most, is capable of wickedness, for he is selfish and insensitive. Now will you please explain yourself?"

"Before I do, I want Juan to tell me what he thinks of Atahualpa. He has been his tutor for years," Aolani said, looking at Juan.

"I think Moche is right. Atahualpa is selfish and insensitive. He has been spoiled and always wants his own way," Juan said honestly.

"Aolani," Moche said, breaking in, "will you please get to the heart of the matter? What happened that makes you want to know what we think about the boy?"

"Last night, Cusi came to my room crying so hard that at first I couldn't hear what she was saying. Finally, I managed to understand a little. Atahualpa had put his baby brother Manco into a dark little room with a rat and wouldn't let him out. She pulled on my hand and I followed her as she ran through the nursery, out into the courtyard, and down the stone stairs to that alcove where the servants keep their supplies. There was no one around but I heard muffled screams behind the thick wooden door. I pulled it open with an effort, for it was heavy, and there was my baby, sobbing and terrified. I held his trembling little body in my arms and carried him back to my room, where I examined his body for bites. There were none. I have never been so angry in my life but I soothed the children until they both fell asleep.

"Still angry and disbelieving, I arose later from my bed, for I couldn't sleep. I aroused my women and the guards in the hall and told them to examine my quarters, including the nursery and the children's rooms, and let me know what they found. In minutes they were back. The nursemaid and Manco's guard had been drugged. Sinchi and Atahualpa were both asleep. I still could not believe that my firstborn son had done this to a baby even though Cusi always tells the truth.

"Then one of my women said she had seen Atahualpa laughing and joking with Manco's guard. She wasn't sure, but she thought he'd had a goblet in his hand. I did nothing further until morning. When Cusi was awake, she told me again that she had seen Atahualpa sneak out of the nursery with Manco in his arms. She'd followed him down and watched him put Manco inside the alcove and then toss in what she said was a wiggly thing. When he left she couldn't open the door. Manco was screaming, so she rushed back to get me. I then proceeded to question the staff."

"Well, what did they say?" Moche said impatiently.

Aolani sighed. "I heard some stories about Atahualpa that made me cringe with shame. But I can't believe all the things the servants said about him, especially since they really had no proof of his guilt."

"Why didn't they tell you what was happening?" Juan asked.

"Because he threatened them. He is the son of the Lord High Inca. They are really afraid of him. Most of them are simple people and they believe he is the son of a god. I can believe this, for I've been around my husband long enough to know that everyone fears him, too. Atahualpa took advantage of them."

Again Aolani closed her eyes and sighed deeply. "But it was my son himself who convinced me of his guilt. When I confronted him, he felt no more remorse or shame for the mean tricks he has played on the servants and my other children than a monkey. He thinks that his pranks are funny and that Manco is too pampered. He said he was only trying to make his little brother tough. As for his treatment of Cusi, he feels he has every right to intimidate her and take liberties with her body. After all, she is going to be his wife in a couple of years."

Aolani rubbed her head while Moche and Juan just looked at each other. "What am I going to do?" she asked helplessly.

Moche put his arm around her and she put her head against his chest and cried. He wiped her tears and forced her to sit up. "Calm yourself, Lani. As you, yourself, said a little while ago, you've always known what kind of a boy Atahualpa is, so let's not overreact to this matter. Let's talk about Atahualpa for a while. He's not a child anymore. If he were in Cuzco what would he be doing at his present age?"

Aolani was silent for a moment. "He'd be attending the college for young Inca nobles and the sons of rulers."

Moche said, "And he would be with his peers, males of his own age at the *Yacha Huasi*. Their training program is primarily centered upon making the pupils great warriors and leaders of men. Instead, Atahualpa is treated like a child and is placed in a nursery ruled over by his mother. The only time he has spent with his father was the year and a half they were together during the war against the Caranqui. I suggest that Atahualpe resents his present situation, and he is taking out his anger on everybody, especially his brother and sister."

In the silence, Juan could hear thunder in the distance. He expected Aolani to show anger at Moche's remarks but she agreed with him.

"You're right," she said. "I know Atahualpe is angry and rebellious all the time. But I have kept him close to me because something terrible happened while he and his father were away. I don't know what it was, but it changed him. Whatever it was, I just haven't wanted to face it."

"From what I know of Atahualpa," Moche said, "I would judge him to be totally male, attracted to the manly arts and little inclined toward history, religion, or the arts. His father should have taken him in hand long ago, but"—Moche held up his hand as Aolani started to speak—"I know! I know that Hwayna Capac cannot give him personal attention right now, but he can place Atahualpa with one of his officers to learn what he needs to know in order to become a leader of men, which someday he might be. Unless," he added, "you want to send him to Cuzco."

"You know that is impossible because of Huascar. He might kill Atahualpa."

"Then I suggest," Moche said, "that we present the problem to his father as soon as possible. He has a right to know. Perhaps tonight."

Looking gratefully at Moche, Aolani said, "You are wise, my dear friend, and perhaps I have been overprotective. I should have thought of my son's needs long ago."

"I would like to offer some more advice. Manco is over three years of age and has always been surrounded by women who cater to his every whim. He may become spoiled, too. Your youngest son needs a male to whom he can look for guidance, since the Inca cannot provide it. I would like you to consider Juan. He is intelligent, perceptive, and kind but he is also a physically strong and powerful man. He is at loose ends most of the time, for he is no longer needed to teach Spanish. Both you and the children are fluent in the language and no longer need him."

Juan was horrified at what Moche was saying. He didn't want to be a nursemaid to a child. He wanted to take his place among men in the Inca world. How could Moche do this to him? Aolani was looking at him with speculative eyes, a thoughtful expression on her face.

Juan said hurriedly, "I'm complimented by your confidence in me, Lord Moche, but don't you think Manco should have a man of his own race, an Inca who could teach him all he needs to know about his world?"

Aolani, paying no attention to Juan, said to Moche, "My dear brother, I agree with you. Juan would be perfect for Manco. He is indeed perceptive and intelligent, and he can provide knowledge of how my son can survive in the new world that may come in the future. Starting immediately, Juan, you will be Manco's lord protector. That means this afternoon. He will have to become familiar with you even though I think he knows who you are. I promised him he would see his Uncle Moche this afternoon, so I will go and prepare him."

Aghast, Juan looked at Moche. "How could you do this to me? I know nothing about young children. I've never been around them. I don't even know what to say to them."

Moche smiled. "You'll learn."

"But I don't want to learn," Juan said indignantly.

Moche suddenly looked stern. "You are behaving like a child. You are not thinking. For one thing you owe Aolani a lot and she needs you. From the first moment you were thrown at her feet she has protected you. Most Inca slaves are placed in the mines and never see the light of day. Others spend years dragging huge stones hundreds of miles. Some deal with the disposal of human waste all of their days.

You were lucky to be her slave. You were taught our language, fed, and clothed on her instructions. Aolani even approached me saying she was terribly worried that you might take your life. She persuaded me to let you ride in my palanquin. She said you needed male friends. She even agreed to provide a woman for you. Now, she needs you."

"I am sorry you were forced to become my friend," Juan said resentfully.

"You are still being childish," Moche said with anger. "I enjoyed your company. I have become very fond of you and I'm only thinking of your welfare right now."

Juan, feeling ashamed, muttered, "I'm sorry. I know what you and Aolani both have done for me and I'm grateful. If she needs me for her son, I will do my best."

"Good. Now you are acting like yourself. Don't you realize that you will be improving your chances? You will be the lord protector of the Lord High Inca's son. It is a great honor and privilege to help shape the mind and character of a child who may someday inherit the Throne of the Sun."

"But I'm not sure that I can help him, much less shape him," Juan said glumly.

"You'll learn," Moche said with a smile. "Don't be so downhearted."

"I can't help it! What do I do with him? Does he talk?"

As Juan asked the questions, there were voices from the hall and Aolani entered with the baby, Manco, on her hip. Nadua followed close behind. The little boy scrambled down from his mother's arms and, with chubby little legs, ran with arms outstretched to Moche, shouting, "Unca Mo, Unca Mo."

Moche picked him up, threw him in the air, caught him, and placed a kiss on the tip of his nose, saying,

"Now where is my kiss?" Putting his arms around Moche's neck, the little boy gave him a kiss on the cheek.

Juan examined the child while Moche talked to him. Manco had Aolani's light golden skin and amber eyes but he had his father's high cheekbones and dark straight hair. He was a handsome child and seemed happy and outgoing despite the previous night's experience. Juan had seen very little of Manco since he was born, for he had a different schedule from the older children. Manco was talking very rapidly to Moche and seemed excited. Juan moved closer to hear him.

"I wuz playin' and den big raindrops fell on my head and I got wet. There wuz a big noise; den fire wuz in the sky, big fire."

"Were you frightened?" Juan asked.

Manco looked over at him, a friendly expression on his face. "Maybe, just a little."

"That's good," Juan said. "You're a brave boy. Storms can be frightening to some people."

"Not me!" Manco said firmly. He wiggled out of Moche's arms, walked over to Juan, and carefully examined his face. "I see you here before," he announced. "You Cusi's friend, Juan."

"*Si,*" Juan said. "That means yes. I am Cusi's friend. I am your friend, too. Friends have fun together. May I have a hug, too?" Manco thought it over and then threw his arms around Juan and gave him a kiss. Juan felt a strange sense of warmth. It felt good to be hugged and kissed by a child.

"All right, Manco," his mother said, "you have seen your Uncle Mo and made a new friend and it's time for your nap. Nadua will take you."

"Juan come, too."

"No, not now. Juan will be there when you wake up from your nap, won't you, Juan?"

207

Did he have a choice? "*Sí*," Juan answered.

As Nadua took him out, Manco was explaining to Nadua, "*Sí* means yes, Nadie. Juan's my friend."

Maybe, Juan thought, I'll be able to manage this child, but please God, not for long.

Chapter Nineteen

Watching the white clouds build up among the far mountain peaks, Aolani saw them begin to darken as the wind of the Storm God whirled and howled about her. Lightning streaked across the sky with the speed of an arrow and the sound of Ilyapa's lightning bolt made a noise like a crack of a whip.

Aolani felt tense and afraid, but not of the storm. She'd been feeling this way for days, afraid of hidden terrors that she could not fathom. Knowing she had to talk to someone, she had invited Moche to visit her this afternoon. He was the only one she really trusted. The wind tossed her hair about her face and Aolani moved closer to Moche and put her hand on his arm. "Let us go inside. I am getting chilled."

They went into her antechamber and sat down facing each other on the bright pillows piled upon the floor. Aolani dismissed her women and poured some wine for Moche. As she handed him the vessel, she said,

Jeanne Nickson

"I suppose you know that I asked you to come for a reason." He nodded. "Moche, I don't know quite where to begin. Perhaps, I am giving more importance to my fears and anxieties than they deserve."

Moche looked at her with concern in his eyes and then smiled a little. "You were always an imaginative girl, but a logical thinker, despite your flair for seeing the unusual. If you have fears, I know they are justified. It is good to talk, to get them out in the open. Now tell me, what frightens you?"

"My biggest fear is about my husband's health. There is something wrong but he will not consult the healers." Tears came to her eyes. "He will not even discuss it with me. He seems to think if he ignores these attacks, they will go away."

"Tell me, what is wrong with the Inca?"

"I think it is his heart." Her words came out in a rush. "Hwayna has attacks of pain that leave him breathless. Then they go away and he says he feels fine but he gets very little sleep and doesn't eat properly. These are all symptoms that his heart is weak. He is moody and strange, not like himself at all."

"It is not rare as we grow older to have such attacks. Air belches from my mouth at times like steam from an exploding mountain, and sometimes I feel pain. My stomach growls and rumbles as well." Moche said hesitantly, "You must think it more than this. After all, you are not a novice when it comes to the healing arts. Our teacher, Lord Pinau, often praised you for your skill with medicines and herbs. He called you a *Hampi Camayoc*, a medicine specialist."

"That is why I am afraid. I have listened to the sound that beats like a drum inside him. It does not beat in a steady rhythm as it should."

"Is there a cure?"

"I don't know, but rest, freedom from worry, and

210

relaxation will help him. I could also give him a mixture of sairi and coca to calm him down but he will not listen to me." Aolani got up and began pacing. "I think Hwayna is brooding too much about the future. He seems to feel he is advancing blindly toward the destruction of the empire. He is obsessed by the problems of what he thinks will be facing us, the invasion of Tahuantinsuyu by the bearded strangers."

"Well, if he gets sick he is not going to be able to solve the problems," Moche said grimly. "I can understand his concerns but the invasion may be years away. Everything else in the empire is going along smoothly. I've been listening to the reports in the last month. The Aymara miners, the Nazca potters, the Cuzco goldsmiths, the builders of fortresses and roads, the farmers, and even the poets and artists carry out their duties to perfection, and precautionary measures and controls work smoothly."

Aolani knelt down beside Moche, her hands twisted together, as she said, "All you say about the empire is true; everything is going smoothly. But Hwayna is thinking like a warrior hit by a stone mace. He is confused. He does not seem himself."

"Why not?"

"Again it is hard to explain, but let me try. Hwayna Capac has always been a reasonable and intelligent man who plans carefully for the future. For instance, my husband used to be indulgent of his enemies, not only because he has a compassionate nature, but because his ancestors have always believed that the way to bind a new province to the empire is not through cruelty, but to help the conquered people have a better life. Now, he frightens me, for he is becoming more and more ruthless and cruel to those who incur his wrath. Do you know what he has just done to the inhabitants of the Island of Punta?"

211

Moche raised his eyebrows. "No, but I know what the warriors of Punta did to his army. I know how the old cannibal chief tricked over fifteen hundred Inca warriors, drowning and butchering most of the Inca's men when he tried to conquer them. I also saw that the Inca was deeply angered about the massacre."

"That is true, but Hwayna retaliated by having all the inhabitants of Punta, including women and children, impaled, cut in pieces, and then thrown into the sea. It sickened me." There was horror in Aolani's eyes as she looked at her friend.

Moche stroked his chin thoughtfully. "I find that difficult to believe. There must be some reason for such a violent action. Hwayna Capac has always been extremely lenient with women and children. Have you talked to him about this?"

"No, I've tried, but Hwayna just changed the subject," Aolani said bitterly. "I asked about the two thousand Caranqui warriors who were cut up and drowned in a lake. He said it was none of my business. Admittedly the Caranqui have inexplicable vices, lower even than the Esmeraldas, who practice sodomy. It was said the Otavalo Lake was so filled with the blood of the Caranqui that the waters ran red. The Inca's own men call the lake by a new name, *Yahuarcocha*, the Lake of Blood. That butchery seems so vicious to me. It is not worthy of the Inca."

Moche was thoughtful for a few moments and then said, "If your lord is tired and depressed at times, that is natural. But you seem to indicate the Inca has been melancholy and depressed for a long time, and that his mood is getting worse, causing a change in his behavior, as well as the strange attacks in his chest. Perhaps he needs a holiday, a rest away from the chaotic schedule here at Tomebamba. Alone with you, he might be able to forget the pressures he is under."

Aolani grimaced then shook her head. "He won't leave now for many reasons but chief among them is the darkness that will descend upon the earth when the moon covers the sun eight days from now. The people become terrified. Hwayna will insist upon being here."

"Well," Moche said, grinning a little, "perhaps we can try a little strategy."

"What are you going to do?" she asked.

"My thought is this. My Lord Inca may not go away for himself, but if you were sick and the healers recommended a change of scene, he just might do it. I think we'll have to bring Nadua and Luasi into our plans. I wouldn't be surprised in the least if they are as concerned about the Lord High Inca as you are. They have known him for an even longer period than you have."

"But what about the matter of the dark mask cast over the sun?" Aolani asked anxiously.

"I have a plan for that, too."

He went on to explain and Aolani laughed. "Moche, you are very clever," she exclaimed.

By midmorning the Inca's entourage was traveling over a high plateau where the bare brown hills undulated into the distance, finally reaching the jagged edges of snow-covered peaks. Juan noticed the land was too hard and the weather too cold for growing potatoes and grain, but it provided adequate grazing lands for the llamas. Not too far away, Juan saw one of the Inca's large herds of these valuable animals roving over the sparse bunch grass.

What a wonderful opportunity this was, Juan thought, as he rode in the litter, to see this magnificent country. How fortunate for him that the Inca seemed fascinated with his tales of Europe and commanded that Juan attend him on his holiday to a hunting lodge in the mountains.

Juan was startled when a fast-moving and extremely large animal raced swiftly past his litter. He wondered if it might be one of the guanacos, for they were similar in size and shape to the llama and the *Coya* had told him they were larger and faster. Juan saw Lord Moche striding at a fast pace past his litter and called out, "Moche, was that a guanaco?"

"Yes. Why? Are you planning on catching one of those during the hunt? If so, I advise against it."

"Why? Are they more dangerous?" Juan asked curiously.

"No, not really, but it is hard throwing a net over them when they run so fast, and a guanaco can drag you quite a distance before you can throw it down and hobble its legs. Why don't you walk for a while? You can see more."

Juan was excited. Despite his new status, he didn't know just how much freedom he had. "Is it permitted?" he asked.

"I will take the responsibility." Moche told the bearers to stop and Juan scrambled out of the litter.

Moving ahead with Moche, Juan felt exhilarated as he breathed the thin, cold air and felt the hot sun on his face. "Would you tell me more about the hunt and just what will take place, Lord Moche?"

"The hunt will probably be held the day after tomorrow, for it takes a little preparation. Beaters will close in on the herd of llamas, driving them toward the hunters and, we hope, to a small ravine or valley. There, they will be easier to capture. No killing will take place, for throughout history our race has been dependent on llamas because they are a source of wool and companionship. You may not know this, but every family in the empire has at least one llama given to them by the Inca. The peasants are forbidden to kill them for food. They must be used only to supply wool for clothing."

Juan was puzzled. "But some of them are used for sacrifices. I heard also that their meat is dried and called charqui."

"Charqui is the name for any meat that is dried, including llama meat. What I meant is that the poor, or those of modest means, cannot kill them. Rules are different for the rich and powerful, especially the Inca. However, he kills llamas only when he feels it is necessary. Most of those we capture on the day of the hunt will be domesticated. The pure white and black ones will be sent to the temples for sacrifice and some llamas will be used by the army as beasts of burden."

Moche stopped at the side of the path and looked down into a small deep valley; a lake gleamed like a jewel in its midst. "There is where we go." He pointed to a black building at the head of the lake near a waterfall. "From now on, it is all downhill. Come, let us descend. We should be at the lodge by late afternoon."

As they moved forward Juan saw a herd of wild pigs rooting in a damp field. They snorted and honked as they ran quickly away to safety on their firm little feet. Moments later the dark shadow of a condor's wing cast a shadow over Juan's face and a strange premonition of danger overwhelmed him as he looked at the valley below.

They finally reached the valley floor and proceeded to the lodge. The main building, Juan thought, was dramatic. It consisted of a central rectangular block with two projecting wings built completely of black volcanic rock. A large, flat outdoor area about three feet above the ground seemed to be an open entrance hall. With the huge columns holding up the roof, it reminded Juan of the pictures he had seen of Greek temples.

As they waited for the Lord High Inca and his *Coya* to enter the building, Juan had an opportunity to examine one of the columns. Carved into its surface was a stylized feline figure equipped with baleful, upturned eyes looking toward the sky. Shown from the front, legs apart and either hand holding an enormous staff, the figure was covered with a pattern of snakes' heads whose fangs thrust forward and faces of fierce jaguars with staring eyes. It was spectacular.

The whole building was simple but sumptuously effective, looking out as it did on a vivid blue lake that reflected the high mountain peaks. Juan noticed the tentlike pavilions in bright colors farther down from the lodge beside the lake.

As he turned back to the group, he saw that the royal couple were already inside and that Lord Luasi was directing Lord Moche, Lord Quis-quis, and himself to follow one of the aides down to the tents. After assigning two people to each pavilion, the aide told them that the Inca expected them for dinner and that a horn would blow at the proper time. Juan was delighted to learn that Moche and he would share one of the tents.

When they reached their pavilion and stepped inside, Juan saw that it was comfortably furnished with two piles of sleeping mats on the rug-covered ground. A pitcher of *chicha*, a basket of fruit, and a small gold container filled with peanuts awaited them on a beautifully carved chest. Moche took off his cloak, tunic, and sandals and said, "I am going to take a swim in the lake. The water is icy cold but I feel hot, sweaty, and dirty from our walk. Do you want to come?"

It sounded marvelous to Juan, who had not been

submerged in water since his arrival in this country. Bathing each day consisted of getting two jars of water, one cold and one hot, accompanied by a clean towel. The thought of a swim filled him with ecstasy. Seeing Moche stride from the tent completely naked but carrying his cloak stirred him to quick action. Stripping off his clothes and grabbing up his cloak, he dashed after Moche, who was already in the lake.

The shock of the cold water made Juan catch his breath, but after a few moments, it became bearable. Delighting in his freedom and good fortune, he swam and frolicked in the water until he was exhausted. Turning toward shore, he waded out of the lake and, feeling breathless from the unusual exertion, sat upon a rock. Moche was still in the water, swimming back and forth in front of him.

Juan felt a sense of shame. During the long years of captivity he had not exercised his body as he should have done. He was dreadfully out of shape. He would have to change his ways in the future and the time to start was right now. Determinedly, he waded out into the cold water again, and while he was swimming, he thought about the hunt and felt a little uneasy. He was in poor shape and he was also unfamiliar with the Incas' weapons. He hoped he wouldn't make a fool of himself.

It was like some kind of gift from the gods to be up here enjoying the peace and quiet of the mountains. After only four days, Hwayna was already like a different person. Aolani rejoiced in seeing her husband's eyes grow bright again without the dark circles under them. His vigorous body was already tanned from the sun to a dark bronze and she could tell by the glint in his eyes that he was having a good time.

It was truly amazing how Moche had arranged the

whole thing. With the support of Nadua and Luasi, who had added their pleas to Moche's, they had convinced Hwayna that his wife was ill and that she needed to get away in order to have peace and quiet. Hwayna had immediately come to see her and found her in bed with pale skin and dark shadows under her eyes, the result of being carefully made-up by Nadua. Hwayna had called in his healer, who examined Aolani and truthfully said there was nothing wrong with her that a good rest wouldn't cure.

Luasi had then suggested that the hunting lodge would offer a pleasant place for her to recover and added that perhaps a hunt could be arranged if the Inca should be so inclined. The Inca, who loved to hunt, had agreed with enthusiasm and here they all were. No, it hadn't been quite that easy. The Inca had said he would have to return for the eclipse of the sun, but Moche had reminded him he couldn't be at every temple in the empire at once, so why favor just the temple in Tomebamba. He then suggested that the Inca inform everyone that he was going to a place high in the mountains, closer to his Father, the Sun, to plead with him to stay on earth. Moche suggested that the Inca could invite some priests and make it quite a spectacular affair. Hwayna had agreed with him and so they were here.

The first day Hwayna had gone sailing and fishing, returning tired, sunburned, and extremely hungry. After making love to Aolani that night, he had fallen asleep and slept like a baby. The llama hunt yesterday had been a huge success for everybody, except poor Juan, who had fallen and hit his head.

Aolani glanced over at Juan as he sat gazing at the lake. He had a bandage around his brow, but looked amazingly handsome in the short white tunic he was wearing. His legs were long, lean, and very well formed.

"How is your head?" she asked.

"It still hurts, but not as much as it did this morning."

Aolani, feeling sorry for him, said solicitously, "It is too bad you had to miss the hunt today. I think you would have enjoyed it. I hate to see the wild animals killed but sometimes it is necessary."

He nodded his head. "Yes, I was looking forward to it. I enjoyed hunting when I was young." He sounded depressed as he went on. "I have been kept a prisoner for so long I was—I was—oh, well, there is no use in moaning about what can't be helped."

"It makes me sad that you feel so unhappy, Juan."

"It is hard for me to be happy here in your land," he said bitterly. "I feel so alone, deprived of those I love."

"I know how you feel," Aolani said quietly. "When I first came to the land of the Incas, I was only ten years old. I, too, was lost and alone. My mother was dead, my father assassinated by my uncle, and I was exiled from the country I knew and loved."

Aolani saw Juan looking at her with questioning eyes as he said, "I'm truly sorry. I didn't know."

Aolani knew she was letting herself get too personal with Juan but she went on. "I was different in appearance, just as you are. With my fair skin, strange hair, and yellow eyes, I was looked down upon by others. I often cried myself to sleep. I was really convinced that I was ugly and prayed to the gods for black hair and dark eyes." She smiled grimly. "In fact, I was told quite often that I was ugly."

"Whoever said so was a fool," Juan said vehemently.

Aolani felt uneasy with the conversation but she did not want to be rude. She stood up. "Are you able to walk? The path along the river is beautiful."

Jeanne Nickson

Juan arose eagerly to his feet. "I would like that very much."

They walked slowly over to the small river and started up the shaded path. Dotting the sides and banks of the stream, tufts of lilies and other flowers created a mass of color while daylight played hide-and-seek amid the overhanging branches. She heard Juan ask, "Are you sure this is safe? Where are your guards?"

"There is no need for protection here in the valley, for the area is entirely surrounded by guards up above. A double ring of them patrol constantly on the rim. It gives us privacy and the restful feeling of being away from many observing eyes. As for the path, it is restricted to all others except for the Inca, myself, and of course special guests when we are with them."

"You mean we are completely alone on this path today?"

She nodded, watching him as she did so, and saw a strange expression cross Juan's face. Aolani realized too late that she shouldn't have mentioned they were alone. She was asking for trouble. She felt a dangerous tension mounting between them. She had known for a long time that Juan was strongly attracted to her. Why had she done this? Had she secretly wanted him to make some move? No, of course not! How ridiculous! She loved her husband.

They reached a beautiful spot where the water cascaded into a misty pool. Aolani stopped, deciding to put an end to this encounter. It had gone far enough. She turned to face Juan and found it hard not to smile. He stood like a bird after rain, its wings hung out to dry, uncertain of what to do. He seemed stunned but his eyes blazed with passion. As he looked at her, she felt a strange excitement in the air. Aolani turned away. She watched a shower of white lilies explode in the dark green of the ferns and felt her hidden emotions explode as well. She couldn't resist looking back and she saw him standing so close to her that she was shocked. Feeling the heat of his body, she grew breathless and weak with desire. Her hair blew across her eyes and she felt him put out his hand and gently replace the strand, caressing her face as he did so. His fingers were as soft as a spring breeze.

"I've wanted to touch your hair and face for so long," he murmured.

Mesmerized by the brooding look in his eyes and the impact of his words, Aolani could feel the wild thudding of her heart and she felt so dizzy that she reached out for his arm. His lips hovered over hers and then descended, demanding a response. She seemed to be floating in a dream, unable to protest. Their bodies closed and fused as one while the fire of his kiss grew out of control. She could feel the throbbing of his heart as his hand roamed over her skin. He held her as if he would never let her go. The tightness of his grip brought her to her senses. She struggled and twisted, trying to get out of his arms. She could not do this. So great were the risks he ran in touching her that it made Aolani tremble with fear. She pushed at him frantically and closed her mouth to his kisses.

"Stop this, Juan. By all the gods, I order you to stop. This is dangerous. Stop it, I say. You could be killed for touching me."

"Aolani, you mean more than life to me. I do not care if I am killed. I awake at night imagining your dear face and fear that dawn will never come so that I may behold you once again. Each day, over these many years, I have looked at you and loved you from afar. I have suffered agonies because you have been blind to what I am: a man who loves you. You have bound me in your silken web of loveliness and now you totally possess me."

"Juan, you must not, you cannot go on. This cannot be. My husband—"

"I know, I know! I hear him lauded by all and know that you love him. I know that I am nothing compared to the mighty Inca, noble and strong—condor, powerful lion of his race. A god on earth!" he cried bitterly. He closed his eyes and to her horror she saw a tear trickle down his cheek. "It is exasperating! There is no way I can compete. I might as well be dead."

"Juan, listen to me," she begged. "I do see you as a man. I am very conscious of you. Why do you think I always keep one of my women with me when you are present? You must know I am half of the Inca world, perhaps even more. But I must admit there is a part of me that is of your world and I am drawn to you. But that is all that it is. I love my husband. The gods know that I get angry with him and lonely when he is gone for a long time, but I do love him. We must not talk in this way again. It is dangerous for both of us. By Mother Kilya, the Moon, don't do this to me. Don't destroy me."

"What do you mean?"

Aolani closed her eyes and shivered. "I don't know what Hwayna would do but my life would change. I heard of one unfaithful queen whose beauty was destroyed, her face carved up by a knife. She was imprisoned in a dark cave and never allowed to see the light of day for the rest of her life. She went crazy."

Juan clutched Aolani and she could see he was horrified.

"God forgive me. Forget what I said. You are right. I will never speak of this again, not because of fear for myself, but for you. I will, however, always love you until the day I die." He brought her hand to his lips and kissed it.

Aolani was disturbed more than she wanted to admit

about her feelings for Juan. The man really affected her deeply. Why had she let this happen today? And why during the long periods when Hwayna was absent from Tomebamba had she found herself thinking of Juan? She loved her husband but she also cared a great deal about this man, an enemy of her people.

Aolani sighed and said softly, "This was all my fault, Juan. I should never have brought you here. We must forget this ever happened but before we leave I want to say something. I am proud that you love me and I feel honored. At another time, in another place, we might have found happiness. Don't ever think you are not a man. You are, and I pray that you will find a woman who truly loves you. Unfortunately, events have laid hold of me and keep me as imprisoned as the water carried in this small river. I love the Inca and he loves me and we must follow our path together. But, Juan, I'll always remember you with frozen tears for what might have been."

Chapter Twenty

Aolani looked at the ring of faces around them: Indians, the beaters brought from Tomebamba for the hunt, priests, and large numbers of warriors with their officers in black-and-red uniforms. She wondered if any of them knew why they were here. Most of the Indians and the native soldiers were fairly primitive and lived in ignorance of what was being discovered by the astronomers, mathematicians, and wise *amautas*.

Right now, most of them seemed more curious than frightened, and somewhat subdued and overwhelmed by the grandeur of the occasion. It was, she thought, quite a spectacular little affair that the Lord High Inca and his staff had managed to put together. Gold-threaded banners of red waved in the air like captured birds. The huge granite boulders beneath had been draped with soft vicuna rugs of black, and on them, gold-crested images of the sun sparkled and gleamed in the light. Musicians in bright-feathered costumes were beating on drums that sounded like thunder while dancers weaved in a convoluted rhythm around them.

On the blood-drenched ground in front of Aolani, the bodies of three llamas lay twitching as the priests ripped out their hearts and placed them upon the sacrificial altar. The drums stopped their incessant beat and the silence was as oppressive as that of the mountain tombs where the Incas buried the dead.

The sky became darker still with a slight greenish cast. It was eerie and Aolani reached out to Hwayna, who took her hand in his and said, "Do not be frightened. The darkness will increase in size as the shadow of the moon draws nearer."

It was beautiful and awesome, Aolani thought, as curious-moving ripples of light and dark bands ranged slowly across the sun. She could feel the air growing a little cooler, and flocks of birds fell out of the sky and began to roost on the limbs of the small stunted trees. As it began to grow darker, she noticed some of the wildflowers had petals that began to close as if it were nightfall. Then, she heard the moaning and the wailing of all those around her as they fell to their knees in terror.

As darkness descended over the earth, the last sliver of the sun broke into a light row of pearllike beads. As the last bead disappeared, it became totally dark. There was a great silence and a gentle wind touched her cheeks as the sun's disk was clothed in black.

She felt Hwayna's arms tighten around her as he whispered, "No wonder all our people panic and think the world is coming to the end. Watch carefully. Now you will see the flashing of a bright corona as the moon moves over the sun and a dark shadow will race across the earth."

All around her people were crying out to the gods. Hwayna whispered, "It is almost over. The glowing sun will soon shine in all its glory and our people will be happy for a while. I must go to the top of the mound before the sun returns." He left her.

As the sun slowly revealed itself once again and its brilliant light descended to earth, it clothed the Lord High Inca in its radiance. The Inca stood on the top of the mound above the watchers, dressed in a cloak to which thousands of small gold disks had been sewn. As he moved, the sun was reflected on their polished surface and he resembled a small sun himself. Hwayna Capac raised his arms and chanted a prayer to his Father, the Sun, thanking him for his beneficence and then knelt to do him honor. The drummers again began to beat their instruments and this time high, haunting sounds of pipes joined in, sending shivers down Aolani's body. She was glad when her husband took his place beside her.

Aolani welcomed him and asked, "I gather you don't believe this to be a bad omen, then?"

"No, of course not, because I understand what causes it," Hwayna answered with a smile.

Aolani was puzzled. "If something like this does not frighten you, why have you called in oracles, priests, and other wise men and discussed the so-called bad omens, like the comets and the exploding mountains? It is as if you are giving credence to them, making them more important than they really are."

Her husband answered. "Lani, the vast majority of people are ignorant and vulnerable. They believe in mystic signs and omens that promise disaster. They also believe in those omens that promise good fortune. In discussing these so-called evil portents with people who are in a position to either spread such fears or calm their followers, I am trying my best to make them see these signs in a natural way, a reasonable way. In other words, I want these priests and oracles to help set fears at rest. It has taken a lot of my time but I believe it may have been worth it."

Aolani supposed that she should have guessed before now that Hwayna Capac would have reasons for what he did. She looked at him with affection. Moche was right. Why did she always believe the worst about her husband? Since he felt like confiding in her she might as well try to ask him again about the Island of Punta and the Lake of Blood. She hesitantly voiced her concerns.

Hwayna surprised her by saying abruptly, "I did not order them."

"But who—no one would—" Aolani stopped. None of his staff would dare order such a thing without consulting the Inca. The only one who might—she stopped and looked at Hwayna with dread.

Before Aolani could voice her thought, Luasi came up and told the Inca that the litters were ready to return to the lodge.

"Good," the Inca said. "Have extra food and gifts of fruit and peanuts sent to the village, as well as to those who participated in the ceremony today. Come, Lani. After our midday meal, we will go sailing on the lake and enjoy the beauty of the sun."

It was their last night at the lodge. Hwayna had dismissed everyone after dinner, for they would be leaving before daylight. Aolani sat humming softly as she watched the moon cast an iridescent film on the water while the wind rippled its surface, displaying its dancing spirit. The spicy fragrance of agi, the red pepper plants, filled the air. She noticed her husband was very silent as he, too, gazed at the lake.

Finally he spoke, and his voice came out of the dark shadow of the pillar against which he sat. "It is very beautiful here. This has been a most pleasing interlude and I am deeply grateful for the effort you took to get me here."

Aolani was taken by surprise. "Hwayna Capac, do you mean to say—"

"That I wasn't fooled for a moment. I've known all along, my dear wife, that this trip was planned for my benefit." The Inca laughed. "And of course, I became positive when I found that my supposedly ailing wife managed a remarkable recovery in a very short time."

"You are not angry then?"

"How could I possibly be angry with such a beautiful wife who has just shown how much she loves me. I am pleased that you were concerned about my health. To tell you the truth, I was worried a bit myself." He moved over and sat down beside her, putting his arms around her as he drew her close. The faint aromatic scent of his body assaulted her nostrils and she felt a surge of desire.

Aolani's hand slid down his bare arm, her cold fingers feeling the heat from his skin. He drew her closer and she heard the knife he wore at his belt rasp against the step. He took her hand in his and brought it to his lips. As he kissed her palm he murmured, "Thank you."

"What did you say?" she asked.

"I thanked you. You are an interfering little witch and I love you for it. I feel so much better—vigorous and more like myself."

"I am so glad, Hwayna, for I have been deeply concerned about you, not only because of the physical attacks but also because of the changes in you personally, and above all the fact that you had grown so far away from me."

His hand lay upon her breast while his fingers gently caressed her nipple. His face came close to hers and his lips touched hers. The kiss was long and satisfying, not passionate, but very loving. As he lifted his head, he said softly, "Remember many years ago when we agreed that it would take great effort on our part to make our marriage work?" She nodded her head. "I want to apologize to you, Lani. I know I have not shared myself with you these past months."

"True," she whispered.

"I have not been responsive to your needs and wishes and I know it. I made a promise to myself the day of the eclipse that I would let you know the depth of my love and I further promise that we will become close together again, for I desperately need you."

When Lani heard her husband's words, she was so overcome with joy at what he had said that the tears she had held back for so long streamed down her face. She felt Hwayna's fingers trying to wipe them from her face and heard him say, "Please, Lani, my little dove, don't cry. What is the matter? Speak to me. Please!"

Sniffing as she tried to tell him, she choked out, "Nothing is the matter. Nothing! I am crying because I am so happy."

As Lani continued sobbing, Hwayna stood up with her in his arms and strode through the large antechamber into his bedroom, where three of his servingwomen awaited his coming. "Leave us," he said.

Placing Lani gently down upon the soft bed of furs, he dried her eyes with the edge of her cloak. Taking the vessel of *chicha* that had been left waiting for him, he held it to her lips. "Take a swallow. I insist. It will make you feel better." Aolani raised her head and managed to sip a little wine. She felt the heat of the liquid as it slipped down her throat and into her stomach. She heard Hwayna begging, "Oh, Lani, please don't cry. It tears me apart."

Aolani managed to pull herself together and gave a choked laugh. "I am such a fool but I've felt so lonely for such a long time, and now I—"

Hwayna's fingers touched her lips to silence her. "Lani, please remember that no matter how distant I may seem at times, or how I neglect you, I have you in my heart always. I could not live in a world without you. Believe me, this is the truth, beloved."

Aolani sighed, sat up, and brushed away the last of her tears, saying, "You know, this is foolish. Here I am, a queen, a mother of three, and a mature woman, but inside I am still a frightened little girl."

"You have never said anything like that in all the time I have known you. I always think of you as my golden falcon, strong of will and brave of heart. Would you believe that at times you even frighten me?"

A small smile curved her mouth. "Frighten you, my lord? I truly doubt it, but let me continue. I have told you about my early years from time to time but I have never mentioned what an emotional disaster it was to me. It was hard enough being born a princess, my father's only heir, and then to suddenly lose everything. But after my father's murder, I became a waif fleeing from my would-be killers, alone and terrified, so I built a wall around myself—my inner self. I pretended to be strong and brave but within I was a rabbit surrounded by voracious beasts. I was afraid of people, afraid to trust them. Then your father sent me to your uncle, Lord Pinau."

With her words winging across his mind, Hwayna sat down beside her and put protective arms around her. "Go on, tell me more."

"I became like a daughter to Lord Pinau, who loved me and gave me back my pride and self-confidence. Moche helped me, too. But that only lasted for about four years and then I lost them both. Moche was ordered to attend the Inca in Cuzco and Lord Pinau died. I was completely devastated. I was back again in a world in which I was unloved—even hated. No one seemed to want me or care about me. Then I met you and everything changed. In the first years of our marriage I began to feel wanted and loved, secure in a world that seemed huge and threatening."

"And then I destroyed that world for you," Hwayna said helplessly. "I sent you out of my life with no explanation and that must have hurt you deeply."

"Yes, at first. Then I tried to forget you and for the sake of the child I carried I tried to become strong. But you returned. At first, I was afraid to trust you, but then you made me believe. I began to feel secure again."

"And," Hwayna said in a sorrowful voice, "we were happy until I began to shut you out again." He looked at her and this time there were tears in his eyes. "By all the gods, Lani, I feel terribly guilty about all this but try to understand. I thought I was protecting you by concealing all the terrible things that were happening all over the empire. I was worried about so many things, especially in here." He put his hand to his chest. "I thought that I might die the way my father did. I thought about leaving this mess for others to face, especially you."

Aolani turned in his arms and took his head between her hands. "But, Hwayna, my dearest husband, as Moche said, if you get sick or die how are you going to be able to find solutions to these problems? You can't let the unseen future frighten you, for none of us know what it will be. Perhaps it will be wonderful." She kissed him with little butterfly touches and then nibbled his lip with her teeth.

Hwayna stopped her and drew slightly away. "I want to love you tonight as I've never loved you before but I want no barriers between us. There is the matter of the Punta and the Caranqui."

Aolani was taking off her tunic and her body glowed in the pool of light cast by the flames in the brazier. She said, "That can wait!" She pressed her body close to his.

He gently pushed her away. "No, my dear, you've pestered me long enough. I want you to know what happened." Taking his hand, she nibbled at his fingers playfully. "Lani, please stop it."

She smiled up at him. "All right, beloved, tell me."

"You already know the Caranqui have been harassing our borders for over twelve years. Thousands upon thousands of our men have been either killed or wounded."

"Are they better fighters, then?" Aolani asked.

"No," her husband said vehemently. "They are sneaky, conniving devils who disappear like smoke into their jungles and wild terrain. They seldom stand and fight like men. They attack with no warning in the dark of the night like ferocious beasts. They fight like wild boars at mating time, completely without fear. When they finally became a threat to Quito, blocking roads, killing workers in the fields, and looting the small villages and farms, I decided enough was enough."

"So you took charge of the armies yourself," Aolani said, "and I didn't see you for over a year and a half."

"Yes, I won't go into detail, but finally I had them cornered in their last stronghold. I sent one army secretly around to the back of the fortress. I had another division under cover of darkness hide behind rocks and trees in the surrounding area. The third division, with whom I remained, prepared for a frontal attack in the morning. The Caranqui, seeing the small group facing them, decided again to attack us at night. They made a mistake. The army behind them took over the stronghold when they sallied forth, and the hidden group of my men joined our main army and the fighting became intense.

"During the fray I was hit in the head by a flying rock and fell. While my guards surrounded and protected me from harm, the war raged on. I regained consciousness to see all the Caranqui in the lake with our men cutting them down. I was dizzy and sick with pain. The lake was a bloody mess. I am not sure I could have stopped the massacre even if I wanted to. That was the last thing I remember before I blacked out again."

Aolani looked at her husband with great sympathy. "I suppose you have been blaming yourself for what happened." He nodded as she kissed him tenderly.

"Just one more thing," the Inca said, "what happened to the Punta women and children was carried out upon the order of our son. I've ordered him back to Tomebamba."

Aolani looked at his grim expression. "I am not at all surprised. Atahualpa has never been gentle, kind, and compassionate like his father. That is why I have always opposed his marriage to Cusi Hwaylas." She helped him take off his sandals and jewelry. "Enough talking! Come, Hwayna, let me take off your earrings."

As he threw his gold chains and beads on the floor he said, "Lani, you know I hate to have you see my ears without earrings. They look disgusting."

"Come on, off with them. They get caught in my hair. Besides I think your ears are rather sweet. Ah, that is better. Now come keep me warm, my Son of the Sun."

And as drops of glistening dew began to cover the ground outside, Aolani went into his loving arms and with mounting passion she became his. Worn out at last, they slumbered.

233

Chapter Twenty-one

Gently scratching the long slender neck of the llama, the Inca was aware of the persistent humming sound made by the contented animal. He was watching his three-year-old son and was pleased with what he saw. Manco was a fine-looking boy, tall for his age, well formed, and with a sensitive face on which expressions changed rapidly.

His son's enthusiasm was obvious as he said, "Father, she is the best llama in the whole world and she likes me, I think."

Hwayna could not help but smile at the boy's pleasure. "Llamas are very affectionate and loving if they are treated right. I am glad you like your gift."

The boy looked at him with sparkling black eyes. "She is the best present I've ever had. Thank you, Father."

"What are you going to name her?" the Inca asked.

A frown appeared on Manco's young face. "I don't know yet. I thought of White Cloud because she looks like a fluffy little cloud but she has black eyes and ears and a very dark nose. Maybe I'll think about it." He changed the subject. "Father, see her use her ears?"

The Inca was amused. He had been around llamas all his life. "Yes, I see, but what have you found out?" he asked with interest.

"She saw a bird this morning and her ears went like this." Manco demonstrated with his little hands on his own ears. "If I go and call to her, just one ear goes like this and the other does this." Again Manco waved his small hands. "Sometimes she turns her head a little to show she really hears me. Then she comes to me and pushes me for some grass. She is so funny, Father. She got so mad when my monkey jumped on her back that her ears went back. She made bad sounds and then she spit! Ugh! It smelled."

Watching his son feed the animal, Hwayna warned, "Your llama is about six months old and will have no teeth until she is two years old, so it is safe to feed her by hand now. But when she gets her teeth, beware, for they will be very sharp."

"You know a lot about llamas, don't you, Father?" asked Manco with admiration. "Look, White Cloud likes you." The llama was nuzzling at the Inca's neck with her black nose.

"I think I like that name, White Cloud."

"Then that is what I'll name her. Father, remember how your llama went in the water with you when you were small like me? Can I take White Cloud in the water with me?"

"Absolutely not," Hwayna said. "The bath is not a big lake, such as my llama had. It is just a small pool for the family to bathe in. Now take your llama back to her keeper while I talk to your mother."

After moving toward Lani, Hwayna Capac sank down beside her on the rug. "He is a wonderful boy, Lani, and

235

I know he is doing well in his studies. The *amautas* bring me such fine reports."

Aolani smiled as she watched her youngest son urging the stubborn llama to pass through the gate. The llama probably wanted to stay and graze in the garden. "Manco resembles you a great deal according to Nadua, who also said he has your same love for animals and adventure. By the way, don't get the idea Manco is perfect. He is always getting into trouble."

She could see Hwayna was not listening to her. He was watching his son. There was a troubled frown on his face and she wondered why. He had been so happy and contented these last few weeks since their return from the lodge, except for the first day when they had learned of Nonie's death. Although saddened by the death they had both known that at last Nonie no longer suffered, and they were grateful that her torment was over. Lani had kept her promise and taken Nonie's younger son into the family. He now studied with the others. In the following days, Hwayna had been wonderful to her, always attentive and loving and, best of all, he had spent more time with their two youngest children. However, something was bothering him today. He had avoided her gaze all morning.

"Hwayna, what is it? What is the matter?"

Reluctantly, Hwayna turned back to her. "Lani," he said with a sigh. "I have to tell you something I know you won't want to hear, but nevertheless, it must be done."

"Well, what is it?"

"I want you to hear me out completely before you say a word." He thought for a moment and then began. "A terrible disease is sweeping across our northern borders and seemingly we have no remedies, according to the healers. In almost all cases it is fatal. Thousands of men, women, and children have died because of it."

"I have heard something of this," she murmured.

"It is rumored among the natives that the disease comes after the strange bearded men visit their villages. From the tales I've heard, it does seem to be related to them in some way. It is spreading rapidly and I believe it will be coming south. I will be sending you and the children to Cajamarca soon."

Aolani gasped. "No!"

"Yes, Lani, and there will be no arguments. I can't do all the things that must be done here and worry about you and the children at the same time. I've ordered Ninian and Atahualpa to return to Tomebamba immediately, for they are close to the danger zone."

In protest, Aolani said, "I won't leave without you, Hwayna Capac. If you are in danger, I want to stay by your side."

"Lani, listen to me. Be sensible." He looked at her anxiously. "I intend to return to Cuzco soon and confront Huascar but I must attend to affairs here and wait for my two sons. In the meantime, I want you safe. I want Manco and Cusi Hwaylas safe. Children are extremely susceptible to the disease. You must go with them and wait for me in Cajamarca. It will only be for a month or so."

Aolani had heard about this terrible disease, which was killing the natives on their borders so rapidly. It seemed impossible that it would come this far. It hadn't even occurred to her that the plague would eventually hit their cities. She looked at her husband with concern. "Are you sure Tomebamba will be hit by this evil curse?"

Hwayna said, "I have asked the Spaniard, Juan de Montaro. He tells me that in the cities of his world this cursed and vicious scourge has wiped out whole cities and the rich nobles; even the kings and queens run from it."

Jeanne Nickson

"Can nothing be done to stop this deadly pestilence? Can't we completely isolate the villages and places where the disease strikes? From what I have heard, it attacks people who live in the same area."

"Perhaps so. I have *amautas* and healers working on the problem, but in the meantime, start making plans, for you and the children will be leaving soon."

From the moment Luasi entered the room, Aolani knew that something dreadful had happened and she was filled with apprehension. All around her, people were laughing and talking, musicians were playing soft music and servants were passing food. Luasi stood with a solemn demeanor, his pale face stark in the gloom at the end of the room. Suddenly, he was walking toward the Lord Inca with a look of compassion and dread on his face.

Aolani moved closer to her husband and placed her hand on his. She heard Luasi say in a low voice, "There is bad news, my dear lord. Perhaps you had better hear this in your chamber."

After looking at Luasi's face, Hwayna Capac rose to his feet. Luasi and Aolani followed him as he headed for his private antechamber. "All right," he commanded, "tell me."

Luasi took a deep breath. "My lord, it is Ninian Cuyuchi. He is dead."

Behind her, Aolani heard the music increase in tempo and the sound of a singer in the distance. A kind of dizziness came over her. Silently, she screamed. No, he was so young! She felt a grief too sharp to bear, for she had learned to love Ninian deeply. She had even hoped he would be her daughter's husband.

Aolani heard her husband cry out in agony. "No, please, not Ninian!"

"My lord, it was the deadly pestilence that roams our

238

borders. Thousands are perishing each day in Quito. There seems to be no cure for this terrible plague."

Aolani went over to Hwayna, wanting to be near him. He was so silent, his face so frozen, that she couldn't bear it. She wanted to comfort him, for she knew Ninian's death had destroyed all his hopes for the future. Aolani took his hand but there was no response.

Hwayna drew away, walked toward the window, and said with his back to them, "Leave me, both of you. Get rid of everyone, Luasi. I must be alone."

"Hwayna, please, let me help you," Aolani begged. "Perhaps we can comfort one another, for I loved him, too."

Without a word he went into his bedchamber. Understanding his grief, but feeling rejected by him, Aolani was devastated. With tears streaming down her face, she retreated to her own chambers.

The next few days were extremely difficult. The embalmed body of Ninian was put in a mummy bag, which was dressed in the finest clothes and seated upon a chair of gold in the Temple of the Sun. Mourners dressed in black did a slow dance around his burial sack, accompanied by muffled drums and dirges. The poets told tales of his life and enumerated his virtues and achievements. Some of them were put into song. A burial place had been prepared for him, a rock shelter in the mountains near the lodge, but the Inca had made no sign that the funeral should proceed. The Lord High Inca refused to leave his dead son's side for three days.

Finally, on the fourth day after the ceremonies had been performed, the Inca returned to the palace and stalked through the building like a crazed beast. He raged at the gods for their refusal to grant his prayers.

He suffered a paroxysm of fury and shouted out angry imprecations at his Father, the Sun, which his servants suffered in silence, but they were aghast at his blasphemy. Finally he had gone to his son's bedchamber and forbidden anyone to come after him.

Many of his servants were concerned and thought he meant to harm himself. They had come to Aolani in desperation, requesting help. His ministers were perturbed, also. Even proud Quis-quis had asked her to intercede with the Inca, for although he could handle administrative detail, he was worried about the rumors that were spreading through the city—that the Inca was seriously ill. He was also concerned about the plague. Two cases had been discovered in Tomebamba.

Aolani, during the past few days, had made several efforts to reach her husband but he looked at her with unseeing eyes, refusing to speak. Aolani gave in to the many entreaties of her staff and decided to try again.

She entered Ninian's room, not knowing what to expect, and found the Inca sprawled across his son's bed, apparently asleep. There were deep lines and dark shadows on his face and it hurt her to see him looking so vulnerable and old. A wave of compassion overwhelmed her; at the same time she felt guilty that she had been so angry with him.

Then she saw the empty beakers of wine that lay scattered across the room. One vessel had been overturned and there was the sour smell of *chicha* in the air. Aolani sniffed one of the containers and detected the faint odor of coca in the wine—a bad combination! She picked up the beakers and stacked them in one corner of the room. She felt Hwayna's pulse and listened to his heart and thanked the gods that he seemed all right, even though she could not arouse him. Taking some pillows, Aolani settled down on the floor prepared to wait until he regained consciousness.

Finally, there was a slight movement on the disheveled bed. After a deep groan her husband's eyes flickered open and then focused upon her. "Go away," he mumbled.

Aolani sat motionlessly, her heart filled with pity. He sat up, pressing his hands to his head. Shaking, he stood up and stumbled to the window and taking a deep breath growled again, "Go away."

Aolani stayed where she was. She said firmly, "I can't, my lord. Your people need you."

He shook his head as if to clear it, then gazed out the window at the garden, saying, "The wind blows hot today, but I am cold." He spoke so low she could hardly hear him. "I feel like a shattered fragment of myself, unable to do anything. How can I help my people?" The Inca started to weep, great sobs racking his body.

Appalled at the violence of his grief, Aolani didn't know what to do or say, so she did nothing. Finally, he seemed to quiet down and sat staring at the rocky ledge. She watched him as he put out his finger and let a small ant crawl up its length.

"A tiny insect. It still lives, while Ninian—"

Shaking the ant off his finger, Hwayna held his head to one side and listened. "Can you hear them? Everything remains the same regardless of his death. The birds still sing, butterflies flit from flower to flower, even the insects live. But I feel dead, Lani, as dead as Ninian. By all the gods, what am I going to do?"

Aolani said in a firm but exasperated voice, "Don't be foolish, my lord. You will survive. You will journey to your end as we all must do."

Hwayna turned his face toward her, but his eyes were closed. Aolani saw a tear roll down his cheek. Suddenly, he hit his fist against the stone wall so hard that she flinched. "His death I could bear, for it comes to all. But the loss of an heir that could have saved the empire I mourn and regret with my whole being. The prophecy will come true." He raised his head and prayed. "Viracocha, Great Creator, help me bear this terrible loss."

Aolani could understand his feelings, but he must be strong. "Hwayna Capac, you are full of self-pity and it will not do. Whatever will happen is beyond your control."

She went to him and put her arms around him, then pulled back. "You can change nothing. Ninian is dead because it was the will of the gods. But you have your own tasks to perform." She raised her voice, maddened by his apathy. "You must be strong and courageous as long as you are Inca, not a coward who hides behind closed doors. You must put your sorrows and worries aside and be the strong man I know you to be. Do you hear me, Hwayna Capac?"

Hwayna said nothing for a few moments. Then he turned and looked out in the garden again. Aolani heard him say softly, "In the name of my Father, the Sun, have mercy upon me and my people." He was silent for a long while.

Suddenly, he spoke. "You are right. I can only do the best that I can for as long as I can. The gods have pity on us all."

She closed her eyes to hold back the tears. When she opened them, he had left the room.

Later that night Hwayna came to Aolani's bedroom and awakened her. He wore only a short black tunic, without jewelry or ornament. His facial expression was grave but his eyes looked at her with warmth. Apparently he had accepted his loss. He said quietly, "Suddenly, I could not bear to be alone another minute. I knew I had to come to you. I'm sorry I awakened you."

Aolani drew his body down beside her. "I needed you also, my love."

He held her close to him, his kiss long, sweet, and infinitely loving. When he finished he rolled over and looked at her intently as if memorizing her face and her body. The look made her apprehensive. "What is it?" she asked.

"Remember the time I was away from you during the Caranqui War?"

She nodded. "How can I ever forget? I was miserable."

"And so was I," he repeated, "and so was I. There were many times when I was alone that I could almost feel you with me. I would see the curve of your cheek in the light, feel the blossomy touch of your fingers on mine, and sometimes even hear the tartness of your voice, as if you were angry with me. How I longed for you." He smiled a little as he looked at her. "I heard that anger in your voice today and it brought me out of my self-pity and misery."

She kissed his bare shoulder and brought his hand up to her lips. "I'm glad," she murmured.

"Do you realize, my beloved, that you are the only person in all the world who ever gets angry with me? Even stamps her foot and yells at me." He smoothed her hair away from her brow. "My friend, Paco, when he was with me showed his anger, but no one else, not even Luasi, well as he knows me, will show me anger."

"Humph," said Aolani. "I have seen Luasi look upon you with disapproval."

"Yes, that is true, but he never voices his disapproval."

"Are you saying you love me because I get angry with you?" she asked indignantly.

"Not exactly, but you treat me as a man, not as a god, which I like, as you know. Without you, love,

243

I would live each day forever and always alone and the gods know this would be a terrible fate. You have given me so much happiness over the years, Lani. I had to tell you this tonight."

He looked so melancholy that she was worried. She said lightly, "You disturb me when you talk like this. You will never have to live without me. We will have many years of happiness."

"Perhaps, perhaps. But happiness is so brief and elusive."

"Stop it, Hwayna. You are getting moody again. We both know that happiness is brief and elusive but still its memory remains, a moment's wonder that warms our souls for all of time."

"That is a poetic thought, my love." He sighed. "Perhaps I am talking as I do because you will leave me tomorrow morning."

Aolani sat up in bed, her heart beating rapidly. "Tomorrow? That's too soon," she exclaimed. "I can't. I won't."

He looked at her with determination in his eyes. "You can and you will! There are now four cases of this dread disease in Tomebamba. You and the children leave in the morning for Cajamarca and then on to Jauja. Nadua and your women are packing tonight. She will go with you along with Moche and one of my aides who will handle supplies and equipment. Quis-quis will escort you."

"By all the gods, you mean this, don't you, Hwayna Capac?"

"I do! I told you I will take no chances on you and the children getting this disease. By all the devils of Hopi-Nuni, don't you know how hard this is for me? Much as I will miss you, I know you must leave. As I said before, I will join you in a few months, if all goes well."

Looking at him, Aolani knew he meant every word he said. With pathetic resignation she accepted what she knew could not be changed. He was sending her away because of his love for her and the children.

"So be it, but my beloved," she entreated in a soft sweet voice, "stay with me tonight."

Hwayna took off his black tunic and threw it on the floor, where it lay like a dark puddle. Aolani slipped out of her sleeping robe and her golden body knelt before him, her glowing skin opalescent in the light from the brazier, her tawny jaguar eyes gleaming into his own.

He drew her tenderly into his arms and wanted to make love to her. He pressed himself against her and held her close to him. But suddenly he felt as weak and as tired as a newborn babe, for the last few days had been physically and mentally exhausting. His eyes closed just for a moment and then he was so deeply asleep that not even the gods could have awakened him.

Aolani lay quietly and contentedly in his arms, his familiar body wrapped around her own. Poor darling, she thought, he is exhausted. Let him sleep. At last Aolani closed her eyes and presently she, too, slept.

Awakened suddenly by an odd noise, Hwayna was immediately alert. The light was dim, for only the smoldering coals were left of the fire in the brazier. He heard a snuffling noise almost beside his head and saw the shadowy form of a small figure. He reached out quickly with his hand and grabbed a small arm and heard a voice say, "Ow!"

"Manco," Hwayna whispered. "What is the matter?"

"I'm 'fraid, Father. I dreamed about being dead in a sack, and I want my Mama." He sniffed.

Hwayna drew him into the bed and put his arms around his son, saying in a low voice, "It is all right,

Manco. Cuddle up. I won't let anything happen to you. No talking. We don't want to awaken your mother."

"All right," said a sleepy little voice. Manco snuggled closer and kissed his father's chin. "I love you," he whispered.

"I love you, too. Now go to sleep."

How wonderful it was, Hwayna thought, as Manco's small, warm body pressed against him, to feel so close to his child. Within his heart he felt a warm, joyous love that kept the aching out. How fortunate I am, he thought, to be loved. Hwayna Capac felt happy as he drifted back to sleep.

Chapter Twenty-two

Juan was on his way to the Lord High Inca's chambers, where he'd been invited to dinner for the sixth time since the Lady Aolani's departure five weeks ago. He felt enormously flattered by the Inca's mark of favor but he also knew he had incurred the wrath of several of Hwayna Capac's jealous advisers and it made him a trifle uneasy. The last thing he wanted to do was to attract the enmity of such a group. But it was rewarding to be held in such high esteem by a man whose power was absolute in this land of the Incas. He had noticed that most of the loftiest nobles came into the Lord High Inca's presence carrying, as a mark of total subservience, some small burden on their backs. It was odd that these men of the highest rank seldom spoke in front of the Inca unless he directed a question at them and then they responded with a nervous and distracted air. Many even refused to look at him.

Juan often thought that the Inca must lead a very

lonely existence, especially with the Lady Aolani gone. Perhaps the reason the Inca seemed to enjoy Juan's company was because he did not regard the Inca as a god, as the rest of his subjects did, for Juan believed there was only one almighty God. Despite his family's apparent conversion to Christianity as a result of the Inquisition, they still believed in Judaism. Juan had discussed his beliefs with the Inca and had been surprised when the ruler asked several questions and seemed accepting of his beliefs. Juan tried to keep the Inca challenged and interested in his world, for he truly enjoyed Hwayna Capac's company. The Inca was a brilliant man and quickly understood new concepts, sometimes following through on an idea just as he had done with the idea of a written language. Plans for the wheel were also moving along. Luasi had come to him a few days ago and asked him how the wheel worked. Juan had shown him by drawing a circular frame turning on an axle. He had also drawn sketches of a simple tumbril and a wheelbarrow. Apparently, they were having trouble getting large pieces of hardwood for the wheels and Luasi had sent for trees that grew in the far south of their empire.

Juan looked around the large chamber as he entered. There was nobody of any consequence with the Inca tonight; not even Luasi was there, which was unusual. The Inca was giving orders to his six aides, one of whom was Sinchi Chacoya, whom Juan had enjoyed teaching because he was a clever and creative boy. He should go far in the service of the Inca.

Servants were scurrying around, preparing the mats on which a large variety of special foods would be placed. Juan knew from past experience that the Inca would point to several dishes; then one of his women would taste and eat some of the food from each of the designated platters before presenting them to the Inca. They never did that from the platters Juan selected; he just had to hope his choices contained no poison. Musicians were playing softly in the background, while dancers moved seductively to the music. The Inca noticed him and beckoned him to approach. Juan came forward and Hwayna Capac indicated with his hand that he should sit down near him.

Examining the Inca's face, Juan saw lines of strain. The Inca had not been happy since the departure of the Lady Aolani and the children. Something was disturbing him deeply, for as water ripples in the wind, his face trembled with emotion as he said to Sinchi, "Take the box away. I'll look at Ninian's things tomorrow and decide if they should be buried with Ninian."

As Sinchi Chacoya lifted the big box and disappeared with it, Hwayna Capac turned to Juan. "Welcome, young man. I have something to show you." He called to one of his aides. "Sahwar, bring me the object my favorite goldsmith just made for me."

Sahwar handed the Inca an object about two inches high and three inches wide, which turned out to be a miniature three-wheeled cart with little wheels that turned around as Hwayna Capac moved them with his fingers. He rolled it back and forth on the stone floor with a childlike grin on his face.

"It really works," the Inca said with glee as he pushed it over to Juan. "This is yours, in memory of your contribution."

Before Juan could even express his thanks for the gold gift, Hwayna Capac had dismissed his aides and begun the process of selecting his dinner. There were several kinds of crisply cooked fowl, a roast of venison, delicately flavored fish of several kinds, fresh oysters, six kinds of potatoes, and many fruits and vegetables brought from all over the country.

When they had finished eating, the servants cleared

the area and brought *chicha* to them in gold goblets, placing a full beaker of the wine beside them. The Inca had not said a word through dinner, which was unusual. He looked sad and depressed and Juan felt increasingly uncomfortable. Why was he here? He wondered what the Inca was thinking about, for he seemed so distant tonight. Juan noticed that everyone had disappeared.

Hwayna Capac was deeply engrossed with his own thoughts, completely forgetting the young Spaniard sitting near him. Like the flight of a bird, the years flew through his mind and the present became the past. He remembered the innocence of his youth when he believed the bright, beautiful sun was a god. He heard the memory of his father's voice, strong in its solemnity, as he proclaimed Hwayna a god, the Son of the Sun.

Then had come the slow disillusionment, the recognition that the Sun, like the stars, received orders from some higher source, a single God responsible for all existence. With that realization had come the knowledge that he was not a deity himself. He had never really thought himself a god, so it was not a disappointment. He had then embraced Viracocha, the Creator of Life, and believed that, as that god had created all things, he would treat his world with kindness. Hwayna had thought that, no matter how great the evil in the world, evil would not win. Justice would triumph and good prevail. It had all seemed so simple and right. But now everything seemed to be going wrong.

Hwayna was no longer certain of his beliefs, for the world seemed ruled by blind forces over which he had no control. God, if there was a God, did not answer his prayers. The world about him was nothing but a vast spiritual emptiness and he was lost in it, without past, present, or future. It seemed Viracocha had no power in this world and neither did the Aztec God, Quetzalcoatl. Was the Spaniard's God the one and only God? These strangers from across the sea seemed able to destroy large groups of people who had done them no harm. Juan claimed that it was because of the Spaniards' belief in their God and His son, Jesus Christ. He said they felt morally convinced that they had the right to invade these lands and convert people to what they believed to be the true faith in the one and only God. Were they right? It seemed impossible to believe!

Yet hadn't Hwayna and his ancestors done the same thing in the name of the Sun? Memories of his own acts gnawed at his heart, bringing unbearable pain. But he had only done what he considered right for his people. He had not been evil or cruel. His head ached with his thoughts. Hwayna felt hollow, empty, desolate. He wished Lani were here. Hwayna tried to imagine what his wife would say. He could almost see her, her golden hair in disarray, her jaguar eyes flashing at him: "You are giving up, Hwayna Capac, crying over your lost ideals. If there is a God, I think he probably expects you to solve your own problems. That's why he gave you a brain. He understands if you make mistakes. No man is perfect! Each and every one of us forges his own destiny and we do the best we can with it. You have made yours. The empire has become more powerful and efficient under your rule. Get on with what must be done."

With an immense effort, Hwayna reached for the beaker of *chicha* and filled his goblet, then drained it. Lani was right! He was just a man. He had done the best he could with his life and would continue to do so. With that decision made, he dismissed his troublesome thoughts. He must talk to the Spaniard.

The room was quiet and empty, just as he had commanded. He looked at the man across from him and said, "My thoughts of the future are so strange, wild, and impossible that I find it difficult to speak of them, but I must. The future seems dark and threatening, not only for me, but for those I love. I am deeply concerned about what I think is going to happen. I need to make plans that are unusual, even extraordinary."

Juan opened his mouth to say something but Hwayna held up his hand. "There is no one in this room so we can be perfectly frank." He paused. He hoped Nadua was right about Juan's feelings for Lani. "First of all, I am aware of your deep feeling for my wife, the Lady Aolani. You love her. Is this not so?"

Hwayna Capac went on. "Have no fear. Speak the truth."

Suddenly, Juan felt a rush of relief. He was almost glad the Inca knew. He had wanted to say it out loud for so long. "Yes, it is true. As my God is my judge, I love the Lady Aolani with all my heart and soul. I would willingly die for her. I assure you, my lord, Aolani is not in love with me. She loves only you."

Hwayna's eyes revealed nothing but his lips curved in a smile. "I have been a fortunate man to have won the love of such a woman. She is very rare. Not only is she beautiful; she is brilliant, courageous, and wise. And, yes, I do know she loves me."

The Inca clenched his fists as he said, "I have a proposition for you that will bring you great wealth in your world and, if fate is on your side, may gain you your heart's desire."

Juan was shocked. Did he mean Lady Aolani? He couldn't. Juan could only gasp. "What in the world are you talking about?"

"I have a premonition that I will soon die." As the Inca saw Juan about to protest, he held up his hand again.

"No, hear me out. If anything happens to me, there will be war between Huascar and Atahualpa. If your countrymen appear while the empire is in chaos, there is a possibility that they may take over Tahuantinsuyu. If this should happen, I want to provide some kind of protection for my wife and our other two children. If the empire falls to Spain—and I do say if—then I—"

Hwayna closed his eyes and Juan saw his face turn gray. The Inca began to cough and he clutched at his chest. Juan went over to him quickly and held the goblet containing *chicha* to his lips. He thought the Inca was choking to death. He started to get up, anxious to get help.

The Inca gasped, "Stay. This will pass."

As they sat silently, Juan felt the weight of the Inca fall against him. He felt strange looking down at the pale face. He didn't understand his deep feeling of pity. He didn't think it possible, but he really cared about the Inca. He didn't want him to die. Over the years Juan had grown to admire and even like this man who had taken him prisoner. Somehow in the last months their minds had touched and he sensed they were alike in many ways.

As Juan sat holding Hwayna Capac in his arms, he thought it very odd. He remembered the absurd thoughts and ideas he had harbored about the New World. He had envisioned the population as being composed of ignorant savages, almost like wild animals. The conquistadors had said they were beyond the pale of man's existence, good only for slaves or to be used as beasts of burden.

Juan looked down at the Inca's strong profile with his high brow, aquiline nose, and the lines of character on his face. Juan knew of the great intelligence and wit of this man, a splendid man, a complete master of his culture. A savage in no possible way!

Suddenly, Juan noticed that color was returning to Hwayna Capac's face and he eased the Inca down on the pillows. He seemed asleep. What should Juan do? Call for help? The Inca had stopped him earlier when he had tried to call the servants. Perhaps he didn't want anyone to know he was a sick man. But if he died and they found him alone with the dead Inca, what would they think?

Juan decided to do nothing yet. The Inca was breathing and seemed asleep. While he sat there, waiting for the Inca to move, Juan kept thinking about Hwayna Capac's last statement. The Inca was right to be apprehensive. The incredible hunger for gold and treasure held by the conquistadors and their followers was well-known to Juan. There was no doubt in his mind that after their raid on Tumbes last year, finding gold as they did, they would be back with more men and supplies to attack Tahuantinsuyu. If the Inca should die, he doubted if young Atahualpa, stubborn and proud but lacking his father's stature, would be a match for them. The Spaniards would swarm like flies over the dying carcass of the empire.

Juan knew he would have to face the problem of just what he would do when his countrymen arrived. He had been 19 years old when he was captured and brought to Cajamarca and he was now 29. Almost all of his adult years had been spent in this land. He had made many friends; he deeply loved Aolani and was very fond of her two young children. He felt comfortable in his life here with the Incas. He had also come to admire the Lord High Inca and appreciate the civilization he controlled. Would Juan have the heart to turn against them and destroy all he felt for the Incas? He knew one thing for certain; he could never turn against Aolani. He would have to protect her. Perhaps he might even have a chance of winning her love. The thought stunned him.

Juan felt a movement. He leaned closer to Hwayna Capac and listened to his heart. It was beating. His skin felt cool. There was no fever. Leaning back on his haunches, Juan watched the Inca. The other man's eyelashes fluttered and then the black eyes were staring at Juan without recognition.

The Inca glanced around and then pushed himself up. His eyes became more alert as he looked around the room. "Has anyone seen me like this?"

"No, no, my lord. No one has entered here since you . . . fell asleep," Juan said gently. "I am immensely pleased that you are feeling yourself once again. Can I do anything for you?"

Hwayna Capac said nothing for several moments, then sighed deeply. "You have seen what happened. Perhaps now you can better understand my apprehensions, why I feel there is a possibility of my death. Therefore, I want to continue with the subject that we were discussing—I think we were discussing." The Inca stopped, looking a little bewildered.

Juan stepped into the breach. "You were saying before your attack that, if the empire falls into the hands of the Spaniards, you want to plan some way to keep your wife and your children safe."

"Ah, yes! I know that, if the country is invaded, my family will be in grave danger, for all royalty will be a threat to the Spaniards. I can hide them for a time, but not forever. You said that you would die for Aolani, that you truly love my wife. The thought occurred to me as I've pondered over the problem that only a Spaniard, a man of their own race, could help my family. Would you consider being a protector to the Lady Aolani, to guard her from evil, from the evil that might be done to her by your countrymen?"

"My Lord Inca, if it is in my power to protect Aolani

and the children, I will do it. I am only one man but I will do everything I can."

Juan could see the relieved look on the Inca's face. The Inca gave a deep sigh as he said, "You will be well rewarded."

Juan looked at the Inca. "I do not want a reward. You have my promise that I will do my best for them."

"You have relieved my mind of one of its burdens but there are many left. You are a good man, Juan de Montaro. I thank you and promise that you will not regret your decision. Now leave, for I am very tired."

As Juan left the room, Hwayna remained seated. He felt as if 1,000 cactus thorns were piercing his flesh and his head weighed heavily. After one of his attacks, it took time to recover. He would wait a bit before calling his attendants. He didn't want them to see him yet. Until recently he had usually had these attacks in private, but they were coming more often. He wouldn't be able to conceal his physical condition much longer.

While he waited, he thought of the one insurmountable problem to which he had gropingly tried to find a solution during the last weeks. The succession! After acknowledging to himself that Huascar was slightly mad, Atahualpa all muscles and no brains, Paullu and Tupa Huallpa weak-minded and unable to rule, he was left with little Manco. But if he publicly made Manco the heir, the others would kill him.

Troubled in mind by a compulsion to find a solution, he had finally made a decision. Now he doubted its possibility of success. Was he fooled by his own conceit to think he could tamper with the future? Well, why not? He would inform certain powerful nobles and priests of his wishes and swear them to secrecy for 12 years. By that time, Manco would have reached the age of 15 and would be old enough to deal with his heritage.

Will my efforts be worse than futile, he wondered, if I seek to mold the future when the present has not even run its course? But isn't it wise to plant a seed and hope eventually for a blossoming tree? It is, he thought, and I will do it.

Chapter Twenty-three

The four days following Juan's extraordinary meeting with the Inca passed slowly and he felt bored and lonely without his work or his friends. There was no word from the Lord High Inca and he missed Moche, whom Juan felt was the closest friend he had made in the Inca world. He tried to contact Luasi, who had always been kind to him, but he seemed tremendously busy and Juan only caught occasional glimpses of him as he went in and out of the Inca's quarters.

Not knowing what to do with himself, Juan contemplated walking into the town of Tomebamba, but in the past when he'd left the palace, he had always been escorted. He was not sure that he was permitted to roam at will. Suddenly, he saw a familiar figure enter the inner courtyard. It was Sinchi Chacoya, his former pupil, who was now one of the Inca's administrative assistants. Prince Sinchi was looking dirty and disheveled, and his tunic was torn. Juan wondered what had happened to him.

As Juan approached the young man he said, "Sinchi, it is good to see you. Where have you been? It looks like you've been out digging up a mountain."

"In a way I have," Sinchi said in a weary voice. "I had to take Prince Ninian's possessions up to the burial site and then seal the cave. It was the most difficult thing I've ever had to do."

"Is that what was in the box you carried away the other night when I was with the Inca?"

"The same. It was sad watching the Inca go through my cousin's things the next day. Almost everything that Ninian saved was a gift from his father and seemed to have been treasured by him through the years. The Inca was quite overcome with emotion and finally placed all the items back in the box, even the lone gold chain he had made for the prince's manhood rites. The Inca ordered me to take the box to his son's resting place and cover it up with dirt to hide the place from curious eyes. It took two days and believe me I am exhausted. You must excuse me, Senor Juan, but I must report to the emperor at once."

"Of course, I understand," Juan murmured as he watched Sinchi Chacoya hurry away.

That evening, as Juan was eating alone in his small room, Lord Luasi appeared in the doorway looking tired, uneasy, and sad. "Sorry to disturb you, Senor Juan, but I have instructions from my Lord High Inca."

Juan's heart jumped. The Inca must want him. Juan stood up respectfully when Lord Luasi came through the doorway. "You look tired, my lord, will you sit with me for a moment and have a goblet of wine?"

Luasi hesitated, but finally sank to the ground, and as Juan handed him the wine he said, "By all the gods I am exhausted. My Lord Inca has not been well today but he has not stopped for a moment. He has kept me busy running his errands." He took another sip of wine and then announced, "I have orders for you, Juan. Tomorrow morning, you and Sinchi Chacoya will leave for the south to join the Lady Aolani. She has reached Vilcabamba as of our last report, and to that city you will proceed. There will be an armed escort awaiting you both at the palace gate at dawn."

Juan's voice showed his astonishment as he asked, "Why this sudden order? Is something wrong?"

Luasi put his hand to his head and pressed his eyeballs. "I really don't know. I am puzzled, too. The lord is acting very strange. I am fearful." He sighed. "He gave no reason for this order and I did not ask him." Luasi rubbed the back of his neck and sipped some more wine. "I am very concerned about my lord. Just a few minutes ago he sent for the healers. They are with him now."

Oh, my God, Juan thought. Is this what the Inca was afraid of? "You believe he is really ill?" he asked with dismay, thinking perhaps the Inca had suffered another attack. "What are his symptoms?"

"He aches in every part of his body and has a great pain in his head. I fear he has quite a raging heat in his body, for his face is flushed and his eyes have a strange light about them." He stopped and then went on. "His son, Ninian, I understand, had the same symptoms and it frightens me. I feel very close to the Lord Inca, for I knew him as a child, so bright and happy as he played in the valley of Sauca Cachi. It was my job to guard him. Later, when he was a young man, I was one of his tutors and later still, his first adviser. For many, many years I have been close to him. All day long my mind has ebbed and flowed like a living sea bringing back a tide of memories that haunt me. I couldn't bear it if anything were to happen to the Inca." Luasi blew his nose on a small square of cotton.

"I must go back. He will need me."

Juan heard nothing else about the Inca during the evening and after a restless night he showed up at the gates just as the sun came up. Sinchi was already there and looked as confused as he was. As the sky lightened the captain of the warriors asked them to get into the litters. As they did so, the sun's bright rays burst in jewellike tones across the palace. Juan felt a little sad at leaving but then his spirits began to lift. Leaving Tomebamba on the great Chinchaysuyu Highway that led to the great capital of the empire, Juan suddenly felt euphoric. He would see with his own eyes more of this incredible world of the Incas he had heard so much about, but then he felt a pang of anxiety. He couldn't help but wonder what awaited him in the future. He cast the thought aside. He didn't know what the future would bring but it would have to be more exciting than being a prisoner in the palace.

During the next few days the caravan crossed the province of the Canari, which had been so painfully won by the Inca. Sinchi and Juan were accompanied by 50 of the Inca's warriors. Bearers carried litters but both the young men decided to walk as much as possible. Sinchi, who had taken this journey before, kept Juan informed about all that they saw.

At first the great highway skirted irrigated terraced valleys, but then it began to climb high godlike mountains that dwarfed their small group. They passed through great snow-covered fields that seemed endless, but no matter where they traveled the road was clean swept and litter free with comfortable lodgings for Sinchi and Juan almost every other night.

The caravan continued through the provinces of Loja, Cajas, and Hwancabamba stopping each night beside the highway. Since they were traveling with very little baggage and with no llamas to herd, they made rapid time. If one of the many Inca lodgings appeared anywhere near nightfall, Sinchi and Juan took advantage of it; otherwise they slept as the warriors did, on mats on the hard ground. Their food was simple, consisting of charqui, potatoes, and a little water made into a stew. Sometimes they were able to add other foods to their diet by bartering with the natives.

One morning they began the descent into the famous Valley of Cajamarca. Juan was more impressed with the region than when he had lived here. The vast cover of mist that filled the valley at night was slowly beginning to dissipate as the sun became hotter. The light cast a golden veil over the lush fields, which spread as far as the eye could reach. Flowers and blossoming fruit trees created a blanket of color over the meadows and orchards. Steam from the Inca's baths—hot springs which bubbled up from the ground on the eastern end of the valley—could be seen rising above the familiar palace.

That night the two young men, after swimming in the warm pool in the Inca's garden, dined outside. They were served the most delicious food they had eaten in a long time. As Mother Kilya, the Moon, appeared in the heavens, a silvery radiance enveloped the garden, creating an eerie, mystical setting. Juan felt tremendous awe, remembering all the wonderful things he had seen thus far, and to his amazement he was overwhelmed again by the feats of the Incas.

Juan turned to Sinchi. "I am continually in awe of the magnificent achievements of your people and how well everything is administered and maintained. Who repairs and takes care of the roads, erects the bridges, builds the palaces and temples, Sinchi?"

Sinchi was silent for a moment. "It is obviously not the work of any one ruler but I think most of the credit must go to the great Inca, Pachacuti, Hwayna

Capac's grandfather. He had great vision and dreams. It was Pachacuti who united the people with common laws and a common language. He gave us a noble capital and a strong fighting force. It was probably Tupac Yupanqui, our Inca's father, who finished what Pachacuti planned." Sinchi looked at Juan. "How much do you know about the organization of the empire?"

Juan thought for a moment. "I have been told that all your people are strictly regulated, even to grouping them into ten age groups and decreeing what each group must do at a certain age. I also know that someone called a *chunca camayoc*, a chief in charge of ten families, is appointed who keeps accurate records on quipu cords of all the families and transmits the information to an overseer who handles the information of a hundred families. He in turn sends it to a man above him, who is in charge of a thousand families."

"This is true and there is even a *hupu camayoc*, a chief of ten thousand families. It is a powerful position and that man is usually related to the Inca. When a man reaches the age in which he must give four years of his life to government service, it is known, and the man is ordered to report for service at some specific location. Untold thousands of man-hours are available to the Inca every year. Some of these men help build the palaces, bridges, temples, and forts under the architects and wise *amautas*; others are placed with well-qualified engineers and work on terraces, aqueducts, roads, and mines. Many are assigned into the army."

"Do any of your people rebel against the enforced labor?" Juan questioned.

"I am not sure. It is possible, especially with a nation that has recently been added to the empire, such as the Canari. But don't forget our people recognize the Lord High Inca as their god and would not think of defying him. Then, too, this service is looked upon as an adventure by the young men. They leave their small villages and go off to see the world."

"Well, Pachacuti and his son, Tupac Yupanqui, seem to have accomplished a lot."

The quiet of the night was disturbed by the distant lonely call of an owl. Sinchi began to laugh softly. "You are right. The great and wise Pachacuti and his son were powerful rulers, but as young children, we detested Emperor Pachacuti. We had to memorize the hundreds, perhaps thousands, of pronouncements made by this greatest of Incas. We were punished if we made any mistakes in quoting him."

"Can you give me some examples?" Juan asked.

"Well, let me see. Here are some of my favorites:

> Jealousy is a worm that gnaws at a man's vitals.
> Rage denotes a weak character.
> A man condemns himself to death when he kills without authority.
> Judges who accept presents must be treated as thieves.
> The peace of a nation comes from the obedience of its people.

I could go on for hours. These maxims direct our society. There are literally rules for any kind of situation, moral issue, or crime."

"I can understand why. He appears to have been a very wise man." Juan looked out over the peaceful garden. "I wish we could stay here in Cajamarca for a few days," he said wistfully.

"Forget such a thought. Capt. Chilandro said we would leave at dawn tomorrow, but I must admit this has been a perfect evening. It is a shame to waste it." Sinchi looked at Juan and smiled at him, mischief in his eyes. "I have an excellent thought. Let us swim for a while in the warm pool. Come on. Bring the wine. I've got the goblets."

The next two weeks passed swiftly. Juan was interested and challenged by everything he saw. Even though Sinchi was over ten years younger than he, Juan enjoyed his company. The young prince was intelligent, mature, and very knowledgeable about his country and Juan could see he enjoyed his role as teacher.

Juan became used to seeing the multitude of travelers on the highway as they approached ever closer to Cuzco. Rich nobles with large escorts were occasionally seen either going to Tomebamba or returning to the capital city. Priests and administrators were numerous, many on their way to officiate at festivals and ceremonies or carrying out the Inca's orders. Then there were the *chasqui*, messengers running almost every hour along the highway to the huts set up at two-mile intervals where they were replaced by fresh runners. Sinchi informed him that the messengers could cover over 200 miles in a 24 hour period. In five days they could cover over 1,000 miles. It was unbelievable, Juan thought.

One day they noticed a pronounced change in the number of runners—almost twice as many as the previous day. Juan called it to Sinchi's attention.

Sinchi didn't seen concerned. "There can be all kinds of reasons for more runners, especially if the emperor wants information in a hurry." Sinchi changed the subject. "Just think, in a few hours we'll be in Bombon, only three days' journey from Jauja, where the Lady Aolani is staying. I can't wait to see the family again." He turned to Capt. Chilandro, who was walking behind them.

"Captain, we will stay in the palace at Bombon tonight." He turned back to Juan. "It is a pleasant city." In a whisper he said, "I have an aunt who is the head *mamacoya* in the House of the Virgins. She will find women for us." His eyes sparkled. "We'll have fun tonight."

Before dawn the next morning, Juan awakened with a start, his head aching and his stomach churning. Gradually he became aware of the wailing sound of many trumpets and the heavy monotonous beat of big drums. He wondered what was going on. Hurriedly he dressed and rushed to the reception room. He found Sinchi, half dressed, there before him, talking to Capt. Chilandro. With them was a *chasqui* runner in his black-and-red tunic.

"What is it?" Juan asked in alarm. He had a strange feeling, a premonition that he already knew the news. Hesitantly he asked, "Is there news about the Lord High Inca?"

Sinchi seemed utterly shaken. He was trembling as he answered in a choked-up voice, "He's dead."

"Oh, my God!" Juan said. "How?"

Capt. Chilandro answered, "The messenger says that there is much confusion in Tomebamba. Rumors and strange stories abound." He took a deep breath and then went on. "The death of a ruler is kept very private but it is thought by many that he died of the same dread disease as Prince Ninian. I was about to learn more when you arrived." The captain looked at the messenger. "Go on."

The messenger was a very young man and there were tears in his eyes as he answered. "I was told that there was talk of a black box sent to the Inca. They said that when our lord lifted the lid, an unending swarm of flying creatures flew into his face."

Sinchi was pale but his voice was firm enough. "That is a ridiculous tale. I saw my lord open the box. There were no insects."

"I wonder about the succession. Who will be Inca?" Juan asked.

Capt. Chilandro answered. "General Quis-quis believes Prince Huascar will have himself proclaimed Lord High Inca immediately in Cuzco but I have no doubt Prince Atahualpa will also declare himself his father's successor. That is why he is ordering all the armies and men to report to Gen. Challcochima in Tomebamba immediately. My men are getting ready to leave now."

"Then you will leave us without an escort?" Sinchi asked.

"I must obey orders," Chilandro answered, "but in my estimation you will be safer without my men as you go farther south. Huascar will be suspicious of all warriors from the north. He will kill all strange men in uniform. Disguise yourselves as priests. There will be many of them traveling to Cuzco to curry favor with the new Inca. Besides, it is only a three-day journey to Jauja."

There came a loud blast of trumpets. "I am going to find out what is going on," Juan said, as he moved toward the door.

The others followed him through the rooms and corridors to the palace gate. They saw a great many people moving toward the Temple of the Sun.

Juan grasped Sinchi's arm and said, "Come, let us go. Perhaps the priests have more news."

In the great flat square in front of the temple, crowds of people were gathered. They had come from all the villages around as well as from the city itself in response to the call of alarm from the temple. As they approached the square, priests poured from the temple doors

267

chanting liturgies in time to the drums as they circled around the large enclosure. When they returned to the front of the temple they fanned out on either side of the high priest. He stood silently in front of the crowd, in golden robes, his hands raised to the heavens.

Suddenly, cold winds came down from the mountains; the violence of their breath blew through the square in a fury, chilling Juan to the bone. He shivered with apprehension. Then, as quickly as they came, the winds departed from the square with one last fearful howl. In the complete silence that followed, the voice of the high priest rose high and clear.

"Hwayna Capac, lord of us all, is dead.
The blessed gods have called our ruler home.
Tenderly they enfolded him and drew him close.
For dearly he was loved by them in life.
Deep sorrow bears down upon our land.
Let us pray to the gods."

The large group of people summoned by the temple drums had anticipated news but not this. They began to moan and scream and there was a look of terror on their shocked faces as they absorbed the horrible fact that their god was no more. Then began an orgy of emotion that was too violent to be believed. Amid the screams, wails, and moans of the many mourners, people began to kill themselves by stabbing knives into their bodies or strangling themselves with their own hands. Some people sank to their knees and, in a paroxysm of grief, tore out their hair, mutilated their faces, and ripped at their clothes. Others just sat in a daze while some joined the priests and began singing with tears rolling down their faces.

Turning to Sinchi, Juan decided to get him back to the palace before he fell apart emotionally. The young prince was looking at the scene before him with frantic eyes. Grabbing Sinchi by the arm Juan pulled the boy along with him. Seeing Capt. Chilandro in front of him he called out and the man came back to him. Between the two of them they managed to get Sinchi back to his room and put to bed.

Returning to the reception room, Juan poured himself some wine and sat down. He was shaking. He gulped the wine down and poured more. Juan wanted to get out of this town as soon as possible. He was very much aware of the promise he had made to Hwayna Capac and he felt it was essential that he reach the Lady Aolani as soon as he could. Juan wondered about Prince Huascar in Cuzco, who was seemingly already accepted as the successor to the Inca. He had heard that when the Inca died his wives and women became the possessions of his successor. Would Aolani's fate be that of a concubine to the new ruler? It was a horrible thought and not one he could accept. Juan made up his mind. He would leave today for Jauja even if he had to go alone.

There was the sound of approaching footsteps and he looked up. It was Capt. Chilandro, looking very worried. "I've had a direct message from Prince Atahualpa repeating my superior's order. I and my men are to return to Tomebamba at once. We will leave within the hour. There is no word about what you and Prince Sinchi are to do. Do you wish to return with us?"

Juan was concerned about Sinchi. He knew he must go on to Jauja but he didn't know about the young prince. He couldn't leave him here alone. Perhaps Sinchi should return to Tomebamba. "Captain, I will not be going with you. Give me a little time with the young prince. Let me see if I can talk to him to see what he wants to do."

269

Jeanne Nickson

The captain nodded, but said, "I can't give you long. We must leave. I'll wait for you."

Juan went into Sinchi's room and called his name. The young man showed no response. He didn't even open his eyes. Going over to Sinchi, Juan placed a hand on each side of his head and said sternly, "Sinchi, look at me. Damn it, look at me." Juan shook him.

Sinchi opened his eyes and said, "Those people! What they did. It was terrible! Nothing is stable or secure anymore. I don't know what to do."

Juan, reminding himself that Sinchi was young, said sympathetically, "I know, Sinchi, how grieved you are that the Inca is gone but I know he would want you to act with courage."

"I felt like killing myself down in the square," Sinchi said in despair. "Maybe, I should. I should be with him in the afterworld. He will need me."

"Sinchi, listen to me. He will have plenty of people with him and don't forget the gods will be there, too."

Sinchi paid no attention to Juan's words, but he did sit up. "You don't know how it was with me. I had no one, no father, no mother, just the Inca and the Lady Aolani. His presence was like a light in my life, showing me what to do and where to go. He was like a father to me, not an ordinary one, but a heavenly father guiding me through life. Now, I have no one."

"Sinchi." Juan took him into his arms. "You still have family. You still have the Lady Aolani. She needs you. Little Manco and Cusi Hwaylas need you. Do you hear me, Sinchi? Aolani needs you."

Sinchi pulled away and looked at Juan with questioning eyes. "She does need me, doesn't she? We must go to her."

Juan said with determination, "Yes, Sinchi, we must go to her this afternoon. Let us go and tell the captain."

PART 3

War Between
Brothers
1527

Chapter Twenty-four

Aolani was immediately aware of the strained and tense silence as she entered the reception room of the palace at Jauja. Moche and Nadua looked at her apprehensively as she approached, while Quis-quis, turning abruptly, walked to the window embrasure, where a vessel of *chicha* was placed. He poured himself a goblet of wine and drank it down.

Feeling there was something unusual going on, she said, "All right, something is wrong. Tell me what has happened."

Moche looked at Quis-quis, who ignored his glance. Then he went reluctantly toward her, his face as pale as a pigeon's breast. Aolani knew there was something dreadfully wrong, and suddenly she didn't want him to speak.

Moche, his eyes full of pain, took her hands in his and said, "Aolani, he is dead! The Inca is dead."

She stood in shock, staring at Moche. "What did you say?"

"Hwayna Capac is dead." Moche choked up, unable to say more.

There was a burning pain in her heart. The meaning of what Moche had said began to penetrate her mind. Her husband dead? It couldn't be. But Moche would not lie to her. Aolani felt cold and her body trembled. She wanted to scream out in anguish. Her breath came in gasps. On the verge of collapse, she sank to the floor and began to weep silent tears.

Breathing deeply, she sought to gain control of herself. Finally she was able to ask, "Are you sure, Moche?"

"Yes, a message just came from Luasi. The Lord Inca died of the same dread disease that took Ninian." Moche knelt down beside her and took her in his arms.

Aolani wept against his chest and in a broken voice she asked, "Oh, Moche, what are we going to do? I can't imagine the world without him."

"Look at me, Aolani," Moche demanded and she slowly raised her head. "My dearest sister, I feel for you. The news has devastated us all, but much as I hate to burden you, plans must be made at once. The unknown and probably unstable situation we face in the empire is fraught with danger, especially for you and the children."

The thought of Manco and Cusi Hwaylas being in danger brought Aolani out of her shocked state. "What do you mean?"

"Tell her, Quis-quis," Moche said.

"Prince Huascar has already taken over the government in Cuzco and is wearing the royal fringe. The priests, the nobles, and the people acknowledge him as Lord High Inca. Prince Atahualpa recognizes he is in grave danger, for his father told him he would rule the northern empire in Quito and Huascar the southern half in Cuzco."

"Both young men knew of this decision. Huascar agreed," Aolani said.

"Well, now Huascar wants it all, claiming he is the eldest legitimate son. He has already ordered your son to present himself in Cuzco and swear allegiance to · him or be prepared for war."

"I see," Aolani said slowly. "I know my son. Atahualpa will not submit to Huascar and so there will be a terrible war between the brothers just as my husband feared. What about the army?"

"The army remains loyal to Prince Atahualpa," Quis-quis said. "The officers know and respect him. They also know the Inca's plans for the succession and feel Huascar has betrayed his father's trust. Besides, the officers have their own futures to consider. If Huascar is Lord High Inca, they will all lose their positions, for the new Inca will appoint his own men to their posts." Quis-quis nodded his head. "Yes, the army will support Atahualpa in his fight for half of the empire."

Moche spoke. "It puts all of us here in a strange position. Quis-quis is positive that, if he and the large detachment of men accompanying us continue on our journey to Cuzco, Huascar will ambush and annihilate his warriors. The new Inca would never let two hundred and fifty armed men, who were Hwayna Capac's personal guards, come anywhere near the capital."

"So you see, my lady, Quis-quis wishes to return to Tomebamba immediately," Nadua said in a disparaging voice, for she had never cared for the general.

Aolani was silent for a few moments and then asked Moche, "What about my husband's body? Is it being returned to his palace in Cuzco to lie in state with the other Lord High Incas?"

Quis-quis answered. "Yes, the Inca's remains are being escorted back to Cuzco by Lord Luasi and the other nobles, as well as members of the Apolina

Council. The funeral cortege left Tomebamba yesterday."

"How long before it will arrive here?" Aolani asked.

"I don't know but it will move slowly. Perhaps two months or more. We cannot remain in Jauja, my lady. What do you wish to do?"

Aolani felt sick. She had to get away. "My lords, forgive me. I must have some time alone. Nadua, come with me." Aolani turned back as she reached the doorway. "Quis-quis, I know you are feeling impatient but I will give you my answer later today."

As Nadua and Aolani entered the queen's chamber, Aolani moved aimlessly to the open window and took a deep breath of air. It was gray and dismal outside and the wind blew hard. As Hwayna had said after Ninian's death, everything just continued on. Clouds passed overhead, trees shed their leaves, birds flew overhead, and flowers blossomed. She watched, as the palm trees thrust their shaking fronds back and forth in the stiff breeze. She felt equally shaken and wanted to collapse on her bed but she couldn't. She was on her own now. Well, she would just have to face one problem at a time. First she must tell the children of their father's death before they heard it from the servants.

Facing Nadua, she tried to sublimate the pain of her husband's loss by taking action. "Nadua, will you fetch my children, please?"

When Nadua left, Aolani's thoughts returned to Hwayna's death. Had he been in pain? If only she had been there to give him what comfort she could. He had died alone, without any members of his family around. It made her want to weep again, but she mustn't, at least not until she had met with the children.

Aolani heard her children's voices, young and eager. Manco raced toward her, crying, "Mama, my llama followed me back to the palace. He wants to stay with me, not with the other animals. Can he, please?"

Cusi Hwaylas in her sweet grown-up way said, "His llama did follow him, Mother. In fact, neither of us noticed him until we were almost back at the palace. I know Manco did nothing to encourage him."

Aolani went to them and, taking their hands in hers, led them to her floor mats. "Come, my dears, sit down. I must talk to you." As Manco started to interrupt she put her finger on his mouth. "Wait, Manco. There is something important I must tell you both." She paused, wondering how to begin, then asked, "Do you remember when your brother Ninian died and we had a long talk about death?"

Cusi Hwaylas was the first to speak. "You told us that death comes to everyone and that we must learn to expect it. The gods decide when they want us to come live with them. They needed Ninian and sent for him. After he died he journeyed to the afterworld, which is a very pleasant and happy place to be."

Manco added his bit. "Yes, and he got to see all of our friends and relatives who have left this world and the gods became his friends. I wonder if the god, Ilyapa, will show me how to throw his lightning bolts when I die."

"Perhaps," Aolani said and then added, "Another person in our family has just died."

"Who?" Manco asked. "Atahualpa?"

"No, my son, it is your father who has died."

"You mean we won't get to see or talk to Father anymore?" Manco asked.

"Not until you, too, go to the afterworld," Cusi Hwaylas said with tears in her eyes. She tried not to sob. "I don't want my father to die."

Manco had tears in his eyes also. "Why don't the gods take Atahualpa instead of Father? I wanted to

Jeanne Nickson

ask him some more about animals, especially llamas. Tell him to come back."

"Oh, Manco," Aolani cried as she hugged him. "Even though you won't be able to see him, your father will be watching over you and taking care of you from afar. If you need help, pray to him and he'll come to you or send someone to you."

"If my llama gives me any trouble, will he be able to help me?"

"I am sure that somehow your father will manage to help you." Aolani decided to change the subject. "Now, when you arrived today, Manco, you asked me about keeping White Cloud here in the palace instead of with the other animals. While we are here in Jauja you may keep him in that small courtyard off of Cusi's room, if that is all right with her." She looked at her daughter.

Cusi nodded her head. "It is all right with me, Mama." She turned to her brother. "But you must take care of him, Manco. You know, feed him and clean up after him."

"Thanks, Cusi." The little boy smiled at his sister. "Come on, let's go tell White Cloud."

As both children raced away Aolani said, "I wish I could accept my explanations of death as easily as they do. Hwayna's death sickens my heart and numbs my will to live. I still can't believe it."

Nadua had been sitting in one corner of the room, sewing a rip in Manco's tunic. She put it down. "This is a sad and difficult time for us all, Quis-quis included. We all loved our dear lord in our different ways. But I know how close you were to him. Your loss must be terrible indeed."

"Only the gods know how much I loved him. True, he made me angry upon occasion and I was often jealous. Sometimes we even fought. But still, to me,

278

he was the most marvelous man in the world. There was no one like him. He made my life very special."

Aolani closed her eyes and swallowed hard, trying to keep the tears from streaming down her face. She had to be strong, she just had to, for all of them. Aolani moved restlessly to the window. It was dismal outside. A thick mist squatted over the city like an ugly toad.

Aolani shivered. "I hate this part of the world. There is always a cold wind sweeping down from the frozen mountain peaks. It chills my body as well as my heart. This window should be covered," she complained.

"I'll see to it. Now why don't you lie down for a while. I'll bring you a hot drink," Nadua said briskly.

"No, I'll be all right. I must decide what to do, where to go."

Nadua interrupted. "Don't let Quis-quis rush you. He is an impatient man. He always reminds me of an eager hunter about to stalk his prey."

She went to the door and soon reappeared with a servant, who went to the window and attached an animal hide over the aperture.

"I know you don't like Quis-quis, Nadua," Aolani said after the servant left, "but give him credit. He is a great warrior-general and has been very loyal to my husband."

"Humph," Nadua snorted.

"I don't think it wise to return to Tomebamba right now with that deadly disease still prevalent. The children might get it. There is also the possibility that if the war begins, the town will be attacked by Huascar," Aolani said.

"Why don't we stay here in Jauja and wait for the funeral procession?" Nadua asked. "The lodgings are very comfortable."

Aolani turned to her. "As I have said, I do not like this town. They say it is the home of the devil, Huari-vika, and I can believe it. However, that is not the reason I don't want to stay here. Jauja is an important administrative base and it will be one of Huascar's first strongholds if war occurs. Huascar and his generals would come here. We would certainly have to give up these comfortable lodgings to them. We would probably be moved to the House of Virgins."

"The heavens forbid! I've had my fill of temple lodgings," Nadua said. "There is always the huge palace of Hwayna Capac in Cuzco. According to Inca law, Huascar cannot take over any of Hwayna Capac's personal property or possessions."

"Of all people, Nadua, you should know how I feel about Cuzco. I was very unhappy there. I know I'll have to stay there during the funeral ceremonies, for I owe it to my husband to be present. But I do not want to stay there any length of time." Aolani was silent as she paced up and down.

Nadua bit off her thread and folded the tunic just as Aolani came to a decision. "We will journey to Sauca Cachi. The villa belongs to Hwayna Capac and was beloved by him. It is close enough to Cuzco, only two days' journey from the capital, but far enough away for privacy. We will leave tomorrow. Nadua, ask Quis-quis to attend me at once."

"What about an escort?"

"I'll ask the general to leave us fifteen warriors, the litter bearers, and enough of the llama tenders and their animals to carry our belongings."

When Nadua left, Aolani slumped back against the pillows, feeling desolate and unsure of herself. Was her decision the correct one? Feeling that a great burden had been shifted to her shoulders with the death of her husband, she wondered if she was capable of handling it. She knew Hwayna had been deeply concerned about what would happen to his youngest son, Manco, if he died. He had told her that it was not unusual for a newly crowned Inca to assassinate not only brothers and half brothers, but even those with power who might threaten him. Huascar was ruthless, she knew, and would not hesitate about killing the boy. How was she going to protect him?

Then there was Cusi Hwaylas. It would be very advantageous for either Huascar or Atahualpa to take her as a wife, for it would reinforce his claim to the throne. It hurt her to think she could not trust her own son any more than Huascar, but Atahualpa had always been ruthless, selfish, and ambitious for power.

Sick at heart, Aolani thought of the only possible solution. She must send Manco and Cusi away from her to Machu Picchu, the hidden refuge Hwayna had told her about. She must stay behind, acting as a decoy, for Huascar and Atahualpa would think she would keep the children with her at all costs. It broke her heart to consider being separated from Cusi and Manco, but it must be done.

How was she to get them to Machu Picchu? She knew of the hidden exit in the cave at Sauca Cachi but who would guide them to the refuge? Luasi wasn't here and Paco, her husband's old friend who lived at Sauca Cachi, was very sick and frail. She would have to send for Luasi. There was no one else who knew where the refuge was. She sighed, for she had no doubt that both Huascar and Atahualpa had spies in her entourage who kept them informed of everything she did. She would have to move carefully.

Aolani heard the sound of a throat being cleared and knew that Quis-quis was present. Telling him quickly of her decision to go to her husband's childhood home, Sauca Cachi, she saw by his expression that he was dismayed and disappointed that she had not elected to return with him.

He cleared his throat again. "You know, my lady, that Sauca Cachi could well be a prison, selected by yourself. It is a narrow valley with only one entrance that can easily be defended, but Huascar could also prevent you from leaving. It would be wise for you to return to Tomebamba and the protection of your son, the Inca, Atahualpa."

"You forget yourself, Quis-quis," Aolani said coldly. "I am *Coya* and must honor my husband at the ceremonies in Cuzco. I cannot turn tail and run like a frightened rabbit to a safe hole. Please leave us the warriors, litter bearers, and animal tenders as I have requested."

Looking offended, Quis-quis left without a word. He had obviously had no orders from Atahualpa to take her and the children back to Tomebamba. She doubted if her son would even think of it. He was not clever and she doubted he would even deem it necessary to order her back.

Thinking of her husband, she whispered quietly, "Oh, Hwayna, beloved, the future seems bleak and all you foretold is coming true. Huascar is hideously exposed for what he is. His ambitions, in the dark of your absence, march the empire toward disaster. I have no confidence in Atahualpa, I am sorry to say. Oh, sweet my love, help me protect and guard Manco and Cusi from their enemies. My loneliness is heavy but you will remain in my heart forever. I long for you and your council. Guide me if you can, and I'll try not to fail you. May the gods bless and receive you with honor."

Chapter Twenty-five

Exhausted by the emotional impact of the funeral ceremonies, irritated by having to endure the critical scrutinies of the nobles, and tired of trying to be diplomatic with Huascar, Aolani hoped that the day would soon be over and that she could return to Sauca Cachi.

In a way, it would be hard to return, for the children would be gone. It made her heart ache but thanks to the gods and Juan's and Luasi's efforts they had reached Machu Picchu safely and Nadua and Luasi would take good care of them. It had been a miracle that Luasi had managed to send her a message of their safe arrival in the midst of all this confusion. Just knowing they were in a secure refuge gave her the strength to endure this traumatic and painful experience. It had been far worse than she'd imagined.

The three days of looking at the effigy of her husband sitting on a gold throne in Haucapata Square with servants flicking flies away from his painted face

had been excruciating. The wailing dirge of the participants in the daily processions that circled the throne
assailed her ears and made her cringe. Having 4,000
servants, concubines, and warriors put to death so that
they could accompany the Inca to the afterworld had
greatly upset her, even though they had volunteered
for sacrifice.

But above all, watching Huascar take over her husband's place as Lord High Inca had made Aolani sick
and uneasy. A man of average intelligence and no wit,
he apparently carried a grudge as big as the fortress of
Sacsahuaman. He had made her fearful of the future.
The new Inca was as undependable as a volcano, calm
and pleasant at times and then likely to erupt with
a fury that was frightening. He seemed to be popular enough with the large mass of people inhabiting
Cuzco, but among his family, attendants, and nobles
there was a feeling of wariness, apprehension, and
even fear. His mother-in-law looked at him with absolute hatred and his two wives both looked fearful when
he approached. In his way Huascar had been cour-
teous and polite to Aolani, seeming to think that she
espoused his right to the throne rather than her son's,
which was not exactly true.

On this, the last day of the ceremonies, Huascar
would become the absolute ruler of the empire.
Lords, ladies, chiefs, and dignitaries from all over
Tahuantinsuyu gathered to witness the actual crowning
of the new Lord High Inca. Even though Huascar had
assumed the royal fringe and declared himself Inca
upon hearing of the death of his father, he would not
be officially crowned until this special ceremony was
concluded.

Aolani sat with Huascar's two wives and his mother-
in-law on one side of the raised dais. On the other
side sat his advisers and the Apolina Council he had

appointed. Looking around her, Aolani could see that compared to the glittering spectacles created under Hwayna's direction, this was quite a shabby affair. There was no music or dancing and it seemed disorganized. The High Priest of the Sun stood directly behind the Inca. As drums began to beat, two nobles in red-feathered robes approached the throne carrying the new Inca's standard, a small pennant about twelve hands around the edge, woven of soft vicuna wool. Embroidered in the center of the pennant was the arch of a rainbow beneath which two serpents lay entwined. Aolani wondered why Huascar had chosen this as his personal emblem.

Following them came two warriors dressed in black and red. They held staves to which the Inca's *champi*, his personal weapons, had been attached. These men took their places on either side of the Inca and held the staves aloft. The high priest and two assistants came forward carrying the *sunturpaucar*, a staff covered and adorned from top to bottom with short red and blue feathers. From the top of the staff three large feathers floated in the breeze. Aolani noted Huascar's staff of office didn't even match his costume. The high priest placed the staff in the Inca's left hand and then, taking the gold scepter from the other assistant, placed the emblem of authority in Huascar's right hand.

As the high priest symbolically took the red fringe from Huascar's head, blessed it, and then replaced it, there were sounds of trumpets coming from all around the square. All the people shouted, "Haille! Haille! Haille!" Then they fell to the ground. The highest nobles formed a line, each one carrying a gift, and moved up the stairs of the dais. One at a time, they knelt before the Inca and repeated the oath of fealty: *"Ancha hatun, opu, intip-chari, conqu zapallopu, tucay parcha ocampa yuau sullull."*

It took about three hours and Aolani was never so thankful in her life as when it was finally over. At last she was able to withdraw to the back of the dais and walk down the stairs to where Moche and Sinchi were waiting for her. The three of them hurried back through the throngs of people to the palace of Hwayna Capac.

As they reached the gates, Aolani, slightly breathless from pushing through the crowds, stopped and said suddenly, "I can't stand any more. I must get back to Sauca Cachi. We will start back tonight."

"You mean walk all night?" Moche asked.

"The road is clear and there will be no people on it tonight. They will be too drunk. Don't forget there is a full moon tonight," Aolani said.

Moche nodded. "We will do as you command, eh, Sinchi?"

Sinchi said with youthful exuberance,. "It sounds like fun. I'll get the bearers and everyone ready to go."

Later that night, as Aolani's palanquin moved quietly through the night, a great weariness descended upon her spirit. She felt that the gods had forsaken her and that her entire life had changed in that one moment when Hwayna had breathed his last. The star-encrusted curtain of the night glittering above offered no solace. The moon, in luminous splendor, was remote and cold. For months Aolani had felt just as remote and cold. If it hadn't been for Manco and Cusi, she would have joined all the others who died in order to accompany their lord to the afterworld. She moaned. How could she continue, so forsaken and alone?

Aolani closed her eyes and prayed to Viracocha. "O, Lord, troubled in spirit, I seek your help. Give me the strength to bear my loss, and the courage to go on."

She closed her eyes and sleep descended upon her. When she awakened, the sun was almost directly overhead and the gates to Sauca Cachi were swinging open. She noticed immediately that the number of guards had doubled.

Sinchi came up to Aolani, looking concerned. "It appears that Sauca Cachi is to be your abode for quite some time. There are guards inside the valley as well as out. Shall I object or say anything?"

"No! I don't want you or Moche to get into any trouble. It won't do any good. Huascar has apparently decided I am a hostage worth keeping. Tell our bearers to move on."

As they entered the long narrow valley, with its precipitous rock walls rising to tremendous heights on each side, Aolani thought of Juan. He had arrived at Jauja with Sinchi a few days after she had learned of her husband's death. She had not seen him, but knew that he had accompanied them to Sauca Cachi, where she had formulated her plans for her children's escape to Machu Picchu. She had asked Moche to enlist Juan's aid in getting her children to safety and now she wondered if he had made it back to Sauca Cachi or if he had been captured. Thinking about him upset her. Why was she so worried about him? He and Sinchi had made it all the way from Tomebamba to Jauja without incident, and without her permission. Juan had promised her that he would stay with the Inca. He'd had no right to run away. Sinchi had told her that the Inca had ordered Juan to Jauja, but that didn't make sense to her. Hwayna had known that Juan was in love with her and her husband had been jealous. He would never have sent Juan after her—or would he?

Golden ribbons of light fluttered through the trees on the other side of the river while the sunlight above poured like a warm blanket over him. Juan had caught five fish, which reposed in a reed basket placed in the cold shallow water. Juan, lying on the grassy bank above the stream, knew he should be feeling happy and content but in truth he was miserable. It had been months since he had first entered the valley of Sauca Cachi and not once had he had an opportunity to talk with the Lady Aolani in private, not even when Moche had asked him to help Manco and Cusi escape to Machu Picchu. In fact, he seldom saw her at all. The little news he had of her he picked up from Moche or Sinchi Chacoya.

Juan looked down at Sinchi, who was still fishing in the Inca fashion, holding a spear, examining the water for movement, then thrusting deep into the pool. Apparently Sinchi had been unable to pierce any of the agile silver fish. Sinchi finally threw his spear down in disgust and after climbing up the incline, lay down on the ground.

"By all the gods, this fishing is a monotonous and tedious business. I don't have the patience for it," Sinchi said with a smile.

"Perhaps you should try the Spanish way, using a stick and a hook with bait," Juan said absently. Juan's eyes followed the flight of a condor in pursuit of food. A flock of pigeons took wing from an old carob tree nearby. Alerted, the large bird swooped down and, with clutching talons, grasped one of the birds and rose in triumphant flight to the sky above. Sinchi was also watching the birds and looked morose.

Noticing Sinchi's expression, Juan wondered about him. He did not seem to fit the mold of the other Inca boys Juan had seen. Personally, Juan had enjoyed traveling with Sinchi, for he was interested in everything he saw. Sinchi meticulously studied all forms of life, many times surprising Juan with his observations.

Juan had also noted that Sinchi was a gentle and sensitive young man who was reluctant to hunt and kill the wild animals needed for food. Good as he was with his weapons, he had always let Juan make the final kill.

Without thinking, Juan asked, "You didn't want to stab a fish, did you?"

Looking embarrassed, Sinchi compressed his lips as he said honestly, "I never have liked to kill living things. I've always felt that their lives are as important to them as mine is to me. I would have been ashamed to admit this a few years back, especially in front of Atahualpa, but I am old enough now to stand up for what I believe. Don't misunderstand. I am not a coward. If I had to protect my family or get food because I was starving, I would do so. But to kill wantonly is difficult for me." He looked worried. "There will be a war soon, I know. I do not think I will make a good warrior. I hope I don't have to fight."

"How do you know there will be a war?"

"I do not know for sure, but I know that my uncle, Hwayna Capac, expected it to happen upon his death, and after watching Huascar when I was in Cuzco, I believe there will be a war."

"What is Huascar like?" Juan asked.

"I found him a cold and unlikable man," Sinchi answered. "I heard from my cousin in the palace that he is cruel, untrustworthy, and greedy for power. He will challenge Atahualpa, who is as bloodthirsty as he is. There will be many battles with Incas fighting Incas. I don't want to be involved in it but I don't see how I can avoid it."

Juan thought about what the boy had said. He felt rather the same. He had no desire to be part of this war. Two greedy men, hungry for power, would tear this empire apart. And what would Juan do when his own countrymen arrived, knowing that this group of predators would spill even more blood and cost many lives? What would he do? Well, he didn't want to think about it.

Juan jumped up. "Come on, Sinchi. Will you take the fish up to the cooks? I've promised to help some of the men in the village repair the llama enclosure."

When they neared the villa, Sinchi went off with the fish and Juan started for the woven bridge that spanned the river. The bridge needed repair soon. He would have to remind the village elders again. Sitting down, Juan put on his sandals and tied them. Suddenly he heard a scream. It sounded like the scream of a child. Racing toward the river, Juan saw with horror that the footpath over the straw bridge had broken through about halfway across. A figure hung from the heavy cable as the bridge itself swung back and forth above the churning water below.

"Hang on," Juan shouted.

Then he moved cautiously out on the woven footpath and reached the torn opening. Reaching down he grasped the wrist below the hand that still clutched the cable and he lifted the body through the hole up beside him. Only then did he see that it was Aolani looking at him in shock.

Carefully holding her close, he walked back along the bridge path to the riverbank, heaving a sigh of relief when they were off the bridge. Juan could feel her heart beating next to his own and see her hair falling in a molten mass over his arm. Gently he placed her on the grass and asked, "Are you all right?"

"Yes," she said breathlessly, "a little shaken, that is all."

Aolani smoothed out her tunic and brushed some pieces of straw off her gown before looking at him. Her unusual eyes of yellow gold gleamed up at him through the thick black lashes.

"I want to thank you for rescuing me. It was brave of you. I was quite frightened for a moment, I admit, not of the water, but of the sharp rocks below me. But now I must return to the villa, for my hand is burning and is badly scratched. Thanks again, Juan."

As she turned to walk away, Juan grabbed her by the arm and turned her around, saying harshly, "Lady Aolani, why have you been avoiding me as if I had the plague? What have I done that you should treat me like a stranger?"

She looked at him in contempt. "Why did you sneak away when my husband was ill and couldn't stop you? Why did you come here, anyway?"

Juan said bitterly, "I did not sneak away. The Lord High Inca sent me to you."

Aolani looked at him with distaste. "You lie! My husband would not send you to me, for he knew of your feelings of—"

"Of love, Aolani," Juan said. "You are right. The Inca told me that he knew I loved you. He did ask me to come after you."

"What a lie! Why would he do that?"

Juan said quickly, "The Inca felt that I might be of help to you when the Spaniards come. He felt that you and the children would need me and you do. He offered me a fortune to be your protector."

As he uttered those last words Juan knew he had said the wrong thing. Her eyes looked at him with disdain. "And men of your race do anything for a fortune, don't they?" Aolani drew away from him and ran up the path toward the villa.

Chapter Twenty-six

Juan was just about to leave the guest house, a small three-room building across the stream from the villa, when Sinchi came running across the stone bridge. Juan greeted his guest, his eyebrows raised. "Good morning, Sinchi. What are you doing here so early?"

Smiling a little slyly, Sinchi said, "I have a surprise for you, Juan. My beautiful aunt desires your presence in her chambers as soon as possible."

After yesterday's experience with the *Coya*, Juan was not pleased at having to face her again. He asked curiously, "Have you any idea why she wants to see me?"

Hesitating, Sinchi replied, "Not exactly, but last night the Lady Aolani did question me about our trip. Perhaps it has something to do with that. Come on, Juan. She told me to bring you to her at once."

Juan's sleep during the night had been troubled by the thought of Aolani and her scorn and disbelief in what he had told her. He reluctantly followed Sinchi, his face grim, feeling a little angry. Why in God's name had Aolani sent for him after showing him how little she believed in him? He was not in the mood to listen to any further accusations. Sinchi left him at the entrance to her reception chamber, formerly the Lord High Inca's quarters.

Juan entered the room. The floor was covered by a huge gold-and-silver mosaic, tapestries adorned the walls and the far side of the room opened onto a pool with exotic gardens on the other side of it. The scent of flowers filled the air with a delicate fragrance. Aolani turned toward him as he entered and her beauty hit him like a blow, as it had so often in the past when he'd had to be silent in her presence. He took a deep breath, refusing to be intimidated. He was no longer a servant and he refused to act like one. He looked at her steadily until she suddenly dropped her eyes.

"You sent for me, my lady?" he asked without emotion.

As Aolani moved toward him, the sun from the open door touched her hair with sparks of gold. She stopped a few feet away from him and said straightforwardly, "After talking to Sinchi and to you yesterday, I believe I may have misjudged you. I have asked you here to tell you that I am sorry. I have not been myself for many moons."

Juan said more gently, "It is understandable. The death of your husband and the separation from your children must have been difficult for you."

"I must admit I have been so absorbed in my own grief I have given only slight thought to others." Aolani moved away from him and stood by the open door, her face in shadow. "When you arrived in Jauja after Hwayna's death, I was still in shock. I could understand why my husband sent Sinchi to me. He knew I loved my cousin like a son. I was sure Hwayna had sent him here to protect him from the pestilence, but I—"

"But you wondered why I had come with him," Juan finished. "I assure you that I was sent by the Inca."

"I know that now. Sinchi told me that my husband ordered you to join me but I am still puzzled. You see, I know my husband was aware of your feelings for me." Aolani said hurriedly, "Not that I told him, but there was very little that he didn't know. Aware of his jealousy, I find it hard to believe he would send you to me. I am bewildered, unable to understand it."

Wondering just what to tell her, Juan was beguiled as always by her presence. The sadness in her eyes and the confusion on her face made her seem more vulnerable and approachable than he'd ever seen her. She was very thin and the deep shadows under her eyes made him aware of her agony. The air of command was gone; only the woman was present, her scent making him ache for her. One thing he knew. He was not going to tell her that the Inca had intimated to Juan that he might win her love. She would never believe him. He wondered if he would ever be able to tell her.

Juan started to speak. "Let me tell you what—"

"No, not here," she said. "Let us go outside." Aolani led him out to the pool, where pillows had been placed in the shade of a blossoming red tree. "Do you want *chicha?*"

"No, it is too early." Juan sat down after she did and watched the two streams of water, one hot and one cold, splash into the pool. Feeling comfortable with her now, Juan began telling her of that strange night when he was alone with the Inca, repeating as much as he could remember of the conversation, both before and after his attack.

Aolani listened with rapt attention, and when he concluded, she was silent for a few moments. "Yes, most of what you have told me I can understand. He really believed in that old prophecy. He believed that after his death Huascar and Atahualpa would both seek the royal fringe. He felt that the blood of thousands of warriors would flow like a river throughout the land and would weaken the empire. If the Spaniards come, they will be able to invade and conquer Tahuantinsuyu, encountering little resistance. For months before he died, the Inca followed what was happening in countries to the north of us as they were taken over by the invaders. They killed the men, raped the women, took everything they could, and finally destroyed the mighty civilizations they had invaded. He was dreadfully afraid the same thing would happen here in our own empire." She was thoughtful. "He probably thought a Spanish protector might ensure some kind of help for myself and the children in case of such an event. You mentioned yesterday that he had promised you a fortune. I—"

Juan interrupted. "I don't want a fortune. I told him so. I am very fond of the children. Why else would I have helped them get to Machu Picchu? I have already told you of my feelings for you. Do you think I would let my countrymen harm you if I could possibly stop them?" As Aolani attempted to speak he raised his hand. "I know you loved your husband and love him still. You need feel no obligation to me. Do you understand? I made a promise to Hwayna Capac, a man I admired, and I will keep that promise."

"I believe you, Juan, and I am grateful. I am grateful, also, for the part you played in helping my children escape to safety. Were they frightened the morning I left for Cuzco?"

"No, they thought it was a great adventure, especially Manco. He loved climbing through the tunnel at the back of the waterfall. Cusi got wet and was cold but Nadua wrapped her in a shawl. The ones who were frightened were Luasi, Nadua, and myself, especially when we saw the hazardous trail we had to climb down."

Aolani's face was somber. "I was frightened, too, not knowing what awaited me in Cuzco at the funeral, hoping no one would question me as to why the children were not with me, and above all, fearful that the children and the three of you would be captured."

Juan said with admiration, "Luasi is a genius at organization. No wonder. He was head of the Inca's household. Everything was arranged. Clothing, food, safe shelters, and guides. I wore a priest's hooded robe, provided by Moche, I understand."

"Yes, I know. In fact, it was my suggestion. I also provided an ointment to darken your skin. Did you use it?"

Juan nodded as he went on. "We traveled mostly at night, especially south of Cuzco, where multitudes of people were converging on the city."

"Did you have trouble east of Cuzco finding the trail that led to Machu Picchu?"

"No, but as I said Luasi had planned everything. He was even thinking of your escape. He made me memorize all the landmarks so that I would be able to find the Weeping Rock, where at each full moon someone will always be waiting to guide you to your children."

"How I pray for that!"

The shade had disappeared as the sun climbed ever higher in the sky and Juan felt warm. He noticed beads of perspiration on Lady Aolani's smooth forehead. It must be late morning. Juan suddenly remembered his promise to Aroqui, a man in the village. "Will you excuse me, my lady? I promised the village elders I would help harvest the quinoa with them this week."

"How interesting," Aolani said. She was surprised and touched that Juan was helping the farmers. Most men she had known would not labor at such a lowly occupation. They thought it beneath them. Many years ago when she had lived at the Temple of Viracocha with her foster father she had worked in the fields and helped the priests with all the household tasks and had enjoyed the activities. She admired Juan for what he was doing; she was also chagrined that he was leaving her, for she had enjoyed the morning.

"Leave, by all means." Aolani watched Juan as he stood up. By all the gods, he was a fine looking man. How he had changed! Gone was the pale, thin, rather intense young man she had first seen. Now, he was tall and straight with a powerful physique, his muscles rippling under his tan skin. As Juan bowed, his dark hair fell in curls about his face and she wanted to touch them. The thought appalled her. By all the gods how could she be thinking such a thing?

She said abruptly, "Thank you again for being so understanding." As he reached the door she added, "Moche is having his evening meal with me tonight. Will you come?"

"Yes, my lady, I will be here."

"Come as soon as the sun begins to sink below the mountains."

As he left she began to feel more lighthearted than she had in weeks. Then she thought of Cusi and Manco. Oh, how she missed them! But she'd done the right thing— they were safe. Someday with the gods' help she would see them again. She'd have to wait until it was safe for her to go to them. It would take time. But right now she was hot. She would swim and soap her body.

297

*   *   *

During the following year, Aolani began taking more interest in the life of the village, and when she found that there was no *Hampi Camoyoc* in the valley, no one with any knowledge of medicine amongst the villagers, she decided to make herself available. It was rather far for the people to come up to the villa, so she asked Juan to find a small hut and have it cleaned.

Aolani then asked Sinchi to help her find the different herbs she would need. She explained to him that they would need molle leaves and bark for cuts and wounds, sarsaparilla to kill pain, chillca for painful joints and pains, manioc for rheumatism, sairi for headaches, matecclu for eye treatment, saltpeter for stones in the liver, and many other simple remedies. She even sent to Cuzco for coca and the cinchona bark to use for chills and fever.

At first, she spent one morning a week in the small hut loaned to her by Aroqui, brother to her dear friend, Paco. During those beginning weeks the smell of animal dung and human excrement and the smoke of the cooking fires were offensive to her nostrils. The screams of the children, the loud chatter of the women gossiping as they filled their baskets with water from the river, and the loud shouts of the men assaulted her ears.

Soon Aolani became oblivious to the sounds and smells. She was happy in what she was doing, feeling worthwhile as a person, enjoying the sense of being useful again. She also enjoyed the admiration she saw in Juan's eyes whenever he saw her. Aolani continued to be amazed by Juan, or Senerhuana, as the villagers called him. Not only did he work in the fields; he helped in other ways. Juan was teaching the youngest children how to swim, working with Sinchi in helping the older boys develop skills with weapons, herding llamas, repairing walls and buildings, and just generally making himself useful.

The men looked to Juan for leadership and direction, the women adored him and giggled and laughed at his jokes, and the children followed him everywhere if they were not working. Aolani had also fallen under his spell. His warm concern for her welfare was evident, and she accepted his assistance gratefully. He had cleaned the small hut, built an object called a table on which she placed her medicines and other equipment, and found or made the tools and splints she needed.

One morning after the last patient had left and Choque, her headwoman, was cleaning up, Aolani saw Juan eagerly approaching her. There was a gleam in his dark eyes and he was smiling as he said, "I have a splendid idea, Aolani, but I need your help. The harvest is almost over. The last of the maize will be brought in tomorrow. All the men, and the women and children, too, need a fiesta."

For a moment she looked at him blankly. Then she understood. "Yes, a fiesta—a celebration! The people would enjoy it."

"I know they would but I don't know what to do, how to organize it." He looked to her for help.

"We must have music, dancing, food, *chicha*, and of course games and contests." She clapped her hands. "It will be wonderful."

Juan grinned at her. "Where do we start?"

Aolani looked at his expectant face. It was ridiculous how happy and lighthearted he made her feel. She said with a smile, "This is the time of year when the greatest feast of all is celebrated in the empire. It is called *Hatun Raymi* and is always held after the harvest is in."

"What happens at the feast?"

"First of all, thanks and praise are given to the great god, Maker of Heaven and Earth, Tici-Viracocha, but other gods are included as well. In Cuzco the people celebrated for about ten days."

Juan frowned. "I was thinking of one day or, at the most, two."

"You are right. We couldn't do what they did in Cuzco for ten days." She could picture the festival in her mind. "In the middle of the great square they built a grand three-tiered image of Viracocha and everyone passed in front of it and blew his breath toward the image, including Hwayna Capac and myself. That was to let the gods know that we lived because of them. A great many dances were performed in the square below the gods, and sacrifices were made. There was music, food, and much drinking of *chicha*."

Juan said with a question in his eyes, "I notice there is plenty of *chicha* in storage at the villa. Can we use some of it?"

"Of course." She smiled. "Now, we will let Moche make a shrine to Viracocha and plan the sacrifice. I'll take care of the music and the dancing. Choque can take charge of the food and wine and help you organize the women. You and Sinchi will handle the games and contests."

"Well, let's get busy. I'll go get Sinchi and tell Lord Moche."

As Juan rushed away Aolani marveled at the way nothing slipped by him. He was as sharp as a thorn from a cactus. She liked his new name, Senerhuana. It seemed to suit him.

The dark clouds she had noticed all morning were now directly overhead; they looked threatening. There was a sharp clap of thunder that made her jump. It shocked the birds off their perch in the caiminto tree and she watched them fly away into the distance.

It made her think of Cusi and Manco so far away.
How they would have enjoyed planning the celebration. Tears came to her eyes. How was she going
to escape from Sauca Cachi and make her way to
Machu Picchu? She had to get out of here. She
must find a way to get back to her children. But
there were guards at the main gate and also in the
valley itself, supposedly to protect her but that was
nonsense. Huascar's real reason was to keep her as a
hostage.

Just after midmorning on the day of the celebration,
when the sun was hot in the sky, Aolani and Juan
made their way across the small area to the right of
the dais Juan had built for the statue of Viracocha.
Rugs and pillows had been placed on the ground for
them to sit upon. A large piece of bright yellow cotton
shaded the space. As Aolani sat down she could see
that all the villagers had crowded into the small area,
their expressions somber but their eyes bright with
anticipation of the day.

Exactly when the blazing sun was directly overhead,
the soft beat of drums could be heard coming from
many different directions. Six men came in playing on
their drums, each with a single stick; they took their
places on either side of the dais.

A handsome boy of about 12 advanced toward the
drummers. Aolani had selected the boy and could see
he was nervous but proud of himself and his attire.
He was richly dressed in a costume Aolani had made.
His knees from the legs down were covered with red
tassels and so were his arms. On his body he wore
many chains and ornaments of gold and silver. In his
right hand he carried a tool used by the farmers to till
the soil and in his left hand was a big woolen bag that
was usually used to carry potatoes.

On the boy's left side came a pretty girl, still a child, wearing a long knit skirt with a train carried by a handsome woman. Behind them, village women performed a slow and stately dance taught to them by Choque. As they came closer, Aolani could see that the little girl wore the puma skin that had belonged to little Manco. It hung proudly from her shoulders and completely covered her back. She grinned at the people and they smiled back. She, also, carried a beautiful woven bag covered with ornaments of gold and silver. Behind the dancing women came six Indians who represented farmers, each with a plow on his shoulder; on their heads were beautiful feathered headdresses of many colors, which Aolani had made out of one of Hwayna's cloaks. She could hear the sounds of pleasure coming from the spectators as they watched this unusual show of costumes and color.

The actors stopped in front of the dais and then silently moved backward. There, the farmers sank their plows into the ground and hung the sacks of potatoes on their frames. From time to time as the stately dance went on, the farmers lifted their bags of potatoes to the sky.

It was a simple ceremony to the gods, asking them to bless the next planting season. It was so different from the formal ceremonies in Cuzco. Aolani wished her own children could have been present. She prayed every day that they were safe and happy. She tried to keep her tears back. Suddenly there was total silence and everyone sat down.

Juan knew it was Aolani's turn to take part in the ceremony and he saw Moche moving forward in his priestly robes. Moche extended a hand to the *Coya*, who stood up and walked with him to the dais. Aolani looked as a queen should look, in her tunic of silver that glittered like clear water in the sunlight. Blue-and-gold embroidery decorated the neckline and the hem and she wore a headdress of shimmering blue feathers. She was so beautiful that Juan felt breathless.

Suddenly, Aolani commenced to sing a song to the gods. Her voice was so sweet and high that it sent chills along Juan's spine. He had heard her sing before and knew her voice was unusual but this song had an eerie quality that seemed to belong to the spirit world. There was a deathly silence when she finished, and a low moaning sound came from the throats of the Indians.

Moche used the dramatic moment to move toward the white llama standing between two men. His hand, moving as quick as lightning, stabbed the animal. As blood spurted forth, Juan saw Aolani avert her eyes, for she hated to see anything killed. However, Aolani was aware that the animal would furnish meat, a rare and delicate treat for the villagers.

The formal ceremony was over and everyone but the actors rushed to the llama enclosure, where the contests and games would be held. Juan was glad to see Choque collecting all the costumes and the valuable ornaments. He saw Aolani put a hand to her head. She took off the feathered headdress and let it fall to the ground.

Knowing something was wrong, Juan came over to her. "What is it, Aolani?"

"My head is throbbing with pain," she said. "I am sorry, Juan, but I must return to the villa."

Moche and Choque had both noticed Aolani's pallor and came toward her. Moche had overheard their conversation and said in a worried voice, "I will come with you, my dear Aolani."

"No, I forbid it, Moche. You and Juan are needed. Choque, you have all the food to supervise. I will be fine. Tia and Aranis will be at the villa to attend me."

303

Juan said abruptly, "Your ladies will not be at the villa. You gave them permission to attend the festivities, don't you remember? I will come with you, for both Moche and Sinchi are needed at the games and Choque has things to do. I, fortunately, am free. Come, Aolani."

As the others reluctantly left, Aolani turned to Juan. "I will not have this. I am not a child. I can take care of myself."

"Come, Aolani." Juan took her by the arm.

Stamping her foot, Aolani said, "By all the gods, Senor Juan, what makes you think you're in charge of the valley? I do not want you, do you understand? I just want to be by myself."

"All right, but I will escort you to your chambers."

Aolani threw up her hands in disgust and said, "You are as obstinate as a llama with too much weight added to its load. It just will not budge."

Juan said nothing, but followed her closely across the bridge, past the lake, and up the hill to the villa. As they moved into the reception room on the first floor, Juan saw a stranger, a man with so sour an expression he looked as if he had just swallowed some of that nasty vinegar that was made from the fruit of the molle tree. Since he wore gold earrings in his ears, he was probably an Inca of some importance.

Aolani saw him, too, and asked the invader in an imperious voice, "Just what are you doing here?"

"Lady Aolani," the man said coldly. "I've been sent by the Lord High Inca, Huascar, to escort you and your retinue to Cuzco as soon as possible."

"Why?" she demanded.

"I did not ask, my lady. I just obey orders," the man responded without expression.

Aolani looked quickly at Juan. He noticed that her eyes were full of fear but it did not show in her voice as she commanded, "Senerhuana, take this man to the guest house and see that he and his men receive food and lodging. We will leave in the morning. Please arrange everything."

Juan watched her sweep from the room and was proud of her, knowing how she feared Huascar. Turning to the stranger he said politely, "Will you follow me, my lord?"

After showing the man his quarters, summoning his servants, providing refreshments, and showing him the path to the guest pool, Juan went quickly into the village and summoned Aolani's women and Moche, leaving Sinchi and Aroqui to carry on. He told all three of them what had happened.

"You ladies must prepare to pack and have food ready for tonight and tomorrow morning. Moche, will you be sure the litters and the bearers are ready in the morning at sunup? We don't want them drunk. Perhaps you had better find them now. Choque, have the servants return here immediately. I'll take care of the llamas and their tenders." He watched them leave to follow his instructions before going back to the villa.

Aolani nervously paced, panic-stricken. Why had Huascar sent for her? Did he suspect something? Had he found the children? Her head ached so painfully that she felt sick. She couldn't think. Then she heard a slight noise at the door and froze with fear. Seeing Juan, she felt a sense of relief. Why, she didn't know. What in the world could he do that she couldn't?

He brought a goblet to her and said, "You told me sairi was good for headaches. Drink this." He handed over the goblet. "I put the sairi in some *chicha*, which I think you need."

She made a face as she drank half of the brew. "You know I hate *chicha*."

"I've never understood why you didn't like it. Drink the rest of it."

She did as he told her. "Ugh! You deserve to be told. The women in the temples chew molle leaves a good deal of the time in order to make this wine. When the leaves are ground fine by their teeth and well mixed with with their saliva, they spit it into a bowl. When there is quite a good amount of spit in the bowl, they cover it and leave it to ferment." She watched his expression with amusement.

Then he laughed. "It still makes you feel good."

Something about him attracted her, but it wasn't love. No, her deep love was for the man she had lost. What she felt for Juan was a physical attraction, lust, perhaps. He was so lighthearted and happy most of the time, not taking anything seriously, that he brought her out of her black moods. Hwayna had been so different. He had grown so serious with the years, absorbed in the problems of the empire. But still she knew he had always loved her.

Putting down the goblet, she mused aloud. "I don't know what's the matter with me today. I must have anticipated Huascar's return, for I've felt fearful all day. All through the celebration I felt so sad. I kept thinking of my children, wishing they were here. They are growing up without me and I ache for them. Every day I wonder how they are getting along without me. I pray to the spirit god every day, hoping my wish to be with them will be granted." She looked at Juan. "Do you think I'll ever see them again?"

Juan couldn't endure her anguished expression. "Of course," he said earnestly. "I'd say in about ten days."

Aolani looked at him as if he were a chattering monkey without a brain in his head. But he was smiling so cheerfully she almost smiled back. "Can't you be serious?"

"I am being very, very serious, Aolani. For the first time in months I think we might have a chance to escape." He smiled. "Will you return my love if I help you reach your children?"

"I don't know whether I can return your love, but I might seriously consider it," she said, flirting with him.

Lifting her up, he whirled her around. "Consider it done, my lovely, adorable Lani. I would move mountains for you. You will see your children again, I promise."

She made a face. "Don't bother with mountains. Just take me to Manco and Cusi, and don't call me Lani. That was my husband's special name for me."

Juan ruffled her hair and kissed her forehead. "Who knows? Perhaps Mother Kilya, the Moon, may help me win you as a wife. May I call you Lani then?"

Aolani had to laugh at him. "You've made me feel better, Senerhuana, but I am still fearful about returning to Cuzco. What will the Inca do to me if he is aware that I tricked him?"

"Do not worry so, Aolani. Let your imagination rest. The Lord High Inca has sent an Inca noble to act as your escort. He does not act like a guard ordered to bring a prisoner back to Cuzco. Now, rest my lady. Your women are here to attend you."

Chapter Twenty-seven

They left Sauca Cachi the next morning and Aolani spent long hours thinking about her present situation as bearers carried her litter toward Cuzco. What would happen to her there? She felt a great fear of Huascar and wondered why he had sent for her after leaving her alone for a year. She did not know if she had the courage to face him. So many changes had occurred since her husband's death that she was uneasy and unable to take charge of her life.

Thoughts of Hwayna still occupied her waking hours, and even at night she would wake up thinking of him and her former life. Aolani missed the world she had known as *Coya*, the comfort of familiar surroundings, the luxurious beauty of the palace, the care and concern of all those around her. She missed above all the warmth of her husband's devotion, the love and protection he had provided.

During the first two months after his death she had

refused to face the facts and concentrated on keeping her memories alive. For a time, Aolani had deliberately refused to face the reality of Hwayna's death, for if she did, she knew she would fall apart. But life was not so easily avoided and certain concerns began to impinge on her self-willed isolation. The needs of Manco and Cusi had demanded her attention. Not only had they needed her during that tragic time, but they were in danger as well. She was aware that her husband's death would precipitate a confrontation between Huascar and Atahualpa that might affect her younger children. A primitive instinct for survival had forced her out of her dreamlike existence, and she had become stronger as she met the demands on her time.

Then, with Juan's help, she had begun to find herself again as a person and she was grateful to him for that. She had been mentally stimulated by working with the villagers who were sick or injured. It had made her feel proud of herself when she was able to help them. She had actually taken pleasure in planning the celebration and making the costumes for the delighted participants.

Aolani realized she had finally accepted the past. Hwayna was gone. For almost 22 years she had been obsessed by him, living in a world protected by wealth and power. She had been bathed, dressed, and attended to like a child's doll; her every want had been catered to before she had even known she had it. Even her children had been taken care of almost completely by others. Aolani felt a moment of guilt and sorrow. Could she have exerted more influence on her oldest son if she had tried? Was it her fault he was selfish and lacking in concern for others? Could Atahualpa, with more help from her, have become the son Hwayna needed? Well, the answer to that was gone, too. She would never know. With that conclusion she felt her eyes close. She had not slept last night. She would try to sleep, for she needed to be rested if she was to face Huascar.

When they arrived in Cuzco they were taken to the palace of Hwayna Capac. The big courtyard, always so crowded, was deserted. As the others followed Aolani through the empty palace, she felt more strongly than ever a sense of isolation. It was as if her family, the servants, attendants, and palace functionaries had never existed. They were the ghosts of the past.

She stopped at the door of her old chamber and walked in. Memories of her arrival 20 years ago came flooding back. She had been so strong and determined, confident that she could do anything she wanted to do. When Hwayna Capac had come into her life she had known that he was the man she wanted for a husband and she had won him. When they were first married, Aolani had felt that they were invincible, that they had everything the world could possibly give them and always would. But it wasn't true. She had found out the hard way, just five years after their marriage, when Hwayna Capac had taken a new wife and sent her away. She had discovered life was as uncertain as were the storms in the mountains. The gods could change her whole life in one fleeting moment. Why hadn't she learned her lesson then?

Suddenly, something Moche had said came into her mind. "As water in the river flows and is reshaped by rocks and monstrous obstacles, so our lives follow along an unknown path and are changed. Slowly and pleasantly life moves along until some terrible or tragic event drops us in a crashing descent, leaving us gasping, torn apart. Still, as the river runs ever onward, despite all nature's barriers, until it reaches the sea, so our lives move inexorably to our end."

In this dark time Aolani thought it was true. Along with the pleasant, one had to accept the unpleasant in life and do the best that one could under the circumstances and get on with life. She intended to try to survive this catastrophe and help her children survive as well.

As the sun rose over Cuzco, Juan watched the shadows from the high mountain peaks linger for a moment over the city. From his vantage point on the hill above the fortress called Sacsahuaman, he began to see that the design of the city did resemble a puma. The large fortress was the head, the palaces, temples, and huge plaza the body, while the Tullumayo River with the small abodes lining its banks was the tail. As he watched, the sun began to bathe the entire city in light and the gold-thatched roofs of the temples and palaces sparkled in the sun.

Juan had hiked to the highest place above the city for a definite reason. If Aolani and the rest of her party were going to make an escape, there were many things he had to know. Being familiar with the city was one of them and trying to find the sacred *huaca* known as the Weeping Rock was another. The shrine was the spot where Luasi had started the climb that led to the hidden trail leading to Machu Picchu. On the day when the children made their escape, Luasi had emphasized to Juan the importance of recognizing different landmarks all the way up the mountain, for there was no marked trail. At last Luasi had pointed out the strange configuration in the rock that marked the spot where Juan should wait if he ever returned with the Lady Aolani. Luasi had told him that at the full moon each month someone would be there waiting to guide them to the hidden refuge.

It had been well over six months since he had left

Luasi, Nadua, and the children. It was hard to remember exactly where the Weeping Rock was, although Juan knew the approximate location. Luasi had told him that it was a shrine dedicated to Mother Kilya, the Moon. Women came to the shrine with their troubles. Perhaps if he waited and watched, some women from the city would show him the way. Otherwise it might take him hours to find the spot.

Juan could see the four great highways that converged in the center of Cuzco. Early as it was, he could see several travelers already on the Chinchaysuyu Road leading from Cuzco to the far north. On the Condesuyu Road leading west to the sea there was a lone priest making his way. A thin veil of fog hung over the far eastern slopes and the Antisuyu Road leading to the rain forests in the east was concealed in a lavender mist. Juan couldn't see the highway south because of the buildings.

Juan sat quietly watching the city come awake. At first the cobblestone streets were almost empty, save for two Indian women in colorful shawls who trotted with bare feet toward the Huatanay River for water. There were signs of activity in the great palaces as servants began the day's work. A group of soldiers emerged from Huascar's palace and walked down the square to the stone bridge and, crossing it, turned in the direction of *Coricancha*, The Temple of the Sun.

A woman emerged from Hwayna Capac's palace and Juan knew it must be Choque on her way to the market. He knew Moche had given her the last of the coca leaves he had left to trade for food last night. It was incredible to think that with all the gold, silver, and jewels in the palace they were unable to trade them for food. It was forbidden by law, for all these items belonged to the Lord High Inca and could not be bartered.

A movement on the other side of the Tullumayo River attracted his attention. Three women were walking along the east side of the river, which was extremely desolate, so he assumed they must be going to the shrine. Perhaps fortune was going to smile on him after all. Juan watched closely and saw the women veer toward a sharp fault on the mountain's face. Then they disappeared.

Jubilantly, Juan started down the hill, thinking about the river he would have to cross. As he remembered, the stream had been shallow enough then to walk across, although it had been up to his waist in some parts. He had carried Cusi in his arms and Luasi, who was shorter than he, had carried Manco on his shoulders. Nadua, in her usual forthright fashion, had made her way across the swirling water without a complaint or a call for help.

Today when he reached the river it appeared swifter and more turbulent than he remembered. Nevertheless, he started to wade through the water, but soon found he had to swim. It wasn't easy, but he made it. When Juan pulled himself up on the bank, he had to rest for a few moments. The cold air hit his body and even in the hot sun he shivered. He'd be warmer if he kept moving. He ran swiftly toward the spot where the women had disappeared, his sandals squishing as he ran. Following them, he turned quietly into the canyon and up ahead saw the shrine and breathed a sigh of relief. He skirted the *huaca* to avoid being seen by the women and made for the faint path above.

Sharply outlined against the sky, the jagged crests and enormous peaks of pale blue hung over him. Somewhere up there was the place he was looking for. After scrambling up the steep slopes for over four hours Juan stopped. He was tired and out of breath. The sun hovered high overhead. If he didn't find the landmark soon, Juan was not sure what he was going to do. He didn't want to attempt descending these precipitous slopes in the dark, nor did he want to give up, for he might have to hole up for the night. He decided he had to take a chance and keep climbing for a while.

Fortunately, just a few minutes later he rounded a formidable cliff and there it was, a notch or pass, shaped like half a circle, in the rocky wall above. As he started back down to the city, he fervently hoped there would be a guide waiting for them the night of the full moon. If not, the chances of keeping Aolani safe would be very slim, for Huascar would probably locate them and return them to Cuzco.

After listening all morning to the ranting and roaring of Huascar, who sounded like an angry lion in a cage, Aolani arrived back at Hwayna's palace in the late afternoon feeling hungry and tired. She was as weak and wobbly as a newborn llama as she and Choque made their way through the empty halls to her own chamber.

Moche, who had been anxiously waiting all day for her to arrive, asked, "How did it go, my dear?"

Aolani made a face. "Of all the swarthy, long-faced, graceless, and unpleasant men I have ever met, the new Inca takes the prize. By all the gods he is a despicable man."

"Why?" Sinchi asked. "What did he do?"

"Can you believe he left me sitting over four hours in the reception room?" Aolani said in an irritated tone of voice. "There was nothing except a bare stone floor to sit upon. No refreshments, no excuses, nothing. Is that not true, Choque?"

"Yes, my lady. All true," Choque said.

Sinchi laughed. "Come on, my dear aunt, many is the time my uncle, your husband, kept people waiting for days, not just hours."

314

Aolani sighed. "I have not been subjected to this kind of treatment, I suppose. I know I have been spoiled after being *Coya* for so many years. I have come to expect deference but I must become accustomed to my new status of being nothing but a useless widow. I have resolved to change and accept my new position, but it is hard. Sometimes I think I'll never adjust."

"You are not a useless widow, my dear, far from it," Moche said. "Tell us, what did Huascar want? Why did he send for you?"

Aolani sank down on her pillows. "Choque, bring me a drink of cold fruit juice." Looking at Moche, she shook her head. "To tell you the truth, Huascar screamed so much I found myself confused. However, I think he apologized because he couldn't find Cusi and Manco. Apparently he believed my story. When I arrived in Cuzco for the funeral, I told him that the children had been kidnapped by Atahualpa."

"His anger is understandable, my dear," Moche said smoothly. "According to the gossip, Huascar's army apparently got as far as Tomebamba, took Atahualpa prisoner, and subdued the city. Then Atahualpa escaped, rejoined his forces, and recaptured the city."

Aolani was so pleased that she smiled. "So that explains it. I thought he said something about Atahualpa being a snake who escaped through a hole, although I am not sure." She smiled again.

Moche went on. "If my information is correct, Atahualpa was captured in the midst of the battle that was going on in Tomebamba. The officer who captured him put him in a windowless hut with a guard in front. Atahualpa managed to find some sort of tool, dug himself out of the adobe hut, found his men, and returned to do battle, chasing Huascar all the way to Cajamarca." Then he added, "They say Huascar's army was all but destroyed and had to return to Cuzco."

315

Aolani could not help but be glad. "It serves him right." Then the serious aspects of the situation struck her. "He claims that he is going to raise an army of three hundred thousand men and return north to squash Atahualpa like a bug and kill his entire army. Do you think he will?"

Moche shrugged. "From all I have heard, Huascar is a strong but evil man whose dark power would destroy the empire and all who live here. He is like a rotten piece of fruit that contaminates all those close to him. His entourage abounds with those as cruel and corrupt as he is. Yes, he will certainly try to kill all opposition." He paused. "I worried about you all morning, my dear Aolani. Thank all the gods you are safe."

"Huascar is not through with me yet," she said soberly. "He wants me to remain in Cuzco and join him when he has raised his army. He expects me to go north with him to fight Atahualpa and get my children back."

A new voice entered the conversation. Juan stood at the doorway, filthy dirty, his tunic torn in several places, but a triumphant look on his face. "We shall see about that. We must escape, and we will. I've solved the first problem today. I know how to get to the meeting place. Tonight I'll go through the tunnels to be certain I know the way and to make sure they are safe."

"Good," Aolani said. "I'll go with you. I know how the door opens in my husband's bedchamber, the one that leads to the House of Concubines." She licked her lips with her tongue. "I am parched. Choque, where is my drink?"

Choque handed her a jeweled goblet. "It is only water, my lady. We have no fruit."

"We have no fruit?" Aolani looked amazed and puzzled. "Why not?" She wondered why they were all looking at each other in such a peculiar fashion. "What is the matter? What is wrong?"

Juan broke the silence. "It is a little embarrassing to explain to a queen, my lady, but the sad fact is that none of us has a thing we can barter for food and the merchants will give us no credit. Choque has barely been able to feed us on the few coca seeds Moche happened to have."

Aolani found what she was hearing hard to believe. For years, food of all the most exotic kinds had been available whenever the Inca and his family desired. Now it seemed there was no end to the number of changes she would have to make, she thought. But this situation couldn't continue. She could ask Huascar for help but she didn't want to. Suddenly she remembered there was a huge marketplace in Cuzco where every kind of food could be had for a price.

"What form of trade will the merchants accept in exchange for food?" Aolani asked.

Juan answered again. "They are interested in acquiring food or merchandise that is easy to carry and will not spoil. The most popular things are cacao beans, peanuts, seeds of maize, coca leaves, feathers, pieces of cloth, rugs—"

"I believe that I can solve this problem," Aolani said. "Feathers were one of my husband's weaknesses. He adored feather cloaks. He always kept sacks of them around. Choque, come with me." Aolani started for the door and then turned around. She wanted company when she entered Hwayna's chambers. "Why don't you all come? I can show you how to open the tunnel, Juan."

They followed her like a group of eaglets being led by a mother bird to another part of the palace, pausing beside a life-size puma carved in stone that guarded a door. It eyed them suspiciously with its jeweled eyes as they entered a musty, dark chamber that had obviously belonged to the Inca.

Aolani did not pause, but entered another large chamber that was as stuffy as the first one. A little light filtered in through the hides that covered the windows. The others followed Aolani into another room but it was even darker than the first two.

"Juan," Aolani said, "will you and Sinchi take the hides off the windows in that last room?"

While they waited, Aolani told them that this was one of the Inca's dressing rooms. It had no windows. Suddenly the room lightened and a cold breeze wafted through the room. They could see the chamber was filled with beautiful cloaks and headdresses. Along one side of the room were many large sacks, each marked with a different colored feather.

"Well," Aolani said, smiling. "I thought they might still be here. Take all you need, Choque. It might be a good idea to take some of these sacks with us when we make our escape. They are very light. Are there any servants left in the palace? I haven't seen any."

"There are two caretakers, my lady," Choque answered.

"Take them with you to carry these sacks." Aolani's eyes returned to her nephew. "Sinchi, I forgot to bring my herbs and we may need them. Take some feathers and buy what I need."

Moche interrupted. "That won't be necessary, Aolani. I can get all the herbs and things you need at the Temple of Viracocha. Besides, I think Sinchi should go through the tunnels with Juan. It would be safer in case anything happens to Juan. It is darker than a black devil's eyes down there. By the way, Sinchi, there are some torches in the cooking area. Perhaps you'd better come with me to check and see if they are usable. If not, we may have to buy some. Thank the gods, we have two days."

After Sinchi dashed away, followed by Moche and Choque, Aolani walked over to the large stone shelf that ran the length of one side of the room. "Some of my husband's most prized possessions," she said as she lightly touched them. Picking up a huge conch shell, Aolani held it up to her ear. "When Hwayna was a small boy, his father took him along when he went to inspect a great fleet of balsa-log rafts. It was the first time Hwayna had seen the vast ocean that extended far into the distance and he was enthralled by it. His father, later that day, gave him this shell, which he always treasured."

"What is this?" Juan asked, picking up the huge jawbone of an animal, the like of which Juan had never seen before.

"It is not the bone of any animal we know, so it is rare. One of Hwayna's exploring teams found it in a faraway country. My favorite object has always been this great green stone that seems to pulse with life." Aolani caressed it and then moved to the other side of the room, where she pulled aside a tapestry, and secured it to the wall.

Looking at the wall, Juan was as impressed as always by the way the boulders were cut and fitted into a perfect polygonal pattern, each stone interlocking closely with its neighbors. Aolani seemed to be looking for something. Juan moved closer and saw her hand run carefully over the surface and stop at the design of a small sun etched in the rock. As she pushed it, a dark aperture slowly widened in front of him until it was big enough for a man to step through. He saw that the door was not as large and heavy as the other stonework in the palace, but as thick as three fingers.

"By God!" he said. "It is a miracle. How does it work?"

"Look up at the lintel," Aolani said.

319

Following her advice, he saw a smooth, well-polished piece of green rock, which had been slightly rounded, then attached to the horizontal crossbar of the doorway. A similar stone appeared at the base, allowing the slab of stone to move smoothly over its surface. The faint light showed steps disappearing into the darkness below.

"Ingenious!" He moved to the aperture. "Let me take a look."

"You can look but you will not see much without a torch, just stairs going down into darkness. Wait for Sinchi to get back." She pushed the door shut. "Are we going down when he returns? It is getting rather late."

"It will take time for Choque to cook our meal. The more we do today the better. But, Aolani, please listen to me. I ask you not to go into the tunnels until we can inspect them."

"Why?"

"They could be dangerous. It is also possible that the Inca might send for you or that someone might come to see you. If you are here it would avert suspicion. Besides, Sinchi and I can more quickly accomplish our mission. Please, Aolani."

Aolani found it hard to resist his pleading voice and the concern in it. She also remembered that Huascar's wife had said she would call sometime. She doubted that meant tonight but she said, "All right, Juan. Perhaps this time you may be right, but if you are not back in a few hours, I am coming after you. Agreed?"

Juan took her hand in his and brought it to his lips, giving her an intense look from those burning dark blue eyes of his. She felt breathless as he said softly, "Agreed, Aolani."

Chapter Twenty-eight

The small group, led by Luasi, had been walking along the trail that led from the mountains above Cuzco to Machu Picchu for three-and-a-half days. Now they were nearing their destination. Juan had enjoyed every minute of the journey. Scrambling up the narrow canyons, skirting scarps of bedrock, traversing narrow rock paths along precipitous cliffs, falling and stumbling down steep talus slopes of loose and unbalanced rock had all been dangerous and hard, but exciting. A part of the paved path had run through steep forested hills where an occasional condor with wide-spread wings would soar gracefully above them. What a magnificent bird it was! There was nothing like it in Spain, Juan thought. He had been amused by the wild alpacas and llamas that glanced curiously at them as they passed by. White butterflies had fluttered over their heads.

Glancing at Aolani, who was smiling as she walked beside him, he could imagine what she must be feeling. In another hour or two she would see her children again. No wonder she had a sparkle in her eye and a flush on her cheek; she must be excited. A small stream crossed their path and he saw Aolani leap across it like a doe in flight. Juan took Choque's arm and helped her wade across. As they reached the other side, the long, wailing sound of a conch shell came from a distance, the eerie call sending a chill down his spine. Aolani started and came hurrying back to the group.

Luasi said abruptly, a look of concern on his face, "Someone approaches. Hide yourselves."

They all jumped off the path and found refuge behind trees. They waited silently, their eyes peering up and down the path. Oh God, Juan thought, they didn't need trouble now, not when they were so close. Suddenly, he heard a small scream and Aolani jumped onto the path and started rushing down it. Was she out of her mind? Juan started after her and then saw the figures. He heaved a sigh of relief. She must have recognized Manco and Cusi even from a distance. They came running toward her with Nadua puffing along in the rear.

Manco reached her first and flung himself into Aolani's arms. Juan could see that she was crying even as she smothered him with kisses. After a few moments she put him down and held out her arms to Cusi, who joyously threw herself into her mother's embrace.

Aolani drew back and looked with wonder at their faces. Through her tears she said, "Stand back, Cusi. Let me look at you. Oh, my dear child, how beautiful you are. You are almost grown-up."

Manco tugged at her arm. "Look at me, Mother. I've grown big, too."

Laying her hands caressingly on his cheeks, Aolani said, "So you have, my son, so you have. Just look at how you've grown. You are up to my shoulder."

"All right, children," Nadua's familiar voice broke in. "Let me greet your mother."

Both women put out their arms and hugged each other, and Nadua said happily, "My lady, it is so very good to see you. We, both Luasi and I, were terribly concerned when we heard that you were being held prisoner at Sauca Cachi. Thank all the gods, you have made it safely here." She looked around and found Luasi. "There you are, husband. How dare you sneak away to rescue my lady without taking me?"

Luasi came toward her smiling, holding out his arms. He held her close and kissed her. "And what possessed you, wife, to bring the children away from the refuge? Besides, you almost frightened me out of my skin when the sentinel announced there were other people on the path."

Juan watched the scene, relieved and happy that they were all together again. It felt good to know they had escaped Huascar. After resting for a while so that everyone could catch up on what had happened, Luasi insisted they proceed, for he was anxious to get his charges inside the citadel. The path at this point was wide enough for them to walk two abreast. Manco, Cusi, and Sinchi dashed on ahead with youthful exuberance. Moche and Luasi, talking earnestly together, followed close behind them, leaving Nadua and Choque walking at a slower pace.

Aolani had waited, hoping to talk to Juan. As they followed the rest of their group she said gratefully, "I wanted to thank you again, Juan. I doubt if we would have made it here if it had not been for you. It was because of your leadership that we escaped safely through the tunnels. I was deeply concerned when we came to that turbulent underground river.

How did you find that passage across the water?"

So she had noticed that. Juan was pleased. "I admit it wasn't easy. After that first night when Sinchi and I explored the tunnels, I was worried myself. I went back the next day, and in the semidarkness, I almost didn't find the rock protuberance. It was just luck. Once I did find it, I was able to roll a couple of boulders into the gap and the rest was easy."

"You say that, but I doubt if it was that easy. I don't know how you managed to move those huge rocks." From Juan's silence, she guessed that he didn't know either. "Then, too, you were the only one who knew the path up the hill."

"Thank the good lord, Luasi was waiting. I was anxious and frightened, wondering what I would do if there was no one there." Wanting to change the subject he said, "How Manco and Cusi have changed."

Aolani agreed. "Manco, despite his height, is still a child, but he is much more self-assured. Cusi has grown into a beautiful young girl, hasn't she?"

"She looks a lot like her mother but she is not as beautiful in my eyes. I know a young man who looked absolutely dazzled when he saw her."

"Sinchi," Aolani said. "I noticed his expression, also."

Juan asked curiously, "Is Cusi to wed one of her brothers?"

Aolani was silent for a few moments. "I don't know what the gods have in mind. It may be out of my hands, but I will do just about anything to keep her from having to marry Huascar or Atahualpa."

"What about Manco?"

"Please, Juan, enough of this subject. I am happy today for the first time in months. I am back with my children at last. I cannot and will not think of such problems at the moment."

With that statement, Aolani moved ahead of Juan and walked alone up the path and rounded a rock cliff. A small stone hut stood a short distance away. She walked over to it and stood looking at the spectacle before her. Aolani saw majestic snowcapped mountains rising above the clouds and splendid precipices of colored granite looming in the distance. Thinning mists touched the surrounding peaks of the city with shrouded hands. The gleaming silver thread of the Urubamba River, thousands of feet below them, broke the silence with the savage roar of its waters. Gazing down at the tiered city, Aolani was awed and overwhelmed by what she saw. So this was Machu Picchu, the city in the clouds.

Aolani felt Juan standing beside her. She moved closer to him, wanting to touch another human being. "Oh, Juan," she breathed, "it is awesome, magnificent. It is everything Hwayna told me it was."

Juan was awed, also. "I wonder how he built this mountain-locked citadel. It is the most spectacular city I have ever seen."

"Hwayna was not the only Inca responsible for this. His father started building this refuge in the sky after he had a terrible vision of brothers fighting brothers and strangers from another world destroying our empire. In his dream the rivers ran with blood, our cities were destroyed, and our people enslaved."

"Your husband believed in that vision as well. I hope it does not happen, but if it does, they certainly built a splendid refuge. Now, we had better follow the others or we might get lost," Juan said.

Aolani's heart was beating rapidly from excitement. The place was beautiful, her children were safe and well, and her dearest friends were with her. Manco insisted on taking her on a tour of the city. She was so busy just looking at him, rejoicing in his enthusiasm and delight in telling her about what he called his city, that she hardly listened to him at first. But then Aolani saw that he was very serious about what he was saying. She tried to concentrate on his words. Suddenly he stopped talking and looked at her.

He was waiting for her to comment. Aolani said tentatively, "This is the upper center of the city, you say, and I am staying in what is known as the House of Kings. By the way, even if it is somewhat small, the rooms are really quite nice. My chamber has water that comes through a channel, runs through my room, and empties into the garden. It makes a pleasant sound at night."

Manco's face showed his delight at her praise. "I chose that room for you myself, Mother. Did you see the garden? I know how you love a garden. Cusi planted many of the flowers."

"It is beautiful, but where is Cusi?" Aolani asked curiously. She had expected her daughter to be with them.

Shrugging his shoulders, Manco said, "I told her I wanted to show you around first." He waved his hand around the area. "We are standing in the largest square. There are three of them. This is the lowest one." He pointed with his finger. "Over there is the Stairway of Fountains. It drops in sixteen big steps and goes through the lower city, bringing fresh water to everyone by means of its cisterns."

"How remarkable," Aolani said with interest. "What is that round wall over there?"

"That is important, Mother," Manco said solemnly. He seemed almost condescending as he added, "It is a bastion that contains a sacred and holy shrine. There is a secret about it that only the high priest and myself know about. Perhaps someday I'll show you the secret if you promise to tell no one." He pulled her hands and demanded, "Come on, Mother. We are going to see my llama."

"In just a moment, Manco. I need to understand a bit more. Are your quarters in the same building that I am in?"

He looked surprised at her question. "No. See the white granite temple with the three windows in back of the shrine?" He pointed with his finger.

Aolani looked at the building he described and said, "I have never seen windows of that size and shape before. They are magnificent!"

"My room is there, Mother. I can see almost everything that goes on in the city from my windows," he said eagerly.

Aolani was puzzled by the temple's size. "It seems like a big place. Are you not lonely over there?"

Manco looked thoughtful. "No—no, not much." He paused. "Well, maybe sometimes. But I'm not alone. The high priest and my two *amautas* live there and I have three servants."

Aolani wondered about the situation. "Is not Cusi there with you?"

"No, Mother, Cusi lives in the House of Kings."

"Oh," Aolani said, "I am disappointed. I thought we would all be together as we were in Tomebamba."

"I am grown-up now, Mother, and besides I have a yard there for my llama. Come, let us go and see him."

After they left White Cloud they spent two hours going up and down flights of stairs and into buildings. Aolani called a halt. "That was a wonderful tour, Manco. I am proud you know so much about Machu Picchu. But if there is more to see, it will have to wait for another day. I am quite tired from our trip. How about continuing tomorrow?"

He looked at her, his face serious. "I don't think I can. I want to, but I have a lot of things to do. I am sorry, Mother."

Manco looked so concerned and worried that Aolani said gently, "It is all right, Manco. I understand."

But she didn't understand. Manco was not like himself. He seemed so much more serious than the joyous little boy she had known. Perhaps he had just grown older but she sensed there was more to it than that.

Going back to her own chambers Aolani decided to take a short nap before the evening meal. She had just begun to relax when she heard someone sit beside her. Opening her eyes she saw Cusi looking forlorn and lonely. Aolani sat up quickly and took Cusi in her arms, where she promptly burst into tears. Rocking her to and fro, Aolani waited for her daughter to calm down.

"Come now, my sweet girl. What is the matter? Why are you crying?"

Cusi pushed her hair back from her damp forehead. "Mother, I've been so lonely and miserable. I prayed that you would come back to us and make it like it used to be in Tomebamba. I hate it here, hate it, hate it." She hit her fist into the pillows.

Surprised at her daughter's outburst, Aolani said tenderly, "All right, Cusi, calm down. I can't help unless I know what is wrong, can I?"

Cusi began to quiet down a little. "I don't know how to tell you without sounding like a hateful, jealous little fool. I've tried to be understanding but it has been so hard," she said with a sob.

"What has been so hard?" Aolani asked. "What are you talking about?"

"Since we first arrived in Machu Picchu, everything has changed. Sometimes I feel I don't even like my own brother anymore, even though I know it is not really his fault."

"Please, Cusi, I am trying to follow you but I can't make sense out of what you are saying. What has Manco done?"

"It is hard having to give in to him all the time just because he is the true Lord High Inca. This is his city and everyone in it worships him. He can do no wrong. If he wants something he gets it. It is not good for him, Mother. Sometimes he behaves like a little beast."

Suddenly, Manco's attitudes and statements became more understandable. "I see," Aolani said.

"And, Mother, you know we always had the same *amautas* to teach us things and you know I loved to study. Now they say—" Cusi broke into sobs again.

Aolani's heart went out to her. She knew what they must be doing to Cusi. Not many Incas were like her husband, Hwayna Capac. "Stop crying, Cusi. Crying will not help. Are they saying you are only a girl?" Cusi nodded. "And that you must learn womanly skills?" Her daughter nodded again. "And I suppose you spend your days weaving, embroidering, and working with the women. Am I right?"

"Yes, Mother, and I hate it."

Hugging her daughter to her, Aolani knew how hard it must be on this intelligent child, who loved learning. "Cusi, listen to me. Things will change. I promise you they will change."

That evening after dinner, Aolani asked Juan if he would like to walk and see the city by moonlight. She was happy to see him jump up with alacrity, eager to go with her. They walked up to the watchman's hut where they had stopped yesterday. They moved away from it and stood gazing at the glimmering buildings, terraced fields, and silver-crested peaks in the light of the moon.

Aolani broke the silence as an animal howled in the distance. "See the shadows on the moon. There is an old story that tells how Mother Kilya received her blemishes. There once was a wolf who fell madly in love with the great shining orb and whenever there was a full moon he would howl out his love for this lovely bubble in the night sky. Mother Kilya, the Moon, took pity on him and brought the wolf up to her bosom. In his excitement at being with her, the wolf bruised and scratched her, so the moon, in anger, threw him back down to earth, for he had ruined her beautiful face. But still, always faithful, the wolf howls of his love at night, especially at full moon."

The lonely silence of the mountain and the immense feeling of isolation brought Juan close to her, his fingers gently touching her face. When she didn't turn away, Juan brought his lips down to hers. He kissed her gently at first and then with keen delight as she responded to him. With his passion mounting, he felt her soul touch his and in silent ecstasy he felt she loved him at last.

Then he felt her push him away and he felt like howling to the moon. He tried to draw her back to him but she would have none of it.

"Please, Juan, don't rush me. Perhaps in time but not yet. I loved once and I followed my husband gladly. I experienced great joy and great pain. I feel something for you, Senerhuana, but I don't know whether it is love or lust. Please, my dear friend, don't push me."

Juan felt bereft as he said, "I understand, or at least I think I do."

"I need your help, Juan."

"What do you want of me?"

Aolani quickly explained about Cusi and Manco and what was happening to them. "I must help Cusi, Juan. I really must." Her eyes were gleaming like jewels in the moonlight. "Will you teach her about your world? I think it will interest her. I intend to teach her about herbs, medicine, and other things. I must get her out of this so-called woman's world they want to keep her in. She is a bright, intelligent girl."

"When do I start?"

"The day after tomorrow. I will arrange it. Keep up her Spanish, also. In the meantime I must do something about Manco before they mold him into an arrogant little monster who thinks he can do no wrong. Juan, tell me, do you think the people who work in the fields and labor in the city need my help as a healer?"

"I am sure they do," he said tenderly. "I have yet to see any sign that they are receiving any medical help. They rely on the little knowledge some of the older women have picked up. I will look into it further and try to find a place for you in which to work. Do you wish that?"

"I would be grateful to you," she said simply.

Chapter Twenty-nine

While Juan waited impatiently for young Manco at the watchman's hut, he looked over the landscape with a disillusioned eye. It was beautiful, but a prison. He noticed for the first time how the river below circled the city like a moat, reminding him of the castles of Spain. It made him feel homesick. Sometimes he longed to see his family and the small village where he had been born. Despite his beautiful surroundings and the indisputable fact that he enjoyed his life here most of the time, he had been feeling more and more depressed of late. Aolani seemed to have moved out of his reach. Three years in this remote area seeing a woman every day, a woman whose very presence absorbed all his waking thoughts, and there was still no response from her. He was a friend, nothing more. He was no closer to her than he'd been in Tomebamba when her husband was alive.

Aolani had been quite pleasant with him during their stay at Sauca Cachi, and later when he had helped her escape from Cuzco she had been grateful, even affectionate. Then she had changed. She didn't seem to want to be in the same room with him anymore. Sometimes he thought he was wasting his time in this country. The Spaniards were arriving by the hundreds, disembarking in Tumbes. It should be possible to get a ship out of there for Spain. If he lost Aolani, there would be nothing here for him. But then he remembered his promise to Hwayna Capac. He should make sure Aolani would be safe before he left.

His thoughts were interrupted by the sound of footsteps approaching. Smiling, a triumphant expression upon his face, Manco flopped down beside him on the grass. "I am sorry to be so late, Juan, but the high priest stopped me and ordered me to stay in the temple."

Juan had become very fond of Manco, almost thinking of him as a son. He was becoming aware of the problems Manco would face as the Inca's legitimate heir, not only with his brothers, but with the Spaniards, too. When Luasi had first told Juan that Manco was his father's heir, he had worried about the young boy, wondering what was going to become of him. Manco was already the most important person in this small community, deferred to by the nobles and worshiped as a god by all. The people here considered him the Lord High Inca already and Juan didn't think it was good for Manco.

Manco could, and sometimes did, take advantage of his position, quite shamelessly if he wanted something. But on the other hand, he had generosity, consideration, and kindness, which were admirable qualities. Manco was really a remarkable young boy, tall, handsome, quite strong for his age and very intelligent, like his father in appearance and character. Juan could see that Manco was still looking

Jeanne Nickson

quite pleased with himself. How did Manco get away from Villac Umu, the only man who still treated him like a little boy? The high priest was an overbearing and intimidating man, accustomed to being obeyed by everyone.

"Well," Juan said, "you look as pleased as a monkey with a banana. Tell me how you dealt with Villac."

Manco looked at him, a serious expression on his face. "As you know, Juan, I am almost twelve. I am the Son of the Sun and I've been told that I'm a god on earth." He made a face. "That man treats me like a baby. I have resented it for a long time, even though I know he is loyal and means well. I was really angry and said, 'Enough, Villac. Do not order me about again. I will do what the gods tell me to do and you will accept my commands.' Then I turned and walked out."

Juan was astounded. "You are right, Manco. That really did take courage on your part. But I must warn you that, although you are not a child, you are still not a man. Listen to the advice of those older and wiser than you."

Juan sucked thoughtfully on a blade of grass. "Don't be too anxious to leave your childhood behind. Someday you'll wish you were a child again. I know I often do."

"Why, Juan?"

"I don't know. Life gets to be too much for you, too complex—like a maze that you can't escape. Then you remember the times of your youth with affection. Everything seemed so simple then and others solved your problems for you."

"You seem sad, Senor Juan. I don't like to see you like this." Manco looked worried. "Usually, you are so happy and cheerful. Are you sure there is nothing I can do?"

"Thank you, Manco, for your concern but this mood will pass. I'll be all right." Juan could see Manco was not convinced.

The young man said hesitantly, "Forgive me, Juan, but—but sometimes a man needs a woman. Could that be your problem?"

Despite his unhappy mood, Juan felt slightly amused. Manco was absolutely right. He did need a woman, but not just any woman. He needed Aolani, the boy's mother. How would Manco feel if he knew that? Juan stood up and changed the subject. "All right, Manco, let's get on with the training."

As Manco got up he said nonchalantly, "Just a minute, Juan. I want to say something. Just in case you ever need a woman's comfort, feel free to ask me. I have many girls. I can't use them all. I would gladly give you one."

Juan was surprised and touched by Manco's words, but not shocked. He knew that the young Incas were introduced to women at an early age. Even here on Machu Picchu there was a House of Chosen Women. Was Manco already involved with them?

By Manco's knowledgeable looks, Juan guessed that he was. Looking at the sun, Juan saw that it was getting late. It was high time they got on with the exercise program.

"Manco, thank you. Now enough of this for a while. Let's work out. We'll run the course first, carrying and throwing stones. Find four pebbles twice the size of duck eggs. I've set the targets in place. See if you can win this time."

After a good two hours of physical exertion they both fell limply on the grass. Juan said, "Your running has improved. You are very proficient with the mace but you are still not slinging your stones with enough power. You must develop your arm muscles. I suspect you are not doing your push-ups, or at least not as many as you should. Come on. There is no time like the present. Let's see how many you can do."

With a groan Manco obeyed.

Covering up her emotions and keeping them deeply hidden had been difficult for Aolani during the past few years. Many times she had wished it were possible to let down her defenses and just admit she wanted Juan and live with him. If it had been feasible she would have done so, but in a small community such as this one, it would have been impossible to keep a love affair a secret. She was aware that she would have been considered nothing but a harlot in the eyes of the high priest, the nobles, and even members of her family. Perhaps some women could live with that, but she could not.

But marriage was another matter. This, too, presented many problems. Realistically, in the eyes of the nobles Juan was a captive slave. A marriage to him would create a scandal that would have harmed all those around her. Aolani doubted that any priest would even perform the marriage ceremony.

So Aolani had done the only thing possible: avoided Juan as much as she could and kept herself busy with her work, knowing she was hurting him. But she was getting older and her only hope of resolving her problem was the death of Huascar. Then she could approach Atahualpa. He would be Inca for a short time. He had the army and few knew about Manco yet. If she could reach Atahualpa, beg him to free Juan and make him an Inca by privilege, a marriage might be possible. That is, if Juan still wanted her. It was worth a try if all she thought came to pass but she would have to talk to Juan alone sometime soon. Suddenly, she remembered she must remind Manco of

Cusi's birthday dinner tonight.

Knowing that her son worked with Juan late this afternoon up by the watchman's hut, she made her way to the grassy top of Machu Picchu. She saw that Juan and her son had just finished some exercise and were sitting with their backs toward her. Aolani wondered where Manco's bodyguards were and discovered them standing a short distance away, in the shade of the cliff. She moved quietly across the grass and stood listening to Manco a moment.

"Senor Juan," Manco was saying, "in our last Spanish discussion, we were talking about the Spaniards and their conquest of our neighbors to the north. Some questions occurred to me later. How is it that your countrymen can come into a new land and conquer the many savage tribes so easily? Even my father had great problems with the Canari and he had a very large army."

"Weapons for one thing," Juan answered. "Their guns and cannons are not only frightening, but powerful, shooting sparks and raining fire. Their trappings protect them, for they are made of metal and cover their bodies so that spears and arrows do not penetrate their armor. All the men do not have horses, but those who do have them are even more powerful, for they are able to move faster and protect the foot soldiers." Juan paused. "However, more important than weapons are the tactics they use."

Manco looked puzzled. "I don't understand the word tactics."

Juan rubbed his chin. "I'll give you an example. Their first goal is to kill the local chief or ruler. This tactic leaves the people without a leader and they are as confused as birds in a windstorm. Then the Spaniards appoint a chief or king who will obey them. They call this leader a puppet ruler. They can control him. I think this tactic was used in a different sort of way by your father, Hwayna Capac, was it not?"

"True," Manco said. "You know many things, Juan. I think I will need your advice if I become Inca. Perhaps you would like to be a lord of my realm."

Juan was not listening. He had turned around, sensing someone behind him, and discovered the graceful figure of Aolani. He felt a shock of excitement. "Your mother is here, Your Highness."

"That means I am a prince, doesn't it? When I become ruler you will address me as Majesty and you'll be an embassy."

Juan couldn't help laughing but stopped when Prince Manco, his eyes flashing, his gold earrings sparkling in the sun, asked, "Are you laughing at me?"

"No, of course he is not," Aolani said. "It is just that Juan couldn't be an embassy. That is a word for a building." Manco began to laugh, too. "The word you need is ambassador."

"Thank you, Mother. Why are you here?"

"My son, I have seldom seen you lately. You have not been with us for an evening meal for a long time and I've missed your company. I knew you would be here with Juan and so I came to remind you that it is Cusi's birthday today and Nadua has made a special meal including your favorite honey cakes."

Manco noticed that Juan couldn't keep his eyes off his mother. Suddenly, he knew what was wrong with Juan. He was in love with her. Manco had never thought of it before, but now that he'd had some experience with women, he was aware of what was going on. He could feel the tenseness between them. There was something there. Perhaps they needed a little help.

Manco thought quickly. He knew Juan was going hunting tomorrow.

"Mother, you are looking pale. You are working too hard with the Indians. I think you should take a holiday and get a little sun. Juan, why don't you take my mother hunting tomorrow?"

Juan immediately said, "I would be honored to have you come along, Lady Aolani."

"I would like that," she said taking Manco's arm. "Now, my son, how about walking down the hill with me?"

A heavy mist had blanketed Machu Picchu, muting its usual noise and covering its narrow streets and steep staircases with a thick gray mantle that disguised and changed the appearance of familiar landmarks. As Juan moved slowly up the eerie silent stairs, which he hoped led to the House of Kings, he wondered if anyone else was out on an evening like this. While he'd been helping the old priest he'd been so preoccupied with thoughts of Aolani and tomorrow's hunt he had not realized the mist was coming in thicker than usual. By the time he put his work down and reached the upper town, the mist was so thick he could barely see his hand in front of his face.

The welcome odor of roasting venison assailed his nostrils and he suspected he must be approaching his dwelling place, for he had shot a deer yesterday and left it with Nadua last evening. It smelled good and he knew he was hungrier than usual after that session with the young prince. Using his hands to guide him, he felt a curving wall and knew he was at the shrine, the only curved wall in Machu Picchu. Turning to his left, he moved tentatively across what he hoped was the great square. Juan felt as if he was traveling through a thin pale soup, for he could neither see nor feel anything around him. He followed his nose and the succulent odor made his mouth water. Keeping one arm extended in front of him, he felt a sense of relief when he saw the subdued glow of a fire ahead of him.

Then Juan heard indistinguishable voices, but as he grew nearer he recognized them. Moche, Sinchi, and Luasi were discussing the dangerous situation that existed in the empire. They were arguing as usual about the events that had precipitated the war between Huascar and Atahualpa. Juan stopped at the open doorway, out of breath, not quite ready to go in.

"It is too bad," Moche said, "that Huascar's advisers told him to order Atahualpa to present himself in Cuzco immediately after he first assumed the royal fringe. If the Lord High Inca, Huascar, had left well enough alone and consolidated his already strong position, and appointed Atahualpa the Governor of Quito, this war would never have started. Besides, at that time, Prince Atahualpa was only seventeen. Knowing him, I think he would have been satisfied with governing Quito for that is what his father promised him."

"You are right, Uncle," Sinchi exclaimed, "but I'll tell you where that fool, Huascar, made his second big mistake. Returning Atahualpa's emissaries of peace, mutilated and dressed as women, was a big error. My cousin is young but an insult like that would make him fighting mad and also stir up the anger of his armies. The warriors were never loyal to Huascar anyhow. No wonder the officers proclaimed Atahualpa King of Quito."

Luasi said thoughtfully, "But you can understand that action placed Huascar in an impossible position. He could not allow such defiance. It is against Inca law. He had to raise another army and defeat his brother or he would have lost the respect and support of the people. Well, we know Huascar has reached Tomebamba according to our last report but I wonder what has happened. I hope we get some information soon."

"I would be willing to bet on Atahualpa's armies defeating Huascar," Sinchi announced.

"Why?" Juan asked, coming out of the shadows where he had been standing. "Atahualpa is very young and inexperienced."

"Greetings, Juan," Sinchi said. "I admit Atahualpa is young but he is ferocious and has the greatest army and the most experienced generals. You can't beat Quis-quis and Chalcuchima."

"Perhaps you may be right, but I don't think that will be the end of it," Juan answered.

Nadua came into the room. "My lords, it is almost time to break your fast, and thanks to Juan, we will have venison. Believe me, you can't solve the empire's problems tonight. Besides, this is a birth celebration and we must do our best to make this a festive affair for Princess Cusi Hwaylas. This is a special birthday for she is eighteen, a woman today. Moche, where is your pipe? Luasi, go get your drum. Juan, you need to clean up. Go quickly. Prince Manco will be here at any moment." With her orders given, she bustled back to the cooking area.

Juan excused himself and went quickly to his room to wash up. Wiping himself with a cotton cloth, Juan put on a clean tunic and went out to join the others. As usual, he glanced around, but noticed Aolani had not arrived. Sometimes he thought he must be mad to love a woman who was so indifferent to him. He wondered why she was so late. He was hungry.

Unknown to Juan, Aolani was busy adorning herself. In her bedchamber, the second largest room in the House of Kings, she tried to see herself in a small mirror but doing so was almost impossible, for it was too dark. A twisted tow, dipped in a black substance, and giving off a wavering light, was attached to a sconce in the wall. She missed the bright torches that had been available in Tomebamba. She pulled the comb through her hair after putting on a warm, long-sleeved tunic of soft white vicuna wool. She fastened a necklace of emeralds around her neck and placed a cap of green feathers on her head, knowing that they curled provocatively around her face.

Why was she going to so much trouble? Aolani asked herself, but in her heart she knew why. She enjoyed dressing up and looking her best when Juan was around. There was no point in fooling herself. She was attracted to him. However, Aolani was having second thoughts about going hunting with him tomorrow. Could she trust herself?

Aolani asked herself another question. Why was she always in such a quandary about Juan? Perhaps it was the whole desperate impossible situation in which she found herself. She had many self-doubts in the first place; perhaps they were foolish, but they were there. How could she possibly be happy married to an outcast who had no position in this world? She was used to the best and Juan had nothing. And then there were Manco and Cusi. How would they be affected by such a marriage? But her deepest fear was the belief that she could never really love again, that what she felt for Juan was just lust, a physical need for a man.

Linked with these problems, however, was this strange sense of excitement whenever she was around Juan, a desire to be with him that overshadowed even her desire to be with her children. A touch of his hand would send messages to all parts of her body, which would respond in a way she could not control. Perhaps it really was love. There was no reason why she couldn't love more than one man. So she had come to a decision. They were both unhappy, but why should it remain that way? She would have to risk taking Juan as a lover, and by the earth-mother's devils, let other people think what they wanted.

The fast-beating throb of Luasi's drum accompanied by the melancholy notes of the pipes played by Moche provided background music for Aolani's song. The poignant story of a lovesick queen's love for a shepherd boy was popular with the Incas but it sounded a little foolish to Juan, besides reminding him of his own unrequited love. He tuned out the music and looked at the people with whom he had lived for the past three years, all of them in the same house, except for Manco.

It had been a good evening, a night of friendship, good food, sparkling conversation, plenty of wine, and lots of laughter. He felt very close to them all, especially Moche, who had been his first real friend. He was such a good and gentle man, wise beyond his years. Moche had always been exceptionally kind to him, but then he was affectionate with everyone. As Aolani said, there were no demons eating at his soul.

Juan's trip with Sinchi had brought him close to the young man. He thought of him as a younger brother, full of fun and a wonderful sense of humor. He knew Sinchi was in love with Cusi Hwaylas and suspected the young princess was in love with him. Sinchi's love probably didn't stand any more chance than his own, Juan thought morosely. Sinchi had spent months collecting all those beautiful feathers he had given to Cusi as a birthday gift and risked his life for them but Juan doubted if Cusi even realized the effort Sinchi had made to please her.

When the song was over, Juan watched Prince Manco make his excuses, first taking leave of his mother, and then kissing his sister, who threw her arms about her brother's neck. Cusi had been delighted with the beautiful pearls and gold bracelets Manco had given her. Juan wondered where the boy had found them. Perhaps there was truth to the rumor that there was a hidden treasure buried somewhere on this mountain. As Manco came past him and said good night, he winked at Juan. The young devil! He must be on his way to his women. For a moment, Juan felt a stab of jealousy, but then had to smile. He wasn't envious of Manco's youth. He wanted only one woman and that was Aolani.

With Manco's departure the party seemed to be over. Cusi came across the room and Juan stood up as she kissed him with affection and thanked him for the carved jewelry box he had made her. Then she went to Moche, who was standing next to Juan, and thanked him for the set of pipes. Moche left with her, offering to carry her things back to her room.

Juan poured himself some more wine and sat down again as Nadua and Luasi left, followed by Sinchi. A storm must be brewing. Juan dimly heard a crack of thunder and the screaming of the wind. He was glad there was a wooden door on the entrance to the House of Kings or drafts of air would be sweeping through the large room. It was cold enough in here as it was.

Shivering, Aolani drew her wool cloak around her and walked closer to the brazier. The hide on the windows moved with each gust of wind, even though it was pulled tight and fastened. The gale howled like an angry god outside.

"As wild and unreasoning as the wind is tonight, perhaps it will blow away the mist and I'll be able to go with you tomorrow," Aolani said.

"You are shivering. Should I put some fuel on the fire?" Juan asked.

"I don't think so," Aolani said wearily, "for I intend to retire before long. I want to talk to you tonight, so

344

come sit beside me for a few minutes and keep me warm."

"Just exactly what do you want me to do to keep you warm?" Juan asked her with a twinkle in his eyes. "I am prepared for anything."

Looking into the hot coals, Aolani said softly, "Just hold me, Juan. I am cold in body and spirit tonight and crave human warmth."

Lying down against the pillows, Juan put out his arms and pulled Aolani gently down beside him. He held her close and wrapped his body about her shivering form. "What is it, Lani love? Tell me what is wrong."

Sighing deeply, Aolani said, "It's everything! The empire is groping like a blind man in the midst of a catastrophe, frightened, uncertain of where it is going. I don't know what I am or where I am going anymore. I see nothing but sorrow and unhappiness in front of me. I am lonely and tired of fending for myself."

"My poor beautiful love, you are not alone." Juan lightly kissed her forehead. "You will always have me, the children, and your friends."

"But can't you see, Juan? We are living in a dreamworld up here. It is unreal and everything on the outside is in chaos. I like you, maybe I even love you, but I don't know. What could we do in the real world? How could we live? You have nothing. At the moment, I have nothing—no home, no possessions, no nothing."

Juan heard the despair in her voice and he couldn't help but agree with her. What future could he hope to have with her, even if she loved him? What future could he have in the empire if Atahualpa became Inca? None! Her son would never consent to such a marriage. And if—no, when—his countrymen came, what then? Holding Aolani close, so that her body nestled up to his, Juan wanted to make her feel that he was invincible but he could not. He had as many fears as she did, perhaps more, but he wasn't going to let her know. The day was coming soon when they would have to leave this mountaintop. It seemed like a prison after nearly three years.

Finally Juan said, "If Atahualpa becomes Inca, perhaps you should plan on talking to him. After all, he is your son. Maybe he would give you Sauca Cachi. You were happy there, were you not?"

Aolani was quiet before she said softly, "Juan, I've been thinking of that same thing and if Atahualpa becomes Lord High Inca I think I will go see him. Will you go with me?"

"Wherever you go, I go. I promised Hwayna Capac I would protect you. But think about it, love. There could be problems, especially for the children."

He held her for a while and she made no sound. He didn't care. It was just such a joy to be close to her. Finally he looked down at her face. It was calm and peaceful even though there was a trace of tears on her cheeks. She was sound asleep. He pulled another fur over them and soon he, too, fell asleep.

Chapter Thirty

The next morning as the sun began to rise above the cloud-capped pinnacles, Aolani followed Juan past the watchman's hut onto the path that had first brought them to Machu Picchu. Aolani, deep in her own thoughts, paid no attention to nature's spectacle before her. She was thinking about the cataclysmic changes that had disrupted her life since Hwayna's death. Just as she'd told Juan last night, she had no home, no roots, no stability in her life; even her children were pawns of fate. Aolani felt as if she was in the midst of a perilous sea, prey to unknown dangers, buffeted by the winds of change. There was no security that she could see either now or in the future with Huascar, the Lord High Inca. If Atahualpa won the war and became ruler, perhaps he might help her. He might give her one of Hwayna Capac's many palaces, for according to Inca law, her son could not inherit his father's personal wealth but he could distribute it as he liked.

In thinking about her past, Aolani knew that she

should have been wiser and planned for the future better. Perhaps she should have asked Hwayna for a palace of her own, for land, for servants and valuable objects, but she hadn't even thought of a life without him. She had never considered herself as being just the Inca's *Coya*, of importance only because of him. As long as Hwayna was alive she had felt wanted and needed. Aolani felt that in the past she had led a useful life, but now she felt powerless. She had become an older woman without a place in life. Of course she had her children, but she was too weak to help them. It was depressing.

And then, what a stupid and mindless idiot she had been about losing her own country. Without Hwayna, her position as Queen of Chachapoya was not recognized, nor would it be supported. Neither Huascar or Atahualpa would ever let her claim her country, for it was too valuable, with its gold and silver mines, emeralds, and its fine weavers who made some of the best cloth in the empire.

To Aolani, the whole situation was intolerable. It made her angry at fate, angry at herself, and even angry with the friends who tried to help her, especially Juan. He'd said he loved her so many times that she had lost count, but he didn't seem to understand the problems that must be overcome. The approval of the Inca must be won immediately.

Juan was important to her. He was kind and good. He loved and helped her children. He was always there whenever she needed him. He showed daily concern for her welfare and constantly showed by his actions that he found her desirable, and she needed that reassurance. Above all she wanted him as much as he wanted her. Yes, she decided, she would go along with last night's plan and encourage him to make love to her today.

Knowing she had been silent for a long time, she finally spoke. "Where are we going?"

"Do you remember that small stream that we passed just before your children met us the day we came?"

Aolani nodded.

"There is some lovely country around there," he said. "It is a good place to hunt, for wildlife abounds in the lower valleys."

Aolani glanced around her. It was good to get away from Machu Picchu. The morning smelled fresh and fragrant. In the distance, a shore of clouds, underlit by the rising sun, were turning beautiful shades of orange and pink. She heard the sound of ducks quacking overhead and watched them fly through the sky. Along the path were many unusual plant forms: clusters of creamy white flowers; large clumps of bear grass; wild quinua, its red heavily seeded stalks bright against the rock; soft green strands of a plant she did not know; and yellow daisies in the hollows. The air was fresh and crisp but it was rather cold this early in the day. Aolani knew from experience the hot sun would soon smile on them and banish the chill. Then she would be complaining about the heat.

They seemed to get to the stream in no time. Juan turned off the path and moved downward along its banks. The foaming water tore its way through granite cliffs. Soon they entered a narrow valley, where the cold wind did not blow so hard and the stream moved slower. In the sheltered area the sun began to feel too hot on Aolani's back and she could feel the perspiration breaking out on her face. Just as she had expected, she felt like complaining. Suddenly, Juan stopped so quickly that Aolani almost bumped into him. She saw him scan the area below.

"There do not seem to be any animals at the pool. They are apt to come here when they are thirsty," he said. He pulled her up beside him.

They were standing above a turbulent waterfall, looking down at a forest pool that gleamed like an emerald in the dappled light of the overhanging trees. It was good to see trees again; Aolani couldn't see trees in Machu Picchu, which was above the timberline. It gave Aolani pleasure to see a large number of them growing in this small valley. There were a few she didn't recognize but the immensely trunked ceiba growing near the water's edge was a splendid sight. It stood like a king amid the thornbushes, briars, and small thickets.

She clutched Juan and pointed. "Look, there is a molle tree. We must get some twigs for cleaning our teeth before we head for home."

Juan smiled at her enthusiasm. "Come on, follow me down." He had been concerned about Aolani earlier this morning. She had seemed downcast and depressed. Juan was delighted that she seemed to be in a better mood.

Slowly she made her way down, jumping from rock to rock until she stood on a boulder directly behind Juan. He put out his arms and swung her down beside him as he said, "It is getting hot. We will stop by the pool to cool off."

When he reached a shady area under the ceiba tree, Juan took off the pack he had been carrying and threw it on the ground. Then he removed the studded mace that hung on a short rope from his belt and placed it beside the pack, keeping his knife in his belt. After withdrawing a rug from the bundle, he unrolled it and placed in on the grass beside the pool.

Aolani sat down. "Why don't we go swimming? It has been ages since I've had a chance to immerse myself in water." She looked longingly at the pool and then impetuously slipped off her leather moccasins and leggings and wiggled one shapely foot.

Juan watched in amazement as she suddenly took off her tunic and stood up. He stared. It was incredible that she was doing this. Her beautiful, smooth skin gleamed like a golden pearl. Her shining dark gold hair hung in waves over her breasts. As she turned toward the water, the hair floating down her back touched her rounded buttocks, and Juan noticed her legs were as long and shapely as he had suspected. He couldn't believe this was happening. He had dreamed of this moment for years.

She jumped in and splashed him. "Come on in, Juan. It is cold but it feels wonderful."

As she swam across the pool, he tore off his belt, and his knife dropped to the ground. He couldn't pull his clothes off fast enough. After kicking off his sandals, he headed for the water. Seeing that Aolani was already on the far side of the pool, he hesitated, wondering if he should join her. Suddenly he felt uneasy. He looked around and as he did so he saw the reflection of a huge cat in the water staring down at him with fierce eyes. Shocked, he saw the tawny orange-and-black cat and heard a growl. Juan dove into the pool and swam toward Aolani. A jaguar, he thought. Jaguars loved water and could swim. What was he going to do?

Seeing Aolani ahead of him he grabbed her by the legs. "By all the devils of Hopi-Nuni, take your hands off of me, Juan." Her angry eyes glared at him.

He was so cold his teeth chattered. He was also frightened. "Lani, there is a jaguar in the tree over there and all our weapons and clothes are under him."

"Don't call me Lani," she protested. Then his words made an impression on her. "What did you say?"

Juan pointed and her eyes followed his finger. "Look at the tree over there where your clothes are. Now take your eyes up to the first limb and follow it out to the water."

Aolani took a look and clutched him. "Oh, my! Let's get out of here."

"We can't go out the way we came in, and if we get out on this side of the lake, that jaguar could make it over here in two leaps. I think we had better try to ascend the waterfall until we can decide what to do."

The rocks were slippery and the water was strong as it poured over them. Their wet bodies touched constantly as they moved upward. At last they were standing on a large boulder that overlooked the small lake. Water was falling on either side of them. It was hot and sunny on the rock. It felt good, for they were blue with cold.

"Is it still there?" Aolani whispered.

"Yes, I wonder how long it's going to stay there."

"Don't you think the cat would have attacked us before now if it were hungry?" Aolani asked anxiously.

Juan didn't have the heart to reply. The jaguar might be full now, but how long would it be before the animal became hungry?

The boulder was slippery and narrow. Juan was holding her close to him so she wouldn't fall, and her breasts kept brushing against his body every time she turned toward him to say something. He couldn't keep his eyes off them, even in this predicament. He could feel a stirring in his groin.

"It feels warm and pleasant here on this rock," Aolani said, "but we have to do something." Suddenly she clutched Juan. "I think I'm slipping."

Juan pulled her back, drawing her close to him. "Move over. You've got room on your side. I can't think with you so near me, Lani."

"Don't call me—"

"Lani," Juan said. "All right, but move over."

As she made more room for him, Juan stood up to get a better look at the tree. The tawny animal was still there, but it looked as if it might be sleeping. A jaguar was rare in these parts. Juan had not seen one in all the time he'd been there. But it was just his luck to find this rare specimen and to have brought Aolani into this dangerous situation.

They couldn't stay here much longer. The cat would soon get hungry, and with its sense of smell, it would know exactly where it could get a delicious dinner. They were not safe here and they certainly couldn't stay until nightfall. They would freeze to death. Juan had to do something. He looked at the falls on his side of the boulder and tried to peer as well as feel his way through the water, but it came down with such a powerful force that Juan felt it must be the main channel. It would be less forceful on Aolani's side.

"Lani," he said in a low voice, "step in front of me. I'll hold on to you. I want to change places with you."

"What did you say?" she shouted.

He explained again in a louder voice and she complied. He put his hand under the foaming water. He was right. It was not as forceful on the other side. If he could make his way out on this side, he would try to circle around and get his weapons. It would be dangerous but he had to make the attempt. It was ridiculous to sit here naked, just waiting for that cat to pounce. Juan turned to Aolani and explained what he was going to do.

Aolani looked at him with deep concern. "Isn't that terribly dangerous, Juan? The animal is downwind from us. He will be alert to your approach and this valley doesn't seem wide enough for you to circle around him without his detecting you. Have you considered any other possibilities?"

"Of course I have," Juan said indignantly. "Retreating back up the trail is out of the question. We lack clothes and weapons and that animal would surely come after us. We'd be extremely vulnerable on that narrow path."

"How about fire?" she asked. "Animals are afraid of fire."

"True, but how are we going to light one?" he asked with exasperation.

"Well, perhaps, if we just stay here, it'll go away."

"Why should it? Its dinner is right in front of it. It can swim across the pond and join us before you'd know it. After all, it is a climber as well as a swimmer. Believe me!" Juan put a hand to his head. "Even if it didn't attack us, we'd freeze tonight if we stayed here."

"I think I know a way to escape," Aolani said thoughtfully. "Can jaguars swim under the water?"

"I don't know," Juan said in a puzzled voice. What was she getting at?

Aolani went on. "If we swam underwater, there would be no body odor to betray us below the surface. Is that not true?"

Juan looked at her in surprise. He hadn't thought of that possibility. If he swam underwater until he was past the ceiba tree and emerged on the other side, he might stand a good chance.

As he examined her idea Aolani watched him intently. He had a very expressive face. For a moment he had eyed her with hope but now he was looking doubtful. "What's wrong?" she asked.

"I'm not that good at swimming underwater."

"Well, I am," she said confidently.

"Oh, no!" Juan exclaimed. "It's too risky."

"Nonsense, you were willing to take an even bigger risk than this. Now listen to me. When I am safely on the other side and start approaching our site, I will try to signal or let you see me. I want you to make a loud noise and throw rocks at the jaguar." She looked over at the ceiba tree and saw the animal. The big cat was awake, crouching low on the branch, as if it was about to leap, it tail twitching. She said, "Juan, look."

"Holy Mary, Mother of God, it is a miracle."

A deer stood alert at the water's edge, ready to flee. As the jaguar sprang from the tree, the deer took off like a winged arrow through the trees, the cat following behind.

"Come on, Lani, let's go," Juan cried.

Moving quickly down the rocks to the pool, Juan dove in and swam toward the ceiba tree. He could hear Aolani behind him. As he reached shore, he ran forward and picked up his weapons, his heart beating rapidly with excitement. A tremendous feeling of relief came over him as he saw Aolani come ashore and grab her clothes. In a few moments she was dressed. Glancing up at him she said impatiently, "By all the gods, Juan, let's get out of here. Don't just stand there. Get your clothes on."

As they rushed back over the trail they had come down so eagerly only a few hours before, they were both silent. When they reached the path leading to Machu Picchu, Aolani, out of breath after the steep uphill climb and the thinner air, asked, "Are we safe yet, Juan?"

"I would think so. Besides, we have weapons now," he said in a weary voice.

"Then let us find a place to sit and rest. I'm starving," Aolani said.

Realizing he was also tired and would welcome a rest, Juan led Aolani to a place he often vi ited after a day's hunting. The view was wonderful and exciting.

Aolani looked at the small grassy area surrounded by rocks and the view in front of her. It was magnificent. The lonely peak of Hwayna Picchu rose before her on the left and, on the right, a great granite cliff rose sheer from the roaring white rapids of the Urubamba below them. Machu Picchu between the two spectacular rock formations was surrounded by great green precipices stretching into the distance. Where Aolani and Juan were seated a few yellow blossoms on delicate sprouts grew in the crevices of the rocks around them.

Juan handed Aolani the packet of food Nadua had wrapped in a piece of clean cotton cloth. There was a pottery jar of *chicha*, two plantains, corncakes, and charque. Taking off the cotton rag that was tied across the top of the jar of wine and removing the plug of bunchgrass, Aolani handed it to Juan, who took several swallows. He didn't touch the food. She wondered why he looked so despondent.

Aolani attacked the food with voracity, for she hadn't felt so hungry in a long time. As she finished her meal she looked at the splendid scene before her. "I love this spot, Juan. It is truly awe inspiring."

"Well, I am glad something turned out all right today," he said in a dispirited voice. "Do you want some *chicha*?"

"No, thank you. Drink it yourself. You sound as if you need it." Aolani watched him gulp it down as she took off her moccasins. Here was the perfect setting for a love scene. She was ready, but he was as morose as an old bear and twice as moody. It was not like him at all. What on earth was wrong with him? She kissed him lightly on his cheek, then reached over and did something she had been wanting to do for a long time. She ran her fingers through his thick, dark curls. He pulled back as if he'd been stung by a bee. "What is the matter, Juan? You look feverish."

"Nothing is the matter," he said glumly. "Everything is the matter."

"What, tell me?" she asked.

"I wanted this to be a perfect day for us alone, just the two of us. We haven't had much time alone, you know. Then that damn jaguar had to be there. He ruined everything. The whole thing was ridiculous. We will probably both catch colds from spending hours in that icy water."

Aolani moved closer to him and put her hand over his. His fingers began sensuously stroking hers. "Juan, I think it's been a wonderful day. It's been exciting and different."

He went on as if he had not heard her. "I behaved like an idiot," Juan said furiously, "leaving my weapons like that, not even looking around for signs of danger—just dashing after you because I forgot everything. Seeing you swimming next to me, I thought my dream had come true."

"When did you dream that?" she asked with interest.

"The last time you were in Cuzco and I was alone at Sauca Cachi. I swam for hours in your pool, dreaming that you were by my side. It was a very erotic fantasy."

"Juan, look at me. I am beside you now," she said in a voice husky with desire. She trailed her fingers over his bare arm.

He turned hesitantly toward her, feeling a tremor of delight as her fingers lingered and caressed his cheek. For the second time that day she began to take off her tunic, but stopped, her eyes on his. "Help me, Juan."

As he slowly took off her tunic, gazing at her in wonder, his hands and tongue began exploring her body with growing passion. After all these years, it seemed unbelievable. Juan couldn't help himself from murmuring, "So perfectly beautiful, more so than I dreamed. Your skin is softer than the most delicate flower petal. Your form, even a goddess would envy."

Aolani could feel all the pent-up desire he had for her. His lips kissed her breasts, and as he sucked and caressed them with his tongue, his fingers were fondling her with an urgency that Aolani could feel deep in her being. His tantalizing touches were sensuously attacking her in places that sent lightning-like shivers of passion through her body and the intense heat of his desire warmed her like a flame. She begged him to enter her. His lips sought hers and his tongue incited a wave of roaring desire that flowed through her body like a torrent.

Pressing herself close to him, feeling every little movement of his body, she felt she was a part of him and he was a part of her. Her heart seemed bound in the coils of his joy and the knowledge that he loved her was a powerful force that had penetrated the empty shell of her life. She heard him murmur, "I love you, Aolani, with all my heart and soul." He moved within her, slowly at first and then ever faster until the heavens themselves seemed to explode around them.

Finally exhausted, they lay quietly in each other's arms. Aolani felt a strange sense of wonder. She had learned to love again. There was something deep between them, she thought, something more powerful than she had ever believed possible.

Juan rested awhile, and then, incapable of resisting Aolani after so many years of being unable to touch her, he began to slowly seduce her once again. The second time was not as intense as the first, but so sweet and wonderful that tears ran down her face. Juan wiped away the tears with his hand.

"Oh, my sweet, dearest Aolani, please don't cry. Did I hurt you? Aolani, answer me. What did I do wrong?"

"You idiot, Juan. Don't you know that you did everything right? It was wonderful. Can't you see that my tears are those of happiness and contentment? Oh, Juan, I—"

"What, beloved Aolani, what is it?"

Aolani said gently, "I love you, Juan, very much." She gave a deep sigh of contentment. "Why don't you call me Lani?"

Chapter Thirty-one

As dawn's soft fingers touched the dark sky of night, Aolani awakened. Today the sun was shining and she could hear from the garden the sound of feathered birds bursting out in song. She felt wonderfully warm and happy as she remembered her day with Juan. She stretched out like a cat and moved her hands over her warm body. Soft and smooth to the touch, her skin seemed alive and more sensitive today than it ever had before. She felt loved, wanted, more optimistic than she had felt in years, and most important of all, she was in love. Calling to her women, she asked for hot water. While she waited, she sang to the birds, attempting to duplicate their sounds.

As Aolani bathed, Nadua appeared in the open doorway and said with a twinkle in her eye, "Something, or should I say somebody, has made our sad little *Coya* into another person. Did you enjoy the hunt yesterday?"

"We almost caught a jaguar, or should I say the

jaguar almost caught us. Senerhuana was upset and disappointed. However, I had a very successful hunt and managed to capture my prey, who in turned captured me." Her face grew tender. "Nadua, I do believe I am in love."

"It is about time. You've spent years grieving for someone who can no longer be a part of this life."

Speaking quietly, Aolani said, "I don't regret those years of grief, for I needed time to mourn, to let my deep and loving memories of Hwayna Capac become pale shadows that blend into the merciful past."

"I know, I do know, my lady." Nadua picked up the comb and started to get the tangles out of Aolani's hair. "I have information for you, my dear. Something momentous is happening here in Machu Picchu. I feel it in my bones. I don't know what it is all about, but my husband goes around with lines of worry on his face."

Looking at Nadua with concern, Aolani asked, "What are you talking about? Ouch! Don't pull so hard."

"I am sorry, my lady, but I think you need to be forewarned." Nadua put down the comb and sat opposite her mistress. "Villac, the high priest, returned yesterday afternoon from Cuzco with two men whom I haven't seen as yet. Villac sent for Luasi and Moche and they met all last evening and then again this morning, discussing or should I say hatching up some scheme. Word has come that they would appreciate your visiting the temple as soon as possible this morning."

Suddenly all Aolani's happiness disappeared. "Oh, Nadua, what now? What new trouble do we face?" She pulled at her hair. It was a mess. "You had better finish my hair quickly."

Wearing one of her most imposing tunics of dark blue, embroidered with silver and orange flowers, and covered by a blue-feathered cloak, Aolani walked across the square to the Temple of the Sun. Luasi was waiting at the entrance and gave her a warm smile, but his dark eyes looked serious. Nadua was right, for he seemed worried as well. The stone staircase was narrow, and as they had to walk up single file, she had no opportunity to question him.

It was late morning and the hide coverings had been removed from the three windows. The sun coming through the open apertures cast splashes of light across the gold mosaic floor. Manco's bedchamber was on the right but his lessons were conducted here in this elegant room. These chambers had been given to him when he first arrived in Machu Picchu. It seemed strange to Aolani that her baby, now almost 12, was considered a god by these old and experienced men.

Luasi conducted her to the dais covered with bright handwoven rugs and pillows at one end of the room. He bowed and returned to sit with the others. Aolani recognized the two men that Nadua reported had returned with Villac Umu, the high priest. Who could forget Quis-quis and Chalcuchima, the greatest generals in her husband's armies? She nodded to them as they inclined their heads in her direction. Why were they here? she wondered. It must have something to do with the war and Atahualpa. The high priest, a slender man with an intensely serious face, was even more intimidating than usual. Moche and her son's two *amautas* smiled at her.

Villac spoke up. "We are waiting, my lady, for the young Inca. He is with his llama, I understand. However, he is on his way. It will only be a few moments."

"Are you sure my son should be present at this meeting? From all appearances, this must be a momentous matter."

"The Lord High Inca is the subject of this meeting. He must be present."

By all the gods, Aolani thought, he called Manco the Lord High Inca. Her face paled. Atahualpa must be dead. Aolani was about to question Villac when she heard a sound at the entrance and Manco walked into the room, dressed simply in his everyday tunic. It even had a smudge of dirt upon it. Aolani was proud of the way her young son reacted to the sight of all these men staring at him. He walked proudly with his head high, taking his place on the dais without hesitation. With his high forehead, cleft chin, and high cheekbones, he looked so much like his father that a shiver ran down Aolani's spine. Then she noticed that everyone without exception had bowed his head to the floor.

In a clear voice, Manco asked, "Why have you summoned me here, Villac Umu?"

The men all returned to their former positions and Villac spoke. "There are things you and the *Coya*, your mother, should know before I can answer your question, my lord. Chalcuchima, one of your father's generals, will first bring us the latest information on the state of the war. If you, my lord, or anyone else wishes to question him, do so. Please, General, begin."

"I understand that you already know that your brother defeated Huascar's army at Tomebamba. Our warriors followed the remnants of Huascar's army south and won another tremendous victory at Ambato. However, we had many wounded and dead and it was close to a year before we could proceed. We headed for the area north of the Apurimac Gorge. Huascar's army in the meantime had been reinforced with countless new recruits."

"Was Huascar with his army?" Manco asked.

"No, my lord. Huascar was in Cuzco and Atahualpa remained in Cajamarca. Huascar was determined to keep us from crossing the mighty Apurimac River and his huge army defended the river on the north side. It was a lonely plain, interspersed with rocks that rose like jagged pillars all around us. During that first day of battle, our eighteen thousand men were overwhelmed by the sheer might of Huascar's army—close to fifty thousand men we figured. That night we could hear their drums and jubilant shouting as they celebrated their victory."

Manco was leaning forward, obviously interested in the battle. "Did my brother's army lose then?"

"No, our men worked all night building ambushes, digging holes, and covering them with brush, stringing ropes between boulders and other such devices to delay them when they tried to follow us. Men were hidden around the ambush areas to kill Huascar's men as they fell. Well, we won, almost destroying their huge army. They ran so fast they didn't even pause long enough to protect the Apurimac crossing by burning the bridge. We followed them to Cuzco and took Huascar prisoner."

It was such a waste, Aolani thought, so many thousands and thousands of men killed on both sides and all because of greed for power. It was amazing how men, even Hwayna Capac, convinced themselves they were at war because of their belief in the rightness of their cause, giving reasons as ambiguous as their logic. The history of war repeated itself over and over again. She listened as Chalcuchima went on.

"In order to frighten and subdue Huascar's people, we sacked the city, burned his grandfather's mummy, and paraded Huascar through the city streets wearing women's clothes."

Moche interrupted. "I understand you murdered his wives and children."

"That is true, my lord, but this is war and I had my orders from the Lord High Inca, Atahualpa. Huascar usurped the royal fringe against his father's wishes and started the war. He and his supporters were to be punished." Pausing for a moment, Chalcuchima then attempted to justify his acts. "The things I have to do in war incense me, sicken my senses, and disturb my sleep, but I do what my lord commands. He believes in punishing his enemies ruthlessly as an example to others."

Aolani felt more and more horrified. How could Atahualpa have done such a cruel thing as ordering the deaths of women and children? She felt ashamed. The crass stupidity of her son's actions appalled her. This act would alienate his people.

"Where was my son when this happened?" she asked.

"Atahualpa was on his way to Cuzco but he could not continue his journey. He received word that the Spaniards had left Tumbes and were on their way to Cajamarca. Atahualpa's army, about fifty thousand strong, marched with him to meet them. You must understand the Inca thought of the Spaniards as being minor bandits, of little consequence with their small number of men. He was very curious about their strange attire and above all he was determined to acquire their horses. Atahualpa even sent gifts to them so they wouldn't go away. He did take the precaution of evacuating the city of Cajamarca. He arrived and took up residence at the palace outside the hot springs before the Spaniards arrived.

"The first day they met, everything went very smoothly and the Spaniards invited him into the city the next day to see all their horses and equipment. We urged him not to go but the Lord High Inca would not be deterred. Well, they kidnapped him easily, for it was a well-planned surprise attack. We were stunned. I sat with our huge army and could not make a move for fear they would kill the Inca if I did. They allowed me to see him and he commanded me to do nothing. Atahualpa said the Spaniards merely wanted a huge ransom in gold and silver and told me to send out teams of men to gather the metals and bring them to Cajamarca. He needed enough treasure to fill the large reception room."

"How did they treat him?" Aolani asked.

"I went to visit him every few days at first. He lived in the lower palace. His women served him; his wife was there. Many times a banquet was in progress and there were dancers and other types of entertainment. He even invited a couple of the barbarians to take their evening meals with him upon occasion."

"It was unbelievable," Quis-quis said angrily. "He would not listen to us. We had many reliable reports from our people who had learned the Spanish language and worked for the barbarians. They talked openly among themselves about killing the Lord High Inca and Chalcuchima, leaving the army and the people with no leadership. Pizarro, their leader, was cunning. He sent emissaries to Cuzco announcing his support of the dead Huascar's legitimate claim to the throne, thus ensuring their support. Huascar's supporters were ecstatic and sent word that Cuzco would welcome Francisco Pizarro and his men with the open arms of friendship."

Chalcuchima interrupted. "The Lord High Inca wouldn't believe us when we reported this to him. I told him that he shouldn't trust his captors, that the Spanish were rapacious and formidable barbarians, indifferent to right and wrong. But the Inca continued to think of them as a few bandits who would be satisfied with a ransom that he would soon recover from them. He thought they were too few to possibly take over the empire."

"You have not told us all yet. My son, Atahualpa,

is dead, is he not?" Aolani asked, and both generals nodded their heads. "How?"

The two men looked embarrassed, confused and sorrowful. Quis-quis finally answered, but doing so was an effort. "Your son, my lady, to—that is, to avoid being burned alive, embraced the faith of the barbarians."

Aolani was shocked. "In other words, he denied his own right to be one of the gods."

"Yes," Quis-quis said. "He was strangled eighteen days ago."

Aolani had thought all along that Atahualpa might be dead but that did not lessen the blow when it fell. What a terrible ending for her son. Filled with anguish, she wanted to cry but she knew she could not do so yet. How he had died was somehow understandable. He had been severely burned as a child, and since that time, he had hated fire. Poor Atahualpa! He had committed a terrible blunder, however, and caused another blow to the empire. He had denied he was the Son of the Sun, a deity on earth loved by the gods, by adopting the Spaniards' God. But then it was true. Her eldest son was not his father's heir, not the Son of the Sun, and he knew it. But neither was Huascar Hwayna's heir. How cruel fate had been to both young men.

Knowing what she must say, despite her grief, Aolani said, "My lords, I know why you are here and what must be done. Our people, our empire, our way of life—they are predicated upon the belief that the Lord High Inca is the Son of the Sun, appointed by the gods to help his people live in wisdom and light. He is descended from Inti and shares in his divinity, and his word is law."

"True, my lady," Villac Umu said. "There is chaos throughout the land without a rightful heir. There is no law and order in the empire. The people do not know where to turn. They are like animals in a forest fire, trying to get away, but unable to escape the flames. As a result there is an epidemic of suicides, whole families doing away with themselves. The Spaniards are enslaving the people, forcing them to work in the mines and fields under impossible conditions. We must do something."

Aolani tried to imagine the anguished bewilderment of the people. She spoke simply. "It frightens me, for my son, Manco, is young but he is Hwayna Capac's heir, as you all know. Huascar was not my husband's son and Atahualpa was not qualified."   .

"Yes, Manco is young, Aolani," Moche said, "but he is his father's choice. All of us here, as well as three other nobles, were told by Hwayna Capac that Prince Manco was to be his successor. We all swore we would protect him until he gained strength and wisdom."

Aolani heard the quiet, determined voice of her son. "I, too, have always known I was my father's heir, for he told me to prepare myself. I am your Lord High Inca and I must now assume my responsibilities. I know I am young and will need help but I will do what I can to save the empire."

"There is one thing more you should know, my Lord Inca," Quis-quis said. "The Spaniards have put your half brother, Tupa Hualppa, in Atahualpa's place as Inca."

"By the sacred Mother, the Moon," Aolani exclaimed. "I hate to be unkind but poor Tupa Hualppa is the son of a concubine and the poor child is lacking in wits."

"The Spaniards selected him for that reason, no doubt," Moche said sadly.

Manco stood up. "I know there are many decisions to be made but I want some time to myself. Please, leave me. We will talk later." He placed his hand on Aolani's shoulder. "Stay."

When the men had all left, Manco went to the middle window and stood looking at his magnificent and awe-inspiring country. "I am a little frightened, Mother. I had not expected this to happen quite so soon."

Aolani, feeling a need to lighten her son's mood, walked over and stood beside him. She put her arm through his and she could feel how nervous and tense he was. "My dearest son, I never realized that your father had told you of his plan for you."

Manco said, "My father discussed this with me several times. He even told me how he felt when my grandfather, Tupac Yupanqui, informed him he was to be the next Lord High Inca. Father told me that he had been so frightened that his knees shook and his hands trembled."

"I was so proud of you today, my son. You did not show your fear." Aolani squeezed his arm. "Can you believe that, after hearing all those terrible tales today, I am ravenous? I was too nervous to eat this morning. As Lord High Inca, do you think you could possibly get us some food?"

He looked at her in surprise and then laughed. "To tell you the truth I didn't eat much either. I knew something important was about to happen." He went to the door of his bedchamber, called his women and told them what he wanted. Three very pretty young girls, one extremely pregnant, left the reception room. Noticing the glances cast back and forth among the women as they passed Manco alerted Aolani to what was happening. Startled at first, but then amused, she was suddenly aware that her son was more mature than she realized.

Coming back to Aolani, Manco said, "I am going to need a lot of help, Mother. I especially want people around me whom I can trust, like Moche, Luasi, and you. Perhaps Senor Juan, also. I'll need him in dealing with the Spaniards."

"What about Villac?"

"Sometimes he frightens me," Manco said. "He is intimidating. His mind runs on a narrow path, one that is obsessed with the Sun God and my position as the Son of the Sun. I think he is planning to be my chief adviser but I have other plans."

"Hwayna Capac had problems with his priests and nobles at times, but just remember, Manco, you, not they, are the Son of the Sun."

"Do you remember my father's prayer to Inti?" Manco asked.

"Of course. I'll always remember it. When your father was informed of his father's death and knew that he was to be the Lord High Inca, those were the first words he spoke:

'Oh Lord, happy and fortunate Lord of the earth and those who dwell in the spirit world, have pity upon men and hold them in affection.'"

Hearing Manco's voice joining hers, she stopped and let him continue.

"Transmit to me the power to serve thee, the poor, the wretched, those whom thou hast created and set upon earth. Give me the wisdom and the strength to bring peace and safety to our people that they may, with their children, walk in the path of righteousness, living long without interruption and disaster. In the name of my Father, the Sun, have mercy upon these thy people."

Aolani was moved by Manco's remembrance of his father's words but then an eerie feeling swept over her as she thought of his future. A strange, faint chill made her want to warn Manco against accepting his high position. She wanted to tell him of the perils of being a ruler, of being constantly buffeted by the dark winds of fate, of the great weariness of being alone. But she knew she could not. Each person received a challenge when born and had to fulfill the tasks the gods had given them.

PART 4

Eclipse
of the Sun
1532

Chapter Thirty-two

Lately, Cuzco depressed Aolani, even more than it had in the past. The weather, of course, was still miserable. The cold winds sweeping down from the high summits penetrated every corner of the palace and the heat from the braziers was lost in the large rooms. After all the years spent in the warm and pleasant climate of Tomebamba, she was always cold. Then there was the city itself. Now that all the gold and silver decorations had been ripped from the temples and palaces, the city had assumed a ghostly appearance, its dark somber walls a specter of their past glory. The formerly clean streets were filled with debris, the refuse and excrement of men and animals and the destruction left by the Spaniards. Since most of the Inca nobles and dignitaries had left for either their country houses or their own provinces, an ominous silence hung over the city like a smothering cloud.

Aolani longed for her home in Sauca Cachi, the simple beauty of the terraced fields, the warmth of the sun shining down on the deep valley and the cheerful faces of the people, unaware of what was going on elsewhere in the empire. The valley was well hidden and the narrow entrance artfully disguised by rocks, trees, and brush. It was well guarded and she fervently prayed that it would not be discovered. She was so grateful that Manco had presented it to her as a wedding gift when she married Juan but Manco wouldn't let her live there alone, since Juan was gone. He said it was too dangerous. Wearily, she sank down on her pillows. There was so little to do in Cuzco. Aolani wished she were back in Machu Picchu with Cusi and Sinchi, for even though she had often felt the wind blow cold in the citadel, there was usually the intense heat of the sun during the day. Even more important, her days there had been busy and rewarding and the atmosphere was pleasant.

As she thought of her daughter, Aolani's heart was filled with joy as she remembered Cusi's happiness when Manco had approved of her marriage to Sinchi. Aolani gave a deep sigh as she thought about all the other things that had happened after that last eventful meeting when she had learned that her eldest son had been killed and that Manco had become the Lord High Inca.

During those first weeks after hearing of the death of Atahualpa, gradual but enormous changes began to occur in Machu Picchu. They could all be attributed to her son, the Inca. Overnight Manco had become a powerful force, a man to be reckoned with, absolutely sure of himself and well aware of his responsibilities, as well as his power. Villac Umu, so intimidating and authoritative with others, was like a tamed puma, obeying all orders given him by the young Inca. Luasi, always fanatically loyal to the royal family, was like a piece of clay in Manco's hands. Even Sinchi and

Moche were under his spell and obeyed him without question.

There was so much activity going on: strangers came and went like silent shadows, seemingly busy on various errands. Manco, Villac, Moche, and Luasi disappeared for a whole week, and when they returned, the Inca immediately sent Luasi out on some mysterious business. Nadua was as curious as Aolani was but the men told them nothing.

Five weeks passed and then one day Aolani had been summoned to the Inca's presence. She was surprised to see Juan there. Her heart beat rapidly as it always did when she saw him. The gods only knew how she loved him, more so every day. Manco came forward to greet her and kissed her on the brow, then led her to a seat beside him. Juan also sat down. *Chicha,* small peanut cakes, and a vessel containing hot cocoa, a favorite drink of Aolani's, were brought forth. It was thoughtful of Manco to remember how fond of the beverage she was.

Beginning the conversation, Manco said, "I have brought you both here because I have plans for you, Juan, and a great concern for my mother. First, I am going to approve of your marriage, which will take place tomorrow." Aolani gasped as she took a fast gulp of the cocoa, which burned her throat. Manco continued. "The estate of Sauca Cachi, belonging to my father, but not one of his private palaces, I give to you, my dear Mother."

As Aolani opened her mouth to express her gratitude, Manco held up his hand to stop her. "Not yet, Mother. Perhaps you will curse rather than thank me when you hear what I want in return. Juan, there are conditions attached to these offers and the decision will be up to you."

Wondering what the young Inca was up to, Juan

377

Jeanne Nickson

asked bluntly, "What do you want of me? What are the conditions?"

"You can do me a great favor, Juan. I don't believe that it will be too dangerous, but I may be wrong. You are a clever man, adept at adapting to new situations." Manco looked at Juan, an entreaty in his eyes. "Here is what I want you to do. I will send you to Tomebamba and supply the proper clothes and a horse. You will mix with the Spaniards and keep me informed on all they are doing, thinking, and planning."

"Oh, no!" Aolani exclaimed. "That means we will be separated. No, Manco, no!"

"Juan is the only man who can do it. He is a Spaniard. He should have no problem in mixing with the leaders." Turning back to Juan, he asked, "Will you do it, Juan?"

What choice did Juan have? Aolani thought. Manco was giving them everything they had ever dreamed of but what was she going to do for months and months?

She heard Juan say, "I agree."

That memory brought Aolani's thoughts back to the present and to her new husband. She worried about him constantly. Juan had been gone nine months, and there had been no word from him, at least to her, for over a month. And where was Manco? He had disappeared silently in the night with Luasi just about a month ago. Was there some connection? Something was going on and she was being left completely out of it. Hwayna had always kept her informed. How maddening it was!

Gazing down into the small garden she felt heartsick. Everything seemed wrong. The memory of Juan gnawed at her constantly and she endured, with increasing dismay, the reasons for his absence. Aolani knew that Manco was obsessed by the bearded men and appalled at what they were doing to the empire but he never talked to her. Was he planning another war? She presumed that was the reason behind his need for information and the many meetings he was holding with high-ranking officers and various dignitaries from the four quarters. Could the empire endure another major war?

She heard a slight sound, the sound of metal striking stone. She turned toward the entrance.

A tall, black-bearded Spaniard stood at the door. Aolani had never seen one of the barbarians up close. He was the strangest sight she had ever seen. A metal bowl sat on top of his head with yellow and red feathers floating above it. His chest was encased in metal and great bulging sleeves came down to his wrists. His hand was clutching a great shiny weapon that looked very sharp. What was he going to do? Kill her? She prayed to her Mother, the Moon, to save her. Aolani had heard that the Spaniards raped and savagely ravished every woman they encountered. She drew back against the wall wondering how she was going to escape. She swallowed and her heart beat so rapidly she could hear it.

Then the man spoke as he came toward her. "Don't be afraid, Lani. It's me, Juan."

Aolani couldn't believe her ears. But suddenly she saw his eyes gleaming with mischief, like dark coals. Then he dropped his weapon and held out his arms to her. By all the powers of heaven, it was Juan! Aolani ran to him and he crushed her into his arms. She let out a yell. He was hurting her and he smelled like a dead fish.

"What's wrong? Why did you yell?" Juan asked in surprise.

Aolani was angry. Like lightning her surprise and pleasure turned into indignation at the scare he had given her. First he had frightened her out of her wits

379

and now she felt as if her ribs were broken. "You hurt me, you barbarian. I feel as if I've been squeezed by a giant armadillo." She sniffed the air and put a finger to her nose. "Besides, you smell. Get out of that ridiculous costume while I call for bathwater."

"I am sorry, Aolani. I forgot I had on the armor. I was just so glad to see you," he shouted after her disappearing back. He took off his helmet and threw it in the corner; then he untied his offending breast plate, tossing it after the helmet in disgust. He sat down on the floor and tried to pull off his hip boots. He couldn't manage them. Usually a comrade helped pull them off. Aolani was right! This costume was ridiculous.

Aolani saw his problem on her return and attempted to help, but found it impossible. The boots wouldn't budge. She was becoming angry again and tense. She picked up a knife from her weaving basket and mumbled, "A husband comes back after a long absence and he can't even manage to get his stupid clothes off."

Nadua came in at that moment and was surprised by Juan's appearance. "My, you are a funny sight to see in that outfit. My lady, what are you doing with that knife? You may cut your husband and you'll ruin those leg coverings. Let me see what I can do."

"Ladies," Juan said, getting angry himself, "here I'm back safe and sound after nine months of dangerous work and not a welcome do I hear. If you'll just get out and leave me in peace, I'll manage myself."

Paying no attention, Nadua was working the leather down and finally succeeded in easing the boot off his leg. The other boot came off much more easily. By this time, Juan felt sorry that he had frightened Aolani by coming through the tunnels dressed as a Spaniard. It was just that he had been so anxious to see her. He had left Francisco Pizarro's group this afternoon, not wanting to wait until tomorrow, when the general planned to enter the city.

Watching him as he bathed, Aolani found him as handsome as ever, even with that funny beard. She was already beginning to feel aroused, and when he stood up, she silently handed him a cotton towel. She couldn't help herself. She buried her face on his naked chest and began to kiss him lightly all over.

Then she said brokenly, "I'm sorry, Juan, that I behaved so badly but I was frightened and shocked by your arrival. You didn't even look like yourself."

Juan said nothing. He just picked her up in his arms and carried her to the bed rugs. After all this time, he felt too choked up with emotion to speak. Gently he began to remove her clothes. When he had done so, he stroked her breasts, his breath coming unevenly. Then he raised his lips to hers and kissed her slowly, enjoying the familiar movement of their tongues. She giggled and caressed his soft beard as she kissed him back. When he touched her in all her favorite places, he could sense her passion reaching out to him and was filled with such warmth and love that he thought he would die if he ever had to leave her again. He could wait no longer and plunged into her.

Later, as she lay in his arms, Juan murmured, "My beautiful Lani, so loving and passionate, and as unpredictable as a volcano threatening to erupt. But, oh Lani, my Lani, how I love you."

When Aolani awakened early the next morning, she reached for Juan to make sure she hadn't dreamed. She saw his eyes open slowly and look into hers. Then he drew her deep into the curve of his body.

"I am sorry, my love, that I rushed you last night. Let me try again."

Aolani felt the hardness of his erection against her

Jeanne Nickson

soft buttocks. His kisses burned the back of her neck and ears; then he sipped at the pulse in her throat, which sent shivers of desire running through her body. A wave of intense pleasure engulfed her as his sensuous fingers traced the curves of her body. She wanted him and abruptly turned to face him. His first thrust was like a flame of light as he entered her. Small tremors swept her away in a tide of pleasure.

Later, with breakfast over, they lay quietly together, her fingers still playing with this strange new beard that curled around his chin and floated above his mouth.

"Tell me, Juan, about your trip."

He said bleakly, "In many ways it was a rough experience. But I am not going to tell you a thing unless you quit pulling on my beard. It hurts." She stopped what she was doing. "You cannot imagine what it is like in Tomebamba and every place else my countrymen have been. I felt shocked by what I saw. There is no order; the city and streets are a mess. People exist only by robbing and looting."

"How could everything have changed so radically in a matter of months? I don't understand," she said.

Juan attempted to explain what had happened. "During the civil war between Atahualpa and Huascar, a great deal of the administrative detail was neglected and the empire was not running as efficiently as it had when Hwayna Capac was ruler. After Huascar and Atahualpa were killed, the empire was like a large body without a head. Since that time both the Spaniards and bands of your own people have raided and destroyed the warehouses, storage huts, palaces, and temples wherever they went. They have also stolen and slaughtered thousands of llamas for food."

Aolani said grimly, "You mean, our civilization, as I knew it, is dead?" Juan nodded. "What happened to you in Tomebamba? Did the Spaniards accept you?"

"I had no trouble in that respect. Manco had arranged that a horse, clothes, two servants, and gold would be waiting for me in Cajamarca. How he got them there I do not know. My guards took me over back roads and we seldom saw any people. When we reached Cajamarca I changed clothes. I had a little trouble with the horse the first few days but I soon learned how to handle him. Wearing that armor is like being in hell, especially when it is hot." She kissed him lightly all over his chest and he moaned. "Do you really want to hear or shall we play games?" Aolani cuddled next to him.

"Shortly thereafter, I fell in with three of my countrymen and a lot of Indians escorting a treasure back to Cajamarca from Cuzco. Aolani, you just wouldn't believe what the people of Cuzco let this small group take away with them. There were almost three hundred loads of loot from Cuzco and over a hundred loads from Jauja. There were chalices, necklaces, nuggets, and even dismantled altars and fountains. I just couldn't believe it. By the time I reached Tomebamba the leader of the group, one of Gov. Pizarro's most trusted soldiers, had become a good friend of mine."

"Why do they call Francisco Pizarro Governor?"

"He is the leader of my countrymen here. The king appointed him in charge and his title is governor. Anyhow, when they found out that I could read and write, I was recommended to the governor and I became his secretary. I still am. That's why I must get back. I should be with Pizarro and Manco when they enter Cuzco this morning." Juan got out of bed and went to the door shouting for Nadua.

Holding a blanket around her to keep warm, Aolani asked, "Did you say Manco? Is my son a prisoner?"

Nadua entered the room bringing Juan's Spanish

Jeanne Nickson

clothes. "I cleaned them as best I could. Those queer metal pieces are over in the corner where you left them."

"Nadua," Juan said with a smile, "how in the name of the gods did you guess what I wanted?"

"Well," Nadua said as she left the room, "you've had a bath, food, and a woman. From what I've heard, there are people coming and I suspected you might want to get out of here."

"Juan," Aolani demanded, "answer me. Is Manco a prisoner?"

"No, Aolani, he is not." Juan struggled with his underclothes, shirt, doublet, and tights, talking as he did so. "Manco walked into the governor's camp four days ago. He was disheveled and there was blood on his tunic and on his body." He went on quickly, seeing her expression. "No, it was not his blood."

"I don't understand. Why in the world would he walk into the camp of the Spaniards?"

"Manco told Pizarro that he had escaped from General Quis-quis and he begged sanctuary with the governor, claiming that Atahualpa's army was trying to kill him." Juan sat down and began pulling on his boots. "The governor seemed willing to believe his tale. I don't believe that he connects Manco with Chalcuchima. In fact, Pizarro thought Manco's arrival was a miracle, a stroke of good fortune."

Looking puzzled, Aolani asked, "Why did he think that?"

"Because Tupa Hualppa had died and Pizarro desperately needed an Inca ruler he could control."

Aolani was skeptical. "Do you mean they think Manco is going to obey his commands? That is ridiculous!"

"They don't think so. It is my belief Manco sent Chalcuchima to kill Tupa Hualppa. Manco wants to take Tupa Hualppa's place for some reason."

384

Aolani was disturbed. "Did Chalcuchima really kill that young boy?"

"The Spaniards think so," Juan said. "Anyhow they burned Chalcuchima alive."

"What an awful way to die!" Aolani rose from the bed and walked over to Juan. "I wonder what Manco is really trying to do. What is he up to?"

"I would be willing to wager that he is not planning to be the governor's puppet Inca for very long and that he has a good reason for what he is doing," Juan said grimly. He stood up, fully dressed in his strange clothes, and went to Lani. "Give me a kiss, wife, before I put on my armor."

Aolani clutched him tenderly around the neck and kissed him. "When will I see you again?"

"Not for a few days but I'll work something out. I do not think it wise to come to you directly here in the palace, so I will use the tunnels." He kissed her gently, grabbed his armor and was gone.

Chapter Thirty-three

The sound of someone calling her name and shaking her shoulder awakened Aolani out of a deep sleep. Opening her eyes, she blinked a couple of times; then in the flickering light of the torch, she focused on a familiar face. She sat up quickly, reaching for the fur-lined cloak she kept beside the bed. Clutching it around her she said, "Moche, what are you doing here?"

Even before he answered she knew something dreadful had happened. Unable to control her fear, filled with a sudden terror, she knew that danger loomed before her like an untamed beast. By all the gods, what terrible news could have brought Moche to her bedside in the middle of the night? Oh, please, she prayed, please, not Juan!

Moche's eyes were deeply shadowed and he was obviously in great distress as he said, "It's Luasi, Aolani, he's—he has been killed."

She looked at him in shock, unable to believe what she had heard. Who would want to kill Luasi? Why? "Does Nadua know?"

"Yes. She is on her way to the temple where they took the body. Juan is with her."

Aolani arose from her bed and faced him, her voice trembling as she asked, "How, Moche? How was he killed?"

"It was terrible, Lani!" He began to speak slowly, forcing the words to come. "The Inca, Luasi, and I had just finished the evening meal and were sitting, just talking. Suddenly, there was a commotion in the hall and five drunken barbarians sauntered into the room. I sensed something was about to happen and knew there was absolutely nothing I could do to prevent it. The men demanded wine and laughed among themselves, talking loudly and pointing to the Inca." Moche closed his eyes.

"What were they saying?"

"My Spanish is poor but their words of insult could not be mistaken. From what I could gather they called Manco a woman, a coward, and a man without male organs."

Aolani was aghast. How could they treat a young boy so shamefully? She shuddered, for she knew Manco had understood them. She asked fearfully, "What did my son do?"

"Nothing, but I could see by his eyes that he was furious. They then raised their legs at him. One of them even opened his pants and pissed on the floor," Moche said in disgust.

"Well, go on!"

He swallowed hard. "Then a man grabbed one of the Inca's servingwomen, threw her on the ground, and tore off her clothes. The next moment Manco was standing there looking like the thunder god himself with a sword in his hand, saying in an angry voice, 'Leave her alone.' "

Aolani groaned. "Where did he get the sword?"

"It was hidden under the rugs. The Inca has other weapons hidden all around the palace. Perhaps he anticipated something like this would happen. A hulking brute of a man came toward us with a sword in his hand. He said, 'So our puppet wants to play, does he?' With that he lunged toward the Inca. Luasi jumped in front of Manco and the sword pierced his heart. It all happened so quickly. I saw the Spaniard pull out his weapon and the blood gushed out of the wound. Then Luasi fell to the floor. The Inca turned pale and let out a cry as he sank down beside Luasi and held him in his arms." Moche wiped at the tears falling from his eyes with his sleeve.

Aolani said quietly, "Go on."

"Suddenly, a harsh and commanding voice said to the Spaniards, 'Drop your swords and leave this room.' It was Juan. Someone must have sent for him when the trouble started. I rushed over to Luasi but he was dead, and I—I—" Moche was crying, his voice thick with emotion. "Death had hit him like a stab of lightning. He had no chance at all."

Aolani, too, felt the sorrow of Luasi's death. His loyalty and devotion obliterated by a single blow. Her thoughts went to her son. How horrified Manco must be! Luasi had been like a father to him. She shook her head in despair. "Manco," she said. "Where is he? What can I do?"

"The Lord Inca stood there in shock with blood all over his tunic. I heard him whisper, 'That's it! I can bear no more.' Then he turned to me and said, 'Go to Nadua and my mother. Tell them what happened. I will be there soon.' "

Wringing her hands at this new tragedy that had

come into their lives, Aolani wondered how it was all going to end. Walking the floor she wished there was something she could do. Anything! It was terrible to sit around, unable to help in any way. Men, she thought in despair, what was it in their natures that made them so aggressive? The killing seemed to go on and on. Would there never be an end to it? This time it had been Luasi, one of their own, killed by a barbarian, but Aolani remembered the many wars the Incas had fought just in her lifetime with the Chachapoyas, the Canaris, and the Caranqui. So many innocent men, women, and children killed—for what?

The night seemed endless to Aolani as she sat waiting for her son. She did not feel like talking and Moche, too, was silent. At the sound of approaching footsteps in the hall, Aolani stood up and watched Manco enter the room followed by Juan.

Her husband came and stood beside her, whispering, "Do you know?" She nodded. He put his arm around her and held her tight.

Withdrawing from his embrace, Aolani moved toward her son. Manco was only a young boy; Luasi's death must have been a terrible blow to him, for she knew he had loved the man. She took Manco's hand. "I am so very sorry, Manco." She wanted to hold him in her arms but she knew she must not. He would be embarrassed and offended.

Aolani felt his fingers grip hers and then he released her hand. "I know how a llama feels when that last ounce has been added to his load and he balks," he said bitterly. "I am through being a puppet of the Spaniards. No longer will I obey them like a lowly slave or endure their abuse. I want to avenge the terrible inequities to which they have subjected our people and the wasteland they have made of our empire. I am leaving Cuzco for good as soon as Luasi is placed in his tomb in the Yucay Valley. Then I will disappear."

Aolani gasped, and the others stared at the Inca. "I can't believe what I'm hearing," she said. "Disappear where? They will find you and kill you."

"No, Mother, they won't." Manco walked to the window and saw the sun's early morning rays drenching the rooftops and washing the city in a bright mist. He turned toward his mother, aware of her fear and concern. "I have been preparing for this moment for a long time. I have willingly played being a puppet Inca in order that I could prepare myself to withstand the barbarians. Those in this room have been helping me, as did Luasi and many others."

Suddenly, Manco's actions made sense to Aolani. She had wondered for a long time how Manco was able to endure the life he led with the Spaniards. Then there were the many mysterious disappearances of Moche, Juan, Sinchi, and Luasi. Oh, yes, and Villac Umu and Quis-quis as well.

"Tell me what has been going on?" she asked.

Manco said proudly, "A while ago I ordered there be a large planting of crops, a gathering of weapons and clothes, and the mobilization of troops throughout Tahuantinsuyu. I needed time to prepare for war and so I've allowed the Spaniards to think me weak and willing to do their bidding. I've guarded my plans from all but a few, Mother. I would have told you but I feared for your safety if I were caught. Also, I did not want you to worry."

"Ha! I worry anyhow," Aolani said with a touch of asperity in her voice. "I should have been told. It might have made this ordeal more bearable."

Manco looked a trifle taken aback. "I am sorry, Mother. I meant well. But to go on. I now have many storehouses filled with the things we need for war. I have over one hundred thousand men trained in tactics of fighting armed men on horses. One group is stationed not too far from the Yucay. I will leave with my men after the funeral ceremonies."

"Will they let you leave Cuzco?" Moche asked.

"I discussed it with Francisco Pizarro tonight after what happened," Manco answered. "He is feeling quite guilty about what his men did this evening and said he would provide me with a suitable escort, meaning that I will be under guard, of course, but I will escape. I was suitably grateful for his help and promised him a life-size statue in gold of Hwayna Capac. His greed will ensure my leaving," Manco added cynically.

Aolani could understand and sympathize with the actions Manco had taken but she was fearful for him. She was well aware, however, that war had always presented an opportunity for highborn Inca youths to prove their manhood and win glory, fame, and riches for themselves and their families. Manco was Lord High Inca and must prove himself just as his father had. She remembered Hwayna Capac at 16, when his father had sent him in charge of a huge army to quell a rebellion initiated by the Chachapoyans. Hwayna had thrown himself into the war with the same spirit, as eager as Manco was to prove himself a great warrior. Realizing the futility of wars and aware of the risks he would be taking, Aolani was heartsick over his decision.

"I don't believe I could change your mind about your course of action," Aolani said sorrowfully, "but let me remind you that the poetic tales of great battles and the exploits of courageous warriors which you have heard from the storytellers in your father's palace have given you only a partial view of war."

"I know of your feelings, honored Mother, and perhaps that is another reason why I was reluctant to tell you my plans. But please understand, I have to do this.

I want to feel proud of being an Inca and show the barbarians our strength and our courage. It is a path I must follow."

"So be it, my dear son. May the gods support you in your efforts and the devils of Hopi-Nuni plague your enemies. You will always be in my prayers." Aolani wondered what she was to do. "Tell me, am I to go with you? Or am I to stay here in Cuzco?"

Manco said in a hesitant voice, "Mother, I have a great need for your help on an important matter. You are the only person in the empire who I can call upon to do this." He paused, looked at her, then went on. "You know the condition of the empire, the plight of our people, and the cruelties inflicted upon our populace. Above all, you speak Spanish fluently and eloquently. You are a queen who could talk to the King of Spain on equal terms and let him hear the truth about what is happening. Would you be willing to go to Spain with Juan and try to gain the king's understanding of our problems? Perhaps you could gain his support for our cause."

Leave the land she knew, sail across the sea to a strange and unknown country, and speak to the king who had sent these barbarians? Could Aolani help her people? She shivered at the thought. But it was not a shiver of fear—it was one of excitement and wonder! Could she do it? Why not? Aolani thought. If men from another world could sail to this land, why couldn't she, a woman, sail to theirs? If she could only persuade the king to show justice and mercy, it would help her people. It was better than sitting here doing nothing.

Taking a deep breath, Aolani announced, "I will do it."

As Manco took one of her hands and raised it to his lips, Aolani looked over his head and saw Nadua standing in the dark doorway. When she moved into

the light, Aolani saw her face. Despite her pallor and
dark-shadowed eyes, she seemed to be in control of
herself. What a valiant and courageous woman she
was, so strong of spirit. Aolani went to her friend and
took her in her arms, too choked up to talk.

"There is no need for grief. Luasi died the way he
lived, serving his god, the Inca," Nadua said.

As Aolani lifted her head, she saw Manco approaching them, his eyes filled with anguish. His voice trembled a little as he said, "I am so very sorry, Nadua. I
swear by my father's *huaca*, that if I had known what
would happen, I would not have lost my temper and
picked up that sword. May the Creator forgive me."

"I know, my lord, I know. I heard what happened."
She patted his hand. "I have a favor to ask."

"Anything! Anything I can do, I will," he said sadly.
"Not that I can do very much at the moment."

"I want to go with my lady on her journey," Nadua
said, looking at Aolani with pleading eyes. "I want to
get away."

Manco said with concern, "You know it means fleeing
to a place beyond the sea. It may be dangerous."

"I want to do it. There is nothing for me here,"
Nadua answered.

Aolani said quickly, "Then you will do so, Nadua.
I will welcome your coming. I will need you, dear
friend."

How much you will not know for a while, Aolani
thought. No one knew her secret yet, not even Juan.
She could hardly believe it herself. She had thought
herself barren after all these years and now at 42, she
was pregnant. One of Juan's miracles. The thought of
another child pleased her. With Nadua at her side she
would feel less concerned about the birth of the child
and more confident about the future. It was possible
that Spain might be a better place to rear the babe

than this mountainous, war-torn land, which would always lay under the shadow of the condor.

As Manco took Juan aside and quietly began speaking to him, Aolani went to the open window. Sacsahuaman, the splendid fortress, loomed against the stars in the early morning sky and she thought of the many years of labor and the countless thousands of men compelled to work on this huge monument to war. Of what use had it been against the barbarians who controlled most of the empire? She shook her head. Such a waste of human effort.

Her thoughts were interrupted by the sound of temple bells calling the chosen women to prayer. She saw the running forms of two *chasqui* arriving at the palace gates. A squad of warriors on guard duty in the courtyard were marching back and forth. If she didn't know better she could almost imagine that she was young again, standing here with Hwayna Capac. She recalled being with him on this very spot looking over his city so very long ago. Thinking of Hwayna she remembered what Juan had told her about the Inca's final instructions to him. He had asked Juan to guard and protect her and the children from the Spaniards and even implied he should marry her.

Aolani had been touched and humbled by the unselfish love Hwayna had shown in planning for her future happiness. Tears came to her eyes and she stifled a sob. She felt the pain of his loss again as she stood looking out at Cuzco from his palace. Suddenly Aolani felt a powerful sense of Hwayna's presence. She could almost feel him touching her with gentle fingers. The morning breeze ruffled her hair and she heard the murmur of his voice in the wind. She strained to hear his words but she could not.

Wanting to feel the warmth of his embrace, Lani put out her hands, but could not touch him. She felt dizzy, lost, and very alone. She stood silently, smelling the scent of his skin, the air cold and damp around her. Struggling to shout out his name, she cried out, but all she could hear was the wind screaming down from the mountains. Just as she was despairing of ever reaching him she felt strong human arms around her and heard Juan saying her name.

"What is the matter, Lani? Tell me," he said in a frightened voice.

Tears filled her eyes and then she felt Juan draw her close in his embrace and was comforted. It felt good to be close to him and feel his need for her. She also needed him. With his help she knew she could have the strength and courage to face this strange new world of his. But Aolani promised herself she would always preserve the precious past in her heart and with the gods' help return someday to Tahuantinsuyu. But for the moment, she would look to the future, not the past. Aolani took Juan's arm and guided him toward the inner chamber. It was time to tell him about the child.

Three captivating stories of love in another time, another place.

MADELINE BAKER
"Heart of the Hunter"

A Lakota warrior must defy the boundaries of life itself to claim the spirited beauty he has sought through time.

ANNE AVERY
"Dream Seeker"

On faraway planets, a pilot and a dreamer learn that passion can bridge the heavens, no matter how vast the distance from one heart to another.

KATHLEEN MORGAN
"The Last Gatekeeper"

To save her world, a dazzling temptress must use her powers of enchantment to open a stellar portal—and the heart of a virile but reluctant warrior.

Bestselling Author Of *Yesterday's Dawn*

Talon has stalked the great beasts of the plains, but he has never faced prey more elusive than the woman he has stolen from his enemies. In her pale eyes, he beholds a challenge that will test beyond all endurance strengths he has thought indomitable.

As courageous as any man, yet as delicate as a tundra flower, Summer has longed for Talon's embrace; now, she will fight to the death before submitting to him. A terrible betrayal has turned Talon against her—only a bond stronger than love itself can subdue the captor and make him surrender to Summer's sweet, gentle fury.

__51952-6 $4.99 US/$5.99 CAN

HISTORICAL ROMANCE
HUNTERS OF THE ICE AGE:
YESTERDAY'S DAWN
By Theresa Scott

Named for the massive beast sacred to his people, Mamut has proven his strength and courage time and again. But when it comes to subduing one helpless captive female, he finds himself at a distinct disadvantage. Never has he realized the power of beguiling brown eyes, soft curves and berry-red lips to weaken a man's resolve. He has claimed he will make the stolen woman his slave, but he soon learns he will never enjoy her alluring body unless he can first win her elusive heart.

__51920-8 $4.99 US/$5.99 CAN

A CONTEMPORARY ROMANCE
HIGH VOLTAGE
By Lori Copeland

Laurel Henderson hadn't expected the burden of inheriting her father's farm to fall squarely on her shoulders. And if Sheriff Clay Kerwin can't catch the culprits who are sabotaging her best efforts, her hopes of selling it are dim. Struggling with this new responsibility, Laurel has no time to pursue anything, especially not love. The best she can hope for is an affair with no strings attached. And the virile law officer is the perfect man for the job—until Laurel's scheme backfires. Blind to Clay's feelings and her own, she never dreams their amorous arrangement will lead to the passion she wants to last for a lifetime.

__51923-2 $4.99 US/$5.99 CAN

LOVE SPELL
ATTN: Order Department
Dorchester Publishing Co., Inc.
276 5th Avenue, New York, NY 10001

Please add $1.50 for shipping and handling for the first book and $.35 for each book thereafter. PA., N.Y.S. and N.Y.C. residents, please add appropriate sales tax. No cash, stamps, or C.O.D.s. All orders shipped within 6 weeks via postal service book rate. Canadian orders require $2.00 extra postage and must be paid in U.S. dollars through a U.S. banking facility.

Name _____

Address _____

City _____ State _____ Zip _____

I have enclosed $_____ in payment for the checked book(s).

Payment <u>must</u> accompany all orders.☐ Please send a free catalog.

Timeswept passion...timeless love

FLORA SPEER

When he is accidentally thrust back to the eighth century by a computer genius's time-travel program, Mike Bailey falls from the sky and lands near Charlemagne's camp. Knocked senseless by the crash, he can't remember his name, address, or occupation, but no shock can make his body forget how to respond when he awakens to the sight of an enchanting angel on earth.

Headstrong and innocent, Danise is already eighteen and almost considered an old maid by the Frankish nobles who court her. Yet the stubborn beauty would prefer to spend the rest of her life cloistered in a nunnery rather than marry for any reason besides love. Unexpectedly mesmerized by the stranger she discovers unconscious in the forest, Danise is quickly arroused by an all-consuming passion—and a desire that will conquer time itself.

_51948-8 $4.99 US/$5.99 CAN